The Errant King

The Errant King

The Dark Sea Annals

Book 2

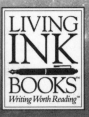

LIVING
INK
BOOKS
Writing Worth Reading

WAYNE THOMAS BATSON

The Errant King

Volume 2 in The Dark Sea Annals™ series

Copyright © 2011 by Wayne Thomas Batson

Published by Living Ink Books, an imprint of
AMG Publishers, Inc.
6815 Shallowford Rd.
Chattanooga, Tennessee 37421

This is a work of fiction. Names, characters, places, and incidents either are the product of the author's imagination or are used fictitiously. Any resemblance to actual persons, either living or dead, events, or locales, is entirely coincidental.

Print Edition	ISBN 13: 978-0-89957-878-0	ISBN 10: 0-89957-878-1
ePUB Edition	ISBN 13: 978-1-61715-255-9	ISBN 10: 1-61715-255-2
Mobi Edition	ISBN 13: 978-1-61715-256-6	ISBN 10: 1-61715-256-0
ePDF Edition	ISBN 13: 978-1-61715-257-3	ISBN 10: 1-61715-257-9

First Printing—October 2011

THE DARK SEA ANNALS is a trademark of AMG Publishers.

Cover designed by Daryle Beam at Bright Boy Design,
Chattanooga, TN.

Interior design and typesetting by Reider Publishing Services,
West Hollywood, California.

Edited and proofread by Jeff Gerke, Christy Graeber, and Rick Steele.

Printed in the United States of America
16 15 14 13 12 11 –D– 7 6 5 4 3 2 1

DEDICATION

To Him who counts my tears and weighs my sorrows;
to Him who lifts my chin and promises that things will
not always be this way; and to Him whose ironclad word
assures me that until the Day comes, even tragedy will not
be wasted—I give to you the labor of my mind and my hands.
—September, 2011

CONTENTS

Prologue

From the Personal Journal of High Shepherd Sebastian Sternbough, 18 Muertanas, 2219

*T*wo ships left Anglinore City that fateful eve. The next morning, under a blood red sunrise, only one returned.

Of course, that had all been planned. For his traitorous deeds, inciting war with the Gorrack Nation, King Morlan and his minions had been forced to sail across the Dark Sea, renouncing the known world of Myriad forever. But, when the command ship returned, I discovered that all had not gone according to plan.

A sweat-soaked courier had given me the news that Aravel, High King of Myriad, my liege and my friend, had been stricken with some grave sickness. According to King Ealden of Llanfair, General Alastair Coldhollow, and the others who sailed on the Dark Sea, High King Aravel became ill with some constricting fever. It had worsened mightily as the ship wrestled with the winds and sailed back to Anglinore.

We exhausted ten of our strongest guards getting the king to the medical ward. Doughty men to be sure, and valiant, but the careful journey from the docks was arduous. I arrived at the ward and wondered that Queen Maren was not yet there. I sent urgent word with the guards to fetch the ailing king's wife as quick as could be.

Inside, the doctors and surgeons swarmed around the stricken king. I mixed the mightiest herbal remedies I had yet discovered: rulemarr, essence of flouris, even merriander, but nothing seemed to work.

"Sebastian," Aravel cried out. "Sebastian, it is burning . . . inside!"

I flew to his bedside in the center of the low-ceilinged ward. "Easy, my lord. Rest your head."

Aravel coughed, and some kind of black spittle trickled from the corner of his mouth. "Shepherd, if I've told . . . you . . . once, I've told you . . . a thousand times: do not call me lord! I am your friend, for Stars' sake."

I smiled grimly, wiped the fluid with a clean towel, and felt his forehead. He was burning with fever, something hotter than anything I had ever felt. A lesser man would have been consumed. But not Aravel. His eyes were still clear, and thoughts raced behind them.

"Where is she?" he asked. "Where is she, Sebastian?"

"She is coming," I said, praying I was right. "Maren will be here."

He wrenched suddenly and hacked, spraying his chest with the black liquid. A stench leaped up, and First One as my witness, I believe I saw steam.

"Aravel!" cried a voice from the south corridor.

"She comes!" I told him. "Your wife is coming."

"Please," Aravel said, "please get this wiped up. I don't . . . want her—"

"Of course." The doctors and I swabbed and cleansed the last of the foul liquid from the king's bare chest, just as Queen Maren entered the room. She bore baby Lochlan with her.

"Oh, Aravel," she cried at his shoulder. "What . . . what happened?"

He blinked at her. "Keep Loch back. I . . . I don't want to give this to him . . . or to you."

Maren stared at me. "What is it? What sickness is this? Can it travel?"

"We are trying to figure it out," I said, feeling ignorant. "It's like nothing I've ever seen. But to be safe, keep Lochlan away."

Maren handed the child to a medical servant, and she bore him toward the greenery on the east side of the ward. Lochlan wailed softly.

King and Queen spoke in private whispers as the doctors continued to swirl. I tore through my medical journals, especially Treatments of the Seven Races, compiled by Mosteryn the Old. Page after page of pestilence that could affect mankind, and nothing sounded remotely like what Aravel was suffering.

"Shepherd!" Queen Maren cried out. "Look at his skin!"

I spun around and went to the table. Aravel seemed in a swoon. And the skin on his face and chest glistened with sweat, but there was something else there, small pinchings of skin. "LIGHT!" I demanded.

Stewards brought more torches and I gasped. The pinches were darkening as I watched, blisters filling with black fluids. Some grew larger and popped, draining down the side of his face.

"Hot," Aravel muttered. "So hot . . ."

"More cold water!" I called. But even though it had been drawn from the basement wells that went far down into the coldest stone, it was never cold enough. The welts and blisters continued to form.

"M-Maren," Aravel whispered. "I am fighting . . . so hot . . . I am sorry."

"Hold on to me!" she cried, taking his hand. "You feel my touch. Hold on to me, Aravel!" Queen Maren turned and looked to me, desperation burning from her eyes, burning into me.

I went back to the medical journal and scoured the pages. There had to be something. Then, I thought for a moment that I'd got it. I found a sickness, an allergic reaction actually. The sting from a kind of gaelfish mostly found in the Wetlands of Chapparel could cause welting and a very high fever, but still, no mention of black fluid.

"Shepherd!" called a man as he roared into the ward. He was one of the medical servants I'd seen when we first came in with the king. He'd torn out of the room just after the king's blisters appeared.

"What is it? I have no time—"

"You're looking in the wrong book," he said, and placed a very old copy of Canticles on the table. "Read here in End Things, right after the big section on the Convergence." He pointed to a heading for a new portion of text.

I glared at the man. "But this is The Sevenfold Curse."

"Just read!"

I did. Among the terrors to come in that dark chapter of Canticles was a plague. This plague brought burning, burning from the inside. With dread twisting like a thorny vine inside me, I read on. A burning, blistering sickness . . . unworldly fever, black puss, and great pain. I glanced at the king. It was the same. It had to be. But search as I might, there was no mention of a cure.

"What is your name," I demanded.

"Vrenith," he said.

"How did you know to search here?"

"It's end times prophecy, Shepherd," Vrenith said. "I study it."

"Good, good," I said. "Do you know . . . is there any treatment? Is there any cure?"

"No, none that I've read about."

"What about the prophecy here, does it ever lift? Does this curse ever lift?"

Vrenith frowned. "That is a question left in doubt. We argue about it all the time in Canticles study. Either way, it seems in the hands of the First One."

I rubbed my temples. "Then, go and pray. In fact, find anyone and everyone you can, drag them to Clarissant Hall, and pray until your knees bleed!"

"Yesssir!" Vrenith sprinted out of the ward.

"Shepherd!" It was Aravel's voice, if voice it could be called.

I turned back to him and gasped. The black blisters were everywhere now, seeping and oozing. The king's flesh was streaked with rivulets of dark fluid. He trembled and shook. I could feel the heat from his body.

"I . . . I am leaving," he said.

"No, Aravel, no!" Queen Maren still clutched his hand.

"For my part," said the king, "I am sorry. I should have seen Morlan's treason faster. I should have known. But . . ." he coughed several times. "I worry about . . . the First One."

"The First One?" I asked. "Why?"

"I am afraid," Aravel said. "I left Him . . . I tore down the Altar." He looked longingly at Maren. "I am sorry, my wife . . ." Tears mingled with black puss drained from his eyes. "I should have listened to . . . you."

"Aravel . . . no . . ."

The king lurched up a few inches and winced. He spoke now through grit teeth. "You know . . . I never stopped believing . . . in Him. I just . . . didn't understand . . . I just gave up."

Feeling somewhat intrusive, I said, "You may have given up on the First One, Aravel. But He has not given up on you."

Aravel smiled through the pain. "Ah, you bring . . . me comfort." He stared at his wife. "I . . . love you . . . my sweet Maren . . ."

And then, King Aravel the 48th High King of Myriad, breathed his last.

I write these words and must fight to keep from snapping the pen. This was Morlan's doing. My heart, my Shepherd senses, all told me it was so. I've never believed in coincidences, and I wasn't about to suggest such a thing now. Aravel contracting a swift and lethal disease just after sending his brother into exile across the Dark Sea spoke of premeditated violence just as if Morlan had signed his name in blood on Aravel's chest.

How I wish Aravel would have slain Morlan on the battlefield. He'd had the chance, I knew, at the end of the Gorrack War. Twin brothers had met, face to face, in combat. A bitter, exhausting struggle, through which Morlan had practically dared Aravel to slay him. But even when provoked by treachery, Aravel would not finish Morlan. He cut off Morlan's hand, when he could have had his head and been done with it. It might have been the mercy of a benevolent king. I knew my friend Aravel to be such a man, gracious, humble, and kind. But, I wonder.

I wonder when Aravel had his sword's point just inches from Morlan's heart, if it was not mercy at all that stayed his hand. And when Morlan dishonorably struck with his dagger, I don't believe there was anything honorable in Aravel's decision to spare Morlan. It feels like betrayal to write this about my dear friend, but I suspect that fear kept Aravel from killing his brother. Fear and weakness. Some misguided reluctance to be rid of such pure evil, I may never understand. I shudder to think of what it might mean.

Aside of his dear wife Maren, there is no one who knew Aravel as well as I did. But some men keep things locked away so deep in their hearts, that even Shepherds cannot discern them. Whatever his true reasons, Aravel's choice to leave Morlan alive likely cost him his life.

And there is, within me, a creeping dread that Aravel's choice may cost us all in the end.

CHAPTER 1

THE GRAY HOUR

All folk are afraid of the dark.
Be they biggin or wee, the unseen
world casts doubt upon reason, scratches
worry into even the bravest warrior's mind.
But night holds no terror like the gray
hour, the time before stars, when shadows rule
the twilight world. In the gray hour, things appear
and things vanish. Do not fear the dark, but lock
your doors in the gray hour. For it is neither day
or night, and in its shades, foul things walk.

—From Chaparrel Tales, Bard Gregan Whellanhall

10 SEDWYN 2238

I was just seven when my childhood ended.

Nights like this one . . . where dusk seems to last forever, make me remember. And I find myself loosening the stone on the left side of the fireplace and digging out my journals. As I sit here now, reading, writing and . . . remembering that night, I find myself not wondering why they came, but wishing they would have taken me too. I know that is weak. It's just that I miss my family, and the village has never been the same, really. I've never been the same.

It was an hour before dusk on the 27th day of Solmas in the year 2226, twelve years ago. I had just come back from a pretend hunt with my childhood friends and found the Wetlands, my village, bustling as usual. Fishermen brought their last catch back from the lagoons, the tavern keepers lit their lanterns, and the real hunters stood in clusters, slapping each other on the back and bragging about their exploits stalking in the deep woods. I found my father chopping wood with his great axe in front of our cottage. That axe had been a gift from the village Elder. My father, you see, had done something very brave in the great war, the war against the Gorracks. But it was before I was born, and my father wouldn't speak about the war or about what he had done.

He was a big man, brawny, with wild coppery hair and beard. I loved the curly hair on his muscular chest. I liked to pull them out one at a time to make him yelp. I watched him work now, marveling at his strength. "I am all out of arrows again, Daddy," I said, holding up my empty quiver. "See?"

"Again?" he said with mock anger. He swung the axe and split a huge stump. "Well then, young Ariana Kurtz, either your aim has grown dull or you'll be bringing your mother and me a cartload of game for the storehouse." He put down the axe and winked.

"Oooh, you always know just what to say to make me angry!" I growled, beating at the leather armor on his legs with my little fists. "My aim is better than ever! Why, I could shoot the whiskers off your chin if you'd ever stand still! And you know the Elders won't let me join the hunt . . . the real one, that is."

He picked me up while I was still swinging, but I stopped when he held me in his twinkling, blue-eyed gaze. "Ariana," he said. "You're a better shot than some of the bigguns, and your eye is the best in this village, I deem. Don't you let them keep you from using your First One-given skills just because you'll never grow a beard. I know that you will do great things one day." Father hugged me then, and I didn't resist. He also knew just what to say to give me hope.

"But, darling daughter," he said as he put me down, "a true hunter doesn't go round begging for arrows, either."

He laughed. I laughed too, but I said, "I'll go ask Mom."

I opened the cottage door, and the savory smell of my mother's stew welcomed me. She boiled the venison with potatoes, carrots, onions, wild garlic, and sea salt. My mouth watered. She sat near the fire and tested the pull on a bow she had just strung. "It looks strong," I said.

"It is," mother replied. "It'll put an arrow half way through a felsa tree. Maybe all the way through."

"Speaking of arrows, Mother, could I have a few of yours? Mine are spent and broken."

"Daughter, I have shafts a'plenty," she said. I felt a *but* coming on. "But . . ." she said. "I made them for your father—and for me. You know how to make them. Go down to the shore, fetch some reeds and goose feathers. Just get back before gray hour. I wouldn't want a bogle or a banshee to run off with my little Ariana."

"Mother! I'm too old for those littlin' stories," I said bravely. "But I don't feel like going all the way down to the shore. Can't you just loan me a few arrows? I'll make some this weekend."

"Nay, dear daughter," she said. "Get your reeds and feathers—and get back before gray hour."

The endless white shores lay on the other side of the woods and fell between the Bay of Taranaar and the black waters of the Dark Sea. I knew all the wooded pathways, but if I was to get to the shore, harvest reeds from its mires, gather goose feathers from its banks, and get back before gray hour, I would need to run.

So run I did, barefoot, over root and under fallen trunk, along the green paths. I imagined myself as a young deer, only faster. I wasn't really afraid of the gray hour. I'd been out during that shadowy, dusky time on a few occasions . . . with my parents.

I always figured that sneaky parents just made up the whole gray hour thing to frighten us littlins into getting home before dark. Once, I even caught my parents winking about it. "Oh, the sun has sunk behind the trees," said father with a wink.

"We had better get our precious Ariana safely into the house, for gray hour is upon us!" My mother had replied, winking back. That pretty much settled it in my mind.

But . . . one could never be too careful about such things, so I sprinted all the way to shore.

I discovered that I was not the only Wetlands villager visiting the shore that late afternoon. There were many of the town Elders, dragging their chain nets along the banks. They sought to harvest the butter crabs that burrowed in the soft mud. A few hunters waded out into the marshy, tall grasses in search of sections of reed straight and hard enough to make arrow shafts. I knew better than to get in the way of those tall, proud men, and besides . . . I had an advantage.

At low tide, I liked to wade out in the muck so far beyond the banks that I could catch a glimpse of the open sea. The hunters didn't like to get their prized cloth armor all mucked up. And they certainly didn't want to be seen without their armor on. But I waded out even up to my chin to the very last rows of tall marsh grass. There I found the choicest reeds in unlimited numbers. Of course, when I went that far out, I also often found the sting of the gaelfish. They leave a red, bubbling rash that is most painful. But I can take it.

A few of the Elders waved at me as I came by. A few of the hunters sneered. It was low tide, so I ignored the hunters in the shallowest parts and made my way out to gather the best reeds. Up to my waist in water, I went to work. I could hear the crashing of the waves on the distant sand-bars, and I looked out to the whitecaps beyond the shore.

The Dark Sea was mysterious and beautiful, and its music lulled me into a trance while I worked. I planned to collect so many reeds that I'd never run out of arrows, but I lost track of time. A sharp pain scraping my toes shook me out of my trance. A gaelfish the size of a pumpkin had snuggled up next to me and decided to play footsie. That hurt! I scurried away as fast as the water would let me. It was then that I noticed the sun had gone down behind the trees.

It was the gray hour.

My heart skipped a beat. I almost dropped a handful of about thirty good reeds. But when I looked back to the banks, I couldn't believe it. The Elders, the hunters . . . they were all still there! They weren't even trying to leave. Well, I thought. If they aren't worried about the gray hour, then I'll just go back to work. And back to work I went. I had enough reeds to make a hundred good arrows, but I kept going, stuffing them into the quivers I had brought, into an empty satchel, even down the back of my shirt! I noticed the tide began to come back in, and a cool breeze came came with it. I looked out to the open sea once more . . . and froze.

In the shadows that lay thick upon the Dark Sea, black ships drifted. Great sailing ships with tall masts and black sails—the sea was full of them. It was as if all the shipwrecks from all the reefs of the sea had risen up and now sailed for the Wetlands. I dropped my handfuls of weeds and raced for shore, screaming as I went. "Ships!" I cried. "There are great black ships on the sea!"

The hunters mostly ignored me, but not the Elders. One of them, a graybeard I knew by the name of Jasek, came running out into the water to meet me. "What is it, child?" he exclaimed, his white eyebrows raised in alarm. "What do you say?"

"Elder Jasek, there are ships out beyond the reeds, out in the sea!" I yelled, choking on emotion. "Dark ships! I'm scared!"

"How many?"

"Too many! And they had black sails!" I cried, looking back over the marsh grass, but it was now too dark to see what was out there. "I want my father! I want my mother!"

"All right," Jasek said, and without asking, he hugged me close. Then, he picked me up out of the water and started back to the hard ground. He yelled at the hunters, "To the village, you haughty fools! There are ships on the Sea! Tall ships with black sails! Get your bows and swords! There may be enemies already ashore."

Then Jasek sprinted up the bank and into the forest. I couldn't believe how fast he ran. The Graybeards I had known before had been anything but quick. Perhaps it was fear that drove his aging body beyond its normal limits. Or perhaps he knew somehow what was about to happen.

We reached the village in moments, and I heard Jasek's sharp intake of air. I tried to see what had frightened him so, but Jasek covered my eyes. "What's happening?" I cried, panic running through me like snake venom.

Jasek did not answer. Suddenly, we were thrown forward with unimaginable force. I hit the ground once and rolled into a patch of ferns. I stood up screaming, but my voice stopped. I saw something standing over Jasek's body. This thing was manlike but huge and gray with skin cracked like sun-baked mud. It had enormous pale eyes and a scowling wound of black for its mouth. It seemed to carry its own aura of malice and hate, something that laced my bones with ice and made it hard for me to breathe. My head felt weighed down, like a cruel invisible hand was forcing my head down to the ground. I fought to look up for the Elder once more.

Jasek slowly rose. He drew his sword and swung at the creature. But this monstrous thing seized the blade in its gigantic crumbling paw of a hand. The creature pulled Jasek towards itself and bit into his shoulder. Jasek screamed. The monster then slung Jasek to the ground like a toy. There was a hideous crack, and Jasek did not move. The earthen beast grabbed Jasek by one foot and dragged him away toward the row of cottages near the old tavern on the northern edge of town.

Stumbling, crying, mad with fear, I ran into my village. But there was no refuge to be found there. Stepping from the ferny forest edge was like crossing an unseen barrier into suffocating terror. I shook from head to foot, and my limbs were nearly too heavy to move. I tried to call out, but my words were strangled away. I struggled to the corner of Hazor's, a kind of clubhouse where the hunters gathered, and tentatively peered around the edge. Everywhere I looked there was fighting. Hunters, Elders, and dozens of villagers were there in the public square defending against those giant clay beasts and other dark things I couldn't quite see. The folk of my village fought with sword, axe, and bow. Each clash, clang, and twang startled me like a sudden blast of thunder.

Something came at me out of an alley between two buildings. It was something half wrapped in black tatters of cloth and it flew as if its feet were not touching the ground. In its hand was a long pole made deadly with a curved iron blade on the end. I knew it to be a scythe. With a shrill cry, I dove for the ground, and the thing sailed above me. I felt a piece of its dark garment touch my bare leg, and that spot went icy cold. There came an agonized scream, and I turned and saw that this apparition had struck a villager to the ground.

I raced behind some cottages and skirted the village, trying desperately to get to my cottage. Then, there came a sound like a gale wind when it shrieks in the midst of a storm. Only this was no storm. This haunting wail rose in pitch until my ears could not bear it. I fell to the ground and clutched my ears. At last the sound ended. I rose to my feet and ran heedlessly toward my cottage. I tripped over a dead man's leg, screamed, and stumbled on. I saw an alley I recognized. I knew my cottage was just around the corner.

I felt something behind me, so I ran with all I could muster. I turned the corner and slammed into the door of my home. It was locked.

I banged on the door so hard the skin on my knuckles split. "Father! Let me in!" I wailed. "It's Ariana! Oh, please let me in!" Suddenly, the door opened and I was yanked in so hard that one of my quivers tore free from my back.

"Darrow, bar the door!" my father yelled, holding me close. She lunged and slammed home the slab of wood.

"I'm so sorry!" I cried. "I shouldn't have stayed out so late! It's all my fault."

"No, Ariana," my father said. "No, this night was not your doing. It is something foretold long ago."

I never got to ask him what he meant by that because suddenly, the roof over our cottage shuddered. Then a section of it was torn free. And a huge thing, one of the giants with cracked gray skin, looked down into the opening. But this one was twice as big as the others I'd seen. It reached in and grabbed my mother right off the floor. Even as she was pulled through the ruined ceiling, she drew a dagger and stabbed the thing's enormous hand. I heard a roar, and before I knew it, my father had raced out of the front door after the creature. I ducked my head out of the door, terrified of what I would see.

I saw my father with his special axe, hacking at the knee of this creature that still held my mother. The beast roared again, dropped my mother, and fell to one knee. My father did not hesitate. He swung the axe with both hands in a circle above his head as I'd seen him so a hundred times when he needed to split a tough piece of wood, then he slammed the axe down onto the creature's neck. Something black gushed from the wound, and the earthen beast went down.

My father dropped his axe and knelt at my mother's side. He put two fingers to her neck, just under her chin. Then he clutched her to himself and wept. I stood in the doorway of what had once been my home. And I watched as my poor father cried out in a rage over my mother's still form. But suddenly, that shriek, that blood-freezing, ghostly wail blasted all thought. It was very close. I clutched my ears. Then, I saw it.

On the other side of the fallen monster, something hovered in the air. It looked like a woman's form, but it was clad in some kind of rough, studded armor. She held no weapon, but her fingernails were long like claws. Her hair swirled slowly around her head almost as if she was underwater. But her eyes were the worst. Where the whites and pupils should have been, there were only sockets full of fire. My father reached for his axe. The creature shrieked and came at him with supernatural speed. She hit him, lifted him off his feet, and carried him screaming into the distance. My mind left me, and I saw no more.

I'm nineteen years old now, almost twenty. The village has been rebuilt, but I'm still not a real hunter. Not according to the Elders, that is. I am the surviving daughter of the great Hagen and Darrow Kurtz, but I've made no name for myself. I'm just Ariana.

We don't talk much anymore about the black ships, about the nightmarish forms that invaded our village, or even about those who were taken. But I know we all still think about it.

I do. Especially on nights like this one when the forest comes to life with insect chatter, and tendrils of mist roll in on the inlets and the bay. Nights when dusk seems to last forever and the Gray Hour puts ominous shapes in every archway, under every tree, and in every cleft of rock. In the Wetlands there are many nights like this one.

I put my journal away with the others and then locked my door up tight.

CHAPTER 2

KING'S REST

The discovery of vaskerstone in 2706 AO was considered a blessing of the highest order. There seemed no end to its uses: triggering doors to open, lighting a room, providing clarity of thought, healing, even giving its owner the ability to perceive things at a distance. But there were also misuses. In fact, the purest mature vaskerstones could, if used often enough, be bent to the will of its user. Some hunks of vaskerstone seem to lose their power after their original owners die. It is certainly worth more study. While immature vaskerstone—that from which we craft emberstones—were quite common, fully aged vaskerstone was a rare find, more so even than cyrium. Most rue its scarcity, but there are some who believe it is for the best that we have so little.

—Cravat Mervis, *The Many Facets*
of Myridian Stone, Volume 3

41 SEDWYN 2238

In a cloud of worry, High Shepherd Sebastian Sternbough left the throne room in Anglinore castle to continue his search. Sebastian's Shepherd gifts gave him unique powers, and several hundred years of study and experience had given him wisdom beyond most beings in Myriad. But none of that made it any easier to find one person in the labyrinthine corridors and chambers of Anglinore Castle.

Of course, thought Sebastian, *descending a spiral stair to the barracks, it shouldn't be this hard to find the queen.*

The temperature was markedly warmer on the lower floors. The furnaces, kilns, and ovens were all already ablaze even at this early hour. The smell of hickory and bacon filled the air. Sebastian found the barracks empty, but the mess hall full. No queen, but definitely someone who could help.

Sebastian raced to the table and dropped onto a bench seat next to an older soldier. He wiped sweaty dark locks off his forehead and said, "Skappy, I am looking for Queen Maren. Have you seen her?"

The man at the table looked up suddenly, and porridge dribbled down both sides of his gray mustache. "Wha-what? Sebastian?" He wiped his face with the padded sleeve of his arming doublet. "Whatever happened to, 'Good morning, Skap, mind if I sit down?' Or 'Pardon me, Guardcaptain, but I wonder if I could interrupt your meal?'"

"I am sorry about that," the Shepherd said. "But I'm afraid I am in haste. I cannot find Queen Maren."

Skap slurped down a spoonful of porridge. "Saw're in Clarissant Hall. She came in durin' morning prayers."

"Ah," said the Shepherd with some surprise. "Good, very good. She's spent so little time there of late. I almost thought, ah, nevermind."

"Almost thought what?" asked the Guardcaptain.

"It's nothing," Sebastian said.

"Mm, hmph." Skap stroked his beard, and a few crumbs spilled out into his porridge. "She didn't look good to me. Kinda pale, I thought."

"Keen eye as usual, Skap," the Shepherd said. "She's not had enough sunlight."

"More'n that." He let his spoon sink into the porridge. "There's something unwholesome about her these days, dark even."

Sebastian nodded. "So I have thought also. Since the coronation, she's fallen into some kind of impenetrable murk. My elixirs have little affect on her humor. Now, I get the distinct impression that she is avoiding me."

"Seems like the only time she's herself is when Lochlan's around."

"Hence my mission this morning," said the Shepherd. "King Lochlan is going to spar Adelbard today. It would do her good to watch. So . . . if you'll excuse me, Guardcaptain, I will take my leave. Hopefully, I'll find her still at prayer."

The Shepherd hurried to the door, but paused at Skap's call. "Sebastian, I don't know what she was doing in Clarissant Hall this morning, but I don't think she was there to pray."

The pews in Clarissant Hall were nearly full, but the queen was not there. Sebastian inquired. Many had seen her there, but no one knew where she might have gone or even saw her leave. Sebastian stared absently at the stonework of the "Altarwall" where of old the lords of Myriad had placed their crowns in rich wood settings to honor the First One. The immaculately carved altar had stood in that place for more than a thousand years before Aravel had it removed. Queen Maren had refused to have the altar rebuilt. And that troubled Sebastian greatly.

So Sebastian gazed at the Altarwall and said a brief prayer. He thought he might know where the queen had gone, but he hoped he was wrong. The living should never spend so much time among the dead.

King's Rest was a courtyard cemetery built along the far eastern wall of Anglinore Castle. There, within view of the sea far below, ten generations of Myriad's High royalty rested. Sebastian stood on the balcony entrance and gazed over the yard. Tree canopies and stone architecture obscured the view, and the crashing of the Dark Sea on the castle mount far below made it difficult to hear anything with precision. If one listened for long, it was all too easy to imagine distant whispers among the graves.

Sebastian shuddered and descended the rampart into the yard. Rubbing the upper arms of his cloak for warmth, he wound through the plots and monuments. The morning sun was climbing high in the steel gray sky, but it had done little to warm the land. "That's all it is," Sebastian whispered to himself. "A little cool today. Nothing more than that."

He barely strayed a glance from his path. This was no game of hide-and-seek. If Queen Maren had indeed come to King's Rest, there was only one place she might be. Sebastian found the massive granite obelisk toward the back of the yard near the sea wall. Aravel had loved the sea.

Queen Maren was not there. But she had been.

At the foot of the monument lay a care-wrought bundle of white roses, gray-blue forget-me-nots, and silver seneca bells. Sebastian knelt there a moment and touched the stems. He allowed a trace of his power to flow into the already wilting plants. Well fed and sealed now, they would flourish brightly for a long while.

"Loch needed a father," Sebastian whispered as he stood. "Curse Morlan for taking you away." Flashes of that fateful morn, nearly twenty years earlier tried to pierce his mind's eye like a living splinter, but he shook his head. "Not now. I have a queen to find."

Sebastian went to the sea wall, rested his arms upon its cold stone, and stared south down the shoreline. The Dark Sea surged inland, warring against its mighty undertow and curling into raging fists, waves tall and relentless. They slammed upon the shore and then stretched like claws, clutching the sand, desperately trying to hold on before being sucked back into the black water. It never ceased to amaze Sebastian that, except for the whitecaps and foam, the water was so dark, even in the shallows. Hence the name, he thought.

A pair of white horses raced along the beach, bearing their riders rapidly across the sand. A group of townsfolk sat nestled in the high grass between dunes. And just below, walking hand in hand, a couple strode just out of the water's reach. None of these could include Maren, of course. She would be alone.

Sebastian watched the couple walk north until they disappeared around a bend in the castle mount. There the Shepherd's heart caught in his throat. The vaporous low clouds parted a moment, allowing a clear view of the Seat of Kings . . . the great stone chair at the cliff's edge. For ages it had been a place of contemplation for the High Kings of Myriad. Lochlan had not yet used it. The Seat had remained empty since Aravel's passing. But is was not empty now.

Sebastian fled the graveyard and flew through the castle corridors wishing he knew if any Windborne were in town. He didn't know, and he wouldn't waste the time to look. Instead, he drove his legs as hard as he could until he came to the stables. His mare, Suranthis, stamped as he approached. He leaped upon her and cried, "Sura, bear me with haste!"

The Elladorian mare descended from a line of swift mounts, and was considered by most to be as close to pure-blooded as could be. She thundered across the grounds, past a dozen gawking guards, and out of the main gatehouse. Then, through Anglinore City they raced, taking only the back ways and alleys to avoid town folk. And soon, he rode outside the city and turned north. In an instant, they traversed the flat plain that aproned the castle and charged up into the foothills toward the cliffs.

At last the Seat of Kings came within sight, as did a nightmare beyond Sebastian's blackest dreams. Someone was on the high stone seat, but standing on its edge . . . a mere step from a three-hundred foot plunge.

"Ya, Sura! Go!" The mare responded and bore Sebastian over the uneven ground as if it were a cobbled stone avenue in Anglinore City. They clambered up the hills. The cliff's edge rose up perilously to Sebastian's right. He tried not to glance. He needed to focus on the Seat of Kings. And now, there could be no doubt. It was Queen Maren. She stood on the very edge of the seat. The wind lifted her drapes and fluttered her long dress. She seemed to sway.

Sebastian urged his mare forward. With the staccato beat of hooves clattering in his ear, he wondered what he would do once he got to her. If she was as unstable as he suspected, the wrong words or actions might literally push her over the edge. Of course, who knew what the wrong words or actions might be? Anything could set her off. I'll leap up there and tackle her if I must, he thought.

The massive Seat of Kings came up quickly, and Sebastian saw the queen turn her head. Just twenty yards away, he brought Sura to halt and called out, "Maren, what are you doing?"

As if in a trance, she turned her head. "Testing the First One's will," she replied, her voice flat and empty.

"T-testing His will?" Sebastian felt as if he'd just been gut-punched by a Stonehand warrior. "Surely no good can come of that."

"Good?" she echoed and stared at him with sad incredulity. "Why should I expect anything good to come of the First One's will? Nay, Shepherd, I am simply testing if He would rather me live . . . or die. Either event is fraught with sorrow."

"Queen Maren, who has stolen both your wisdom and your will?" Sebastian subtly shifted his legs, nudging Sura forward. "Your life is not sorrow. Lochlan loves you. He needs you. Indeed, I have been looking all over Anglinore for you so that I could tell you of Lochlan's late morning tilt with General Adelbard."

She blinked, and her expression melted. Sebastian saw a glistening on her cheek. But still, she wavered on the edge.

"Lochlan . . ."

"Your son," the Shepherd suggested gently, "is breaking his fast as we speak, complaining about the oatmeal, as usual."

A weak smile came and went. "He complains . . . unless I make it. Particular that way, he is."

"You may need to rescue him from Daribel's wrath. You know she cannot abide anyone preferring a recipe above her own."

Sebastian brought Sura as close to the Seat as he dared. The terrain beneath the mare's feet was so narrow, that one wrong step would send them careening down the side of the cliff to the dashing rocks. He could hear the Dark Sea crashing upon them. It was hypnotic . . . in a way.

"Maren," he said, holding out a hand, "please come down from there. You and I both know this is no way for a Stormgarden to leave this world."

Her expression slackened once more. She stared out to sea. "Neither is boiling to death in his own blood," she said. "His own . . . black . . . blood."

"There is a difference, my queen," he said. "Aravel did not choose that end."

"No . . . no, he did not. It was ordained . . . the First One took my beloved Aravel. . . . Took him."

"Do you really believe the First One wanted Aravel to die like that? That was no more His doing than the Gorrack War. If blame you must cast, cast it upon Morlan who put it all in motion. Aravel's poisoning was Morlan's doing, not a work of the First One."

"Perhaps the First One did not cause Aravel's death." Queen Maren wobbled. Sebastian started, but she steadied herself. Tears streaked, forming droplets at her chin. "But He allowed it. What is the difference?"

Sebastian swallowed hard. "It is all the difference in the world, Maren. One is love and mercy. The other is malice and manipulation." The Shepherd glanced upward. The sun had burned off a patch in the mantle of gray, and hazy beams of light shone down on the Dark Sea. "There is wickedness in this world, yes, including our own. Why the First One allows any of us a next breath defies my reason. But He does. Perhaps, unlike we who call ourselves wise in Myriad, it is because He can see all ends."

Queen Maren blinked, and for the first time, it seemed to Sebastian that she had the steely focus of old. "What do you mean?"

"Take Alastair Coldhollow," he said. "Myriad has rarely seen such a frost-hearted killer. Hardened, despairing, and enslaved to Witchdrale, he nearly took his own life. Can you imagine if he had? The Gorracks might have slaughtered half the world. Morlan might sit now on the throne of Anglinore. You and Lochlan would have died at Cythraul's hand . . . or worse."

Queen Maren slumped backward and sat on the stone seat. "I . . . I love my Lochlan," she whispered.

"I know you do. I know. Why don't we go and see him?" He held out his hand. She took it, and he helped her step over to sit behind him on Suranthis.

"But Aravel," she said, weeping on the Shepherd's shoulder, "I miss him . . . so much."

"It is a hurt I can scarce imagine," he said. "A deep wounding . . . but it need not be the end of you also." Sebastian turned the mare and said, "Ya, Sura! Let's go home."

CHAPTER 3

WHEN MOUNTAINS TREMBLE

Why don't some folk believe in legends? Don't they know that a legend is only a truth, wrapped in a cloak of years, shrouded by fancy, and nearly forgotten? And while I'm asking questions, here's one that's daunted me for some time now: why don't the littlins mind their elders? I venture to say that all a' Myriad would be spared a great pile of trouble if we all remembered the legends . . . and our elders.

—Gaffer Aeldis, overheard at the hearth
of The Wandering Boar in Ellador (2229 AS)

6 SOLMONATH 2238

Cool wind from the south whispered through the endless firs and pines on the slopes of Mount Falchion just west of Hammer's Gap in the eastern Hinterlands. Young Tanneth Goliant, or Tango as his friends called him, ignored the wind and the distant thunder. He crouched behind a boulder, blew an unruly stripelock out of his eyes, and stared at the entrance to the Haunted Cave.

"You shouldn'a go in there!" his little sister Melienne said, tugging at his tunic so hard the garment slipped off his shoulder.

"Cut it out, Meli!" he growled back, adjusting his sleeve. "How is anyone supposed to know if it's really haunted if'n no one ever goes in the cave t'look 'round?"

"Well, Da said for one thing!" Melienne replied. "You know the legend about the Red Queen and the Dragon. Da told us!"

"Of course, I know it. He tells us every time it storms." Tango snorted. "If we were home right now, he'd probably be tellin' us all over again." Tango's eyes grew wide, and he spread his arms like wings. "Greedy for gold and precious cyrium, Raudrim, the lord of all wyrms, dug too deep. The cold breath of the underworld's vaults put the dragon to eternal slumber, and he lay there sleeping for many an age."

Meli squinted. "Eww, I hate this part."

Tango went on. "Escaping the rebellion of her tortured people, Quevara the Red Queen of Cragheath Tor, sailed the river still streaming with peasant's blood. Her ship aground near the mountain, she escaped into the stoney depths where her soul became one with Raudrim's. There they wait for someone to disturb their slumber."

"It might be true, Tango. It might. No one is allowed to go in. Da even said that Proconsul Braeger kept armed knights out front to guard it."

"There haven'a been guards here since I've been alive," Tango replied. "And besides, it's just a silly legend to scare us littlins out of a dangerous place."

"Tango!" Melienne cried. "That's just it! Legend or not, haunted or not, caves are dangerous!" Just then, the wind picked up and hard drops of rain splashed through the needly boughs above. Lightning flashed, and a sharp crash of thunder echoed in the mountains.

"Ya know what Da' also told us?" Tango asked. "He told us, the bravest of the brave earn great reward by facin' danger, not runnin' from it."

"And just what reward do ya think we'll be gettin' for goin' in there?"

Tango lowered his curly eyebrows, narrowed his eyes, and whispered, "Cyrium."

"What? You really think there's cyrium down there?" Meli rolled here eyes.

"I'll wager that was why the Proconsul posted guards there, so's no one could get in an' find that cyrium."

Meli sighed. "A ton of cyrium ore does ye no good, if yer dead. Ah, and it's probably just part of the legend anyway. Who needs the trouble?"

"Look, Meli," Tango said. "You can stay out here if you want, or you can run back through the storm to the village, but I'm going in!" His sharp axe in his hand, Tango flew out from behind the boulder, dashed down the rain-slicked gully, and disappeared into the inky darkness of the cave.

"Tango!" Melienne cried, and she sat there for a few moments getting wet. "Wait 'til I tell Da!" she growled into the rain. "Oooh, Tango, it's all your fault." But the promise of legendary cyrium and her older brother's stubborn streak was too much to resist chasing after. Melienne darted out into the storm and raced into the cave.

Meli found Tango six long strides into the cave. "Help!" he cried, whirling round and round, hands flailing. "I've run through a patch a' spider webs. Eck, eck, eck!"

Meli laughed. "Serves you right. Tol'ja, didn'a?" She pulled fistfuls of web off his chest and shoulders and wiped it away on jutting stones. "See now, there's nothin' t'be afraid of. No spiders anyway—wait, uh, maybe I was wrong. Hold still."

"What?"

"Hold still! You've got one in your locks."

"Get it off me!"

"I'm tryin', now shush-it!" Meli gently moved one of Tango's locks aside. The spider clambered slowly under a different lock. It was palm-sized and had red and black stripes. In Bugs 'n Beasts, Da had always said, red means deadly. So Meli was careful.

She moved another lock aside and then swiftly brushed the spider onto the cave floor. It started to skitter back toward Tango, but Meli stomped it into greenish pulp. "There, got it!"

"Thanks, Meli," Tango said, still pulling strands of web out of his locks. "But I thought you weren't comin' now?"

"Looky for you I did, eh?" She frowned. "Let's just take the spider as a warnin' and get out of here."

"No, Meli. You don'na have t'come. But I'm gonna look around a bit."

"I don'na get it. You jump like a girl for a spider, but you're gonna go lookin' for a dragon?"

"Jump like a girl?—You are a girl! And I did'na jump anyway. Besides, there's not likely any truth to the dragon. If it's down in the mountain, why has'na come up?"

"I dunno," she replied. "Maybe it's sleepin'. But we know about the Red Queen. She was real."

"Was real," said Tango. "Dead an age at least, I'm sure. Probly fell off an edge an cracked her noggin. Nothin' but bones now, but I'll wager the cyrium she was after's still in here. I'm gonna find out."

The rain increased in earnest, blowing sheets into the cave's entrance to spatter at their feet. Tango dug a flickerstick out of his satchel and scraped it along a stone like a gigantic match. It sparked twice and kindled into a bright, pure yellow flame. As its name denoted, it flickered as if by an unseen breeze and cast dancing shadows even as high as the cave ceiling.

"A dragon could fit in here," Meli said.

"Just stop. You'll scare yourself silly." Tango took a step toward the back of the cave. "You comin'?"

Meli followed at his heels, even holding on to the bottom of Tango's tunic. They picked their way along the toothy cave floor, and it wasn't long before it angled down and curled away to the left. Light from the cave's mouth was soon swallowed up by their depth. They depended completely on their flickerstick now.

"Ow!" Meli went to one knee.

"What's the matter?"

"I'm alright," she replied. "Turned my ankle a bit in a hole."

"Ruts," Tango said. "They're all over. Deeper than I thought. Sorry, Meli. Can ya get along?"

"If'n I said no, can we go back?"

Tango shook his head. Little sisters.

They continued on in silence. The ceiling above lowered to about thirty feet and, though there were still a dozen paces on either side of them, it felt as if the passage was constricting. The air was stale. Each breath was heavy.

Having descended continuously for twenty minutes or more, Tango began to wonder about his plan. Legends aside, Meli was right: the Red Queen had been a real person. Da had told him all about her, even read the official records from Hammer's Gap town hall. Queen Quevara had ruled over all the lands west of the Impass Mountains called the Curtain for more than a hundred years. A ruthless, remorseless matriarch, Queen Quevara enslaved the neighboring Stonehand tribes and quelled any opposition with her black army of Stalkers. Whether she was mad when she took the throne or her sanity ebbed away slowly over the years, no one really knew. But she had clearly lost her mind. Within her royal city gates, atrocities piled up. Queen Quevara began pitting Stonehands against wild beasts and reveled in the slaughter. Public executions were rampant. Some claimed that, for her own wicked pleasure, Queen Quevara had scores of peasants slaughtered so that she could watch their blood color the stream that ran through the capital city.

Tango shuddered. Meli's hand found his belt, and she stayed right behind him as they descended. It was treacherous, slow-going. There were many more ruts, sudden changes in footing, and uneven stone. Fences of sharp stalagmites rose up before Tango and Meli, forcing them to meander. Monstrous, knobby shapes loomed suddenly in their path, and the siblings stopped for a breathless moment, only to realize it was some jagged formation of stone.

Worst of all for Tango was the eerie silence. The storm's voice was a memory. There were no living creatures chirping, squeaking, or scritch-scratching. The dead stone all around them seemed to suck away all sound. Every footfall, every breath seemed as loud as a cannon blast. Tango's nerves had frayed to a hair. The hair snapped.

He heard something. He froze, and Meli banged into him. The flickerstick fell from his hand and sputtered to a weak glow at his feet.

"Tango!" Meli mewed. "Why'd ya—" Then they both saw it.

Another light, a bouncing, will-o-the-wisp. It danced in the unknown distance. Tango grabbed up the flickerstick and dragged Meli behind an alcove of stone.

"Tango, what is it?"

"Shhhh . . . I dunno," he said. "It's getting closer." He desperately scraped the business end of the flickerstick into the stone, willing it to go out. But it didn't. And the other light grew near.

"C'mon . . . c'mon," he whispered. He could hear footsteps now and a strange muted padding.

He scraped and jammed the flickerstick, but it was made too well. Probably one Da' mixed and loaded, he thought angrily. No matter what he did, he couldn't get the glowing embers to go out. He glanced up desperately. Hard to tell exactly, but when Tango looked up, the oncoming light seemed almost upon them.

Nothing good's coming up out a' the bowels of this mountain, he thought. *The flickerstick'll give us away.*

Not knowing what else to do, Tango slammed his bare foot down onto the burning end of the flickerstick. Pain lanced up Tango's leg, and he grit his teeth. It felt as if tiny strands of liquid fire were winding their way up his ankle and around his calf. He thanked the Starmaker that he'd toughened the soles of his feet on innumerable hunts over the years. The sharp, biting pain was nearly more than he could bear, but he didn't shut his eyes. Even as he ground the last dying sparks of the flickerstick under his foot, he stared through the stoney fence.

A tall shadow, a man-shape, walked beneath the bobbing light, and beside him was something else . . . a hump of twilight, sleek and stalking. Tango had seen such shapes before in the mountains before: a wolf. But unless the darkness was playing tricks on him, this creature was bigger by far than any wolf he'd seen in the wild. The torchlight came to a halt not forty paces from Tango and Meli's hiding place.

The ghostly figure placed the torch on the ground, and Tango saw his face. Beneath a snake's nest of unruly, long gray hair, the man bore a high forehead and equally prominent chin. Raised cheekbones and cords of tendon stood beneath large, thinly hooded eyes. Tango could not tell their color in torchlight, but somehow the man's eyes reminded Tango of graveyard stone.

"Who is—" Meli began to ask, but Tango clamped a hand over her mouth.

The man stayed in a crouch, removed something from a coat pocket, and began scrawling something on the cave floor. A wet snort drew Tango's attention. The wolf. He could see it now. Massive hackles of rough fur on its shoulders, sleek fur on its thick frame of muscle—and moonlight yellow eyes. Tango watched in horror as the creature sniffed and snorted, and slowly began to move in the direction of their hiding place.

Tango dropped to his knees and frantically began to search by feel through his many pockets and satchels.

"What's goin' on?" Meli whispered urgently. "Another spider?"

"N-no-no," Tango breathed back. "C'mon, know I've got some." He stiffened and peered through the stone. The beast was out of the torchlight, a black shadow and glistening eyes advancing in the darkness.

"What's going on?" Meli pleaded.

"A wolf," Tango whispered. "A big one, and it's on to our scent . . . coming this way."

Meli sucked in a breath.

Tango found the oblong tube he was looking for, snatched it from the leather pouch on his hip, and uncapped it. A harsh pine smell filled the air.

"Ugh, what is that?" Meli asked.

Tango felt for her hand, found it, and plopped a gob of paste in her palm. "Sapeline," he said. "Smear it in your armpits, behind your ears, and—"

"Smear it? Armpits—wha?"

"It's got t'go where ya smell," Tango said. "Do it! Oh, and ya have t'put it . . . uh . . ."

"Ewww, Tango . . . there? Do I really haf'to?"

"If ya' don'na cover your smells, that wolf'll get us."

Without another word, they both went to work smearing themselves with the pungent paste. The reek was powerful, like snorting evergreen needles and munching on pine cones—enough to make them gag—but they both managed to hold back the reflex. There was something prickly in the paste as well, maddeningly uncomfortable, especially in certain places. They endured it, fearing the wolf, fearing discovery. Tango slowly raised up to look between the fangs of stone. The wolf stood right there, nothing but the stone fence between them.

It stood motionless for a moment, but Tango heard its wet breathing. It snuffled and sniffed. Its semi-luminous yellow eyes seemed riveted on a lower plane as if it could see Meli through the stone. Then it suddenly snorted and rose up a little taller. It shook its head and trotted quickly away, back to its master.

"Stop fooling around, Sköll," came a voice like an echo of thunder.

Tango ducked down but watched through the tiniest sliver between the jutting stone. The massive wolf sneezed twice and kept shaking its head. The tall figure hissed, "Quiet!"

He returned to a crouch and seemed to be drawing symbols of some kind. Short, scraping movements, but without a moment's pause or any visible indecision. Then, he withdrew six red candles.

One at a time, he lit them, dribbled wax onto the stone floor, and then anchored the candles in place. He stood and backed away from his design. "Sköll, at my heel," he commanded. "I need you alert for this."

Meli joined at Tango's side and found a crease she could see through. "Who is he?" she whispered.

"I don' know," he whispered. "Too tall for Hammer's Gap, not a Stonehand, either. Human, maybe. Never seen his ilk before now."

The stranger uncorked a tube the length of his forearm. He cried out something in a language Tango and Meli didn't understand. He waved the tube around, and a glistening powder feathered out into the air. Like dust motes in a ray of sun, the powder cascaded downward toward the flickering candles. There came a whoosh and a red flash, and all the powder ignited. Suddenly the air around the stranger seemed filled with crimson serpents. They whirled a moment and then streaked off into the unknown depths of the cave.

The wolf pacing around his legs, the man stretched wide his arms and cried out in a voice, deep and resonant . . . like an avalanche somehow finely tuned. "Striack, felsom durim a Sabryne! Raudrith et Quevarith, sooth felsom durim a Sabryne! Vangsurrow mar, vangsurrow mar, VANG-SUR-ROW-MAR!"

There came a terrifying silence. More than silence, it was as if all sound had been torn away, leaving a raw, bleeding emptiness. Tango and Meli fell to the stone floor and clutched their throats. They gasped for breaths but felt nothing. Numbness flooded over them.

But then, the ground began to tremble . . . the movement strange and irregular. Bouncing, then slewing, then a rapid tremor. All at once, the sound returned with a great roar. Impossible wind gusted out of the darkness. Tango and Meli clutched at each other and the floor. The invisible surge tore at their hair and their clothes. A monstrous cry rose above the gusting air current. It was a guttural, deep scream that throbbed with the ringing of heavy bells.

The wind ceased just as suddenly as it came. Tango and Meli, weeping but daring not to make a sound, slowly rose to their knees. Wide-eyed and trembling, they stared at each other and then dared to peek through the stone. The thunder-voiced man was still there. With one gloved hand on the hilt of a sword at his side and the other in the wide pocket of his long black coat, he stared into the distance and seemed to be waiting. His wolf companion paced nervously behind him. The red candles somehow stood and were still lit.

From the black distance came a rumbling thud. Then another. And each time, the cave shuddered. Somewhere beyond what Tango and Meli could see, stone cracked, and rock fell against rock. The cadence of the deep thuds was slow but continuous. It grew louder and louder. Tango and Meli struggled to see, but there was nothing there beyond the candles' light. A pair of knobby stalactites snapped off from the cave's high ceiling, tumbled through the air, and came to a jarring rest far from where they should have landed.

"Be still!" the man hissed at the wolf. The wolf froze in its tracks directly behind the man.

The crushing thuds stopped, but still there was nothing. And yet, Tango felt there was something there. The air itself felt thick and close like one might feel in a crowded chamber. But without any warning, three jets of crimson flame burst from the darkness and engulfed the man. The flames were unlike any blaze Tango or Meli had ever seen. Like burning ribbons of incandescent blood, the licks of fire danced and writhed.

And when the streams of fire ended, Tango and Meli gasped. The man had turned to stone. His wolf was singed but still alive. It crouched behind the stone figure and emitted a muted whine.

"Pretty . . ." came the deep voice. "But your vaunted red flame cannot penetrate skin of stone." The man melted back into fleshly existence. "Raudrim-Quevara, I summon you."

The darkness bulged and wavered, and then a titanic form crawled forth. It was wreathed in darkness and seemed to be growing. Tango and Meli had heard many dragon stories. They'd read books and seen drawings. But aside from the long neck and folded, bat-like wings, this thing, this monstrous thing looked nothing like the dragons they'd seen. Horns like a ram's. A flourishing mane of hair like a stallion's, only deep red. And torso of human-shape and musculature but with feminine curves.

"I am Cythraul," the man uttered, and then he ran at the creature. Something like a chain slung down from his hand, and he cast it at the beast. It arced up and over the creature's raptor-like head and then wrapped around its neck. The man who called himself Cythraul, vaulted into the air, swung on the chain, and dropped onto the creature's neck right behind the flowing crimson mane on its head.

Tango and Meli watched in awe as Cythraul drew a long, subtly curved blade and lanced it into a sleeved pocket of bone behind the beast's jaw, deep into what must have been the creature's ear. The creature twisted and rolled, knocking down stalactites with its wings as it came to a calamitous rest on its back. "Be still, or I will end you!" Cythraul thundered. The creature, easily fifty times the man's size, fell motionless except for a tremor in one wing.

Cythraul kept the blade in place and drew his mouth up to the beast's ear. He whispered for a great while, but Tango and Meli could not make out his words. At last, he leaped down off the creature and asked, "Do we have an understanding?"

"Weeee, doooooo." The creature's voice reminded Tango of the searing hiss that escaped from flowing lava whenever the mountains west of Hammer's Gap erupted. "But I will take what isss mine firsssssst."

"As you wish," he said. "I care nothing for Cragheath Tor. But do not miss my deadline by even so much as a day. I know your secrets. I know your debts, and I know the one you fear."

With unfathomable speed, the creature rolled to its feet and charged past Cythraul and the wolf. Its wing clipped the stone on the ceiling above Tango and Meli. A large hunk of rock fell. It landed well away from the cowering pair, but crashed into fragments. Several caromed toward them. Tango jerked Meli away, but it was too late. A stone the size of a nerfa gourd glanced off of the back of her head.

She fell limp in his arms.

CHAPTER 4

IMPROVISATION

I found him sweaty from exercise in the long yard. "It's time you had a real sword," *I told him.*

The lad mistook my meaning and went eagerly to the barrel and started to sift through the blades. He selected a shiny short sword that looked new and relatively dangerous. But he barely had the sword out of the barrel when he yanked his hand back, stung. He dropped the blade and tried to rub the pain away. I daresay it happened so fast that he had no idea what had happened. But there it was, a ruddy welt rising on his knuckle.

He turned and looked at me then. I could see his slowcoach wheels in motion: Had Synic really rapped my knuckles? Could the old man really move that fast? *I had, and I could, but I enjoyed keeping him guessing.*

"Do you not remember?" *I asked him, giving my best glower.* "A used sword is of no use to a true swordsman. Next time, listen. I don't like to repeat myself."

The lad ran off to his quarters, and so help me, he came back with another blade dangling by his side.

"What is that?" *I asked him, my fury mounting.*

"Why, it's my sword," *he replied, drawing the weapon and swooshing it this way and that with a flourish.*

"Your sword?" *I asked.* "Did someone give it to you?"

The lad replied, "Yes, my nuncle did. He fought for King Mendeleev in the Gorrack Wars."

"If it is your nuncle's blade, then give it back to him."

"He's dead, sir."

Impertinent lad. "Then mount it on your wall to remember him or else throw it away! It will not serve you in the least. Cast it aside, and join me at the anvil."

"But I thought . . ."

"You thought you would learn to fight with a sword that you did not make. Now, peace, and join me at the anvil."

And that was how I began to train the greatest pupil I've ever had: Alastair Coldhollow.

—From the Journal of Synic Keenblade,
Entry #156, 4 Octale 1922 AS

41 SEDWYN 2238

Sweat dripped from High King Lochlan's square jaw and poured down his already glistening chest. He extended his left arm for balance, lifted his fencing blade vertically to his forehead, and bowed slightly to his opponent.

General Alfred Adelbard, Loch's tutor, did the same.

"Once more!" Queen Maren cried from the balcony overhead. "Show what you've learned, Loch!"

Loch smiled at her. He could almost feel the radiance of her expression. He thought he knew why she glowed. She was certainly proud of her only son, but it was more than that. Much more. How often had she told him he looked so very much like his father, Aravel, when he was young? It was very true. Loch had seen portraits, especially the one in their private chambers.

But often, he wondered about his mother's grief. *More than twenty years gone,* Loch thought. *And still . . . she has not let him go.*

General Adelbard cleared his throat. "Are you going to duel or just sit there slackjawed like a Sidonese chimparoo?"

"I can do both," Loch replied. He faced his instructor. "You've taught me everything you know, old 'Bard. You just make sure you don't get your beard caught in your crossguard."

Adelbard smirked, lowered his sword, and said, "Savat?"

"Savat," Loch replied. He let his blade fall to horizontal and dropped into his fighting stance.

Adelbard moved fast. He was left handed and struck with a hard, high chop to Loch's right shoulder. The young king blocked hard, and his teacher used the momentum to spin. His mossy gray beard whirled and flopped with the lightning quick turn. 'Bard dropped to one knee and swept his blade at Loch's feet.

But Lochlan Stormgarden had seen that move far too many times to lose his footing. He leaped the blade and planted a half-strength kick on 'Bard's shoulder. Off balance only a moment, 'Bard cartwheeled out of Loch's reach.

Loch came on the offensive, charging in with a series of sharp slashes. No wasted movement, just crisp strokes . . . onside, off-side, onside . . . developing a rhythm. Loch wanted to lull his opponent into a pattern, a repetitive, unthinking series. All the while, Loch was measuring 'Bard's strength, watching his balance. An opening would come.

He backed his instructor halfway across the fencing room, through the intermittent bands of sunlight from the room's tall windows. The clash and clang of the blades were muted by the rich wood panelling that covered every inch of the room, even the ceiling some forty feet above. Even as he subtly increased the weight of his attacks, Loch caught a breath of that wood. Age-old cedar. But there was something else in the scent. A hint of something musky.

How many high kings had trained in this very room? Loch wondered if he was smelling the manly scent of his father. Perhaps that was another reason why his mother liked to come to the fencing room. It was—

'Bard darted under a weak slash and lunged. Loch had been entranced by his own rhythmic strokes . . . and his wandering thoughts. He'd left his opponent a huge opening. For a lesser swordsman, it would have been a fatal mistake. 'Bard's thrust came at Loch's belt. But such was the young king's agility and strength that he was able to throw himself backward and form a C with his body. 'Bard's stab, even if it had been full strength and to kill, would have missed its mark.

Loch batted his opponent's blade down with a defensive back-hand stroke. He renewed his attack, but was behind in his tempo. 'Bard still maintained the advantage. He came on with lusty downstrokes and dangerous flicking slashes. Loch backed up. He felt his opponent trying to flank him, but couldn't do anything to stop him. Just a matter of time before—

It came faster than Loch expected. 'Bard drove toward Loch's offside, the left side of his body, forcing a weak, backhanded block. Then, with a mighty flourish, 'Bard threw his weight into a devastating upstroke. It was designed to propel Loch's sword high, completely opening his defense for a spinning slash.

The blow crashed into Loch's sword just above the hilt. But rather than letting the powerful stroke take his sword arm up to a useless height, Loch improvised. He let go of the sword alto-gether. 'Bard's mighty upstroke knocked Loch's sword whirling into the air.

Loch dove under 'Bard's spinning attack, caught his blade just before it hit the ground, and then drove a powerful thrust to within an inch of his instructor's chest.

General Adelbard was no stranger to Loch's creative sword-play, but this was something extraordinary. His beard seemed to sag and he said, "I . . . I did not see that coming."

"Wonderful!" Maren cried from above.

"Ah, so-so," came another voice from the chamber door. "Wouldn't have fooled me."

"Nor me," a third voice said.

Loch spun on his heel, looked to the door. "Uncle Alastair! Telwyn!"

A broad shouldered blur slammed into Loch and crushed him in a hug that most bears would envy. Loch returned the mighty embrace until Telwyn pushed him back to arm's length.

"Look at you!" Telwyn said. "The very image of a high king! Wouldn't you say, MiDa?"

Alastair Coldhollow joined them in the center of the fencing room. "Very kingly indeed," he said. "The light beard is new. Going for roguishly handsome, is it?"

"Definitely handsome," Abbagael said, appearing at Loch's side. She ran the back of her hand down Loch's fuzzy chin. He ducked but not soon enough to avoid Abbagael's peck on the cheek.

"Hey!" Alastair complained. "If you are dishing out compliments and kisses, I would think your husband might receive one."

She fell into Alastair's arms and traced a finger on the scars that formed a cross on his cheek below his right eye. "Maidens like scars," she said playfully.

"No wonder you fell for me then," replied Alistair. "I certainly have more than my fair share. Of scars that is . . . not, ahem, maidens."

Loch shook his head and barked a self conscious laugh. But he battled within. Here were his dearest friends in all of Myriad, but at the same time, he rued the attention, the focus on himself. He looked up at Telwyn . . . just 27 years old, but as manly as could be. His largish eyes were a whorl of warm almond and amber, and they radiated understanding, kindness, and compassion. Locks of nearly black hair framed his prominent brow, broad cheekbones, and granite chin. A razor's edge dark beard ran down his jaw and blended into a tight goatee.

If anyone looks like a high king, Lochlan thought, it's you.

"Ah, dear, dear friends," came a soft, matronly voice from the door. Queen Maren stood at the threshold, one arm on the doorframe, the other hugging around her waist. "It has been far too long since your last visit."

Abbagael went to her, and they embraced tenderly. It seemed to Loch that Abbagael handled his mother gently, as if the queen were delicate crystal and might shatter.

"Far too long," Abbagael echoed. "But we wouldn't miss the ceremony."

"No," Maren said, "I know you wouldn't. But there need not be an occasion for friends to visit."

Abbagael glanced sideways at Alastair. "I am sorry, Maren, but it's just that—"

Alastair cut in. "It's just that her foolish husband keeps dragging her to distant lands on searches and other vain adventures."

Gladness danced in the queen's eyes, but her smile was tentative. "I will speak to Drüst about more frequent wind carriage excursions," she said. "Dear Abbagael, might we spend a few moments together?"

"Clarissant Hall?" Abbagael asked. The queen nodded. Abbagael winked at her husband, and then she and the queen left the fencing chamber arm-in-arm.

"I've brought Icetooth," Telwyn said.

"Icy!" Loch exclaimed. "Where?"

"He's in the courtyard."

"You left him there?"

Telwyn nodded.

"Unattended?"

Telwyn nodded again.

Loch suppressed a smile by forcing a frown. "He'll eat all the squirrels again!"

"Well," Telwyn said with an impish grin, "I suppose we'd better go and play with him . . . keep him distracted from the, uh . . . menu."

"Wait a moment," Alastair said. "You lads aren't going to scamper off, are you? What am I to do?"

Loch laughed. "Maybe old 'Bard here would like a lesson from his favorite Anglish General."

"That I would," Adelbard said. "Have you a blade?"

"Always," Alastair said.

"Good, then. Teach me something I can use to deflate this royal whelp."

They shared a laugh.

"C'mon," Telwyn urged. "The squirrel population of Anglinore is dwindling!"

"**D**uck!" Tel warned as he dove and rolled into the kennberry bushes.

But it was too late for Lochlan. He didn't see the swooping snow drake behind him. Icy tilted one wing down and administered such a slap to the back of the young king's head that he spit out the berries he'd been chewing. "Oh, I am going to GET you!" Loch yelled.

Icy snorted in reply.

"That was a snort, wasn't it?" Loch asked, sniffing the air thoughtfully.

"I meant to warn you about that," Tel said, peeking out of the bush. "I did tell you not to feed him any berries. I just never said why. LOOK OUT!"

"Not this time!" Loch crowed. He ducked, felt Icy pass overhead, then leaped. He caught the drake's legs, intending to drag him down and tackle him. But Icy's wings were much stronger than he'd remembered. Icy pulled at the air and took Loch up with him. "Uh, oh," Loch said. "Icy, what are you doing?"

The snow drake spiraled around the courtyard as high as the third floor balcony. "Icetooth!" Telwyn admonished, "you bring Loch back down this instant! He's only High King of the whole realm! Don't drop him!"

Icy curled his neck to see Telwyn and then banked hard to the right and dropped down, gaining speed. "No," Loch said. "No, you're not going to plow me into that bush!" Icy came in low and fast, but Loch put his feet down. His bootheels dug up ten feet of turf before catching. Loch used all of his upper body strength and yanked Icy down. The beast cartwheeled into the kennberries.

Loch laughed triumphantly, until Icy came up from the bush with jaws positively stuffed with clusters of the tiny orange berries.

"Uh, oh," Telwyn said. "This could be rather . . . explosive."

But Lochlan wasn't finished. He leaped to his feet and then dove on top of Icy and wrestled the creature out of the bushes. They rolled playfully on the turf several revolutions until Loch came up panting. "This snow drake of yours is entirely too strong!"

"True," Tel said. "His nature. Can you imagine taking on one of the big dragons of old?"

"No," Loch replied. "I cannot."

CHAPTER 5

SCARS

"Building a comfortable Delshroom is no piece of smerge muffin, I can tell you."

"Nossir! It's a fair lot of work, the better part of a year."

"Raw materials be the name of the game."

"Startin' with yer choice of Delshroom, and bigger is'na always better."

"Snug and comfy is the way to go. And for those, we recommend the shroom forest north of the Tor."

"Round Hammer's Gap."

—A Dialogue between Timmo Tyolar and Aldus Dornlab, overheard at the Spotted Spider Inn, 2141 AS

41 SEDWYN 2238

"Ah, General Coldhollow, they told me I might find you here," said Sebastian Sternbough, High Shepherd of Anglinore, as he ducked into the fencing chamber. "But I . . . uh, thought you were training."

"I have been training," Alastair said, "for the past two hours at least."

"But you don't look very . . . ah, taxed. You're not perspir—" Alastair held up a hand and then pointed to General Adelbard.

The general was bent over, leaning on his sword in the corner of the chamber. Sweat fell from his head and pelleted the floor. "I'm alright," he said. He breathed in ragged wheezes and gasps. "Just need . . . a bit of a rest, 's'all. We'll go again in . . . in a bit."

"No, General, I think we've scrapped enough for one afternoon," Alastair said. "I've taught you all I can in one day. And I daresay I've learned a great deal from you."

Adelbard coughed out a laugh. "I've seen masters," he said. "And I've seen masters of masters. But I have never seen a man with a sword do what you do . . . move as you do. Not Aravel, not Morlan, not even Synic Keenblade. To think you might have learned something from me . . . flattering, but not likely."

Alastair smiled as if in distant memory but then his face grew serious, even stern. "Synic Keenblade was my teacher, 'Bard, did you know? And something he taught me—with bruises and cuts all too numerous—was that every swordsman is worth studying. Every good swordsman can teach you something. For instance, from you I learned that a spinning move can be a most cunning tactic. Oh, I've done plenty of spins in my time, but the way you use it, 'Bard, daring your opponent to thrust at your open backside, all the while shielding your coming strike—now that is genius. It's that kind of skill that keeps you as swordmaster of Anglinore castle, no small feat."

General Adelbard bowed. "You honor me."

"As I should," Alastair said. He turned to the Shepherd. "Now, then Sebastian, well met!"

"Well met," he returned. "Have you a few moments to spare for an old Shepherd?"

"Old?" Alastair laughed. "As men count years, no doubt you would be aged. But Shepherds? Who can tell? You look barely out of your first triniary."

"We Shepherds do like to keep our secrets close," Sebastian said with a wink. "Care to walk with me to my tower?"

Alastair bowed to General Adelbard and followed the Shepherd out of the fencing room into the dark corridor.

Shepherd Sebastian sat in a massive wooden chair near the tower window and absently stroked a large, sleek, orange and white cat in his lap. Alastair sat on a similar seat a few paces away and thought sure the old Shepherd had crafted the chairs himself. Like living roots, the chair legs twisted up from the floor and then meshed into a cradle seat and vertical rests gnarled pleasantly to fit the contours of a person's arms. *I wonder if Sebastian learned his craft from the Willowfolk?*

But no, Alastair knew, that with a touch, the Shepherd could bring the wood to life and shape it to fit anyone perfectly. Sebastian could control all plant life. It was his Shepherd gift.

"The crisscrossed scar beneath your right eye," said the Shepherd, "how did you get it?"

Alastair's fingertips brushed the old furrows. "There are two scars actually," he said. "They are very old, but one much older than the other. The vertical stripe I earned by refusing to follow my sword master's instructions during a duel. It was only Synic Keenblade's great skill that prevented the blade from taking my eye."

Sebastian winced. "And the other?"

Alastair hesitated. "The horizontal cut," he whispered, "was carved by a thorn as I heedlessly charged through the forest after one of Morlan's marked interests. Of that, I will say no more. That part of my life is dead to me now. Come, Sebastian, I'm certain you did not bring me to your tower to ask about scars."

"No," the Shepherd said. "No, I did not. And forgive my prying. It's just that my mind is burdened with . . . ah, so many things that I do not know where to begin. I am worried."

"Well," Alastair said, trying to lighten the mood, "isn't that a Shepherd's primary job—to worry?" He laughed, but cut short his mirth when he saw the Shepherd's unchanged expression. "Share your burdens, my friend, and tell me how I might help bear the load."

Sebastian nodded. He scraped at the arm of his chair with a fingernail, and a small green shoot unfolded until it was about two inches tall. "I have been listening to the voices on the wind," he said. "As I always do. And, in the last twelve years, the voices have spoken almost exclusively of peace and prosperity. But now, I hear a voice that I have never heard before."

"From where?" Alastair asked, leading forward.

"That I do not know. Some place very, very far away. It is an ancient voice full of odd inflections and nuances. And it is a bit garbled as well, at times very strained and hard to discern from the many other voices of Myriad. But, Alastair, one thing cannot be mistaken from this voice: it speaks of . . . of pain. There is, somewhere in our world, an anguish so keen and so profound that I can scarcely endure it for long without spiraling myself into a black mood. It is as if thousands of souls are tortured, flayed in bright red agony, and their cries have bled together into one."

"Is it . . . could it be Morlan . . . across the Dark Sea on . . . on whatever misbegotten continent his ship ran aground?"

Sebastian shook his head so vigorously that Alastair heard the crackling of bone. "Nay, voices from across the Dark Sea cannot be heard here. Not only can those banished from this land never return physically, but they will never be heard from again either. I do not believe the First One would abide it."

"Then who?"

"I do not know," Sebastian whispered. "Perhaps the Hinterlands or the great islands in the far south. Or maybe even something west of the Gorrack Nation"

"Now you speak of strange things beyond my reckoning. The Hinterlands? Does anyone live beyond the Impasse Mountains? And who has dared sail the Tangled Straights to visit those islands . . . and return alive? Hmph, no one even knows if there is anything west of the Gorrack Nation. The Gorracks, if they have even explored, have not been so generous as to share any discoveries."

The Shepherd removed the cat from his lap, gently placed him on the floor, and leaned forward. "These voices are potent and heavy. I am afraid to imagine what calamity they might portend. Now, you partially understand why I am burdened."

"Partially?" Alastair slumped back in his chair. "What else, Sebastian?"

"Queen Maren," he replied.

"Is she well? I thought she looked pale . . . gaunt even."

"Physically, she is undernourished as you see, but nothing else that I can diagnose. My herbs and salves do little to help her." Sebastian paused and gazed at the window. "She bears scars of another kind."

"But so keen, even after all these years?"

Sebastian nodded. He met Alastair's wide eyes with his own. "Time passing seems only to magnify the hurt, rather than heal it. In the span of one horrid day, Maren discovered the remains of long dead King Brysroth in the well and then, as the sun rose that morning, she watched helplessly as Aravel, her soulmate, drowned and burned in his own blackened blood."

"And both murdered by Morlan."

"Brysroth's death was almost certainly at Morlan's hands," the Shepherd said. "Maren tells of how often Morlan visited the well, how often he spoke mysteriously about it. His smug little secret. But how he slew his father and was able to submerge the old king's body in the well with no one noticing, no one knows."

"But Aravel?"

"That is less clear," Sebastian said, staring once more through the chamber window.

"But the way he died, the inner boiling—"

"Is unlike anything I have ever seen. There is no poison in this world that can do that to a man. Even if there were, we were both on that ship, Alastair. Morlan had no way to administer poison of any kind to Aravel."

"But Morlan touched Aravel. I saw him, just before he boarded the fateful craft."

"And Morlan was searched head to toe," Sebastian said. "He bore nothing but the garments we gave him, his flesh, and his chains."

"He did it," Alastair declared. "I don't know how, but he did. Morlan hated Aravel, despised him . . . the wretched man. How many have suffered because of him? Enough of him. What of Maren?"

"She suffers profoundly," said the Shepherd. "At first it was not as noticeable. She had to rule the kingdom after its most disastrous season in many ages . . . and she did so with remarkable serenity. But I could tell. Often she would seclude herself in Clarrisant Hall to weep or wander among the quiet stones where Aravel now rests.

"But now that Lochlan has grown old enough to bear the crown, Maren has steadily declined. She sleeps long and often at odd times. She roams the corridors of this castle like a spirit and has taken to mumbling to herself at whiles. She will not suffer the light of the sun and barely eats. I tell you, Alastair, she is withering before our eyes."

Alastair stood up abruptly. He paced the chamber and rubbed his hands together as if keeping warm. "I may know something of what Queen Maren is going through and it grieves me to imagine one so warm and vital as she . . . now so void of hope. But what of her faith?"

"She doesn't speak of the First One often but, as I said, she spends a great deal of time in Clarrisant Hall where she prays. But I fear she finds herself at odds with Allhaven because of Aravel's loss."

"Whatever life grief will not steal," Alastair said, "bitterness will." Alastair took his seat. "Ah, I am glad Abbagael will spend some time with Queen Maren."

"I am glad of it also." Sebastian scratched at his armrest. "There is one further matter."

"King Lochlan?"

Sebastian's jaw dropped an inch. "How did you know?"

Alastair raised an eyebrow. "I've never known a twenty-one year-old lad without problems."

"True enough," said the Shepherd. "But most twenty-one year olds do not wear the crown of High Overlord."

"Point well taken. What ails the young lord? All accounts say he's ruled well."

Sebastian took a deep breath. "Lochlan is as talented as he is noble. He has governed with remarkable mastery these past four years. He makes good decisions and has the faith of the Anglish Guard. He handles the sword brilliantly, reads and writes brilliantly, leads and legislates brilliantly—as a matter of fact, I don't think I know of any skill at which Loch does not excel."

"So again, what is the trouble?"

"I am afraid . . . he's bored. He doesn't want to sit in one place for long or do one thing for very long."

"But that is his duty, his bloodline." Alastair exhaled loudly. "He should rejoice that Myriad is at peace. Bored!"

The Shepherd frowned. "We all know this—even Lochlan does, I think. But there is another element that he is less apt to reveal openly. Lochlan is troubled by all the attention bent his way. He is especially vexed by others who elevate him to something far above a twenty-one year old lad. It goes well beyond shy to a degree where he doesn't seem comfortable in his own skin. And I do not know what will come of it."

Alastair Coldhollow was silent for many heartbeats. At last he said, "So, Sebastian, to take measure of the things that trouble you: some kind of otherworldly pain and suffering is screaming out from the wind, Queen Maren is slowly dying of grief, and King Lochlan may not want his crown?"

"Yes," the Shepherd said, "that about covers it."

CHAPTER 6

SURE SHOT

Pan-seared blackfin, garlic new-potatoes,
diced fincely root . . . . . . 12 copper, 6 fin
Lightly breaded pepper trout, long-baked cretchin bread,
dashed tomatoes . . . . . . 9 copper
Grilled perch with scallions, rosemary carrots,
and donach berry cobbler . . . . . . 16 copper, 9 fin
Steamed bushel of butter crabs, hush-dragons,
and fried crispins . . . . . . 14 copper, 4 fin

—Asterday's Menu from the Cavaat Inn
(Exclusive Inn for the Elders), Wetlands, Chaparrel, 2137 AS

45 SEDWYN 2238

The banging on my door woke me up before first light. I swayed for a hazy moment in my brell hammock before realizing what I was hearing. "Stars alive," I muttered as I rolled out of the brushed wool netting and dropped to the floor. I slipped on my tattered old robe and padded through the crickety-quiet twilight to the door. But I didn't open it up right away. Since the Gorrack Invasion, Chapparel was as safe as any country in Myriad, but living in the Wetlands on the far northern coast had proved to have its risks. The Dark Sea, even the Bay of Taranaar, hid all manner of threats. This I knew all too well. Moonlight shone dully on the blade of my father's axe, mounted with great care above the ember-filled fireplace. I thought about taking it down.

I listened for a long moment, again beginning to wonder if I'd heard what I'd thought I'd heard. I edged closer to the door, my cheek almost to the wood. One heartbeat, two—

WHUMP, WHUMP! I leaped back, grabbed my father's axe, and swallowed back the reflexive fear.

"Ariana!" came a hoarse, low voice. "Get up! We've plans to make!"

"Mill?" The axe dropping to my side, I went back to the door. "Mill, is that you?"

WHUMP! "Of course it's me! Who'dya think b'banging on your door? Now let me in. We've plans to make."

I threw up the four-inch thick piece of lumber that barred my door and yanked on the cold iron handle. Mill slipped in, not that someone his size could actually slip anywhere. Millard Key, or Millard the Mark as most of his friends called him, stood two fists above six foot. He had broad shoulders as thick as dock pilings and very long arms. The scaled leather jerkin he always wore had stitching and seams in odd places and fit his deep chest strangely, making him look part dragon. His hair, the color of a russet potato, stuck out this way and that in shaggy clumps. As his unruly locks and awkward clothes attested, Mill insisted on doing everything himself.

A happily unkempt mustache drooped on his top lip, and an odd little thatch of whiskers puffed out below his bottom lip. Glad chestnut eyes gleamed when he saw me. And then, as usual, he grabbed me around the waist and whirled me around in a hug.

"Hey," I said. "Easy, big guy, I'm armed!"

I held up the axe, but Mill squeezed me so hard I almost dropped it. "Put me down, ya big goof!"

"Ah, good t'see ya, Ariana!" He thumped me to the ground, but before he let me go, he slapped a very bristly kiss on my cheek.

"Hey," I complained with mock anger. "We're friends, remember?"

"Now there warn't nothing romantic about that little peck. Just a friendship thing, 'sall."

I shoved the door closed, turned to face him, and said, "Well, you've woken me up. Out with it, what're these plans we've got to make?"

He grinned at me. Honestly, he seemed near to bursting with . . . with something.

"C'mon," I growled. "Before I use this axe and knock you down to my size."

"Okay, okay," he said. "Leave it to me to befriend an axemaiden."

"Mill!"

"Okay, sorry. Here it is. How would you like to win the Huntmeet?"

The bottom dropped out of my stomach. "That's not funny, Mill. You know the Elders won't let me enter. I've no beard, remember?"

"An odd duck you'd make with a beard," he said. "But listen, Ariana, what if you could enter? Could you win?"

"Sure I could. You're my only real competition."

"I thank you for that." His eyes narrowed thoughtfully. Not something they often did.

His cuteness made me want to laugh, but I stifled it.

"Now what about this?" he asked. "Could you shoot a bull's-eye from ten yards back a' the firing line?"

"You know I could," I said. "But why? No matter how far away it is, I can't enter. I can't join the hunters."

"Do you know the sourgum shrubs are gettin' quite bushy on the eastern end a' the firing line? I've been noticing that."

"Mill, just what are you getting at?"

We waited until the hunters had gone on their noonday search. With the intense sun overhead, they'd ventured deeper into the wood than usual and took longer than usual to return. We had plenty of time to practice. And it worked like a charm. I had to hand it to Mill. It was a clever plan. And more than that. The only way he comes up with such chicanery is if he's thinking of me. He did that all too often. Much too often for my liking, I thought as I closed my journal.

He'd been smitten with me since, well . . . ever. And he's made no secret of it. But I'm not like the village women who stand around the hunters' barracks all afternoon flirting with anything with facial hair. I've been up front with Mill. I told him directly, "I don't want a man in my life romantically. It's not time for that yet." And, though it hurt him to hear it, I had to be honest. I told him that, even if it were time for me to find a man and settle down, he would not be the one. Mill is a real gentleman, and he's always been very kind to me. A perfect friend, but not a perfect husband.

I don't believe in love at first sight or any of that other sappy nonsense. But I do believe that a woman knows the right man when she gets to know him. He's got to be faithful and honest, strong and witty, adventurous and kind. It's not always definable. But a woman always knows. My mother taught me that when I was very, very young. I would never forget.

I slipped my journal into the hollow behind the fireplace and replaced the stones. Not sure why I hide them. Some people hide treasure. My memories are my treasure.

I passed by the rickety, tall dresser I'd build when I was eleven and stopped short. Dust and miscellaneous smears marred the surface of the round mirror I'd hung there. I don't often look at myself in the mirror, but this time I did. I thought I'd seen someone else in the glass. A ghost. But no, it was only me. The older I grew, the more I looked like my mother. Just not enough like her to be pretty.

I ran my fingers through my long hair. The strawberry tint was gone. Just blond now, combed wheat with streaks of pure gold—my hair was my one redeeming feature. My eyebrows were too thick. My eyes were plain gray-blue. My nose was too big, my lips too small, and the cleft in my chin would be better suited on a man. Not surprisingly, I got that little divot from my father.

I opened the top drawer and took out a brown, weathered tunic—the one with the hood. Absolutely necessary, that hood was. My hair would stand out in the foliage without it.

The shadows on the dusty floor had grown long enough. Night would be coming soon. I'd need my rest to be ready for The Huntmeet. It began noon tomorrow. I had to be in place long before that.

46 SEDWYN 2238

They called him Millard the Mark for a reason: Mill could flat-out shoot. I'd seen him skewer a goose from three-hundred paces, and that with another hunter's bow. Millard didn't need me for the first few rounds, but we'd decided I would take a few early shots anyway. I stayed hunched down in the shrubbery and watched the scene unfold.

The village Elders arrived first to mark off the distances and set up the targets for the first heats. Even though I was certain they couldn't see me, I ducked down and tried to shrivel myself up. I'd not had a very good history with the Elders, and the future didn't show much promise either. Not as long as Plebian Scandeer was High Elder. It wasn't enough for him to put me in my place. No, he always cut me down to size, rubbed my face in it, and then made sure everyone in the village knew. I watched High Elder Scandeer bend over to adjust one of the targets. I had half a mind to put an arrow in his left buttock, but I was able to resist the temptation.

Barely.

The hunters began to arrive and stake out positions along the firing line. Mill better hurry up, I thought, watching the open spaces dwindling. Then, we had a problem: a hunter took up position at the eastern end of the firing line—right in front of me. It got worse when I saw who it was. Choiros Greenshambles. I groaned inwardly. Pudgy, pompous, and patronizing—Choiros was my absolute least favorite hunter. Trouble was, he was a good shot. And now he was standing on the firing line in exactly the place Mill needed to be.

"Choiros, what are you doing?" came a low, gruff voice. Mill at last.

"Preparing for the Huntmeet, peasant," Choiros said. "What does it look like?"

Mill laughed and shook his head. "Looks to me like you're taking the easy way out. Not your usual way . . . but I'm not all that surprised."

"Easy way—what are you talking about, Millard Key?"

"Nothing, oh great and mighty hunter." Mill began to walk away.

Clever, that Mill. He had him.

"Stop, Millard," Choiros practically commanded as he grabbed Mill's bracer-covered forearm. "What do ya mean, easy way? Choiros never takes the easy way."

Mill smirked. "Stars, you know just what yer doin'. Don't pretend ya don't. Every shooter knows the eastern edge here is the flattest ground. Better footing means easier aiming, easier shooting. 'S'fine for ya. Probably the only way you stand a chance."

Choiros' cheeks looked like ripe tomatoes. He strode up to Mill as if he was spoiling for a fight. He tried to get in Mill's face, which made me laugh so hard I almost gave away my hiding spot.

Choiros' stomach kept him many inches from being in Mill's face.

"I see what yer about," Choiros said. "Yer just givin' yerself an excuse for losing. I suppose you'll be shooting from the most uneven ground you can find?" Mill said nothing. "I'll have none of it, farm boy. Just to show you how much better I am with the bow than you, I'll take to the west. You take this easy spot. Even with it, I'll beat ya, I will."

"Ha!" Mill scoffed. "I could shoot left-handed from here and still beat you."

"Proof's not in the words," Choiros said as he waddle-marched away.

Millard glanced into the shrubs and winked.

Crowds had begun to gather on both sides of the range. Not too close. Even seasoned hunters occasionally had misfires. Merchants marched here and there, selling their wares. I could smell the smoked fish, the savory butter crabs, and the sweet honey brews. Ah, my mouth watered.

Torches were kindled on the Elders' platform, and trumpets sounded. Wearing his ceremonial robes now, Plebian Scandeer held up his arms for the already silent crowd to get . . . uhm, more silent. "The day is finally upon us," he declared, his eyebrows raised, eyelids lowered. "Favored and labored, scholarly and lowly, ruling classes and peasant working classes—the Huntmeet begins!" Cheers and shouts. Mugs of ale and willowmeade raised high. "As High Elder, I urge our revered hunters of the Wetlands, the greatest hunters in Chapparel—nay in Myriad—bring us today your most magnificent measure of strength and accuracy."

Stars and sand, the man could yammer! I thought, reconsidering the arrow-buttock temptation.

"For the Huntmeet demands nothing short of excellence— nay, perfection! Seven rounds, lads! Three from ninety paces, three from one-hundred twenty, and one from two hundred. Miss one bull's-eye on any set, and you're out. Do you hear that, people of the Wetlands? ONE missed, and you're out! Can you imagine the tension, the pressure . . ." The hot air. ". . . the stakes? Only a true master will win this day. Only the best of the best shall remain. My only regret on this joyous day is that my crippling injuries prevent me from competing."

Crippling injuries? The man had jammed a willow reed under his thumbnail!

"I light now the green torch! Let the first round of the Huntmeet begin!" The Elder's torch descended in an overly dramatic, slow arch, and bright green flames sprang up from the brazier. The fire danced, and the crowd murmured with anticipation. The field judges took their places, one judge behind every three archers.

I scanned up the firing line. As I thought: to a man, they were all members of the hunting guild. I knew at least a handful of archers better than some I saw on the line, but since they weren't "hunting guild stock"—or weren't male—they were sharply discouraged or completely forbidden from taking part in the Huntmeet. And that was why I was hiding in the bushes.

Oohs and aaahs sprang from the crowds as arrows found their mark. But not all did. Ninety paces was child's play for a hunter, but the pressure of the competition got to some of them. A few shafts found the red instead of the gold, and those disqualified archers slunk away as quickly as they could. But not Mill. I watched as my friend put a tight group of three into the center of the gold circle.

The field judges nodded approvingly. The signal flags went up, and the archers that remained strode across the field to retrieve their arrows. Choiros was a little late getting back to the firing line, but I couldn't tell whether it was because of his bulging girth or that he wanted time to sneer at Mill.

Twenty-nine archers began the Huntmeet, and now it was down to twenty-three. The second round began. Ninety paces still. I got ready, dropping into a crouching stance. Not as comfortable, but no trouble really. Mill and I had agreed that I would take the second shot of the second round. We'd practiced a ton, but still, it was a good idea to shoot under tournament pressure—before the distance increased.

The buzz in the crowd grew, and the oohs and aahs were louder now. Mill calmly put his first shot into the bull's-eye. This was it. I readied an arrow and took aim. So did Mill. I counted to three-butter-crabs, just as we'd rehearsed. We fired. Mill and I had chosen black arrows with dark green fletchings so they would be harder to follow. He'd altered his aim just enough to miss the target altogether, his shaft disappearing harmlessly into a deep thatch of pig-stick brambles. My shot had flown true from my hiding place, whooshed beneath Mill's right elbow, and buried itself deep into the bull's-eye. My heart pounding, I scanned the other competitors, the judges, even up to Scandeer on the Elder's platform. I exhaled. No one had noticed a thing.

The second round ended. Two more hunters dropped out. Those who remained gathered their arrows and took aim for round three. I was third shot in the third round. Mill nailed his first two. I nailed the last one. One more hunter fell out of the competition. And Choiros continued sneering.

As the judges moved the targets back to 120 paces, the crowd's murmur became a dull roar. The merchants had to scream their voices hoarse to be heard. I doubt anyone stopped to buy anything. The action was far too captivating. And all at once, it hit me. I was competing in the Huntmeet. Sure it wasn't legal in the strictest sense, and even if I/we won the whole thing, I'd never be recognized as Huntmeet Champion. But it mattered to me. How many times had the Elders put me down or held me back just because I'm a woman? How many others had the Elders and hunters' lethal prejudices scarred? Anywhere else in the many nations of Myriad, a woman could hunt. Why not here in the Wetlands?

Mill took aim. He was comfortable still at this distance. The firing began. Cheers and screams leaped out of the crowd, as well as near constant applause. Mill made his marks, a perfect set. Four hunters lost out, making the number sixteen remaining shooters. Choiros was one of them. The second set at 120 paces went much the same way. But during the middle of the third set, I heard a ridiculously loud curse. A hush fell over the crowd, and Choiros threw his bow to the ground.

"What do ya know?" Millard muttered. "Old Choiros has put one in the red!"

The judges converged on the target for a closer look, but alas, it turned out that Choiros' third arrow had indeed nicked the gold. The hunter danced with glee. It was actually kind of a wobbling bounce, but still Choiros remained in the field. The same could not be said for more than a dozen other competitors. The third round ended with only seven hunters still alive.

Mill, of course, was one of them, but he was getting a little nervous. I could tell he was relieved on the last arrow in the 3rd round, the way he leaned after the shot, willing it to the gold. He tapped his leg three times. It was time for the final round. The target was moved to two hundred paces. It was my signal to take over . . . totally.

Two hundred paces is a long shot. That distance invites a host of new variables to think about: gravity, wind, bowstring tension, etc. Every shot from here required mental gymnastics, calculations, and instinct. The last is what I had more than any other archer—so my Da told me. Mill told me as well. All I know is if I can see it, I can usually hit it.

The targets were moved back. Crowds moved in. The fishermen had returned from the shore adding substantially to the number of spectators. There must have been five thousand Wetlanders surrounding the Huntmeet. I didn't care. They couldn't see me. I hoped.

Mill took his position. Scandeer gave the signal. The final round began. Tack on fifteen paces for my shots, I was shooting 215 paces from the target. Mill raised his bow. I raised mine. Mill drew back the bowstring until the tips of his fingers were even with the back of his jaw. I drew my bowstring back farther, almost as far as my strength could pull it. The force off the pull and the speed it would generate would help fight its natural descent and the wind. A three-count from when Mill's right hand anchored, and we both released. Mill's arrow streaked low past the target. My shaft plunged into the bull's-eye. The judges looked on intently, offering sympathetic comments to the three archers who missed.

The second pull saw two more hunters forced out. Only Choiros and Mill remained. Silently, I exulted. Not only would

I win the Huntmeet, but I would beat the hunter who most opposed my participating. The thrill surged through me. Every pull of the bowstring made me tingle inside. I could almost feel the wind carved by each arrow and the satisfying thud of the target. It was almost as if I was riding along the shaft. My heart hammered as we prepared for the last pull at 200 paces.

So many judges were watching now. Our timing would have to be near perfect. Mill took aim. It was hard to concentrate with the crowd screaming all around us. Amid the roar, there were random shouts, cheers, and a few jeers even. It was somewhat jolting. I calmed myself and took aim. Mill's right hand stopped. I counted. One, two—

At that moment, everything went wrong. A judge walked behind Mill, directly in front of my hiding spot in the shrubs. I sucked in a gasp. Had Mill fired? I had only a split second. I couldn't shoot through the judge or around him. I gasped again as the idea struck. I reacted. I dropped to the ground, turning the bow horizontally, and fired.

In an instant, I'd calculated the new angle and released the shot. The arrow hurtled between the judges legs, rose steadily, and I lost sight of it. The judge had done a kind of skipping step to the side. I saw him reach down and rub the inside of his right calf. He straightened, shook his head, and shrugged. When he sidled out of the way, I saw the arrow.

Bull's-eye. The crowd erupted. I wanted to do a backflip. Mill glanced back at the shrubs and shook his head. He couldn't believe it either. A deep thumping quieted the chaos. Drums from the Elder's platform signaled that Plebian Scandeer was to speak again.

"Never in the history of the Huntmeet have we had a tie!" he crowed. "And at two hundred paces!" The spectators made a sound so loud that thunder would hang its head in shame at the comparison.

A tie? I felt sick. How did Choiros hit three bull's-eyes at two hundred paces? I guess he was better than I gave him credit for.

I bowed my head. No way the Elders would let this end in a tie. I thought I knew where this was headed. I also knew I had only two arrows left in my quiver.

"And so . . . these two master archers must engage in single combat!" the High Elder bellowed with all the drama he could muster . . . which was substantial. "We will move the targets back ten paces. Each archer gets one shot! If they both succeed, we move the targets again. Here me, Wetlanders! We will continue moving the targets back and shooting until one MAN emerges a winner!"

One man. My blood boiled. Swordplay, I could understand being male exclusive. Wrestling? Sure. But there was absolutely no reason a skilled woman archer couldn't enter. And couldn't win, for that matter. I intended to prove it.

The targets went back another ten paces. The judges gathered round. Choiros fired first. The crowd roared. He'd hit the bull's-eye. Mill took up his bow. We prepared. We fired. There was a hesitant split second, but the crowd went wild again. Bull's-eye. We tied again.

I had one arrow left.

This was it. Either Choiros missed, or I was finished shooting, and Mill was on his own. And there was no way to let Mill know. He would fire into the bushes, and Choiros would win. That got my blood pumping.

I watched as the targets went back another ten paces. Now, it really looked far away. The gold of the bull's-eye and the red of the next circle blended into an indistinct orange. I saw leaves whirling on the ground in the middle of the firing ground. Thank the Stars Choiros was shooting first.

I could only see bits of him through the foliage. But his movements looked a little tight, almost jerky. The crowd's buzzing rose in pitch, but then silenced eerily before Choiros released. It was deathly quiet. I heard the release, the twang of the bowstring. I heard the impact on the target. I closed my eyes. And then I heard the groan of more than a thousand voices.

The First One had favored me. Choiros had missed! Mill looked noticeably relieved. He stood at the firing line with visible confidence. I guess so. He wasn't actually shooting. Choiros hung his head, but only for a moment. He looked up expectantly, gazing at Mill. If Mill missed, they would no doubt shoot again.

Millard raised his bow and took aim. Thankfully, the judges were standing wide to either side of him. Mill's right hand came back. He paused. I counted. We fired. And—

All at once there was a collection of loud and terribly shocking sounds: a scream, the cracking of wood, a gushy splatter, and . . . a collective cry of outrage from the crowd.

CHAPTER 7

River Runs Red

Of course the littlins should mind their elders. And trouble follows when they don't. But lest we give the young snaps too much grief, there's another question to reckon. One that might prove equally daunting . . . but to us biggins. When the littlins come to us and tell us something as dire and serious as the grave, why don't we believe 'em?

—Gaffer Aeldis, quoted just before he left *The Wandering Boar* in Ellador, never to be heard from again. (2231 AS)

6 Solmonath 2238

Grim, weathered, and wrinkled, Tanner Goliant sat at the cedar table in his den, deep in the Delshroom he and his wife had built. *Not quite true*, Tanner reflected. *Of course the Maker of the Stars, Maker of all things, made the Delshroom. Raised it from a tiny sprout to a magnificent Capper.* Tanner and his beloved Dorisse had spent a fair Spriggan spring and summer hollowing it out and carving in the rooms. It had been a rich labor of love, and the Delshoom had become a true home.

Tanner wandered his eyes to the small portrait of Dorisse perched with care atop the dulsichord, her favorite instrument.

His grief for her loss had, over the years, eroded to a dull ache, but he still felt it more keenly now and then. He felt it now. Of course, he still had Tango and Meli—two finer sprigs no one had a right to ask for. So Tanner pushed deeper into his chair and enjoyed his early evening coffee.

Tanner liked the smell as much as the taste: almondy-sweet with a touch of chocolate and rich Alerian cream. The warm vapors from the mug tickled his nose. He took a sip, closed his eyes and savored the body-warming beverage. The storm had gone, leaving Tanner in blessed peace and qui—

SLAM! The front door crashed open so hard that canisters fell from shelves in the pantry, and Tanner spat coffee across the table.

"Da!" came a shrill voice from the front of the Delshroom. "Da, come quick! Meli's hurt fair bad!"

Frozen lightning streaked up Tanner's back, and he fled the den with every father's blackest nightmares chasing after him. The nightmares were faster.

He found Tango cradling his motionless daughter, blood reddening her long blond locks. "Wha-what happened?" Tanner whispered, his husky voice cracking. He started to kneel. "Here, set her on the cradle." He gestured to the long, bowed couch-swing. Tango laid her gently there.

Tanner knelt on the floor beside his daughter. "Oh, my Meli! Tango, what happened, my son?"

"It's my fault, Da," Tango cried, tear streaks running down his dusty cheeks. "I went in the cave, and Meli could'na resist followin' me. A fair big stone fell an hit her sharp on the back a' the head."

Tanner gently rolled his daughter. The blood was frightening, but when he sifted through her hair, he found only a small cut, already scabbed over. "Ah, thank the Starmaker," he said. "There be a welt, but it's nuthin' a young Spriggan can'na handle." He lay her back down. "Fetch me a damp cloth, boy, and . . . some grayroot."

Tango tripped over himself, careening toward the kitchen. He returned seconds later with a damp white dishcloth and a fist full of hairy roots.

"Stars, boy!" Tanner said. "That's enough grayroot to wake a dragon!"

Tango's eyes grew as big as gourds. "Nay, son, don'na you fear. She's just knocked to sleep. She'll be alright." He took the damp cloth and wiped Meli's forehead clean. Then he took one small root and waved it beneath his daughter's nose.

She snorted, blinked, and opened her eyes. "Da, oh, Da!" she mewed, draping herself around her father's neck.

"See, boy? She'll be fine." His eyes narrowed. "Now just what cave were you two explorin' this time?"

"The Haunted Cave," Meli whispered.

"What?" Tanner lowered his daughter to the cradle once more. "What in the Stars possessed ya t'go in there? I've told ya ten thousand times, not to go in that cave. Cursed, it is! Tango, I've a mind t'switch ya til ya can'na sit down."

"I'm sorry, Da," Tango pleaded. "Really I am. And Meli, I'm sorry ya got hurt. I never meant for that."

"Of course ya did'na mean for that," said his father. "But that's the way it is when ya do somethin' ya should'na be doin'. It's an unexpected avalanche, boy."

"Tell'im about the dragon thing, Tango!" Meli urged.

"Dragon thing?" Tanner squinted.

"Ya should'a seen it, Da!" Tango howled, his eyes huge. "We were in the cave fair deep, we were. And this tall man, taller than the royal folk on the Tor, he came up from the cave and summoned up the old Red Dragon you tole us about."

Tanner Goliant's expression changed. His eyebrows rose halfway up his forehead. The tension melted away, and he laughed a boisterous, coughing fit. "Oh ho, you're somethin' me boy. Think by tellin' tall tales you'll get out a'trouble, do ya?"

"No, Da! Ya can tan my hide. Stars know I deserve it and better. But we saw a dragon thing."

Tanner wiped his eyes with his sleeve and frowned. "Tell me yer story then."

Tango, with Meli's timely inserts, told his father everything. Tanner listened patiently, rubbing his stubbly chin and chuckling dryly. But then, came a detail that shut his mouth and chilled his blood.

"The man called the dragon-thing Raudrim-Keveral, Kwiveral, or some such."

Tanner had told his kids about the dragon Raudrim, so that might have been possible to dismiss. But he'd never uttered the name of the Red Queen to his children. It was a horror too dark to speak of . . . until now.

Tanner took his son by the shoulders. "The name, the second name, it could'na been Quevara, could it?"

"Yes, Da!" said Meli. "That was it. I'm sure of it."

"Meli's right," said Tango. "That man said just that: Raudrim-Quevara. He whispered to the dragon thing for a long time, and then it flew off. That's when the stones fell."

"This man," Tanner said. "Did he say anything else?"

Tango nodded rapidly. "He said something about Cragheath Tor. That's what he said, just before the creature took off."

"Can'na be," Tanner muttered to himself. "No, it can'na be."

"What is it, Da?" Meli asked, fear widening her blue eyes.

"Meli-lass, can ya move around now?"

"I think so, Da. I have a bit of an ache back there, but I feel okay."

"Good, good," her father said. "Now listen, both a'ya. I want ya to pack yer things like we're travelin' soon. Pack clothes, light and warm, more than a couple sets. Fetch yer tools too. And then, get to the pantry and pack up anythin' that won't spoil soon."

"But, Da," said Tango. "Why—"

"Mind me, boy!" he said, his tone rigid. "Do as I say, and do it now. We're goin' down to the stream."

The royal guards of Tor Keep were considered elite by any standard of measure for warriors in the Hinterlands. Swift, strong, alert, fit beyond reason, and lethally trained with all manner of weapon, especially the corrusk, the forked blade they'd made famous; the "Cragfel" had guarded the royal family without incident for three hundred years. They were at their posts in the castle tower at the peak of Cragheath Tor, an elevation of more than a thousand feet. Every stair, every passage was guarded, and, at a moment's notice, could be defended with brutal efficiency. The Cragfel were ready for anything.

Except for what came.

Cragheath's ruler, Queen Righel emerged from the washroom to find her husband in their bedchamber with another woman. They seemed in the throws of passion, standing together in a deep and writhing embrace near the corner of the massive bed. Queen Righel dropped her hand mirror. It shattered, sending shards of glass skittering over the dark stone tiles.

"Cordon?" the queen whispered. "Husband?"

There came no answer, but the embrace became suddenly still.

Queen Righel gained more conviction in her voice. "Cordon . . . what . . . what are you doing?"

"Kissing," came a deep, feminine voice, almost a purr.

It was then that Queen Righel first noticed the blood pooling at their feet. The other woman, a tall, curvaceous female with crimson hair turned her head and smiled. Blood trickled from the corner of her mouth, and she released Cordon from her embrace. His body fell hard to the stone, his throat torn, his eyes wide with anger . . . and still.

Queen Righel might have screamed were it not for the vengeance that overcame her at that moment. Her childhood love, her devoted husband of one hundred fourteen years, the valiant Cordon Gildain, lay dead. At the hand of this . . . intruder. Queen Righel's right hand moved like the speed of thought, whipping a formidable dagger from a belt hidden beneath her gown.

"Ah," said the woman. "You bear a weapon. As it should be. As it always has been for the ruling queen of Cragheath Tor."

"Who are you?" Queen Righel demanded, advancing a few steps.

"I am Quevara," she replied. "And I am more." She lifted her arm, and her hand seemed to boil into something scaled and reptilian. A bone-white talon lanced across the distance between the two.

The dagger brattled to the floor. Queen Righel gasped and mouthed the word, "Guards." She looked down at the white spike impaling her chest, and then her head slumped forward.

"Not much of a fighter," said Quevara, retracting the talon. Queen Righel splashed to the ground in a pool of her own blood. Her cyrium crown rolled off her head, spun for a moment, and clattered to rest on the stone. Quevara swooped down to it. She stood, caressing its intricately woven designs. The Spriggan race, ignorant and folksy as they may be, were master metalcrafters—more highly skilled even than their cousins, the Stonehands.

As she stroked the crown, she had a horribly strong urge to take it and horde it, to fly back to her deep vaults and bask in all her riches with the crown as her prize trophy. But no, she knew from whence that impulse had come, one of the baser instincts she'd acquired in The Compromise. There would be time for basking later, perhaps an eternity if Cythraul could be trusted. But for now, there was much work to do and little time in which to do it all.

Quevara went to twin doors at the head of the royal chamber. She placed her palms flat to the wood and felt around for a moment. Then, she smiled. A talon lanced from a finger on each hand and pierced the doors as if they were clay. When she retracted the talons, they returned wet with blood. Quevara yanked open the door. Two Cragfel slumped to the ground at her feet. A half dozen guards had already launched from their posts at the passage openings. Heavy footfalls echoed up from the stairways.

The guards stopped short, coming to a stunned halt before the perilously beautiful woman who stood in the doorway. It was only a moment's hesitation, but it was enough.

Quevara's green eyes glinted gold. She arched her back and threw her head forward. Crimson flame vomited forth, engulfing the guards. They fell in boiling heaps of blood, bone, and ash.

Quevara smiled and, as she took the middle stair, said, "Ah, it's good to be home."

A trail of blood and smoldering carnage in her wake, Quevara at last emerged in the atrium outside the Council chambers. A score of Cragfel guards converged upon her. They, like the others, were strong Spriggans, meaty with thick, hardened muscle, but she'd already fed. She slew them with fire, but pierced one upon a talon. This unfortunate solder she kept alive and writhing like a beetle on a pin. When she smashed in the Council Chamber doors, she flung the man headlong onto the center of the vast table within. He flailed for a few moments, gasping for air and trying in vain to cover the gaping wound in his chest. He died with a final wheezing sigh, and all of Cragheath Tor's Councilmen looked on in stunned horror.

"Good evening, gentlemen," Quevara said, her taloned claw melting back into soft, pinkish flesh. "I would have been here sooner, but I have been resting for . . . some time."

"Who are you?" demanded an older Councilman. He held a mace in his tight fist, and he was strong. Muscle shapes rippled beneath the slate-blue Councilman robes. His smoldering eyes went wide. "How . . . how do you wear that crown?"

"Do any of you bear strength or skill beyond that of your Cragfel?" Quevara asked, strolling into the chamber. She circled the table, tracing her finger's nail across the shoulders of the Councilmen seated there. "No? Then, brandish no weapon in my presence. I have slain every living being between this chamber and Tor Keep and have no qualms about adding a few politicians to their number."

"Outrage!" cried out a younger Councilman. His red hair and beard bristled. "How dare you break into our private chamb—"

The talon pierced him. His eyes became glassy. He crashed half onto the table and fell to the floor out of sight. Almost to a man, the other Councilmen slid backward in their chairs.

"Stay—in—your—seats!" Quevara commanded them. "Try to leave this room, and I will consider it your permanent resignation from the Council."

"But the crown," the older Councilman said, "that is Queen Righel's crown. Where is she?"

"She is dead. But what does it matter?" Quevara laughed. "She was but a figurehead. The real power resides here in the Council, does it not?" No one answered. "I thought as much. Quite a change from Cragheath Tor tradition, isn't it? And I wonder how you convinced your people of this ruse. It concerns me not, for this crown belongs to me. I am Quevara, and I have returned to rule Cragheath once more!"

The Councilmen reacted: gasps, exclamations, pounding fists. One poor man collapsed.

"Silence!" Quevara demanded. "There is nothing you can do. Your world has changed, and your lives belong to me." She glared from face to face. "I have come here to make you an offer. Serve me exclusively. Do my bidding and rule under me."

A squint-eyed man near the west window asked, "Or?"

Quevara's eyes glinted golden. "Or . . . be food for worms."

"I would rather die than serve such as you!"

"Proconsul Braeger, no!" someone yelled, but the old Councilman leaped up from his chair and struck with his mace, a glancing blow on Quevara's shoulder. There was a mind-bending burst of motion and a flash of impossibly large teeth. Quevara flung the Councilman in two pieces at the massive stained glass window. With the torn sleeve of her gown, she wiped a gout of blood from her lips and chin.

"Choose now," she said, her voice a deep hiss.

"My father served under you," came a voice. The squint-eyed Councilman stroked his sharp black beard. "More than three hundred years ago, it was. But he was not some groveler. He was empowered, a member of your personal cabinet, and backed by your authority. If we choose to serve with you—"

"Vilnus!" a Councilman yelled. "What are you . . . you can't—"

Vilnus held up his hand sharply. His squint eyes flashed open. "Do not tell me what I can or cannot do, Cunner Roth. It seems we each have a choice to make. I simply want to know the extent of the choice." He turned back to Quevara. "As I was saying, my queen, if we choose to serve under you, what will we gain in the bargain . . . besides our lives being spared, that is."

Quevar smiled. "I know your likeness," she said. "Your name?"

"Vilnus," he replied. "Vilnus Skevack."

Her eyes glinted, and her grin widened. "Skevack . . . yes, I know that name. Arjen Skevack?"

"My grandsire," he said.

"A reliable servant indeed." She paused a moment. Her eyes narrowed. "You will rule with me, Vilnus. You and any who choose rightly. Of course, your trust must be earned, but once you prove your worth to me, you will never want for anything all the days of your life."

Vilnus stood. "I choose to stand with you. I take up the banner of the Red Queen as my own." He gestured toward the others. "Do likewise, brethren. You serve no one from the grave."

"Well spoken, Vilnus," the queen said. "Make your choice."

The Councilmen stared across the wide table to each other. Blood pooled beneath the dead Cragfel soldier and rolled out almost to the table's edge. Slowly, hands began to rise.

Cunner raised his hand but said, "Queen Quevara, I've no wish to die. My Silenia, my wife that is, and my three daughters have great need of me." He stared at the tabletop. "But could you find some position, perhaps some place for me, where I wouldn't have to . . . I mean, I couldn't look my family in the eye if—"

"You don't want to get your hands dirty," Quevara said. "No stomach for bloodshed, then. Very well. Not all are cut out for greatness. So in exchange for your allegiance, I will grant you what you ask. But think not that you will partake of the greater glory of my reign. You will live and you will dwell in mediocrity. What say the rest of you?"

The rest relented—some eagerly—and so the Council of the Red Queen was formed. Quevara took Vilnus Skevack aside and said, "The peasantry will toe any line I declare. The remaining Cragfel are my only threat. Do you know any of them who might be . . . recruited to our cause? Any whose duty might be purchased?"

Skevack nodded. "I do," he said. "There are more than you might suspect. I imagine I might be able to assemble a detachment even."

The queen placed a hand on his shoulder. "Haven't I chosen wisely?" she mused. "Now, then, *General* Vilnus, this is what I want you to have this detachment do as a pledge, a first act of service to me."

She told him her wish. He grimaced and swallowed. Then, he bowed and left the chamber.

Queen Quevara the Red lay on a ridge of stone about midway down the Cragheath Tor. She dangled an arm over the edge. Her hand dipped into the clear water of the stream that coursed down from the icemelt at the high peak. She wondered if Vilnus had been successful, or if some Cragfel had taken offense and murdered her new general. She rolled over on her back, and her reptilian tail draped across her thigh and dipped into the water.

Quevara watched above where, here and there, the stone thrust outward and misty streams of water fell. Time passed, and she waited, almost in a trance. It had been so long. She wondered if she might dare to believe she could have everything back that was hers . . . and more. She wondered if her blackest inner longing could be slaked again.

Then, she gasped. She thought at first it was some trick of the setting sun coloring the misty water falling. But no, no it was not the sun. Feverishly eager, she clawed to the edge of the stone once more and gazed down into the stream.

"But Da!" Tango complained, hoisting his backsack to a more comfortable spot on his shoulders. "I don't understand. Why are we leaving our home? Why'd we have t'pack all this stuff . . . and our tools?"

"Look boy," his father said, picking his way through the vine-strewn brush. "You and Meli saw something. That I can'na deny. I'm guessin' you saw something maybe ya should'na."

"But why we goin' to the stream?" asked Meli. "We goin' t'fish?"

"That's right, Meli," he replied swiftly. "Just catchin' some fish. If things go well, we'll be headin' back home to fry up some nice hammerhead salmon."

"But, Da," Tango said, jouncing up to hike at his father's side. "This isn't the best branch a' the stream for fishin'. Don't I know it? Too close to the Tor, it is. Fished out."

"Hush, boy," Tanner said.

They broke through the thickest part of the forest and jogged along the stream for close to an hour. At last, Tanner bade his children to stop and unpack their fishing gear. It was nearly dark, a good time for fishing. Plenty of mosquitos, blademites, and gadflies about to attract the salmon. But bites were seldom and catches even more rare.

"Da?" Tango said. "You don'na seem too into your fishin'."

"Huh?" he looked up at his son through a haze.

"Well, I have'na seen ya bait your hook for some time now."

Tanner Goliant looked down at his line. Then, he dropped his fishing tool. He trembled, and his eyes went very wide. "Pack up your gear," he said.

"Whazzat?" asked Meli. "We've only been here just—"

"Pack up your gear, now!"

They obeyed their father's curt command and were travel ready in minutes. "We headin' home then?" Tango asked.

"No . . . not home," their father answered.

"But why," Meli mewed.

He looked down with pity, not knowing what to tell them, not knowing what he could say. "The river," he said. "The river's run red."

CHAPTER 8

POMP AND CIRCUMSTANCE

*Treasure maps can only be trusted so far. So, as we drifted farther and
farther south from the mainland, I began to doubt we would ever find
the so called Aruthredd Pykes. But first light showed me wrong. There
they were: great horns of stone climbing high enough to pierce the clouds.
We moored at the third peak where, according to the map, the treasure
lay. It was an arduous fearful climb. Clumsy Danitus Barnabas fell. At
least it was a quick death. When we first heard the sound, we took it to
be howling, but as we traveled, we soon realized this could not be. The
wind was still. We thought surely it was some creature, some unfortunate
beast trapped in that high cave. But we discovered it was the cave itself,
rather the ore we found in the walls of the cave. Bywydirium we named
it, for it sang like the wind. Fourteen bars and nine ingots we made. My
own share was just as large as my thumb. But it sang to me the sweetest
music. Only in the morning. And only when we were out to sea.*

—From the Pirate Lore Anthology, Dissension Age,
Antonis Fitch, The Corsairs of Trimony

44 SEDWYN 2238

"Stop fidgeting this instant!" Daribel commanded, and then, clearing her throat, she said, "Uhm, that is, if you please, your majesty."

"She's right, my son," Queen Maren said wryly. "The High King Overlord of all Myriad really shouldn't fidget."

"How can I not?" Loch asked, puffing out a breath of pure frustration. "What with all these attendants buzzing around me like yellow jackets on a piece of picnic pie."

"Don't round your back," said the tailor's assistant as she placed the end of a measuring tape between the king's shoulder blades. "There now, chest out, shoulders relaxed, arms at your side."

A seamstress with dozens of colored swatches of cloth draped on her arm held one piece up at a time, letting them hang just beneath Loch's chin. "How's this?" she asked.

"Fades his eyes," Daribel said.

"This?" She held up a slate gray piece.

"Too dreary," Daribel said. "This is a celebration, not a funeral."

"This?" Hunter green.

"Has potential. Save it and keep going."

"Gah! See what I mean?" Loch growled. "I don't need a new tunic for the Feast of Welcome. I have twenty that fit me full well."

"Of course you need a new tunic for the feast," Daribel said, looking to the queen and rolling her eyes.

"Please hold still," said an attendant, stretching yet another measurement tape from his waist down the length of his left leg."

"I think King Loch is still growing," said the royal tailor who himself measured Loch's right leg.

More servants and tailors whisked around Lochlan with materials and samples. A half dozen scribes, their backs pressed hard against the curving walls of the chamber, struggled to stay out of the way as they took down notes and comments being shouted at them.

"Your pardon!" Page Martin rushed into the room with arms so full of scrolls that they nearly tumbled off. "I just need a moment of your time, sire. A few signatures only."

Lochlan had his arms stretched wide in a T for measurements. "With pleasure," he said, lowering his arms and shrugging the tension from his neck. Frustrated attendants glared at the king but kept their measuring tapes at the ready.

Page Martin somehow produced a pen and a bottle of ink, all without dropping a scroll. "Here," he said, gesturing with his rather pointed nose. "Lowering taxes on the fishing guilds again. Hunt guilds won't be happy."

"It's been a hard summer on the fishermen," Loch said. "The severmane have changed their schooling waters, hiding in the perilous reefs and shoals far south. Hmph, deer are plentiful. What are the hunters worried about?"

"Who can say," Page Martin replied. "I am sure I wouldn't know. Now this one, your majesty. Authorizing the new trade route."

"What new trade route?" the king asked, blowing a lock of hair from his eyes and signing the scroll.

"In Vulmarrow, my lord," Page Martin explained. "A diversion really, what with all the bandits camping on the old castle grounds. I'm sure Shepherd Sebastian told you."

"Yes, I'm sure he did," Loch said. "Shepherd Sebastian tells me ten thousand things each day. You know, Martin, I put a great deal of trust in you by simply signing these on your word. You could be selling Anglinore to the Gorracks and I'd never know."

"Perish the thought," the page replied. "But I am grateful for the three hundred gold salary increase you signed for me last week."

Lochlan laughed aloud, but stopped abruptly when a squirrelly looking man entered the room. He had a tray full of small bottles and pouches.

"Oh, there you are," he said, his darting eyes lingering on the king.

"Oh, no," Loch exclaimed. "No, Chesterton, not the herbs. Not now."

"Sebastian's orders," he replied with a toothy smile. "Sebastian's orders."

"Of course it is," Loch muttered.

"Swallow these," Chesterton said, handing the king two blue pills and a cup of water. Loch gulped them down.

"Now these, you chew."

"Grindle berries," Loch said as he chewed. "I like these."

"Well, you won't like these," Chesterton said. He opened a pouch and delicately removed two tiny leaves.

"Basil?" Loch asked.

"You should be so blessed." Chesterton frowned. "Chench fern leaves, your majesty. You must keep these under your tongue until they melt away."

Loch took the herbs and dutifully placed them under his tongue. "Ugh," he said, his face wrinkling. "Tastes bitter."

"That's all for now," Chesterton said. "See you after lunch."

"Mmph, mmpk," Loch replied.

Page Martin shoved another scroll under the king's chin. "Now this one, Lord, is to extend the royal contribution to Anglinore's Sanctuary for another ten years."

"Umph, gumph," Loch said, looking over his shoulder to Queen Maren.

"Yes," she said, nodding. "I suppose the usual fifteen percent will do. That is a great deal of wealth, but . . . it is tradition."

Lock signed the scroll, and Page Martin handed him another.

"Please, your majesty," squawked the tailor. "Can't these scrolls wait? We simply must complete these measurements today."

The attendant darted in and held up another swatch of cloth, this one a deep blue with lavender veins and gold trim. "Ooh, now that one I like," Daribel said. "Very complimentary and appropriate."

"Running a little late, aren't we?" A skinny pole of a man wearing courtly tails and a powdered wig strolled up to the king. He tapped his quill to a tablet of paper. "You're due in Clarissant Hall for your portrait. The painters are a bit nonplussed. You know those creative types don't like to be kept waiting."

"I'm sorry, Galeal," Lochlan replied, trying to swallow the odd taste in his mouth. "But, as you can see, there's a lot going on here. Unfortunately."

"That may well be," Galeal said, still tapping the quill. "But the portrait is almost finished and must be hung in time for the ceremony."

Just then Shepherd Sebastian ducked around the doorjamb and leaned into the room. "High King Lochlan!" he called. "Don't forget Baron Cardiff Strengle's arrival this afternoon. You promised him a game of jacksprite and tea."

"Today?" Loch exhaled. "I thought that was after the Ceremony of Crowns, after the Council!"

"No, mi'lord, today it is. And you know your cousin doesn't care much for waiting." Sebastian vanished from the door.

Loch growled under his breath. He felt like a superheated bubble about to pop.

"I need this measurement for the inseam," said the tailor.

"This scroll," Page Martin said, "is to reopen the southern forest on the Naïthe for lumbering."

Lochlan blinked. His heart suddenly raced, and he felt a bit dizzy. The room seemed to wobble.

"This one?" The attendant held up a burgundy swatch.

"Hm, not sure," Daribel said.

"Please hold still," said the tailor.

"Please sign here," said Page Martin.

"Your majesty," said Galeal, "the portrait?"

Lochlan opened his mouth to speak, but the room seemed to churn. His heart throbbed erratically. A gray curtain fell over his vision. There came a great chilling upon his neck and arms. And all went black.

A quiet knocking at the door was enough to wake Lochlan. The king sat up in his vast ocean of a bed and called out, "Come in."

Telwyn peeked around the door. "Your majesty?"

Loch sat up straighter, feeling a surge of relief. "Tel, come in! Come in, you goof."

"Very sorry to wake you, Loch," Telwyn said, creeping into the chamber. "But your cousin has arrived and you are due to meet within the hour."

"An hour?" Loch's mouth dropped open. "But the tunic, the scrolls . . . my portrait—"

Telwyn held up a hand. "All can wait," he said. "By order of General Coldhollow, anyone who troubled you further today would be cast into the stockade."

"Good old Uncle Alastair," Loch said, leaning back against the headboard.

"What happened?" Telwyn asked, his voice low, his amber eyes large with concern. "They said you collapsed."

"I guess I did. I was standing there one minute. Next thing I know, I'm here in bed."

"Ever happen before?"

"No," Loch said. "Never went out like that anyway."

"But?"

"But . . . all the activity around me, all the fuss . . . it gets to me. I mean, all at once, I had Daribel, my mother, the tailor, the page, the herbalist, and half a dozen others all after me about something. It's not the first time."

"Well," Telwyn said. "You are High King. I suppose it comes with the title."

"I know that, Tel," Lochlan muttered. "But I am just a man, no better than any other in this castle."

"And that is why we all love you so much," Telwyn said. "Your humility will make you a great king."

Lochlan shrugged. "I cannot say with any certainty whether it is humility or just sheer exhaustion. Every day Galeal comes to me with my itinerary, a list of official duties that steal every hour of the day. And in the midst of it, I'm waited on hand and foot whether I want or need anything or not. When it gets like that, my body just goes haywire. I break out into sweats or get cold.

My heart pounds away like Gorrack drums. Loud noises make me jump a foot off the ground. I wonder sometimes if I might be losing my mind."

"Ah, no Lochlan," Tel said, putting a hand on the king's shoulder. "You are most sane. Such a routine would take its toll on anyone. You know . . . in Canticles it says, 'Bear not your troubles alone. There is no shame. For the First One desires to carry your burdens.'"

Lochlan smiled kindly. "I can always count on you to lift my spirits, good friend. I wish I drew as much comfort from Canticles as you do, but—"

"Excuse my interruption," said the silhouette of a man at the door. "It's Sebastian. I was told I could find young master Telwyn here."

"And so I am," Tel said.

"So I see," the Shepherd replied. "Lady Abbagael and Queen Maren send for you. There is some trouble with the wine shipment from Ellador. They thought maybe you could be of assistance."

"I'll do what I can," Tel said. He gave Loch's shoulder a quick squeeze. "See you at the feast."

"Thanks, Tel," the king said.

Sebastian nodded to Tel as he left, but the Shepherd did not leave. "I could not help but overhear some of your conversation," he said. "It's gotten that bad, has it?"

Lochlan's green eyes glistened. With a single swift motion, he wiped his sleeve across his face. "I don't understand it, Sebastian. It just comes over me like . . . like some kind of spell. When people make so much fuss over me . . . it's suffocating."

Sebastian nodded. "Your father often felt the same." The Shepherd smiled from glad memory. "He used to threaten to send me across the Dark Sea if I wouldn't stop calling him things like liege, lord, and majesty."

A smile flickered also on Loch's lips but disappeared all too quickly. "I hate being cloistered up in this high castle. I want to see the land I rule. I want to see the people—nay, not just see them. I want to know them and be among them. But all this?" Lochlan swung his feet out of bed and spun with his arms outstretched. "This station with all its pomp and circumstance—it's not me. Sebastian, I don't think I am cut out to be king. I do not think I can wear this crown."

"A break, your majesty," Sebastian said, sitting on the edge of the bed. "You need a break, not a resignation. Go out, be among the people you love, the people you defend."

"But Shepherd, that will only bring me more of the same. There'll be fawning, cow-towing, and kissing up. Oh, your majesty, how glad we are to have you here! Good King Lochlan, you bless us with your presence! Then will come all the favors. You know we really need a new bridge over the river, sire! Fearfully short of grain, my lord. Couldn't you reduce the quota this year? More bandits on such-and-such a road, your grace. Wouldn't posting a few more of the Anglish Guard be appropriate? Gah!"

Sebastian's shoulder's slumped. "You've made a good point, there."

"Such journeys are always more taxing than they are worth."

"Your people wouldn't think so. They enjoy meeting their king."

Lochlan rubbed his neck. "Ah, I know they do, and I'm grateful. But there's no camaraderie, no fellowship, no real relationships. I long to be real with people and have them be real with me. Everyone's so polite and correct around me . . . so careful."

Sebastian nodded. "Still, it would get you away from here. Consider it, Lochlan. Maren and I could manage here without you for a few weeks. We are at peace."

"I'll think about it, Sebastian, thank you." Lochlan went to one of three wardrobes and pulled out several tunics. "Which one do you think will drive Daribel crazy if I wear it to the Feast of Welcome?"

"The one in your left hand, by far!" The Shepherd laughed. "By the Stars, where in Myriad did you find such an odious tunic?"

"Family secret." Loch grinned.

Sebastian shook his head. He stood and went to the door. "Cardiff is here, you know. He's limbering up in the jacksprite courts. I'll tell him the match can wait until after the—"

"No, Sebastian, I feel well enough now," Loch said. "Maybe the exercise will do me good."

"It may," Sebastian replied. "And maybe your cousins rampant ego will drive you mad."

"It's about time!" came the voice on the sunny side of the jacksprite court. "I hear you were napping. Napping! Dear cousin, tell me it isn't so."

Loch was tempted to roll his eyes, but in general, he knew kings should not do such things. It didn't help that Cardiff leaned against the jacksprite net post and smiled smugly like he owned the place. Resisting all urges to the contrary, Loch said, "Good cousin Cardiff, welcome back to Anglinore. It has been too long."

"Not long enough is what you mean, isn't it?" Baron Cardiff Strengle replied.

"Nonsense, Cardiff, really." Loch held out his hand. Cardiff grasped it, and they shook . . . much longer than was custom.

Cardiff's hand was like a meaty vice, and Loch struggled not to wince as his cousin did his level best to crush his hand. Loch gave him time to put forth a good squeeze, and then Loch turned on his own pressure. It was then that Loch was thankful for all the blacksmith training and gardening. He knew his grip was much stronger than Cardiff would expect.

He met his cousin's eyes. The man was as handsome as Myriad had to offer, a real ladies man. Square chin, square shoulders, square fists too. His muscle wasn't bulky but thick enough to make any clothes flatter the man. His hair was closed cropped and naturally curly, golden brown with roguish sideburns cutting down almost to his jawline. But right now, this handsome baron was red-faced and sweating profusely.

"Quite the grip, uh, ahhh, Loch," Cardiff said. He let go and flexed his fingers. "Hmph, much stronger, eh? How's your jack-sprite game these days?"

Loch thought there was a hint of worry in the man's voice. Good, he thought. Serves him right. "I have practiced up . . . a little," Loch said.

"Well, well, that's good. Wouldn't want to continue your streak, would you? Thirty-nine losses to me in a row." Cardiff took off his burgundy cape, folded it neatly, and laid it on a bench a few feet from the net post. "I'm rather looking forward to making it an even forty."

"We'll see, cousin," Loch replied. "We'll see."

"Limber up?"

"I'm plenty warm."

"Why don't you serve then," Cardiff said. "Show me what you can do."

Loch selected a wooden jacksprite racket, the stiff rosewood with a black leather grip, his favorite. He had to dig through the barrel of jacksprite balls to find one that hadn't already been abused too much. He gave the ball a good bounce, and it thudded back into his palm with ample force. The ball, made from the elastic casing of the magellan nut, contained a single three ounce lead shot sealed in by heat. The lead gave the jacksprite ball the peculiar bounce for which it was named—after the fabled Willowfolk hero Jack'o Sprite.

Loch took his position behind the service line and stared across the low cut grass, to the three-foot net, to his opponent and beyond. The court itself was only forty-two feet long, but it was sixty feet wide. And behind each player was the six-foot high scoring wall filled with scoring pockets from one to thirty-nine. The goal was to get a ball past your opponent and into one of the scoring pockets, the higher number the better—though the higher point pockets were much smaller than the lower point pockets. The 39-pocket was only a fraction of an inch larger than the jacksprite ball itself.

Players would hit the ball back and forth, trying to maneuver an opponent into leaving a section of the scoring wall open. If done well, the player could blast the jacksprite ball into the open section of the scoring wall. Netting a ball or hitting it out of the sidelines gave your opponent a free shot at the scoring wall; not a good idea since a ball in the 39-pocket would be a game winner.

Loch bounced the ball once, decided to serve side arm, and then tossed the ball up. He let it fall to chest height and then slammed the racket face into the ball, flicking his wrist at the end for extra pace. The ball hummed over the net, struck the ground, and blasted at the wall. But Cardiff backhanded the ball with just enough force to career across the net at an untouchable angle. It hit the grass and skidded into the 9-point pocket.

"That was a good serve!" Cardiff crowed.

"And an even better return," Loch grumbled. "But don't forget, I have two more serves." Loch rolled his shoulders and turned his back to Cardiff. "Let's see him get this one," Loch whispered.

He tossed the ball and then simultaneously spun around and uncoiled a sidearmed serve. The ball went a couple of feet over the net and then dove down like gull after a minnow. Cardiff played it well, putting himself in perfect position for the return—that is, if the ball had normal drive and momentum behind it. But Loch's shot carried with it the twisting power of his uncoiling body. The ball hit the grass and—bounce-thud—dove under Cardiff's outstretched arm and into the twenty-one pocket.

Cardiff waddled slowly to the scoring wall and removed the ball. He stared at it for some time, and then tossed it back over to Lochlan. "I . . . I've never seen a serve like that," he said. "Is it legal?"

"Perfectly," Loch replied. "And don't worry, you'll get to see it plenty more."

With the score 119 to 67 in Loch's favor and Cardiff just about to serve, Loch asked, "So, cousin, what brings you to Anglinore anyway?"

"Cermony of Crowns, of course," Cardiff said. He fired off a powerful overhead serve.

Loch was there in plenty of time and gave the ball a sharp cut-stroke. "Yes, but you haven't always attended. Mother says this is the first time in years."

"But this is your year!" Cardiff sprinted toward the net and deftly flicked his wrist. The ball zipped across the net and threatened the 39-pocket. "You kingship authority is already in place, but the people need ceremony, don't they?"

"Of course," Loch replied, merely blocking back a return. "I supposed they do."

Cardiff took a wrong step and couldn't reach the ball in time. It bounced between the 6-pocket and the 18. A "rube" as it was called when the ball failed to enter a scoring pocket, or no score. "Close one," Cardiff said. He set up to serve. "Do I detect some disdain for ceremony, Loch?"

"Is it that obvious?" Loch asked.

"Somewhat," Cardiff replied. He smacked a serve wide to Loch's backhand. "But beyond that, you're very young."

Loch returned with another cut shot. "What's that supposed to mean?"

"Nothing against you," Cardiff replied, sliding easily into a forehand drive. "But at your age, you shouldn't be shut up in a musty throne room, not when there's so much life out in the world."

Loch took two steps toward the ball and stopped short. The ball slammed into his 12 pocket. Loch absently removed the ball. "I must admit, I've often thought such things," Loch said. He went to serve but paused. "You rule over Avon Barony, have you ever felt that way?"

"Me, no . . . no not really. I actually enjoy the ceremony. But I am 116 years old. Different seasons for different loves."

Loch nodded and served. The ball caromed into Cardiff's body, but he shuffle-stepped and lanced a speed return low across the net.

"I've heard," Cardiff said, "that you've been troubled of late."

Loch fired back a return but said nothing.

"And truth be told, I thought I'd come before the Ceremony to see if I could help." Cardiff reached Loch's shot, but sprayed his forehand out of bounds. "Ah! That is another free shot for you."

"I don't see how you can help me," Loch said. He tossed the ball and knocked an easy open shot into the 39-hole. "That's game, cousin."

"So it is, so it is," Cardiff replied, walking to the net and holding out his hand. They shook and sat on the bench. "But, ah, perhaps I can help in ways you cannot see. I am a blood relative, you know."

Loch squinted. "But . . ."

"You don't have to bear the burden of all Myriad on your own," Cardiff said. "I could rule with you. Call me a Chief General or some such, but I could take care of the politicking while you rule? Or, if you want to leave for some years, live out your youthful interests, I could occupy the high seat until you wish to reclaim it."

Loch stood up. "I may be young, Cardiff," he said. "And I've only known you for a few years. But I've known of you for many years. My mother has told me much, especially about how you badgered her when my father died. That alone is more than enough to make me leery of your offer."

"You misunderstand me, Loch," Cardiff said, hands spread wide. "I only wish to help. I—"

"I was born with a responsibility that is hard to bear," Loch said. "But bear it, I must. Death may take my throne, but I will not give it away."

"Loch, no!" Cardiff exclaimed, standing up quickly. "I don't want to keep the throne . . . only to occupy it for your freedom. It—"

Loch walked to the court gate. He looked back at his cousin. "It's a shame you threw the game away to manipulate me," Loch said. "You probably could have beaten me and made it an even forty in a row." Loch turned the corner. "And I'd have respected you more for the honest effort."

CHAPTER 9

GHOST SIGHTING

Witchdrale addiction can destroy a family;
addiction to power . . . a generation.

—Queen Savron Silverwren, ruler of the Vespal Wayfolk,
from her Treatise: The Five Greatest Fears

45 SEDWYN 2238

"That Daribel is something," Abbagael said, brushing her crimson hair in front of the mirror. "You'd have thought with all she's got to do, planning for the Feast of Welcome she'd have little time or food left over for feeding the rest of the castle folk."

Alastair stretched out on the bed and drummed his fingers on his stomach. "I've never eaten so much in my life," he said. "The roast chicken was superb, but the chived potatoes with rosemary and garlic gravy—I just couldn't stop eating them."

"Hmmm," Abbagael replied, braiding and tying off her hair with practiced speed, "I suppose when we return to Llanfair, you won't want anything cooked with my meager skills."

Alastair tried to sit up, thought better of it, and flopped back into the pillows. "Meager? Hardly. The meals you've prepared for me and Telwyn have been glorious, as my expanding waist can attest. But Daribel's hands have been touched by the First One."

They both laughed. Abbagael turned out the oil lantern and climbed into the moonlit bed. She snuggled close to her husband and lay her hand lightly on his chest. Her breathing slowed, but then her eyes popped open and she said, "Did you check in on Telwyn?"

"He's a grown man," Alastair grumbled.

"Still polite to say goodnight to your son," she teased back. "Oh, wait, I forgot: men don't do polite very well. Ill-mannered bores that you are."

In answer, Alastair belched loudly.

"I think that rattled the windowpanes," she said, delivering a quick slap to Alastair's chest.

"Just being a bore," he replied. "But if you must know, I did check in on our son. He was fast asleep. Worn out from another afternoon of sparring with Loch and chasing around with that confounded snow drake pet of his."

"Thank you," Abbagael said, closing her eyes.

"For checking on Telwyn?"

She nuzzled into his shoulder. "No . . ." she said, her voice taking on a dreamy, light lilt. "For peace of mind . . . knowing that you're always here, looking after us."

Those tender words, words that were meant to share love and kindness, somehow slid between Alastair's ribs like a sliver of ice.

He lay very still, the skin tightening in the corners of his eyes. His stomach felt bloated and it churned from much more than the rosemary and garlic gravy. Alastair and his family had been in Anglinore for several days and, each day, the battle had grown stronger, the pangs more insistent. It was maddening to feel it again after years of victory. But he could not deny its presence. The Witchdrale was calling again.

Alastair wanted to scream in anger, but instead ground his teeth. Fermented from witchroot and distilled with fruit or grain elements, Witchdrale was as strong a drink as any in Myriad. It was also bitterly addictive, especially to some. Because of this, it had been banned altogether in most of Myriad's nations. But in some places it could still be obtained. Even the vaunted Anglish Guard would wink about it, meeting in secret while off duty to partake of the "black," as they called it.

Abbagael sighed and rolled so that her back was to her husband. Alastair crossed his arms. He could count on one hand the number of times he'd slipped and found himself in Witchdrale's poisonous embrace. But now, he began to think, *Brayden Arum is in town for the ceremony. If anyone knew where to find a stray bottle, Brayden would.* Alastair found himself grinning. *Just need to steer clear of Katya,* he thought, momentarily picturing Brayden's wife. *She would eviscerate me for even mentioning Witchdrale.*

Alastair clenched shut his eyes and ground his teeth more. *What am I doing?* he screamed inwardly. *I am laying next to my beautiful wife, whose forgiveness changed my life. And I'm thinking of such betrayal?* Instantly, he began to pray. Pleadings came from his heart, out of desperation. He tried to focus on the words, tried to drown out the whispers that told him it was a losing battle. Somehow, even while he enunciated the words of his prayer, he found the other voices speaking with greater clarity. They urged him to remember the past, to remember the faces of the innocent people he'd murdered while in Morlan's employ. They urged him to seek the conscience numbing vacuum that Witchdrale could provide.

Alastair shook his head and began to mentally recite verses from the Book of Canticles. *He will come and be washed clean of his former deeds. And the filth shall drain away. He shall be called free, and no chain will hold him. The First One is rich in mercy and will surely rescue him.* This he said to himself over and over again. And yet, moments later, he found himself creeping down the torchlit corridor that would eventually deliver him to the castle gatehouse and the teeming city beyond.

A shadowy figure loomed in a doorway to the right. "Good evening, General Coldhollow," came the deep voice of a night guard named Jaavere. "Going out for the night?"

Alastair nodded cooly. "No, not for the night," he said. "Just going to visit an old friend in town for the festival."

"You have a good night, sir."

"You too, Jaavere," Alastair said, and he raced away to the stairwell.

Alastair found the capital city of Myriad still very much awake. It wasn't the merry chaos that would erupt after the Ceremony of Crowns, but still, many people walked the streets, a few traders hawked their wares, and several taverns were open. Alastair found Brayden Arum in cozy little, L-shaped pub called The Whistling Pig.

Alastair waved off the tavern keeper's attention and took a seat by his old acquaintance. "Long time, Brayden," he said. "How's the Hammer and Bow these days?"

Brayden turned and started to speak. Then he realized who had sat down and he said, "Alastair Coldhollow, is it? Long time indeed. Here for the ceremony?"

"Wouldn't miss it," Alastair said. "Lochlan's been High King for a few years now, I know, but to have everyone here and see him crowned will be something."

"It'll be somethin' alright," Brayden said. He took a long pull from his mug.

"You don't approve?"

"He's young," Brayden admitted. "Don't misunderstand me. He's good stock, strong, smart, good-hearted . . . but there's something to be said for age and experience. I'd just as soon see Queen Maren keep the throne a bit longer."

Alastair nodded. A group of men raised a toast and cheered. Alastair and Brayden looked up.

"What're ya toastin' lads?" Brayden called.

They turned and a fair-haired young man said, "It's young Duskan here. He just found out he's havin' a baby!"

A dark-skinned man emerged from their happy clump. "Excuse, Anthalos here, good sirrahs," he said. "But it is, in point of fact, my wife Laeriss who is going to have a child." They all laughed heartily, raising their mugs once more. But the broad-shouldered father-to-be drew close to Alastair's table.

Alastair stood and held out his hand. "Duskan Vanimore, so you finally wed Laeriss Fenstalker after all."

"Professor Tolke—it's General Coldhollow, isn't it?" Duskan took Alastair's hand and shook it hard. "So good to see you, sirrah. And as to Laeriss, yes, we have been married for two years now. Beside me all that time, and yet the most elusive quarry I have ever hunted. And still the greater treasure for having made the effort."

A gilded picture of Abbagael flickered in Alastair's mind. "Well, good for you both!" Alastair said. "Here, let me buy your next round." He tossed three gold coins onto the countertop. "Keeper, fetch these lads whatever they like." The happy group grew happier, cheering and slapping each other on the back.

Duskan made a half bow. "Still kind as ever, sirrah. I am deeply in your debt."

"Nonsense, Duskan. It's the least I can do to celebrate old friends. How marvelous that Laeriss is with child! You will make fine parents."

"You misunderstand me," Duskan said. "My debt to you delves far beyond a tavern kindness. Laeriss and I will never repay you for your teaching." Duskan glanced from Alastair to Brayden and back. "You saw something in us. You gave us a chance to show ourselves what we could do—that important deeds were not out of our reach."

Alastair smiled but shook his head. "Much as I would love to take some credit for the fine people you and Laeriss have turned out to be, I would be callused to do so. Your quality of character was in you, there long before I came along."

Duskan smiled politely but said, "But gold that stays buried can never shine."

Alastair couldn't help the pride bubbling up within. His breathing felt suddenly thick, his eyes misty. They shook once more, and Duskan said, "I should return to my friends. Laeriss and I will be returning home to Ellador in a few days. We've a nice cottage in Riand . . . even a guest room. Come and visit?"

"We would like that," Alastair said.

He went to turn, but Duskan took his arm. He glanced furtively and whispered, "Did you find him?"

"Find whom?"

Duskan frowned as if Alastair had uttered the most childish nonsense. "Him . . . the Halfainin. That is why you were testing us."

Alastair was suddenly all by himself, in a private stillness that allowed him nothing but thought. Prophecies from Canticles sparked to life, connected, and blinked like flickering stars in the endless night sky. Telwyn seemed to fit so many of those prophecies, but not all. Morlan's exile at Aravel's hand, while Telwyn was but a child, stood as chief among the uncertainties. The Halfainin was foretold to throw down the Dark King, after all. The stars seemed to blink out, one-by-one, and so the night sky won. "I . . . I thought I did," Alastair said at last. "But, I'm just not sure."

Duskan searched his face. "Well, sirrah, should you find him, I should very much like to meet him." They shook hands once more and then returned to their present company.

"That was amazing," Brayden said. "No one ever says such things to me."

"What?"

"Saying thank you, fer one thing. Singin' yer praises like that. Amazin' really."

Alastair settled back in his seat and stared at his hands. He could feel the heat from the fireplace a few feet behind him, and a knot of burning oak popped. He'd left his chamber, left the castle, and come all the way down to the heart of the city. Now, he wasn't so sure he could go through with it.

"Ya just going to sit there with empty hands?" Brayden asked. "How 'bout I fetch you a pint of ale. Or were you lookin' for somethin' else?"

Alastair put his hands to his face and let them slide down until they scratched on his stubbly chin. "It's getting late," he said. "I should get back to my family."

He stood, but Brayden put a thick hand on his arm. "You sure?" he asked. "When you came in . . . well, you looked like a man on a mission."

"Maybe," Alastair said. "Maybe I was." He stood up. "Thank you, Brayden, but I need to go. See you at the ceremony."

It had been very close.

Alastair's thoughts whirled all the way back to the castle. But the vaporous whispers of the Witchdrale had been silenced. He passed through the main gatehouse and began to think about what might have been if he had fallen. He remembered the other times he'd succumbed to the Witchdrale's call. During the worst of the Gorrack War, Alastair had joined a couple of knights trying to drown their misery and grief. Consuming the "black" had only led to more. If it hadn't been for Hagen, First One rest his soul, I'd have drunk myself to death that night.

Alastair climbed the spiral stairs of the castle's western turret and, because of his height, had to occasionally duck torches. There had been two other times he'd returned to Witchdrale. Once, on an ill-fated mission for Queen Maren, Alastair had led a detachment of Anglish Knights into the Felhaunt. They had been hoping to catch up to a slippery gang of cutthroats who had been terrorizing the main trade route to Llanfair. They hadn't found the bandits, but uncovered a hidden cache of Witchdrale. Around the campfire that night, a bottle had been passed around . . . and then a second. Alastair had managed to keep his consumption light. But one of the other knights had not. Alan Grell was his name. He'd had far too much of the black poison and wandered off into the wood. They'd found his remains the next morning. He'd apparently stumbled into a spirax nest, and they'd had their way with him.

Memories of the third occasion, Alastair would not permit into his conscious mind . . . though, at times he had nightmares. Loud voices tumbled Alastair's thoughts altogether as he turned the corner. Four guards moved about in the hall up ahead and there were more shouts. Alastair realized with a twist in his gut, that they were outside his chamber. As he started to run, he reached down to his side, but hadn't thought to bring the Star Sword. "No, no, no!" he growled as he sped forward.

One of the guards raced to meet Alastair, but he brushed the man aside and went to the chamber. He found his wife weeping into Tel's shoulder. "Abbagael," he said. "Oh, thank the First One you both are okay."

She looked up, her face red and miserable, her eyes small and somehow mean. "Where . . . were . . . you?" she demanded.

"What? I . . . Abbagael, what happened?"

She did not answer, but released a kind of shrieking growl and turned her head away. Alastair looked from Tel and then from guard to guard. "Will anyone tell me what has happened?"

"While you were gone," Tel whispered, pointing at the window. "Mi Ma saw Cythraul."

CHAPTER 10

ADRIFT

How alluring is the siren call of power?
She promises so many things and fulfills so few.

—An Elladorian Proverb

45 SEDWYN 2238

I blinked in surprise. My aim had been perfect. I'd figured in the swirling breeze and accounted for the natural drop along the shaft's would-be path. But there was one thing I hadn't accounted for. I gazed through the shrubs in disbelief, even as figures crashed through the branches behind me and strong arms yanked me from my hiding place.

As the guards dragged me up the firing line, I saw the scene plainly, and it finally registered what had happened. Struggling to his feet and covered in pinkish-orange pulp, was an old, shaggy-haired merchant. His crate of gorgle mellons had been utterly destroyed by my arrow. Loosely attached shards of wood and melon hunks lay all about. Everyone within fifteen paces had been splattered with melon juice. Worst of all, I saw Millard. The guards had him by the arms as well, but no one dragged Mill anywhere. He did not resist them and trudged along with the guards.

But it was his helpless, dejected gaze that brought me crashing in upon myself. What a fool I'd been. And now my best friend would pay for it.

They dragged me past a seething Choiros Greenshambles and at last dropped me in front of the High Elder. His face. Ah, his face! A thousand years would never wash that ugly, gloating expression out of my mind. Plebian Scandeer stared down at me and glared. His mouth hung agape, his bald pate went beet red, and his dark eyes bulged. But somehow, at the same time, every nuance of his countenance was somehow positively dripping with smug triumph.

"OUTRAGE!" he cried. He lifted his arms so that his many robes wavered like the wings of some agitated rooster. "The integrity of the Huntmeet has been most egregiously violated!" I heard hissing, jibes, and other clamor from the crowd. I felt the glare of them all on my back even as I bowed my head to avoid the burning gaze of the Elders.

A guard ran up the stairs, shaking the whole platform. "My lords," he exclaimed. "We found these shafts in the thickets behind Millard's target. These were his shots, my lords. The bull's-eyes came from the girl."

"Ariana Kurtz!" Plebian Scandeer bellowed. "You have truly overstepped your bounds this time! How dare you deceive, how dare you invade, how dare you . . . corrupt this cherished and sacred competition?"

"I am sorry," I muttered, my eyes to the floor.

"Sorry?" he echoed. "SORRY?" He laughed maniacally. "Don't you know what you've done? How dare you, a woman, fire even a single shaft in the hallowed Huntmeet! HOW DARE YOU!"

I felt my ire bubbling up inside me like I might pop. My stomach churned from its deepest pits. Every muscle in my body tensed. I wanted to scream and rage and rant out every cut, every sneer, every blow the Elders had dealt me. But, there was no getting around the cold truth that I had done wrong. I had cheated. It was my choice.

"If I had my way, wench, I would have you manacled and tossed in the stockade!" He stopped, and I could just see the greasy wheels turning in his mind. "In such a severe breech of honor," he said, "I believe this does deserve a sentencing. You will swelter in the stockade for—"

Eldar Justinian put a swift hand on Plebian Scandeer's shoulder. He whispered something in the High Elder's ear. Scandeer frowned, eyes hooded in disdain. Scandeer turned to the crowd and said, "I have been informed by my fellow Elder that the Wetland Statutes forbid criminal charges and sentencing for breeches such as this. Just so." He paused to let the crowd's displeasure wash over me. "But, Ariana, think you not that you escape recourse! I hereby charge you with six months labor. You and you alone will do the Elder's washing. Every robe, every tunic, every garment shall be cleansed thoroughly by your hand!"

Rage and disgust mingled sourly in my stomach. My guts lurched and constricted. I very nearly heaved.

"And YOU," Scandeer said, turning to my best friend in the world. "You, Millard Key have betrayed us all! You are a decorated officer in the Hunt Guild. You have turned on your brethren. You have sought to cheat us all and, in the process, have humiliated us with this . . . this—" He apparently couldn't decide on a word vile enough. "This—girl!"

"And what of it, Elder?" The voice was hard, edged like a sword blade. It couldn't be . . . but it was. Millard. "What of a girl in the Hunt Meet?"

The High Elder spluttered and smacked, but Mill cut him off. "This girl, Ariana Kurtz shot better than ANY of us with her bow. Don't think for a moment that her final shot would have gone anywhere but the bull's-eye. Do you have any idea what kind of skill is required for such accuracy? She shot from fifteen paces back of the rest of us—and shot from a bush! Still she outshot us all! Does this not prove that we are but sanctimonious baboons for discriminating against her? Why shouldn't Ariana be a hunter? Why shouldn't any capable woman be a hunter?"

There came an angry, feminine grumble from the crowd, an answering male grumble too. Scandeer's face and bald head were so red I thought he might pop. "You dare speak to the High Elder in this way?" he spat. "You traitorous peasant! Think you that, after your dishonest approach to our hallowed Huntmeet, that you have any voice here at all?"

"Yes, I broke the Huntmeet rules!" Mill growled back, rising up to his full height and casting a menacing shadow on the High Elder. "And know all of you that this was my own idea, not Ariana's. I talked her into it. I showed her the hiding place. I convinced her it would work." The murmur of the crowd rose to outrage. "But, listen! Do you know why I did this? It was not some ploy that I should win the Huntmeet. I'd rather have food on my table than trophies to gather dust on my mantle."

"Gather dust on your—"

Mill didn't let the Elder finish. "I have no need of trophies, Elder. No, I didn't want to win the Huntmeet for myself. I wanted Ariana to win it. For all the sneers and rejection that she and all the other women in this village have suffered, I wanted Ariana to have a chance to show what she can do. What is the Huntmeet anyway, but a chance to sharpen our skills and prove the best hunters among us? The purpose of the Hunt Guild is to provide food for this whole village! Then why, good Elder, would we not want all of the best hunters to be in the Hunt Guild?"

Plebian Scandeer wasn't so stymied this time. I got the feeling he hadn't been listening to Mill at all, but rather forming his own diatribe. "Millard Key," he said. "You have violated your standing in the Hunt Guild. You have slandered all legitimate hunters and cast your selfish ambitions in front of all their hard work and training. You have cheated and you have been caught. And even so, in your haughty insolence you dare to tell the Hunt Guild its business."

Every one of Scandeer's words plunged into my gut like hammering fists of guilt, but none so much as his last. "Millard Key, your name is hereby stricken from the rolebook of the Hunt Guild. Permanently."

"Permanently?" whispered one of the other Elders.

"This is a lifetime ban," said Scandeer, seemingly inflating himself with every word. "It is my final word as High Elder and, as such, is irrevocable."

I gasped, looking between the Elders and Millard. My stomach continued to twist into unbearable knots. I wanted to say something, but couldn't speak. Even the crowd seemed frozen in silent shock.

Millard shrugged the guard's hands off his arms and flexed his neck. He stared down the High Elder and said, "Good riddance to it all, your phony Hunt Guild pride, your posturing, your political tomfoolery! Perhaps . . . perhaps, I'll start another guild. I'll call it Archer's Guild for those who can shoot without their noses in the air!" Mill turned his back to them and began to descend the platform stairs.

"You'll do no such thing, Millard Key!" the High Elder screeched.

"Watch me," said Mill, his voice a low, gravelly tone that would send black bears running.

Plebian Scandeer slammed his staff hard on the floor and glared at me. "This . . . this is ALL your fault!"

I knew it was, and I did the only thing I could think of: I vomited all over the High Elder.

I sat with my back up against the soft trunk of my favorite tree. The cushion of moss beneath me was so used to my presence that it had a permanent mold of my contours. I was in my favorite place in all of Myriad: The Grove of Golden Light. At least that's what I called it. I don't think there was a formal name for the half-wooded plateau just east of the Wetlands Village. So far as I knew, no one else ever came here. And now it was far from golden. Under the half-moon and ten thousand stars, deep into the clear night, the grove was lit only in a pale, twilight blue.

Still, I would sleep here tonight. I didn't want to see anyone. I didn't want to be in the village at all. I needed time alone, time to think. Quiet breeze whispered in the boughs overhead, and I shook. The trembling wasn't from the cold, but rather from frustration mingling with desperation.

"What am I doing here?" I asked the empty grove. What did the Wetlands hold for me anyway besides agonizing memories, gaping holes in my heart, and daily humiliation? My head fell back against the tree, and the tears overflowed their bounds, running hot down my cheeks.

Truth was, I didn't know why I stayed in the Wetlands of Chapparel. It was where I'd always been. Maybe it was fear of the unknown lands beyond the borders. Maybe I stayed because of the High Elders and all the injustice. I always hoped I could change things. Da always told me I could make a difference. And Mom showed me by her example. But with the invasion, the massacre, the takings . . . everything changed. The new Warden of Chapparel, Gander Brow, didn't invest much time or concern in the Wetlands either. Not like Warden Caddock anyway. Now the Elders ruled with granite fists. I hadn't changed anything except for gaining a reputation as a trouble maker, that and hurting a good friend.

I closed my eyes and bounced my head against the tree. It was like the whole world was narrowing, closing in on me like unbreachable walls. And I saw my future unfold before me: Ariana Kurtz, living as an outcast in the village, doing little but laundry and cooking . . . and aging. I'd never break the Elders' hold on my people. The people would stay blissfully cowed, trampled and thankful for it. I'd endure heaping scorn from the men of the village and never find the one who would be strong enough to love me and protect me as I would him. My face would wrinkle, my hair would gray, and I would live, growing more bitter and poisonous by the year.

"C'mon," I told myself. "You're young still. You can do something yet. You can do anything." *Anything, yeah . . . anything but leave.*

And maybe, just maybe, I wouldn't lead the Wetlands because it was the last place I saw my parents. Maybe if I left, they would never come back.

CHAPTER 11

LEGEND AND TRUTH

Behind the Curtain,
So high and cold,
The walls rise up
To vex the bold.
By master Stonehand,
Spriggan, and human craft,
Its high towers and gates
Turn sword, spear, and shaft.
Wearing five white summits
Like a crown of peace,
A cloud-born refuge where
All fears will cease.
No enemy conquers,
Nor beast assails,
The Fortress high
That ne'er fails

—Inscribed on a bronze plaque in Sentry Hall, Steadfeld Keep

21 SOLMONATH 2238

"Make sure that fire's good an' out, boy," Tanner Goliant said.

How many years have we been camping together, Da? thought Tango as he turned over the blackened coals and still red embers in the dirt. And I've never once mishandled a fire. If times were different, Tango might have told his father so. But not now. Now was a time for sharp listening and quiet obedience.

He watched his father nudge Meli awake. She'd fallen fast asleep after a meager breakfast of pan-fried sausage and roots. It took him several gentle attempts. Meli slept hard, especially after traveling days on end and hiking half the previous night.

Tango watched his father's every move. Tango had never seen any man behave this way much less his burly Da. Quick, compact movements, darting eyes, and constant muttering. It was as if every decision he made was life or death. Maybe it is life or death, Tango thought, a chill creeping up the middle of his back. Raudrim and the Red Queen, once only nightmarish legends, had seemingly become real.

Tango stamped down on the damp earth, a shard of lingering pain in his right foot from having to crush out the flickerstick. It seemed impossible that it had been less than a week since they'd been in the Haunted Cave and first seen the creature.

"Ah, she's too tired yet," Tango's father said. "Can ya' handle Meli's pack?"

"Aye," Tango said. "I can, and more besides. Give me a couple of those satchels."

"That's a good lad." He handed the worn leather bags to his son and then carefully hoisted Meli up onto the middle of his back between two large packs. "There's a girl, pig-a-back, just like we used to," he said. Meli murmured something happy and nuzzled into his upper back. She was asleep again that fast.

There was a momentary pause, and though his father had turned away, Tango had seen the look in his eyes. Tango thought he understood his father more now than he ever had. He understood the fierce love his father bore for them, the desperate need to make the absolute right choices, and the abject fear that, no matter what he did, it wouldn't be enough to keep his children safe.

Tango hitched up his own pack, then Meli's, then seven satchels including the two from his father. In that moment, Tango felt a glowing hot surge of pride for his father. This was as good and decent a Spriggan as there was, and Tango would grow up to be just like him if he could. And no matter how his muscles might burn from the burdens, Tango would keep going. He'd made up his mind that he would have his father's back no matter what came.

"C'mon, boy," his father said. "Daylight's wastin'. I want to get t'the thicket before nightfall."

But for a mound of buried ash, they left their campsite as they had found it and charged into forest leagues east of their home in Hammer's Gap. They chugged along in the wood as only Spriggans can, bounding from berm to hollow, surefooted and quiet. No root tripped them up, no vine entangled them, and the lack of a clear path was barely a hindrance.

It was three hours straight before Tango's father announced, "Stop for a breath." They halted under a canopy of leaning maples with fat red, star-shaped leaves. Taneth let Meli slide down his back.

She plopped to the ground and blinked. "Where are we, Da?"

"Awake at last are ya, Meli lass?" He turned and gave her a swift tickle under the chin. "We are just southwest of the Deeping."

"Deeping? What's tha?"

He took out a stick of smoked meat, carved off a hunk with his always-sharp hatchet, and handed it to Tango, then another to Meli. "The Deeping is a grand forest valley that lay in the shadow of the great Impasse Mountains. Deer and other game are so plentiful there, ya fair trip over them. We'll be makin' our home there for a time . . . in The Thicket."

"How come we never hunted there before, Da?" Tango asked.

"I have lad," he replied. "But I deemed it too dangerous there for you littlins, at least til now. All too easy to loose yer way, it is. Blackwolves and other predators besides. Dark things creep down from the mountains and hunt there too."

Meli chewed on the tough meat. "Is it still so dangerous now?"

"I'm countin' on it," he said. "Any luck, it'll keep villains out of our hair. Safer than Hammer's Gap now, that's fer sure."

"Why?" asked Meli. A potent mixture of sadness and confusion, she fixed him with her eyes. "Why'd we have t'leave home?"

The elder Goliant took a deep breath and exhaled slowly. "I suppose you ought t'know," he said. "But, Stars, Meli to tell ya, I feel like I'm stealin' yer Sprighood away from ya. No one ought to have to think on such things as this, not at your age."

"Da, we know the story," Tango said. "The Dragon and the Red Queen."

"No, son, ya don't."

"But you've told us a hundred times."

"I have'na told you everything." They all sat chewing, listening to the sounds of insects, squirrels, and other forest inhabitants busy at their afternoon habits. "First thing ya know," he said at last, "is that Raudrim was a very old wyrm. Ages old. Ten times the span of any folk in all the Hinterlands. He was in the bloodline of first generation dragons, he was. As peculiar as he was wicked and twice as greedy as all that. He kept hoards of precious things in deep mountain caves in every corner a' the land."

"One of 'em was in the Haunted Cave, right, Da?" Tango asked.

"Right, lad. And more than one venturin' fool went in there seekin' after fortune but did'na come back. Now, this was about the 6th Age, dark times even as we reckon it in the Hinterlands. Quevera became Queen of Cragheath Tor by murderin' her parents in their sleep. Two things she never could get enough of, and that's blood and gold. She built an army of terror, bigger'n anything you've ever seen. Filled the moat around her bastion with the blood of peasants, and killed hundreds more every day just to see their blood run in the streams. She had all the nations of the Hinterlands in chains for near on an age, but then she went too far."

"She went lookin' fer that dragon's hoard," Meli said, nodding as if she was as sage as an elder. "And when she found it, she and the dragon fought an' killed each other."

"That's what I told ya, Meli," Tanner said. "And I'm not sorry. I wanted you littlins scared enough to stay out a' that cave, but I did'na want to darken yer dreams for years. See she went a' searching for that old wyrm alright, and she found him. But they did'na fight. Raudrim was on death's door at last, splayed out on his hoard and still aching for more. But those old wyrms could live on, they could. If they could find a mortal willin' to give up his life, they could kinda meld together and live. Quevara wanted the power and wealth it would give her, and the long life, but she wanted to keep her will. Raudrim agreed, and that dyin' wyrm opened up his chest and took Quevara in."

"Da, how'd ya know all this?" Tango asked. "Was'na this long before your day?"

He nodded. "Aye, but not before yer Great Grandsprig."

Meli brightened. "Great Grandsprig Finnel?"

"That's right. See the Red Queen did'na go into the cave alone. She took her generals with her. Most of them died there, but a few got out. Great Grandsprig Finnel found one of 'em half-dead in the Pine Barrens. He told the whole tale before dyin, he did. Old Finnel passed the story on to yer ma and she to me. Now, I'm tellin' you, Tango and Meli. And I've no doubt that the story you told me from your time in the cave is right true. I saw blood in the river last night. The Red Queen is back at Cragheath Tor, somehow, and with all the power she must have, there's no tellin' what horrible things she'll do."

A mournful howl drifted down from the foothills behind them.

"Wolves," muttered Tanner.

"Not comin' fer us, are they?" Meli asked.

Her father stood, eyes fixed, listening. Other howling cries rose. One was much lower, fierce and frightening in its depth.

"They're far away yet," Tanner told his children. "But we can'na be too careful now. Put on your sapeline."

Meli frowned and scrunched up her nose. "Awww, that stuff reeks."

"That's the idea, sister," Tango laughed, squeezing the tube and daubing his fingertips in the viscous paste. "It's gotta smell monstrous bad t'keep the monsters from smellin' us."

"It's not just the smell," Meli said. "It feels fair disgustin'. Especially when I have t'put it down th—"

"Okay, Meli! We get it!" Tango shook his head.

Once Tanner was convinced that everyone smelled like a newly felled pine forest, they set off to hiking once more. The howling continued, a mournful cacophony, a song of danger growing nearer by the minute. And always, chief among the cries, came the deep baying. It made the little hairs on Tango's neck and legs stand on end.

"How far t'this thicket, Da?" he asked.

"It's not more than a league," the elder Goliant replied. "And it's not just any thicket, lad. You've never seen such a fortress of thorns. All the wolves in the world couldn't touch us in there."

Meli listened to the howls and shuddered. She was five years younger than Tango, still very much in the middle of sprighood. But she was as able as her brother in the wood. Bounding from fallen tree to stone, sliding agilely down each incline, and thundering up hills with ease, Meli seemed made for the deep forest.

Their path took them on a decline now, and the angle steadily increased. But so did the threat of the wolves. "Stay close t'me!" Tanner shouted. He ran now with his hatchet in hand. "I do'na understand it. No beast can track through the sapeline. Ya covered yer parts right?"

"Yes, da!" they replied.

"All of them? Completely?"

Tango growled. "Da, if I put any more down there, I'd grow a pine tree out of my—"

"Right, lad!" Tanner barked a laugh in spite of the fear. He looked up and saw that the sun had slipped behind the hills, the knobby, wooded knees of the mountains. "We can'na be far now. A good sprint'll do it. How' ya doin' with that load, lad? Got a sprint left in ya?"

"More'n that, Da!" Tango said, accepting the challenge and charging ahead. This ought t'surprise him a fair bit, he thought. He tore down the hill, dead leaves spinning in his wake.

"Not too far ahead, lad!" Tanner called. "Ya don' know where yer goin'!"

But Tango had raced up a hill and down the other side. "C'mon, Meli," Tanner said. "We'd better catch up with your brother."

"I can manage!" Meli said.

She kept up with her father, bounding along at his elbow. They tromped up the hill, made the turn just as Tango had, and slid to a panicked stop. Tango was ten yards further down the hill. He had his dagger out and he was backing up slowly. At the bottom of the hill, some twenty-five yards, was an oblong clearing. And in the shadows stood three massive blackwolves. Their teeth, all yellow and white, were bared and gnashing. Their hackles bristled. Rumbling growls tumbled from their throats. And between Tango and the beasts, there was only a thin thicket of knotted brambles.

Tanner held Meli back with his arm and felt as if two massive, heavy chains were pulling him apart. He ached to go to his son, but he couldn't take Meli any closer to the wolves. And he couldn't leave her.

"I'm here, boy," he said. "Keep comin' slowly. Keep comin, but keep yer eyes on them. First sign they might lunge, you haul up here behind me."

"I'm afraid, Da." Tango nearly stumbled on a root.

"Don'na you worry, boy. I'm right here. Just keep you comin'."

Tango glanced back at his father. It was only a moment, the barest instant. A stark, wide-eyed mistake. Horrified, Tanner watched the blackwolves crouch, ready to pounce. He couldn't just let them maul his son. Just as the creatures leaped, Tanner shouted, "DOWN!" He pushed Meli to the ground behind him and dove forward.

With a shout, Tango fell backward. All teeth, heavy muscle, and claws, the Blackwolves launched up the hill.

A shadow. Something immense and black hurtled into view, crashing into the blackwolves. Yelps of shock and pain burst from their jaws. As Tango shuffled backward and his father gathered him up, the blackwolves recovered and turned to face the threat.

There stood another wolf, this one a full head and shoulders taller than the others, muscled like a bull and barrel-chested. Its pelt was like that of the blackwolves but had an odd bluish cast. Its eyes were slanted, huge, and yellow. The intruder was outnumbered but growled fiercely at its foes and stepped forward. The other three attacked at once, their leaps staggered and from slightly different angles.

The largest wolf's muzzle shot forward, its jaws snapped shut on the chest of one of the smaller attackers. In a blur, it crushed the wolf in its maw and smacked the other two from the air with a thrust of its mighty head. Before they could recover, the largest creature tossed its first victim aside and pounced on one of the others. The smaller wolf cried in vain. The larger held it down with its heavy forelegs and then broke its victim's back in its jaws.

The last of the smaller wolves leaped onto the monster's back and went straight for its neck, burying its teeth just above the hackles. But the greater beast shook off the lesser as if it were a dead leaf. Before the smaller wolf could spin and attack, the giant was upon it, ripping its belly open with dagger-like claws.

Tanner and his children cowered behind an apron of bracken at the base of a wide tree up the hill. But they watched. Three adult blackwolves had been brutally dispatched right before their eyes. Tanner shook his head as the great beast turned its blood-soaked jaws toward the upslope.

"Tango, Meli," Tanner whispered. "String yer bows and aim for the eyes."

"But Da, we've no chance against that—"

"I know, son." Their eyes met. "I know."

"Intercepted your quarry at last, have you?" asked a voice deeper than the wolf's rumbling growl. "Sköll, at my heel!"

"That's him, Da!" Tango whispered urgently. "That's the man who summoned the dragon."

They crouched further back behind the trunk. "You're sure?"

"Fair, sure," Tango answered. "The wolf's bigger'n I remember, but that's gotta be him."

"Cythal, he called himself," Meli said.

"No, there was an 'r' in it somewhere. Cyrthal, no . . . Cythraul."

"Shhhh," Tanner commanded.

The ring of metal silenced them. They peered through the brambles and saw the man called Cythraul impale the dead wolves one by one and slide them into a sack.

"These ought to please our new friends," Cythraul said.

Sköll ducked his head, growled, and emitted something like a whimper.

"How thoughtless of me," Cythraul said. "You've hunted well, you've tasted blood, but had nothing to curb your hunger." He reached into the sack. "Very well then." There was a crack and a series of wet snaps. Cythraul tossed a meaty haunch to his wolf.

Sköll tossed the bloody hunks back and consumed them in a few quick snaps. Cythraul laughed grimly. "How easily you devour your own kind." He was quiet a moment and then said, "Not so different, really." He patted the great wolf on the hackles. "Come now, we have promises to keep."

Tanner closed his eyes and sighed inwardly.

"They're leavin', Da," Tango whispered.

"Thank the Starmaker fer that," his father whispered back. Meli started to get up. "No, wait. We'll not move from this spot til we're certain they're gone."

Tango felt as if they waited long enough for the seasons to change, but at last they were off once more. Tanner wouldn't let them run, so they moved much more slowly. They heard no more howls. In fact, the forest had grown silent as the mountain's shadow claimed more and more territory.

The trees were still tall in the deep of the valley, but they became more wiry and there were fewer evergreens. The brambles thickened and grew taller. "We're on the doorstep," Tanner said.

They walked a few more yards and then Tanner urged them to stop. A massive hedge of vine and thorn stood before them. Tango stared into it and felt dizzy. It was very hard to tell the depth of the thing, how far away the nearest thorns were, where one could step and where one could not.

"It's hard to look at, Da," said Meli.

"Aye," he replied. He put down one of his packs and rolled up his sleeve. "See this scar? I got this the first time I tried to get even a foot inside this outer ring."

"What outer ring?" Tango asked. "It looks all jumbled t'me."

"That it does," his father replied. "But don'na you worry. We'll not be tryin' t'get by this lethal gate."

"But how . . ."

"C'mon now, boy, what do us Spriggans do better'n anyone?"

"You dug a tunnel?"

Tanner just smiled. He walked a wide circle around the picket and motioned for the sprigs to follow.

"How big is this thing?" Meli asked.

"The Thicket is somethin' on the order of five hundred yards. It gets taller an' taller as you go deeper in. Just grows up on itself. But inside there's a nice little hollow where yer mother an' me built a little something."

Tanner came to a large gray tree that forked about twelve feet off the ground. The elder Goliant walked around for a bit of time and then began hauling armfuls of dead leaves away from a spot near the tree's base. Then, he bent over at the waist, flexed his massive forearms and began to dig. In a few moments, he was three feet into the soil. Then with a groan and a great wrenching heave, he lifted a heavy iron cap from the hole.

He stood up straight in the hole, smiled, and cracked a flicker-stick. "I'll go first," he said. "Clear out all the spiders."

"Spiders?" Tango swallowed. "Great."

Meli laughed.

It wasn't long before they heard their father calling from within. "Come on, my sprigs. Come see your new home."

CHAPTER 12

An Unwelcome Feast

*The Marinaens may be the oldest of Myriad's races. It's rather hard
to say because they are so secretive about their history. In fact, the
Marinaens are secretive about a great many things, not the least of
which is where they may be found. They live in Myriad's seas and
largest bays, but no one knows precisely where. They claim to be
nomadic, moving from undersea home to undersea home. Might there
be pearlescent castles or cities of coral deep beneath the waves? Only
the Marinaens know for certain. In spite of their mysterious ways,
they have ever been more than faithful to Anglinore and always an
ally to the noble nations of the Myriad. The Marinaens have gone
to war, bled, and died for this loyalty. And they are very active in the
fishing trade. When the High King or Queen wish to contact Marinaen royalty, all they need do is toss a message in a bottle into the
Dark Sea. The Marinaens never fail to reply.*

—Letti's Almanac, 2105 AS

45 Sedwyn 2238

King Lochlan Stormgarden, the High King of Myriad, wore an
orange tunic to the Feast of Welcome.

"You look like a pumpkin," Telwyn said, tilting back his mug.

"Perhaps I should have worn a dark green stocking cap," Loch replied, "you know, for the stem."

Telwyn sputtered the sip he was about to take. He laughed and wiped his lips and beard with a cloth napkin. "I think you've vexed Daribel enough already. It wouldn't have been wise to add insult to injury. See there; she's launching more hate darts to impale you."

Loch gazed across the vast table, and the kings and queens gathered there. On the far side of the chamber, standing just to the side of the tall arched window, stood Daribel. The Kitchen High Mistress, Royal Fashion Consultant, and a few other royal titles Loch had given her but never said aloud, Daribel was well known for having her wishes followed, even by kings and queens. She stood now, arms crossed, eyes bulging, sporting a face that would curdle milk . . . and her burning gaze was directed straight at Lochlan.

"You may wish to consider a royal food-tester from here on out," Telwyn said. "To sample your meals and test for poison, you know."

Loch laughed, but stopped short. "You don't think she would, do you?"

Telwyn rolled his eyes. "To think you are High King of the known world."

Lochlan laughed, but it wasn't long until the mirth faded. He stared into his tankard and absently swished the liquid around. He sighed and lowered the drink to the table.

Telwyn tapped on Loch's shoulder and said, "You do know I was joking, right? You are going to be a fine leader."

Loch nodded and smiled with as much confidence as he could muster.

How did I get here? he wondered, his thoughts returning to a familiar quandary. How can they expect me to lead commanders such as these? He scanned the table. Aside from Telwyn and his family, there was no safe place to look. Loch shook his head. Safe, ha! Certainly not the Windborne.

Though in his winter years, King Drüst, Skylord of the Windborne, looked anything but frail. Fierce green eyes, thrice larger than human, angled down towards his sharp nose. A wide arrowhead of sea-gray hair divided his prominent brow, swept back over his head as if permanently blown smooth by the wind, and disappeared behind his disproportionately large neck and shoulder muscle. His iron gray wings flexed and settled behind him as he laughed.

At his elbow sat Jornth, Drüst's nephew and heir to the Skylord throne. Dark skin and darker eyes, black, plaited hair and black wings, Jornth looked bold, mysterious, and powerful. He blinked a great deal as he spoke quietly to his uncle, and those eyes, somewhat shaded by his cliff-like brow, carried a hint of grim sobriety as if he had lived much longer than his twenty four years. Just in his twenties, Loch reminded himself. But given the short life span of the Windborne, Jornth was already well into adulthood.

Just past the Windborne sat the ruler of Tryllium, King Izjaak Kihlbranan, a Stonehand lord—by all accounts more feisty and fun-loving than his predecessor, King Vang, who fell in the Gorrack War. He wore his brown beard in thick braids that stuck out like stalks from his cheeks and chin. He clinked tankards with Gander Brow, the Warden of Chapparel.

Brow bore a pasty countenance: pale blond hair, mustache and beard, weathered, baggy skin, especially under his hooded eyes, and a bell-shaped nose that moved like a rabbit's when he spoke. He rarely spoke, Loch noted, but when he did, there was usually something worth listening to or maybe even jotting onto a scroll for later review. Gander Brow was known for his shrewd, exacting wisdom. He had a way of cutting through the peripheral issues, the volatile controversies that could easily bog a leader down, to get to the things that needed to get done. It was under

Brow's leadership that Chapparel was not only restored but taken beyond its original port-city grandeur.

Loch noted his mother standing to Warden Brow's left. Queen Maren leaned down to speak to Queen Briawynn of Ellador. Loch sighed. He'd had a secret fascination with Queen Briawynn ever since he was a lad. After the War, she had often visited Anglinore to encourage Queen Maren. And she spent a lot of time with young Lochlan, taking walks or playing in the courtyard. She'd always been so kind . . . and that inner beauty had only amplified her stunning outer glow.

I'd best get in line, Loch thought. Queen Briawynn possessed the kind of beauty that could stun a man and leave him wandering aimlessly for several minutes. Creamy white skin, large dark-colored eyes, tiny but full, plum-colored lips, and a fringe of tawny, feather-like sideburns that framed her face into a heart shape—she reminded Loch somehow of a snowy owl, a kind of still and quiet majesty that shunned attention but demanded it anyway. Queen Briawynn daunted everyone by refusing to marry. She glanced up and connected with Lochlan's gaze. His heart skipped a beat, and he looked elsewhere.

Queen Valaril Nascent had only arrived from Fen's capital city of Sennec in the morning. She was willowy and tall, beautiful in the same way that a sheer cliff might be. She had a narrow face with narrow slate-blue eyes, high cheekbones, and thin, curling lips. As she sliced the roasted beef on her plate, her hands moved with the grace of great skill. Scenic, serene, and distant, but with danger near at all times, Queen Valaril was one of the most capable—and lethal—warriors in all of Myriad. The curvy handles of two daggers stuck out behind her shoulders, and Loch knew she had two more sheathed in her boots. But Loch knew that such a strong and potentially violent leader was necessary for ruling a realm with such a dark history. When Vulmarrow, the former capital of Fen had fallen into ruins and been overrun with blackwolves and worse, the city of Sennec on Fen's far eastern border had been rebuilt to be the new capital. Velaril Nascent had deep history in Fen, she had a royal bloodline reaching as far back as King Mendeleev, and she was the only one willing to take the throne right after the war.

Next to Velaril, just visible behind two enormous clear goblets of spring water, were the Marinaen rulers: Prince Navrill and his recent wife Princess Acadia. Of the group, these two were the most personable . . . which Loch thought was ironic because the Marinaens were the least like humans in form. They had dark blue flesh with purple folds flaring from their cheeks to their shoulders. Wing-like fins gathered beneath their arms, and membranous flesh webbed their three-fingered hands. Loch thought they were beautiful in their otherworldly way, but especially because of the love they clearly shared. Even now, they sat close and stared at each other with their bright eyes.

Loch noted too that, of all these high rulers, only Prince Navrill had a living spouse. *What hope does that offer me?* Loch could see himself as many things, but never a bachelor.

A glass tip-tapping made Loch blink. King Ealden, the hale ruler of the Prydian Wayfolk, stood and said, "Venescence, nuvim! I would like to propose a toast!" He held up a large gray goblet.

"Well that depends," Izaak called aloud. "It's not a proper toast unless you've got something a wee bit stronger than spring water in yer mug, heh, heh."

Ealden cast a wry glare at the Stonehand leader of Tryllium. But he otherwise ignored the comment. "We find ourselves on the eve of a momentous and historical occasion. For tomorrow Lochlan Stormgarden will receive the honorary pledge of service being named for all posterity: High King Overlord of all Myriad. And—"

"Here, here!" shouted the Marinaens.

Ealden almost smiled. "Not quite yet," he said. Loch cringed. He hated having everyone stare at him and worse, King Ealden was clearly about to launch into one of his speeches. Loch seriously considered hiding beneath the table or perhaps, diving out of the window.

King Ealden cleared his throat. "Please stand," he said. He waited a beat until everyone rose from their seats and raised their mugs, tankards, or glasses. "We feast together tonight to celebrate the rise of a new world sovereign. But we entrust new King Lochlan to the sovereign of all, the First One who gives the authorities of this world the power to keep this land safe. We raise our glasses to Lochlan who—"

Ealden continued, but Loch whispered to Telwyn, "My arm's getting tired."

Telwyn smiled. "His heart's in the right place . . . most of the time."

". . . so gloriously skilled that we can pledge our full trust in him to lead, to protect, to dispense wisdom from Anglinore's high seat. There may come times of great distress. There may be controversies and skirmishes. There may even be war. But Lochlan will follow in the footsteps of his father, King Aravel and . . ."

Lochlan began to feel a strange heavy pulse with every word the Prydian king spoke. It was as if an invisible bass drum were beating right next to Loch and the vibration was jarring.

". . . bearing the responsibilities of High King Overlord . . ."

Lochlan swayed. Please stop, he thought urgently. No more about me.

". . . with confidence and greater clarity than any other . . ."

Something inside of Lochlan lurched, and there was an agonizing, fearful moment where he didn't feel or hear his heart beating.

". . . long life, peace, and great . . ."

Loch's heart kicked in. He caught a sudden draught of breath as if he'd just surfaced from deep waters that might have drown him. "Thank you, thank you, King Ealden," Loch managed to croak. "But I can bear no more words of praise tonight." King Ealden looked aghast, but Loch quickly added jovially, "After all, you should be saving up for tomorrow!"

The assembly laughed quietly, raised their mugs a little higher, and cheered, "Here, here!"

Lochlan downed a goblet of fairywater and wished the oil lanterns to burn low.

"I'm telling you, Sebastian," Loch said. "I don't know what came over me."

The Shepherd leaned forward in his chair. "And nothing since then?"

"No, nothing. But I can remember it vividly."

"What were you thinking about when the discomfort began?" Sebastian grabbed a thick leather bound tome from his bookcase and began paging through it.

Loch rubbed the muscle in his upper arm. "It was when everyone was staring at me," Loch said. "And with all King Ealden was saying, I just kept thinking about how many responsibilities fall to me and ALL the tasks and ALL that might happen and—"

"Okay, Loch, calm down." Sebastian put a warm hand on Loch's forearm. "If anyone tries to swallow all of the future and every possibility, he will choke. The First One tells us that each day has its own concerns."

"But what do you think, Sebastian?" Loch looked up plaintively. "Will I be a good king?"

Sebastian closed the book in his lap, and his eyes became bright, almost fierce. "Lochlan Stormgarden, you have the heart of a lion. If you give yourself the time to learn and the grace to make mistakes without losing hope, you will be the greatest king Myriad has ever known."

Loch sat up a little straighter. "How can you know?"

"Know?" Sebastian laughed. "That is such a ticklish word. We speak it too often when what we actually mean is we believe it enough to rest our confidence in it. It is faith, really. And Loch, I have great faith in you."

Lochlan thrust his shoulders back. "Thank you."

"But, in the meantime, I believe you need a break. Have you given any more thought to my suggestion?"

Loch nodded. "Quite a bit," he replied. "And after tonight, I think I figured out how to do it."

"What do you mean?" Sebastian's left eyebrow rose very high. "Have you chartered a coach?"

"No, not that, not yet, anyway," Loch replied cryptically. "It was something King Ealden said . . . about my talents."

"Which ones?" Sebastian asked. "Swordcraft? Art? Smithing? Lute? Herb—"

"Okay," Loch interrupted, "that's what I was getting at. I can do things, right? Just about anything I put my mind to."

"You are a prodigy," Sebastian agreed. "Gifted beyond the measure of most."

"So what if I went out to the people of Myriad? I mean what if I went and lived among them?"

Sebastian squinted. "Well, of course, I agree. I'd like that. But . . . ah, what about all the attention and false—"

"No, no. I don't want that. That's why I'm not going to live among them as King Lochlan. I'm going to live among them as Lochlan the blacksmith or Lochlan the tavern keeper or fisherman or whatever!"

"Go in disguise?"

"Well, not exactly. But very few people have seen me in person and most of those only from a distance. If I'm not wearing Daribel's finest linens and such, not wearing a crown, or prancing about while others bow, hardly anyone would know me."

Sebastian sat back in his chair. He tapped a finger on his chin. "Have you spoken to your mother about it?"

"I have."

"And what was her counsel?"

Loch shook his head. "She told me I should come talk to you."

"Ah," Sebastian replied. "Well, that is helpful."

Loch stared out of the tower window. Sebastian had roses and nightbloom trellised there, brilliant dark red, mingling with ghostly white set against the night sky canvas behind it. Loch felt a powerful pull from the outside, but felt a creeping dread that he would be denied. "You don't think I should go, do you?"

"Lochlan, I will tell you what I think." Sebastian stood and began pacing the perimeter of the tower. "I think that the burden of High King Overlord is of sufficient weight to destroy a man. I have seen it take its toll on your father and his father before him. Both Brysroth and Aravel felt the smothering impact of captivity. But even they have not been so cloistered as you have been. From birth, Loch, you have been suffocated with attention and demands. Your manifest talents have only served to tempt the well-intentioned souls around you to pile more upon you. You've been spread too thin for too long."

Loch dared a smile. "Wait, are you saying what I think you're saying?"

"I can only offer you such wisdom as I have. You must make your own decisions."

Loch stood. "I want this," he said. "I really do. But there are many variables to consider." Loch drew a dagger from his belt. "If only this were as easy as a duel," he said. "The opponent moves a certain way, I know immediately how I must counter. If the angle of attack is such, I know just how to block." He moved through the steps, lifting the dagger high, then slicing back across his body. "Simple."

"There are many seasoned warriors who do not find the steps of battle so 'simple,' my lord."

"In a duel, the decisions come because they must—like reflexes," said the young king with a swoosh of his dagger. "But now, there are too many unknowns. I long to be with my people, but I am fettered by duty. I don't know what I should do."

"Sheath that weapon, and hold this instead," said the Shepherd. He picked up an hourglass housed in a cleverly carved wooden frame that made it look like spiral staircases were running to and fro around the bulbous glass. He turned it upside down and handed it to the King. "Watch," said the Shepherd. his voice now deep and resonant. "Each grain of sand is a coin of inestimable value, and no matter how hard you try to save them, they will all be spent . . . sooner or later. To spend or to save—a risk either way. For even a wealthy man who sits upon vaults of precious things knows not whether even one more coin of this kind will come. And when the last coin is spent . . . would you wish it to be for wondering what might have been?"

Loch watched the sand crystals pour relentlessly into the bottom chamber and sighed.

"Think on it," Sebastian said. "Then tomorrow, after the Ceremony of Crowns and the Council, return to Clarissant Hall and pray. Ask the First One for His final wisdom. Then, we will speak again."

"My prayers don't really work that way," Loch said, his eyebrows knit together in frustration. "You act as if the First One will speak something aloud to me."

"Maybe He will," Sebastian replied. "The Silence cannot last forever, can it? But even if He does not speak in words you can hear, He may provide surety in other ways."

Loch nodded and placed the hourglass back on the bookshelf.

"How was your match with Cardiff?" the Shepherd asked.

"Not so good," he replied. "I won."

"Correct me if I am mistaken, your majesty, but winning is the point . . . more or less."

"Yes, but Cardiff let me win. He made his true intentions clear to me after the match. He wants a share of the throne, Sebastian." Loch paused. "Maybe I should let him have it, that is, if I decide to venture out on my own, he could rule in my stead."

Sebastian turned pale. "I don't think that would be very wise," he said. "Cardiff is in the royal bloodline, and he's harmless enough ruling over a barony. But to give him a taste of ultimate power could prove ruinous. No, my lord, if you would take my counsel, I would advise against allowing Baron Cardiff Strengle even a moment on the high seat."

"You've given me much to think about," Loch said. "As usual." As he turned to leave the tower chamber, he watched as the last few grains of sand drained away.

CHAPTER 13

CLARITY

*Contrary to the beliefs of the younger Shepherds who knew him,
Mosteryn the Old wasn't always old. I knew him as a lad before a
hair on his head went gray and before he called down his first bolt of
lightning. Even then, he had an explosive temper. He had no patience
for the rest of us who took so long to comprehend what he mastered
instantly. Perhaps he had a little more patience with me, but that was
only because I'm his brother. And maybe he felt even a little gratitude
because I first figured out how his lightning could make incredible
glass. He told me once that he'd spent an entire stormy spring season
filling a cavern with his lightning glass sculptures. But he never told
me where the cavern was.*

—An excerpt from the journal of Montague Alderlore,
12 Celesander, 1452 AS

1 FEFTIN 2238

The Ceremony of Crowns went by in a kind of anxious blur
for King Lochlan. He had never seen Clarissant Hall so packed
with citizens, not on the previous Ceremony of Crowns for his
mother. Not on Halfindays when Anglinore's faithful came to
worship. There had been trumpets and singing and King Ealden's

benediction. There had been cheers and weeping and the clashing of swords on shields. But more memorable for Loch was the ceremonial placing of all the rulers' crowns on the altars. It was more memorable . . . and more disturbing.

Lochlan knew it was going to happen. As High King Overlord of all Myriad, he would place his crown upon the high altar. Built on a grand pedestal, the altar was covered in lush purple velvet, and there were two perfectly-sized indentations for crowns: Loch's and Maren's. Once it had been done, Loch and his mother found their throne seats on the high stage just behind the altar. But that was only a part of the ceremony. There was another altar, a lower altar. This one was waist high and lined with dark green silk. And, one by one, the other rulers of the realms of Myriad came forward, placed their crowns, and took their seats. The object lesson was lost on no one, especially not Loch. All the other kings, queens, regents, and wardens—no matter their years of experience, their intellect, or might—were of lesser authority than the High King. It was a willing subordination of wills that dated back three ages, many thousands of years, and with just a few insurrections, the system had proven its worth.

But as the ceremony dragged on, Loch found himself staring at the altars. His crown . . . above all others. What have I done to earn such placement? he asked himself. Nothing, he thought. I was born.

Light from the two narrow lancet windows high above shone down on Loch's crown, lingered there a moment, and then gradually spilled off the side of the high altar. Watching that golden light made Loch think of other objections as well. What of the First One in all this? Loch looked about the hall. It might as well be a vast dining room or a barracks or some theater for the day's newest ideas. There was hardly any sign that the room was meant to honor the One who had created it all. For all intents and purposes, they have put me above even the First One. Loch felt his stomach turning.

The singing of the final song went on. Loch glanced at his mother. She looked back, her eyes knowing as always. She'd told him that there had once been a magnificent altar of another kind in Clarissant Hall. That altar, she'd said, was meant to lift the First One above all Myridian authority, to show due homage, and remind all who set foot in the chamber of the proper order of things. The key-like symbol of the First One, the hallowed avain, had been set on high, and the crowns of the High King and Queen, along with all the other crowns, had been stationed beneath it. What Maren hadn't told him, but other attendants and guards had, was that King Aravel had ordered the dismantling of that revered, old altar.

Why did you do that, father? Loch wondered. He had no answer.

The song ended. Queen Briawynn took her seat. It was time for Lochlan to speak. He stood and stepped a few paces forward. He waited for the assembly there to become perfectly still, allowing enough time for them all to dry their eyes after Briawynn's passionate song. And then, he delivered his dismissal speech.

"Citizens of Anglinore," he called. "Sojourners from the farthest reaches of this realm, I am honored at your presence on this day. For I am just a man—ONE man—born into this throne and station. I accept my place and this seat of authority, but I pledge to you, I will never forget the people I am meant to rule . . . to serve." Applause and cheers broke out. Loch spoke on over them. "I see you now. You are hardworking farmers, smiths, tradesmen, mothers, fathers, sisters, brothers—each and every one of you of greater worth than scepters and crowns. I will never forget. And I hope and I pray that I will NEVER let you down."

"Long live, King Lochlan!" one man cried out.

"First One bless you!" a woman declared.

Lochlan nodded his thanks and looked down to the other rulers. "And to you, leaders in your own right, I thank you now for your show of good faith. But I ask much more than that of each of you. I ask for patience. I ask that you endure my growing pains. And I ask that you will share your wisdom and experience with me. I will lean upon you. This I pledge."

King Drüst and many of the lords nodded or clapped. But Prince Navrill and Princess Acadia rose to their feet and applauded. King Ealden was next. Soon, they all stood, and many moments passed before the applause died down.

"Now to all gathered here, well . . . except for my lords who must join me for the Council, I bid a fond farewell. The Ceremony of Crowns has concluded. The Festival of Crowns must begin! Go and make merry, give thanks, and enjoy all that Anglinore has to offer, knowing full well that tonight you are safe!"

When the uproar had died away, and Clarissant Hall was all but empty, Maren put a hand on her son's shoulder. "Your words were well-chosen, my son."

Loch smiled kindly. "Now, all I must do is live up to them."

"Profits from the mining clans are up," declared Izjaak Kihlbranan. He spoke with such vivacious enthusiasm that his finger-thick braids bobbed around his chin. "Stonecrest and Carrack Vale both report opening new veins, ha, ha! We don't have enough doughty folk on hand to smelt it all!"

Lochlan nodded and tried to look thoughtful and kingly. "Will there be new armor for the Anglish Guard then?"

Izjaak grinned. "Course there will be, the usual stockpiles to all the capital cities."

"I too have an increase to report," Queen Briawynn said, a glimmer in her large, dark eyes. "With the additional manpower from Fen, we've finished construction of three new lumber routes. We've managed to move more timber this year than the previous two years combined."

"That's fantastic!" Loch said, a little louder than he'd meant to. "I mean to say that . . . it does my heart good to see how our realms are working . . . uh, together."

"Yes," Queen Valaril Nascent replied. "It is the least we can do. Sennec is one of the most extravagant and beautiful cities in Myriad, thanks in large part to the exquisite timber of the Verdant

Mountains." In a flash, she held a dagger in one hand and a plump Fennish pear in the other. With a flick of her wrist, a hunk of pear popped up a few inches into the air, just high enough for her mouth to snap shut upon it.

Loch swallowed. She was good with that dagger. Hmmm, he thought. Lock drew his own dagger, a shorter, straighter blade than Valaril's. He picked up a pear from the bowl in front of him. He envisioned the motion, the angle of the blade, the force she'd used. Then, he did it. A crescent shaped wedge of pear flew up into the air. He opened and shut his mouth, smiling as he started to chew. Queen Valaril had been watching. She nodded respect to Loch. Loch nodded back.

"How are things in Chapparel?" Prince Navrill asked.

"Yes," said Princess Acadia. "Our people have made great strides, redirecting the schools of stridentia, eh, the silver tuna, as you call them."

Gander Brow seemed to wake from a long nap. "Good, very good," he said, his nose wiggling. "Record hauls all summer long. Will you join us for the Feast of Octale? We would be honored to thank you in person."

"Surely we will," the princess replied. She glanced apologetically to the prince. "I am sorry to have spoken for us, my husband. What say you?"

"You spoke well, Acadia. Gladly we will come. But, good Warden, I give you fare warning: our people have deceptively large appetites. We might eat you out of house and home."

Gander laughed quietly and nodded.

"No other pressing business then?" Loch asked. The meeting had gone much better than he had expected.

The assembly scooted out their chairs.

"Excellent," King Drüst said, springing into the air. "I'd been hoping to spend some time with the glorious stained glass before the sun is full set."

"I wonder," King Ealden said. "I wonder if I might revisit a point of discussion from the last Council."

King Drüst dropped lightly back into his chair and sighed.

Lochlan didn't much care for King Ealden's penchant for ceremony, but there were very few beings he'd ever met with more wisdom or sincerity. The Prydian ruler seemed genuinely concerned, so Loch said, "By all means. Say on."

"Thank you, your majesty." Ealden opened a thin leather binding and slid one page of parchment aside. "I by no means wish to cast aspersions upon the prosperity we are all so enamored of discussing, but it seems to me that there is an outstanding threat that we would do well to address."

"Not the blasted Gray Hour Raids!" King Roth Haradin objected, his skin reddening to the point that it almost blended with the shock of prickly red hair on his head. He stood from his seat and pounded a fist on the table. "You . . . you had to go bringing this up, didn't you!"

The sudden explosion from the ruler of the Vespal Branch of the Wayfolk took everyone by surprise, and shocked silence reigned for several breathless moments. Lochlan felt a chill tingling on the back of his neck. The eyes of the group hadn't shifted to him yet, but he felt sure their thoughts were turning even now to the High King. I'd better say something, he thought. "King Roth," Loch said, carefully moderating his tone. "Your wisdom is held in high regard here, but your tone is not. Pray, speak your objection more civilly and we will hear it."

Beads of sweat trickled down that red hot forehead. Roth's black eyes smoldered, and his pointed ears seemed to bristle like his hair. "With all due respect, m'lord," he said, his volume teetering near respectful. "We've spoken of this before . . . seven years ago, to be precise. The coastal attacks were horrific, yes, but we addressed them sufficiently. My Prydian cousin seeks only to rub my face in failures long past. When will you let it go, Ealden?"

King Ealden leaned forward in his seat but did not stand. "I take no pleasure in anyone's humiliation or grief, especially not yours," Ealden said. "But I will speak when I deem necessary. The

Gray Hour attacks off in Andurin, Kingsmarsh, Arcan Hold, the Wetlands, and Brightcastle were of a particularly worrisome and suspicious nature. Untold lives were lost. We have reacted, and yet we've come no closer to solving the riddle."

"You won't ever let me live down my decision in Brightcastle, will you?" Roth demanded. "Well, I stand by it, even now. It was not, nor is it now an ideal location for a standing army."

"But to leave it without so much as a garrison?" Ealden replied.

"Would you rather that Llanfair's defenses were made weak?" Roth's eyes bulged to the point that Loch feared they might pop. "The greatest city of our people is perilously close to the shore. I rue the loss of life in Brightcastle as much as anyone—"

"Perhaps not as much as the widows and orphans left behind," Ealden said quietly.

The words seemed to strike Roth like a blow from a hammer. He fell back in his chair and was silent. Lochlan felt chills, and his heart beat rapidly. He became deathly afraid that another episode was coming on, but thinking about it only seemed to make things worse. Loch decided on a different course. "King Ealden, King Roth, it seems to me that the blame for these attacks has been unfairly weighing on both of you."

Roth blinked, but his eyes remained intense. Ealden steepled his fingers and waited. Loch spoke on. "If my understanding of history is correct, then you both made tactical decisions in a time of great uncertainty. The Gray Hour attacks struck the Wetlands first, then Arcan Hold in Fen, Andurin and Kingsmarsh in Ellador . . . two years between each. There was no way to predict the next attack and certainly no geographical pattern aside from the fact that they are all coastal villages or cities. The attack might very well have been at the Horn of Ipswich or Avon Barony . . . or Llanfair. Nonetheless, the blame falls on the murderous hands of those who committed the attacks, not yours."

"Well said," Izjaak exclaimed. "You might make a decent High King yet!"

King Roth crossed his arms, but his furious expression had diminished to something akin to mild annoyance. King Ealden said, "You speak peace over us, King Lochlan, and for that you have my thanks. But we are still no closer to unravelling the mystery. Yes, it has been nigh on eight years since the last attack, but we have no assurances. Llanfair might be next . . . perhaps tomorrow, First One forbid. And we still have no idea who is responsible."

"I thought it was pirates," Loch said. "Black ships with black sails . . ."

"So it may have been," King Ealden replied. "But of the survivors who were not terror-stricken beyond the border of sanity, they tell tales of dreadful creatures, wicked, dark things . . . abominations."

"The Gray Hour stories," Loch muttered.

"Seem to have come to life," Ealden said. "Some claim that villagers were not just killed but taken."

Lochlan shuddered. "Perhaps," Warden Gander Brow began, "perhaps, we should do more to fortify our coastal cities."

All eyes turned to Lochlan. His thoughts raced. "Well," he said, "well, that certainly seems prudent. Let me think. At the moment, the Anglish military demands thirty percent of each nation's fighting force. Suppose we reduce that quota to twenty percent."

"Not enough," Roth interjected. "We have many coastal villages to cover."

Loch scratched his chin. "Fifteen?"

Teura, Regent of Keening on the Naïthe, broke her silence. "To adequately fortify the coastline, vast as it is, would require each nation to retain no less than ninety percent of our own troops."

Sebastian leaned in close to Lochlan. "Reducing the quota to ten percent would leave Anglinore with the smallest ready force since before Brysroth."

"Still," Loch said, squinting as he calculated, "that would leave some forty thousand troops, a formidable number and well trained. And, Sebastian, to be honest, the Anglish Military is 'Anglish' in name only. It is really the Myridian Military, meant for the defense of threats to the whole realm."

"Of course," the Shepherd replied. "Anglinore is but a capital, a figurehead for all."

Loch nodded thoughtfully. "Here then is what we will do," he said aloud. "Anglinore reduces its quota demand to ten percent. Each realm will have an additional twenty percent of its troops to better defend its coasts and borders. In addition, Anglinore's navy will redouble its patrolling voyages to be visibly present especially at dusk, and we will arm our merchant vessels. Lord Drüst, might you have Skyflights vary their course to include more coastal routes from time to time?"

The Skylord looked to his nephew. Jornth nodded back. "Yes," Drüst said. "We will see to it."

"And Prince Navrill, can we count on the Marinaens to give us early warning of approaching fleets?"

The folds of flesh flared violet on Navrill's neck and he said, "By fin and fathom, my people shall not let Myriad down again. How it is that these attacks circumvented our scouting nets, I cannot say. But hence forth, this mysterious enemy will have to kill us all to keep us from our duty."

Loch frowned. "In your words, I hear again undue blame," Loch said. "But Prince Navrill and Princess Arcadia, no one in this room expects you to simultaneously guard every inch of Myriad's coastline, especially at dusk when—if I understand correctly—it is most difficult to recognize ships on the surface from below. The Gray Hour Pirates, whoever they may be, have eluded us all. With our troops on the ground, the Windborne in the air, and the Marinaens in the Dark Sea, I am confident we are well protected."

The room whirled with murmurs, but satisfied smiles ruled the expressions there. At last, Lochlan declared, "This Council is adjourned. Please, my lords, depart and make merry as you see fit."

Loch knelt alone in Clarrisant Hall. He'd chosen a spot on the throne steps from which he could see some of the arched stained glass windows . . . if he opened the corner of his right eye, that is. Echoes of the ceremony seemed to linger, but Loch did his level best to focus on his image of the First One. He pictured someone sage and very old, but not frail. Definitely not frail. Maybe in appearance like Mosteryn the Old: silken white hair cascading from his scalp like drifts of snow, bristling white brow, matching mustache and beard; eyes ice blue and frosty clear, streaked through with storm gray. There would be the creases of age too, but not like Mosteryn. More akin to Skylord Drüst, upon whom wrinkles were more like threads though granite. Loch could imagine this great being upon a throne of cloud looking down and listening intently.

Loch asked for guidance, for clear direction, even for permission. But for Loch, prayer was hard. He believed in the First One truly. To Loch, it was the height of absurdity to suppose that everything that is, just happened on its own . . . with no rational guidance. Consciousness, love, time itself—all of it spoke of a superior. But not being able to see Him, to see Him really, made things complicated. He could see his mother, embrace her and be embraced back. Not so with the First One. He could go to Shepherd Sebastian, sit in his presence, and ask all the questions he could manage. And Sebastian would answer . . . aloud. *Why do you give us senses?* Loch asked in prayer. *Why give us senses by which we experience everything in this world, and yet we cannot discern you with any of those same senses?* Silence was his only answer.

The Silence. Sebastian had explained that there was a time in Myridian history that the First One spoke openly to His people. The book of Canticles was full of their dialogues. That was another proof of the First One to Loch. His recorded speech was so different, so out of the ordinary, and so compelling. And the wisdom within Canticles could not be questioned, even by those who shunned the First One altogether.

Loch shifted his posture and placed his head flat on the top step. How he wished the First One would speak to him like he had with others thousands of years ago. But something had happened—no one seemed to know just what it was—and the First One seemed to vanish from recorded history. Loch continued to pray or, at least, he continued to try. Thoughts bounced around in his mind, and distracting thoughts intervened and interrupted. Finally, Loch gave up. He'd asked what he'd come to ask.

He left Clarissant Hall, as night cast the outside world in shadows.

In the long hallway that led to the tower stair, Loch heard voices behind him. Actually, he heard giggles.

"High King Lochlan!" came a fluttery voice from behind.

Loch turned and saw a womanly form. Two women he realized, as a previously hidden maid appeared at the first one's side. As they drew closer, Loch cringed inwardly. Not again.

"Wait here," the taller woman commanded the shorter.

"It was my idea," the other returned. "I should go first."

"You have no chance. No royal blood."

"Not much less than you. What, are you 1/16th Elladorian on your mother's brother's cousin's granduncle's side?"

The tall one glared. "I'm going on," she said with such a sudden ferocity that the other woman drifted away toward the passage wall.

Lochlan knew she was following, but he strode ahead a few more paces before turning. "Good evening, Teresia," Loch said.

"My lord," she purred with a deep curtsey. A little too deep, Loch thought, given the neckline of the scarlet gown she wore. She was a fetching young maiden, a year older than Lochlan. Dark brown hair flattered her appearance no matter how she wore it, but especially when she wore it down as she did now. Locks spilled down the ivory flesh of her neck almost to her shoulders. Her full lips were colored like ripening grapes, and her eyes were golden brown like a parchment map that any man might be pleased to explore. She fluttered long lashes and looked up shyly. "My lord, you walk these dreary halls often enough. Why do you not shirk their chains and join the Festival outside?"

Loch's smile was lukewarm at best. In spite of her ravenous beauty, there had always been something about Teresia that made his skin crawl. "Ah, Teresia, you are kind to remind me that even a king must make merry from time to time."

"So it is, my lord," she said.

"But tonight it is not my lot," he said. "With the ceremony and the council and such, I'm sure you can understand—"

"I understand," she said. "I understand that you are far too tense for kingly decisions. Might I make one easier for you?" She drew near to Loch and placed her palm flat on his chest. "There, see? The Festival carries on in every corner of the city, my lord. Crowds are teeming, but we don't have to be among them. There are are more secluded places that I could take you."

The warmth of her hand did feel good. And her smell, something like apple blossoms and berries, was somewhat dizzying. "Teresia, I . . . I am flattered. But really, I have so much to . . ."

She moved her hand to Loch's shoulder and, with her other hand slid the arm of her gown a few inches down her arm. "I've always found you fascinating, Lochlan," she said. "Do you find me . . . fascinating?"

"Teresia, what are you . . ." Lochlan swiftly pulled the silky material back to its proper place. He took her by the shoulders and moved her bodily a few feet away from him. "Listen to me, Teresia. I don't know what's gotten into you that you should approach me in this way. But know this: that kind of promiscuous behavior is exactly the way to drive me and any decent man away from you. Keep yourself clothed; better yet, wear something that covers you up more thoroughly."

Teresia backed up another step, her expression equal parts anger and disgust. "How dare you!" she hissed. "I'll have you know that men will line up just to stand in my presence. You'll be sorry you treated me like this. I'll call the Anglish Guard, tell them you tried to have your way with me."

"No, you won't," Loch said, refusing to match the rancor of her tone. "The Anglish Guard is already here, and they have no doubt heard and seen all that has transpired. Did you not notice that I let you follow me close to one of the stair gates?"

Loch gestured a few paces up the hall. A tall soldier stood at the corner of a doorway. He lifted a fist to his lips and cleared his throat with sufficient volume to make his point.

"You sneaky—"

Loch cut her off. "Listen, Teresia. Nothing more need come of this. You made me uncomfortable; that is all. You did no lasting harm . . . to me, at least. But if I am given any special wisdom from the First One or from my position as High King, I say to you this: guard your womanly charms. You are beautiful, and within you, in a frightened corner of your heart, lives someone more beautiful still. But if you give yourself away as you tried to do with me, you will wither her away . . . a little at a time until she is dead. I fear then, some desperate, despicable man will hurt you. And, Teresia, I would never want to see that happen."

He released her shoulders and left her there, mouth wide open. His last sight of her, she was adjusting her neckline.

Lochlan didn't see the shadowy form that slithered from the dark passage just after the last guard post.

L och closed the door to Sebastian's tower chamber and stood with his back against the wood.

"Is everything alright?" Sebastian asked. "You look as though you are being chased."

"Not exactly," Loch said. "But I've made up my mind . . . I think."

"You think?"

Loch's head swayed a bit. "The Feast, the Ceremony, the Council—they kind of made up my mind for me. I believe you are right. I need a break from the throne."

Sebastian nodded. "There must be parameters. You do have responsibilities here."

"I will abide by any and all that you name."

"But not just with regard to your role as king," Sebastian cautioned. "There must be limits to what you may do . . . out there as well."

"Name them!" Loch implored.

"I will do better than that," said the Shepherd, reaching for a blank sheet of parchment. "I will put them in writing." He dropped to his desk, whisked a quill from a little jar of ink and began to scrape away on the page. "So, where will you go first?"

"Keening," Loch replied. "All this time, I have lived so close, and yet, I have never seen their endless fields."

"Brilliant choice," Sebastian said. "Not too far away. Make your plan. It will take me some time to complete your parameters and deliver them to you. There are many schedules to consult . . . and Maren."

"Take as long as you need," Loch said. "It is for me a torchlight at the end of a gloomy passage—even if it takes a year to grasp that light. Thank you, Sebastian." He turned and opened the chamber door only to find Cardiff standing there with his fist upraised as if he were about to knock. "Cousin . . . Cardiff, what are you doing here?"

"I came to see the High Shepherd," Cardiff replied. "Is your meeting quite finished?"

Sebastian stood. "It is," he said. "Quite. Baron Strengle, how long have you been standing at my door?"

"Not long," he said. "I was just about to knock. Come now, Shepherd, I am no spy. Besides, what clandestine discussions could the noble High King and his Shepherd be having?"

"Just so," Sebastian said. "Come in and state your business, Baron."

Loch took his leave and closed the chamber door. As he descended the spiral stair, he wondered about the decision he'd just made. And he wondered just how much his ambitious cousin had overheard.

CHAPTER 14

NIGHTMARE'S BLOOM

There are potent herbs to be found in Myriad for remedies and salves. Rulemarr's bitter taste belies its virtues—stopping bloody leaks from the inside, no less. Flouris, when boiled, will steam away lethargy. My favorite is merriander, for with it, I can cure everything from sneezes to snakebites. But I have yet to find a salve to mend a rended heart.

—Treatments of the Seven Races,
compiled by Mosteryn the Old

3 FEFTIN 2238

The mast of The Mynx began to creak with the shift in the wind. Alastair leaned over the rail amidships and heaved his breakfast into the Dark Sea.

A thick hand landed on his shoulder. "I seems t'remember a voyage like this one, a'ways back." Captain Dagspaddle bellowed out in his gravelly voice, followed by his usual cough-laugh. "I thought you'd have sea legs by now, though."

"Very funny, Captain," Alastair muttered, snorting and catching sea spray in the face for his troubles. "Bah, gah! Hate when that happens!"

"Happens when ye stand at the rail in a fearsome storm." Dagspaddle laughed a bit more. "So what be eatin' ye now, General?"

"I've done it again," Alastair growled. "I've gone an hurt Abbagael. That's why I'm sick right now. I cannot bear to have her angry with me. It feels . . . ah, it feels like I swallowed a dozen daggers and they're all trying to get out."

"Right colorful, that is." Dagspaddle looked up sharply at the turbulent sea. "Ah, I'd better go. Join me at the wheel!"

The man was built like a pear and had short legs that seemed permanently bent at the knees, but somehow, he managed to speed across the deck of his ship. He was at the forecastle and grabbing the wheel before Alastair had slip-slid halfway there. When Alastair finally climbed up to the forecastle, Capt. Dagspaddle pointed at some indefinite point beneath his bulbous stomach and said, "Sea legs."

"How do you know?" Alastair grumbled. "You can't even see them—"

The Mynx slammed into the crest of a massive wave and then slewed down into its trough. Alastair slid on the forecastle deck and straddled one of the railing posts. Alastair groaned. "THAT hurt!"

"I meant t'say hold on, but I was finkin' bout which side a' the wave t'sail down. Guess I picked the wrong one."

Alastair scrabbled to his feet. "How long's this storm going to last?"

Dagspaddle rubbed his palm on his stubbly chin, making an audible scraaaatch! Then, he said, "Squall like this? I fegger it's been buildin' all afternoon. We'll be drivin' through the whole line, like as not. Could be most 'a the night."

"Great," Alastair muttered, bracing himself in the corner of the rail.

"So what'd ye do this time?" the captain asked, his eyes locked on to the volatile seas ahead.

"Well, it's not so much what I did," Alastair said. "It's what I didn't do."

"Ah, let me guess . . . it's complicated."

Alastair laughed. "Yes, you could say that. See, we were sleeping in our chamber, at least she was, you know, in Anglinore Castle. But I couldn't get my mind to stop racing. I couldn't sleep. So I got up in the middle of the night and left our room."

"Right. So?"

"So, while I was gone, she had a nightmare and woke up. She's angry I wasn't there."

Dagspaddle's eyes, tiny black beads in narrow slits, slid over to Alastair for a moment. "That's it, eh?"

"No, there's more," he said, looking off the starboard rail. "I went to a tavern down in the city."

"Well, that's no good," Dagspaddle replied. "What kind'a lout goes about drinkin' while his wife's all by 'erself a'sleepin'."

"There were guards around," Alastair argued. "I mean it was the middle of Anglinore Castle."

"Did ye tell her ye was leavin?"

"No."

"See there."

"It's worse than that," Alastair said.

Dagspaddle turned from the seas for a moment. "If you went an' met some lady a' the night, I'll flog ye meself!"

"I did no such thing!" Alastair growled back. "I'd sooner kiss a spirax than another woman!"

"Blast it, lad," Dagspaddle grumbled, spinning the wheel. The Mynx rolled smoothly down the side of huge, lumbering swell. "This isn't as easy as it looks, what did ye' do?"

"Witchdrale," Alastair confessed. "I didn't drink it, but I set out to. The Black owned me once, but I've been mostly free of it for years . . . since the war. Still, I walked out on my wife in the middle of the night . . . with the intent."

"Witch . . . drale . . ." the captain spoke the words as if their texture was vile enough to make him ill. "I see now. I've been bitten by that snake me'self. But see 'ere, General, this doesn't change things. You tell 'er. Tell 'er everything. And you listen too, now. A woman's anger is rarely a simple thing. It's why I married me' ship! Heh, heh."

"Thank you, captain," Alastair said. He clambered back down the ladder and thought, Every man should have a Captain Dagspaddle about.

"Where's Tel?" Alastair asked, finding Abbagael alone in their cabin below decks.

She looked up from the parchments she'd been reading at a little desk built into the port side of the room. "Icy didn't like the waves. He's been making an awful racket down in the hull. Tel went to comfort her."

Alastair perched himself on pile of keenic seed sacks. "What are you reading?"

"Canticles," she said.

"Something about forgiveness perhaps?" Alastair asked, giving his best sad puppy look.

"Actually," she said, glaring up from the parchment. "It's about the First One's judgment of the unrepentant. 'And the fire shall devour those arrogant—'"

"Uh, no need to quote that verse." Alastair held up his hands. "I am very familiar with it already."

Abbagael smacked her hands flat on the desk. "Where were you, Alastair?" she demanded. "Where did you go in the middle of the night . . . when . . . when I needed you?"

Alastair remembered a curved dagger blade in the back that had felt better than Abbagael's words. "I will tell you plainly. I was disturbed . . . my mind was in terrible unrest. The thirst came back."

"Witchdrale!" The fire in Abbagael's eyes spoke only a whisper of rage. But there was hurt, grief, and bitter disappointment.

Alastair wished for several dagger blades now. "Yes, I left our chamber, left you alone—to seek out the black bottle once again. But please hear me, my wife, I did not drink of it. By the grace of the First One, I recognized my madness. I sat with Brayden Arum in a tavern and never even inquired if he had any Witchdrale. But please, believe me, I would never have left you if I didn't think you were completely safe."

"I wasn't completely safe!" She stood suddenly and held out her hands as if they were suddenly foreign to her and she didn't know what to do with them. "He was there again!"

"Cythraul?"

"I know you don't believe me, but I saw him!" She pointed high on the cabin wall. "He was there . . . in the window, standing on the ledge, just waiting for his chance."

Alastair tried to keep his tone even. "But he . . . he is dead."

"He died once before!" Abbagael shot back. "Uncle Jak hit him with his warhammer and knocked him off the castle wall. He fell a hundred feet, Alastair! But somehow he came back to life."

Alastair went to her and took her hands into his. "I don't know what Cythraul is, what manner of being, but some . . . some, like the Windborne, can endure unfathomable trauma and yet live." Alastair waited for her eyes to meet his, and then he said, "He may have survived a fall that would kill most anyone other being, but Abbagael . . . I drove my sword through his back and straight into his heart. Cythraul is dead. He must be."

"How do you even know where his heart is?" she demanded, tears spilling. "He probably doesn't have a heart at all!"

Alastair could feel her terror, a writhing, insistent fear clawing away at her. "Forgive me, Abbagael," he said quietly. "But there are things . . . there are signs, gah, how do I say this? I thrust my blade into Cythraul . . . to kill him. I turned the blade, and there . . . there are sounds the body makes. I am certain I found his heart and . . . destroyed it." He paused a moment and stared at the floor. "Alas that I am a learned student of death, but I am. And I know that I killed him."

Abbagael sobbed in earnest now, and he gathered her in. "It was a dream," he said, "a nightmare . . . nothing more."

Her sobs shut off like a spigot. She drew away from him and turned her back. When she spoke, her voice was a tremulous whisper. "Don't you think I know that it was a dream?"

Alastair blinked. "But . . . but you said—"

"No one could have been on that ledge in Anglinore, not this time," she said. "Maren had keen-eyed archers posted on every balcony."

Alastair was flummoxed. "I . . . I don't understand. If you know he wasn't really there—"

She spun and came to him. Her eyes pleaded. "Don't you see, my husband? Have you not noticed my tossing and turning nearly every night we were in Anglinore? And even back in our home, have you not found me reading late into the night? Do you not see the dark circles beneath my eyes?"

Alastair looked again and at last he saw. Her tear-streaked face displayed more signs than the recent tears. The pale flesh beneath her emerald eyes was discolored, almost bruised. There were lines, creases but not from age. These were worn into her flesh through worry and fear . . . and a lack of sleep. He understood. A woman's anger is rarely a simple thing.

"I am so . . . so sorry, my sweet Abbagael. How long?"

"Six months," she whispered. "Not continuously, but enough that every time I put my head to the pillow . . . I am afraid." She clutched his hands, and her voice gained traction. "I do not understand . . . why, after all these years? But no matter where I am, the dreams will not stop. Cythraul is alive. I don't know how I know, but I do. He's out there waiting, biding his time, and he's going to come for me."

"Listen to me," Alastair said, his tone firm. "If he is alive, if he does come, he will meet my blade again. And this time, I will not stop until there is nothing left."

"What is wrong?" Telwyn asked from the cabin door.

"Ah, son, I am glad you've come back." Alastair gestured for him to enter. "Come, your mother needs rest. Sit by her bedside and hold her hands."

"I will," Tel replied.

Abbagael melted into the narrow bed and lay on her side. Telwyn took her hands. "Sleep now," he said. "And fear nothing."

6 FEFTIN 2238

Alastair, Abbagael, and Telwyn hadn't seen their home in Llanfair in weeks. But it had been a good time to miss. When they'd left their hillside cottage, the flowers had still been far from blooming. But now, under a midday sky of rich azure and wispy white clouds, their deep green dell exploded with color. Broad swatches of rich scarlet, deep purple, night-sky blue, luminous white, and bright yellow washed down the hill, up the other side, and disappeared over the ridge toward the forest. These were not symmetrical rows of flowers carefully planted by hand, but rather centuries old splashes of growth that had crawled and spread until the landscape burst with irises, tulips, ganders, forsinths, crocuses, and lilies. After the war, Alastair had chosen this spot for Abbagael. And, over the years, they had built their home by hand. Now they stood on the edge of their property, hand in hand, and simply stared.

Icetooth, Telwyn's tamed snow drake, escaped the growing warmth of the day by swooping down into the dell and up into the woods where his private cave was hidden. At last, Alastair led his family inside. They found the cottage much as they'd left it, except for a young fox who had gotten into a grain canister in the kitchen pantry. At Alastair's heavy footsteps, the fox made an orange streak, escaping by the same window it had apparently entered.

"I thought I'd sealed those canisters well enough," Alastair grumbled as he strode to the window.

"Let him be, husband," Abbagael said. "We want for nothing."

Alastair nodded. He was happy to hear the cheer in his wife's voice. She'd rested well for several days running, and the difference in her demeanor was marked. And she was right. They wanted for nothing. King Ealden, ruler of the Prydian Wayfolk who dwelt in Amara, had deeded them the property after the Gorrack War. They owned everything they could see from the window and more besides. And for his service in the Anglish Guard during the war—his efforts perhaps changing the very outcome of war—Queen Maren had given Alastair enough kingsgold for generations to live comfortably. Alastair turned round and took Abbagael into his arms. "Thank the First One for you," he said, and then he kissed her.

Telwyn cleared his throat. "I think I'll go take a walk," he said. "Maybe check on Icy."

Alastair and Abbagael laughed. "Since you're going out, lad," Alastair said, "would you unplug the well and check the water. Oh, and would you visit Uncle Jak and see when he wants us to come get the horses?"

"Be glad to," Telwyn replied. "But that'll take a while. I probably won't be back for several hours."

Alastair wondered about the emphasis on Tel's last two words. He watched the tall young man leave the cottage. "I wonder about that lad sometimes. Knows more than he should for his age."

"That's your age talking, my love," Abbagael said. "He is twenty-five now, you know. Just five years from full manhood."

"I know, I know," Alastair said, shaking his head. "Still. He shouldn't be able to guess my plots and plans before I hatch them."

"What ever do you mean, husband?"

"Well," he said. "There is one room in our home we haven't checked on."

A wondrous day of returning to Llanfair had finally come to an end. Uncle Jak and Telwyn had brought the horses back themselves. True to his word, Telwyn had taken a good five hours to return. They'd enjoyed a fabulous meal of baked stag flank, red potatoes, and plum brownies for dessert—Uncle Jak's favorite.

They'd spent the evening before a crackling fire, sipping fairy-water and recalling fond memories of years gone by. With a deep smile etched on his face, Jak had fallen asleep on the couch. The rest had retired soon after. All was right with the world.

Except for all was not right with the world.

Abbagael seemed to be sleeping soundly. But Alastair wasn't faring quite so well. Was it possible? He wondered, his eyes wide open in the darkness. Could Cythraul still be alive? It didn't make sense. Certainly Shepherds had some amazing powers, but according to Sebastian, Cythraul was no Shepherd. Alastair poured over all the ancient folklore he'd ever heard or read, trying to remember a being who could be killed and yet come back. Banshees were seemingly one such thing, but really, according to the legends, they were just hard to kill. Once slain, they stayed slain.

Liches and Shades were supposed to be risen dead, brought back by certain leeching parasites, but they were mindless ghouls. Cythraul was rotten and malevolent to the core, but he was not some decomposing creature with little or no will.

The crickets and peeper frogs' symphony went on for hours more, Alastair was still no closer to an answer. He'd reached the end of his wisdom and could think of nothing that might do what Cythraul did. Perhaps, she's just wrong, Alastair thought. She's endured so many trials, so many terrors. It's bound to influence her dreams. Maybe that's all it was. And yet . . .

I trust her. I love her. I have sworn to protect her. Alastair ran a hand over his face. I have to make sure.

That's when it came to him. Ealden. If there was anyone in Myriad who possessed more knowledge of all sorts of ancient lore than King Ealden, Alastair had no idea who it might be. Tomorrow, then, he thought. I will visit Jurisduro Hall and—

The scream that erupted from Abbagael was so visceral, so intense, and raw that Alastair's flesh went instantly cold, and he bounced as he turned to her.

"Get away, get away, GET AWAY!" she shrieked, staring and pointing at the closet.

For just a moment, Alastair thought there was something there. A glimmer of white, an undulating dark cloak—Alastair dove for his blade, tore it from the sheath and turned . . . to find only clothing stacked and hung in the closet, just like always. But Abbagael continued to cry and yell—now something unintelligible, and she slammed back into the headboard, trying to get away from whatever she saw.

Alastair dropped his sword and went to his wife. At first she screamed louder and fought him. Then she coughed and wept, emitting such a pitiful whimpering moan that Alastair felt his heart breaking as he heard her. "It . . . it . . . was . . . him," she said, her voice wracked and hoarse. "He was here . . . in our home."

She collapsed into him just as Telwyn tore into the room, followed by Uncle Jak.

"What in the Stars!" Uncle Jak exclaimed. "Is my Abbey okay?"

"The dreams?" Telwyn asked.

Alastair nodded to them both. And as his wife's tears trickled down his neck, something within Alastair hardened in a way he hadn't known since the forgotten days in Morlan's employ. Yes, Alastair thought. I will speak to Ealden and learn what I can. But then, I will go hunting. And, this time, I will leave nothing to chance.

7 FEFTIN 2238

After a cross country ride that devoured most of the day, Alastair drove his horse into Llanfair City, the capital of Amara Nation, the home of both branches of the Wayfolk. Jurisduro Hall stood on the southern edge of the city. Alastair rode up to the main gate, showed the insignia of the Anglish Guard to the gatekeepers, and then, with their salute, entered the grounds. He slowed the horse to a trot, dropped lightly to the ground, and tied her off near a trough so she could get water. Then he marched up to the hall's ornately carved, arched entrance. Two guards, each nearly a head taller than Alastair barred his way.

Alastair sighed and pointed to the Anglish Guard insignia once more. The guards didn't so much as flinch. "I am General Alastair Coldhollow, General of the Anglish Guard and, for my part, friend to King Ealden. Please step aside." The guards remained still. Then Alastair tilted his head back and sighed once more. Forward guards were not permitted free speech. Only 'yes' or 'no.' *How many times do I forget this?!*

"I have come to see King Ealden," Alastair said. "Is he here?"

"Yes," said the guard on the left.

"Is he in council?" Alastair asked.

"No," the right-hand guard replied.

"I think I know where to find him," Alastair said. "May I enter?"

"Yes," they answered. Instantly they moved out of Alastair's way. He glared at the guards as he passed.

Jurisduro Hall was alive with light and greenery, but aside of that, it was somewhat like a museum. Plaques and tapestries adorned the walls, etchings and other artwork too, and most were inscribed with quotes from the First One's Books of Lore. Alastair went straight for the second set of stairs, tromped up quickly, and strode down the long hall. The passage seemed to end, but Alastair knew that it was actually somewhat of an illusion. The corridor elbowed sharply and led to an alcove with a narrow door. As he suspected he might, Alastair found King Ealden there, deeply consumed in reading, thinking, and probably prayer.

"Forgive my intrusion, King Ealden," Alastair said, "but I wonder if you might have a few moments to spare an old friend?"

"General Coldhollow!" Ealden exclaimed, a wide smile spreading. He dropped a ribbon of red silk into the crease of the book he'd been reading and then wheeled around the desk to embrace Alastair. "I must say I didn't expect to see you again so soon," the king said as he drew away. "To what do I owe the pleasure of your visit?"

"I am afraid it is not for pleasure," Alastair replied.

"Is something wrong?"

"With Abbagael, yes. I need your vast knowledge of lore."

King Ealden skirted back around his desk and sat down. He gestured, and Alastair took the seat across from his desk. "I will do everything that I can to help. Is it medical knowledge you seek?"

"No," Alastair said, "aside of a little sleep deprived, she is well. But she's been having terrible nightmares. I know this may sound strange, but do you know of any kind of being, creature or man, that is nearly invulnerable to things that might kill you or me? Falls from great heights, crushing blows, or stab wounds?"

King Ealden sat back in his chair. His high brows arched, and he combed his oaken-brown hair back over his pointed ears. "Windborne," he said. "They can fly right into a mountainside and emerge none the worse for wear."

"No, I thought of that," Alastair said. "No, I'm thinking about a being who would appear to be dead but would keep coming back." King Ealden did not answer immediately, but Alastair thought something had changed in the king's expression. It was subtle, perhaps just a hint of discomfort.

"You speak of Morlan's lieutenant," Ealden said at last. "Cythraul."

"Yes."

"But he is dead. You killed him."

"I think I did."

King Ealden leaned forward on his desk. "You have seen him, then?"

"I have not," Alastair replied. "But Abbagael believes he is still alive. Cythraul haunts her dreams. I tell you, she is tormented."

King Ealden frowned. "I . . . I am sorry. Perhaps it is some Sabrynite ploy. Have you been praying?"

"Incessantly. Almost with every breath. But there seems no respite for her. She's convinced Cythraul did not die when I ran him through, and to be honest, I'm inclined to believe her. After all, he did fall from Anglinore Castle only to get up and kill again. When I found him in Vulmarrow, he seemed in perfect health . . . that is, until I stabbed him. What if he is still out there? He'd no doubt be stirring up all kinds of mischief."

"No doubt," Ealden said. "What . . . what do you propose to do?"

"I'm going to hunt him down, or at least make certain he is dead. But if he is still living, I will see to it that there's not enough left of him to fill a thimble." Alastair stood. "I was hoping you might know something, some ancient legend, some lore that might explain what's going on."

"Alastair, I owe you my life and much more," the king said, standing and holding out his hand. "I will explore my resources, all my books, and see if I can find anything that may be of use. When will you commence your hunt?"

Alastair shook his hand. "As soon as possible. We'll need some time to settle back in, and I haven't told Abbagael yet."

"If I discover something, I will send a Windborne courier to your door."

"Thank you," Alastair said. He was quiet a moment. "There is one more thing."

"Name it."

"While I am gone, would you send a few Prydian Scouts to patrol my property. I don't know if Cythraul really is alive, but if he is, he already tried to kill my Abbagael once."

"I will do better than a few," King Ealden said, his tone grim but confident. "Nothing short of a Gorrack legion will have a ghost of a chance of breaking the perimeter my soldiers will set."

CHAPTER 15

SHATTERED HOPES

There is wisdom in knowing when to run.

—A Spriggan Proverb

22 SOLMONATH 2238

After crawling through a freezing cold, twisting network of tunnels, following their father's voice, Tango and Meli emerged in a space that was not only beyond their expectations, but quite beyond their collective imagination as well.

"Wow," Tango said. "Uhm . . . wow!"

Meli emitted a half squeal, half squeak that might have meant something to a squirrel.

Oil lamps burned all the way around a vast chamber, casting warm almondy light over couches, beds, tables, shelves, bookcases, and all manner of other fine furniture. Each piece looked perfectly organic as if it had grown up from the roots of the earth into divinely crafted comfort. In an open pantry stood innumerable jars. They were dusty but dark and full. There were crates too, and barrels. A cobbled stone fireplace stood at either end and small paintings adorned each mantle. Next to each fireplace, rested barrels of kindling and cords of firewood.

"It's . . . it's a Delshroom!" Tango gasped. "How'd it get in this fair nasty thicket? Who . . . who did all this?"

Meli squeaked again.

"Let's just say . . . it was a family effort." Tanner winked.

"You knew the Red Queen was comin' back, didn't ya?" Tango asked.

"Shrewd mind," his father said. "Like yer mum. She could see through walls. 'S why I never tried to hide anythin' from her."

"Da, you knew?" Meli clambered the rest of the way out of the tunnel.

"Grandsprig Fennel told me what he saw. I learned early on never to doubt his word, not on anythin'. We know Quevara went in there. We know what she did. But when she did'na come out right away, well . . . Fennel got to wonderin' what went on. He feared the old wyrm had taken her in and gone into hibernation or some such. He started workin' on this place right off, transplanted a grand shroom, he did. Each of us carried on after that. Fennel and yer mum did the carved wood. Is'na beautiful?"

Meli scooted over to one of the beds, climbed up the recessed ladder, and flounced on her back. "Pfff, dusty! But comfy."

"Glad you like it, Meli," he said. "I truly am. Starmaker knows I had no desire t' leave the Gap, and . . ." His dark eyes misted over and he scraped an arm across his brow. "None . . . a . . . this . . . should'a ever happened t'littlins like you. I'm so sorry."

Tango and Meli flew to their father, nearly crushing him between them. "It's not yer fault, da," Tango said.

"I like it here!" Meli said.

Tanner patted them both on the head and then drew them apart. "Ah, my littlins," he said. "Do ya have any idea how much I love ya?"

Meli thought a moment. "More than a wedge of cheese?"

"Bwah, ha!" Tanner fell backward on the floor and laughed until his stomach cramped. "Of course . . . hoo, ha . . . of course more than a wedge of cheese!"

"Unless it's sharp Ryefield, right da?"

"Ooh, right you are lad, right you are." He sat up suddenly. "Come to think of it." The elder Spriggan bounced off the ground and disappeared into an alcove behind the pantry. He came back in a hurry with wheel of cheese the size of a pumpkin.

"Da," said Tango. "Is that . . ."

"Aye, it is! Come an' join me at the table." The three Spriggans bounded to the table adjacent to the closest fireplace. Tanner took his hatchet and carved through the wax until a large wedge came free. "Ahhhh, smell that!"

He held the wedge out. "Smells like Allhaven," Meli said.

Moments later, still chewing contentedly, the Spriggan family sat back in their chairs and relaxed at last.

Meli rubbed her arms absently.

"Ah, bit of a chill, now that night's a fallin'," said Tanner.

"I'll start a fire," Tango said.

"Nay lad, I'll do it. You two just hop in bed and rest. I daresay yer feet have'na had a beatin' like that since the prowlcats got loose last summer."

"Please don't bring that up," Tango said, clambering up into one of the beds recessed into the far wall.

"Yeah," Meli said. "How were we suppose t' know not to pull their tails?"

Tanner laughed as he gathered up some timber to burn. He crisscrossed the wood on the wrought-iron grate with the kindling on the bottom. *Doesn't much matter,* he thought. *The wood's all bone dry.* He set about scraping his hatchet across a palm-sized piece of flint. Sparks flew. A lick of fire sprang up. And soon the wood began to crackle away merrily. But as Tanner stared into the flames, he felt anything but merry.

As the fire danced, memories burst into his mind. Not his own memories, not really. These were things his father had lived through, stories he'd passed on to his son. And others, he'd heard as a twenager sitting in the local pub in Hammer's Gap. Finnel and his old friends spoke often and mostly in whispers about things that had happened when the Red Queen was in power the first time.

Tanner clutched the poker and stabbed absently at the burning wood. The Red Queen had taken hold of Cragheath Tor and enslaved the Spriggan people. Slaughtering peasants to watch their blood color the mountain streams was only the start. She'd burn whole families just to illuminate her throne room. Always children first, one limb at a time, while the parents were forced to look on. How many had died at her hand, hundreds of thousands, surely.

Tanner had seen old Kai Varidian's scarred stump wrist, but even when the others at the tavern went on and on, the ex-Cragfel warrior never spoke. But Tanner remembered his smoldering eyes . . . the rage, the grief, the utter hopelessness. This Spriggan had clearly lost much more than his hand. The Red Queen had taken everything from him and then . . . left him alive to relive it every day of his grim life.

And now, Cythraul, whoever he was, had come and unleashed the Red Queen once more.

A voice floated out of the fire. *Promise me, boy,* old Finnel had said so many long years ago. But Tanner heard it now plain as the crackling of embers. *Promise me you won't ever let it happen again. We should have fought . . . but we did'na. We rolled over and let her murder our kin. Promise me . . . you'll fight at least.*

An ember popped suddenly, and Tanner fell backward. He realized how hot he'd gotten sitting that close to the fire. Was it the fire at all? He glanced up at the littlins. Not so little anymore. Tanner thought of what he'd be willing to do to keep them safe. He thought of how close they had come to death already, just yards away from the creature when Cythraul released it.

Cythraul.

This outsider had gone meddling with things he shouldn't have. He stirred an ancient menace and unleashed it on a people who thrived on peace but had scarcely had it for long. Why had this stranger done this? And who were these new friends he was going to meet? What if he was planning an invasion? Send the Red Queen to crumble the defenses and then trample the Spriggan under foot. Tanner had no answers to any of those questions. But he knew that, at this very moment, Cythraul was barely a league away. Certainly within tracking range. Then Tanner looked above the mantle and saw his father's old bow.

He stood and stared at the old weapon. That's cured sapplewood, he thought. Know'n my Da, it's strung fair tight . . . enough to put a shaft through a stag's chest and out the other side.

Tanner's exhaustion fled. His muscles felt supple and strong. His heart rate increased such that he could hear the pulse in his head. He looked back and forth between Tango, Meli, and the bow. Then, he went to the alcove behind the pantry once more. There, among the supplies stocked there, he found an old skin quiver filled with arrows. He slung it over his shoulder, returned to the chamber, and quietly took down the bow.

He stole quietly to the beds. Meli had snuggled under the covers on the top bunk. Her golden locks curled this way and that from her peaceful brow.

"Hi, Da," she said.

"Thought you might be sleepin' already."

"Nope," she grinned.

"Me either," Tango said from the lower bunk.

Tanner captured the moment in his mind: the flickering firelight and the oil lanterns casting a rich glow on their still-young faces. They were beautiful, like beings from Allhaven. He didn't want to leave them, not even for a few hours. But he couldn't live with himself if he did nothing.

"I'm goin' out fer a bit," he said at last. "You'll be safe here—"

"Da, we just got here," Meli said.

Tango was quiet, but he stared hard at his father.

"I won't be long," Tanner said, avoiding their eyes. "A few hours. Back before sunup at latest."

"Why?" Meli asked.

"There are . . . some things I need t' check up on." He shuffled in place a moment. "Just to make sure you littlins will be all safe."

"Hokay, Da," Meli said, stretching her arms out, her traditional invitation for a hug.

Tanner leaned over and clutched his daughter to his neck and shoulder. He breathed her in: all little girl and outdoors and pine and woodsmoke. "Ah, I love ya, Meli girl," he said, letting her gently fall back to the bed. He mussed her hair and then knelt to be at his son's bedside.

"Da?" He looked up, questions bouncing in his dark eyes.

"Ah, I'm so proud of ya, boy," he said, giving his son's shoulder a squeeze. "Handled yerself so well with all this. Takin' on extra packs, runnin' hard, and not complainin a bit. Not even a twenager and yet what a man you're becomin'."

Tango grinned back, but Tanner thought it was a careful smile.

Tanner felt an itch around his eyes and turned quickly away. "I'll be back soon. Mind the fire." He took a few hurried steps and dropped down into the tunnel.

But before he could disappear, Tango grabbed the shoulder of his tunic. "Da, please tell me what yur doin'."

"I told you already, lad. I have things to check . . . to make sure you and Meli are safe."

"Da, I saw you by the fire just now. Ya had a strange look in yer eye. And now you've got Great Grandsprig's bow." Tango swallowed as if to speak any more of his thought might be crossing a hallowed line. "You . . . you're going after that man . . . that Cythraul villain."

"My son," he whispered, "this Cythraul, he's the one who woke the dragon, the Red Queen—ah, whatever she is now. I want to know what he's plannin', where he's goin'."

"But, Da," Tango whispered back, glancing over his shoulder at Meli who had closed her eyes again. "That beast . . . that horrible wolf-beast, it fair cowers at Cythraul's heel. He's a threat, and no mistake. Don't go near him."

"I won't lad. I won't."

"Promise me."

"I promise ya, Tango. I won't go near him. Besides, ya know how quietly I can go when I'm hunting."

Tango's lip quivered as he spoke. "Da, please."

"I . . . I have to."

Tango watched his father disappear into the tunnel.

Tanner Goliant had a terrible memory for names and for recipes, but for trails and paths or directions of any kind, he was nearly flawless. He picked his way back to the hill where they'd hidden from the wolves. He found the place where Cythraul's wolf had mauled the others. With all the blood spray and torn ground, it wasn't hard to locate.

And even if Tanner hadn't been tracking in the wood since he was a littlin, finding Cythraul and the big wolf's trail wouldn't have presented much of a challenge either. The flickerstick showed a clear path east, toward the mountains. He was maybe three hours ahead. Tanner smiled. "I'll make that up in no time," he whispered. He looked westward through the forest canopy. Nightfall's onset had been swift, and he knew that he'd have to extinguish the flickerstick before he got too close to Cythraul. That's where tracking would get hard.

He felt a sudden pang of guilt. He'd promised Tango that he wouldn't go near Cythraul. He planned to stay far enough away . . . just within bowshot. But still, it felt wrong. Tanner blinked the thoughts away and raced off, bounding from loose soil to piles of damp leaves, from dew-slick stones to mossy roots, without losing the trail.

What's he want near the mountains? Tanner wondered. *Nothin' there but sheer rock and the occasional boulder to the head.*

He shrugged as he ran. The Impasse Mountains were a seemingly endless range of stone that stabbed up from the ground to kiss the clouds. They were not just sheer. They were impossibly sheer, unscalable, and insurmountable. Spriggans who by race could practically stand sideways on a tree, clinging only by their powerful feet, couldn't clamber more than a few hundred feet up these peaks. Some adventurous Spriggans—mainly the maniacal, thrill-seeking Cragfel—had managed to harness some of the lesser wyrms and attempted to fly over the mountains.

Tanner shuddered. He'd been on one of the recovery expeditions. They'd found the dragon and the rider at the base of the mountain. What was left of them anyway. Apparently, the altitude was too great even for flying beasts. The Hinterlands was a vast and varied land, Tanner knew. So much of it had never been explored. But as far as its peoples had dared to travel, they'd always had to stop at the mountains.

Tanner ran on, wondering if perhaps, he'd missed a change of direction—that maybe Cythraul had turned north to the Stonehand country or maybe south to the waterfront villages where the Cambri dwelled. But every time he stopped to scrutinize the ground and foliage, he found telltale signs that Cythraul and the monstrous wolf had gone due east.

Tanner frowned and shoved the end of the flickerstick into the dampened soil. It sputtered for ten seconds and went out. Too close to the mountains now, he thought. They'll not see me first . . . if I can help it.

He picked his way through the shadowy underbrush, sometimes unable to see anything but rather feeling around for snapped branches or the odd imprint of a boot's heel in the soil. And still the trail went east. The mountains were there. Tanner could see them, a great black curtain looming up ahead with the faintest blue moon glow higher up.

Tanner froze.

He let his eyes adjust, triple checked his perception of depth, and then reached into his pouch. There were lights ahead. Torchlights.

Tanner reapplied the sapeline. His goal was to get close enough to take a shot at Cythraul, but even at eighty yards he wouldn't take a chance that the wolf could smell him.

The pine aroma burning his eyes, he crept forward. Foot by foot and inch by inch, he moved into range. He counted six torches, and now through the trees, he saw Cythraul, standing tall among some others. They were bulky and short, like Spriggans, but broader and packed with hard-looking muscle.

Stonehands, Tanner thought. But what tribe is that? He moved as close as he dared. They had no tattoos, which was very unusual for their race. Each one wore a single scarlet sash, tied tightly between the bulging shoulder muscle and the upper arm. But most peculiar of all, they were all clean shaven. All the Stonehands Tanner had ever met, including some who were good friends or fellow traders, had all fair boasted of their beards and mustaches. It was considered a tribal tragedy if one of their men had an inch of beard singed in a fire or cut off in a duel.

But these strangers with Cythraul had bare flesh, rugged and weathered, but bare nonetheless except for their wiry eyebrows. And one of them, Tanner noticed, had his scalp shaven but for a long-bound tail.

"I do not like to wait," a voice rumbled. Tanner ducked down.

Cythraul was talking to one of the Stonehands in the midst of a small campsite. "He should have been here from the beginning."

"Kegal won't long be," the tailed Stonehand said. "Exploration beckoned him. We cannot deny our nature."

"I suppose I agree with that," Cythraul retorted. "But if Kegal takes any longer, I may have to feed his present to Sköll . . . unless, of course, one of you would like to volunteer for dinner."

Heads shook around the camp.

Cythraul paced toward the glow of a campfire and paused there. Tanner had as clear a shot as he could ask for. The villain was backlit by the fire. Tanner drew a shaft from the quiver and put it to the bowstring. The arrow was pristine, ramrod straight, and had a razor-tipped tempered iron. Perfectly lethal.

He held the bow horizontally, almost letting it rest on the waist-high shrubs. And then, all at once, he drew back the bowstring and raised the bow to vertical. He lined up the shot. The arrow would plunge into the back of Cythraul's skull, probably blasting through an eye socket or his nasal cavity on the other side. He would be dead long before he hit the ground. Tanner tightened his pull, drew it back to the ridge of his jaw, and quieted his heart. The release would come in just a few more breaths.

"It's about time," Cythraul rumbled, striding behind the silhouette of a tree.

Tanner nearly pulled a muscle in his release hand, reversing the process that would have let the arrow fly. Painfully, he let the bowstring return and lowered the weapon.

"What is that to you?" asked another Stonehand, this one appearing suddenly from the east. "Life is taking time, but you tall folk seem to rush it away."

Tanner blinked. *Where did this Stonehand come from?*

"Easy for you to say, Kegal," Cythraul said. "But I have many . . . obligations."

"Shall we then be commencing our agreement?" Kegal asked. His voice sounded like he had been gargling with chips of granite.

"Yes," Cythraul replied.

"I am full trusting that our work is meeting your expectations?"

Cythraul laughed. "Better than I had hoped. Two of them could fit through that tunnel."

Kegal cracked his thick knuckles. The sound was loud, even from Tanner's position. "Ten years worth of work. It better being worth that."

"It will be to your kind." Cythraul tossed something. It glinted briefly in the firelight before Kegal caught it.

The Stonehand's eyes bulged. "Cyrium? I have never seeing so pure. Much of this, is there?"

Cythraul wandered back into plain sight. "Kegal, I've heard your people's vaults are full of breathtaking riches, but I promise you . . . you have never seen such a hoard as this."

Kegal gasped and clapped his hand.

Tanner raised the bow and drew back the bowstring.

"The wyrm is gone then? Occupied?" asked the Stonehand leader.

"Well occupied, I should think," Cythraul said. "Thoroughly content to trouble Cragheath Tor. Pity the Spriggans that."

"But it will taking my people some time to be gathering and transport our spoils. The beast might return."

Tanner breathed out and started to relax the muscles in his hand.

"No," Cythraul said. "Raudrim-Quevara has a long errand for me over the mountain, or perhaps I should say under the mountain." Cythraul strode over to the great wolf and roughly scratched its hackles. "You need not trouble over the dragon. She will be quite busy in other provinces. Keep a weather-eye out just in case she defies me. Otherwise, she will be in Amara on my business. Fact is, she may never return. I haven't decided yet."

Under the mountain? Tanner lowered the bow. *Amara?*

"Our business concludes," Kegal said, gesturing. The other Stonehands began breaking camp. Tanner took aim.

"Oh, there is one more thing." Cythraul tossed a huge sack at Kegal. The Stonehand nearly fell over.

"What is . . ." He opened the sack. "Blackwolves, hmmm, my thanks."

"That is what Sköll did to three blackwolves." The wolf growled menacingly. "Moments ago, Kegal, you said something that smacked vaguely of a threat. If you ever come that close to offending me again, I will let Sköll have his way with you."

Tanner stretched the bowstring back. The muscle in his upper back protested, but he held the pose without the slightest movement. The razor arrowhead was lined up perfectly. Tanner whispered, "This is for you, Fennel." And then, he released.

The arrow whisked through the dark woods, a silent messenger of doom streaking inexorably towards its target. Tanner had already drawn a second arrow to put through the eye of the wolf, but he'd kept watch on the first target, waiting with morbid fascination to see the villain's head explode.

Something deep in Tanner's mind failed to register what he'd just seen. Impossible, he muttered, a sharp finger of ice sliding down the middle of his back. He drew back the second arrow and fired again, this time for Cythraul's throat.

Tanner felt like he couldn't breath. It had happened again.

Then Cythraul turned. His eyes flashed with firelight and he glared into the forest, fixing his venomous stare on a single point. Tanner knew he'd been seen. He did the only thing he could think of and began to run . . . an all out sprint as fast as he could push himself away from Cythraul.

The two arrows, either one of which should have killed him, had shattered.

CHAPTER 16

BREAKING THE CHAINS

My catalogue speaks of only four Master Blades: sun, moon, stars,
and blood. It's no wonder. To make one you need a volcanic forge,
a vaskerstone core owned by the same being for a hundred years or
more, a Shepherd of metalcraft, and—most difficult of all—a vial of
Pureline blood.

—Jacob Shrewsbury, Weaponry
of Historical Significance

15 SOLMONATH 2238

"Rule number one," Lochlan read, his voice a resonant whisper in
his vast private chamber. "Your kingdom and throne are always
your first priority." Loch stared at the parchment thoughtfully.
The Shepherd had taken his good time drafting the document—
more than a month. *Probably poring over it to make sure there*
are no loopholes I might exploit, Loch thought. Still, the first rule
didn't seem too confining.

"Rule number two: Depart only when responsibilities permit and never without Shepherd Sebastian's expressed approval."
More or less a restatement of the first rule, but so exacting. Just like
a Shepherd.

"Rule number three: Go precisely where you say you are going, remain there, and go nowhere else." *Makes sense. They may need to find me.*

"Rule number four: Remain errant for no longer than the time period approved by Shepherd Sebastian. Return exactly when you are due." Lochlan paused on this one a moment. *But what if I am stuck somewhere or in the middle of some adventure? Ah, no argument. I agreed to abide by all of these.*

"Rule number five: Do nothing that would put your life or your honor in jeopardy." Lochlan read it again and then lowered the scroll. He lay it flat on his bed and went to the lone chamber window. He looked out on Anglinore City under the blanket of night. There were seven concentric rings—fortified walls of descending height—each with a heavily armed gatehouse staggered so that there was no straight-line approach to Anglinore Castle. And each ring was filled to bursting with manors, estates, keeps, and cottages, nestling them protectively away from the uncertain lands beyond. Loch didn't need to remind himself.

It was a dangerous world out there.

Aside of the major cities and larger villages, all the lands between were rough and untamed. There were trade routes and major roads, but even those succumbed occasionally to the ever creeping wild, to say nothing of cutpurses and bandits. The rule of tooth and claw was absolute, sudden, and often fatal.

All my life, he thought, *I have been surrounded by enough swords to bring down nations. To venture forth from the outer gate . . . will take me beyond their reach, beyond their aid . . . on my own.*

And that was just to speak of safety. There was also comfort to consider. *I have been pampered, my every need met, my every want granted. I've never gone hungry. I've never been cold or lived without a roof over my head.*

But as frightening as all that was to Loch, it was also exhilarating. The very idea of having to fend for himself, to earn his own keep, and survive . . . it just felt right. *After all,* he thought, *that's*

what most of the people in the world have to do. Why should their
High King be any different?

Loch went back to Sebastian's parchment. There were more
conditions to be sure, but even if there were a thousand, Loch
would agree. Sebastian had told Loch he could depart right
away—if he agreed to all of the Shepherd's cautions. There was a
world waiting, and this set of conditions was the key.

L och couldn't take his own favorite horse, Turinoth. That
would be akin to hanging a tapestry in Clarissant Hall pro-
claiming, "Lochlan has left the kingdom!"

But within the military stables, he found a magnificent Elladorian draught horse that looked strong enough to bear him
great distances and hardy enough to be put to work if need be.
Loch checked the stable manifest and found the that the mare was
unowned. *Chalaren is your name, eh?* Lochlan signed her out
under Shepherd Sebastian's care and went to her stall.

She was a rich, dark chocolate brown with a long mane of
black silk. Below the knees, all the way down to her massive
hooves, she wore white. She had also an exotic patch of white on
her muzzle that stretched up her face before splitting short of her
brow and streaking like bolts of lighting beneath her eyes, down
her neck and shoulders, before disappearing at last beneath her
flanks.

"Well, Chalaren," he said, tightening the saddle belt. "Are you
ready to bear me to freedom?" She ducked her head and stamped
in response. "Good," Loch said. "That's what I'd hoped to hear."
He mounted up, clicked his heels gently and trotted her off.

Gone were his royal garments. Instead he wore courier gear:
burgundy leather jerkin and cap, blackhide breeches and heavily
buckled boots. He had route papers stamped in Sebastian's wax
seal. As a courier for the Shepherds, he'd be given no trouble from
the gate guards. They knew better than to question the dealings
of Shepherds. The only question was would they recognize their
High King in this guise?

Lochlan could hardly contain his thrill as he rode across the castle bridge and into the heart of Anglinore City. "I'm doing it," he whispered. "I cannot believe I'm really doing it." Gooseflesh danced on his arms, and his heart raced. Liquid energy seemed to pump into his muscles, and it felt as if they bulged and strained beneath his clothing and armor. He felt a sudden urge to let out a loud bark of joy, but even with most of the city sleeping, Loch restrained himself. It was an hour before sun up, and a few pale stars twinkled overhead. The first gatehouse loomed up ahead.

"Hold, rider!" called a guard.

"Present your orders," called another.

Loch lifted his right hand in salute as he'd seen the couriers do so often. Chalaren came to a gravelly stop between the two night watchmen. Loch produced his orders and passed them to the nightwatch captain. He read them quickly. His eyes widened a bit, and he looked up sharply. Loch met his gaze and kept his chin up. Let him look me square in the face and see if he knows me, Loch thought.

"From the High Shepherd himself, eh?" the nightwatch captain inquired. "Must be rather important, beating the dawn like you are."

Loch felt the man was fishing for information. "You know the Shepherds," Loch replied, altering his voice a little, raising the pitch and adding a touch of commoner accent. "Things come t'them at all hours, you know. And if the mood's on 'em, they don't seem t'mind inconveniencing the help."

Both guards laughed. "True that," the night captain said. "Off you go, then!"

The thrill redoubled as Loch escaped the first gatehouse. He shook his head and laughed. "They didn't know me!" he exclaimed. "Not even a hint of recognition." He gave Chalaren a light kick. "C'mon, girl! Let's see what you can do!"

It turned out Chalaren could do plenty. For a draught horse, she had impressive speed. Her heavy hooves crackled on the cobblestone, sounding like a small-scale avalanche as they raced north to the next gate. As they rounded the sharpest bend, Loch began to notice a glow flickering behind a few windows. And here and there the smell of baking bread or sizzling sausage wafted by. Loch was half-tempted to delay his journey and break his fast in town, but he shook the thought away. Even an hour's delay would invite busy shops and much more crowded streets, greatly increasing the possibility that he would be recognized.

The second gate and the drowsy guards there came and went more easily than the first. Each gate Loch passed it felt as if a shackle broke and a length of chain fell away. By the time he left the main gate, the sun had broken the Dark Sea horizon behind the cliff on which Anglinore City was built. The road ahead was clear, but in less than a league, Loch spotted a coach drawn by eleven horses with mounted soldiers riding escort. Eleven horses? Loch thought with a start. Then he noted the green and black livery of those knights . . . and he knew. *What are you doing on the road to Anglinore, cousin?* he wondered. *You've been spending far too much time away from Avon Barony.*

A spectacular, radiant glow—pink, orange, red, and purple—poured over the landscape, and Lochlan thought nothing more about Baron Cardiff Strengle. A well-worn path stretched out before Chalaren's thunderous hooves. The High King Overlord of all Myriad had left the borders of Anglinore and his throne behind. And he didn't look back.

16 SOLMONATH 2238

After a colossal breakfast at the first tavern he'd found, Lochlan sped due south, crossing the unseen border of the Naïthe, even as the sun marched past midday. Soon the rocky edges and jutting fists of gray stone were all left behind, replaced now with gently sloping ground and clumpy hummocks of long grass. The slanting, hilly terrain dove down into a vast green hollow, and long, green spring-grass stretched east to west as far as the eye could see.

Lochlan brought Chalaren to a stop in the midst of it, just to watch. Wind that he barely felt through his clothing and light armor had its way with the endless grass. Waves undulated hypnotically through a thousand-stride patch only to become utterly still just moments later, as the unseen air exerted its touch elsewhere. Lochlan felt he could linger there all day, just watching, what seemed to him, a natural spectacle. He patted Chalaren on the neck and said, "I need to get out more."

Lochlan nudged the mare back to a trot and enjoyed the slow passage. Here and there, long channels of dark blue water divided some of the great fields of grass. Fishermen in low boats floated about lazily. Some waved to Loch as he passed. Large fenced in homesteads began to appear . . . and windmills. Loch had heard often of Keening's windmills, but seeing them sent a thrill shooting through him. They looked like towering mushrooms: the stalks made of timber that had been weatherbeaten to gray and dotted with small round windows; the caps shingled with dark red or green. But the blades were more magnificent still, each almost as tall as the mill itself and nearly brushing the ground with each downward sweep. Canvas covered half of each blade, a sturdy lattice making up the other. Both simple and brilliant, Loch thought as he passed close to one of the larger windmills. And he thought of how many man-hours of work these massive wind harnesses saved each day . . . each year.

The sun began its descent, and fishermen hauled their boats up from the water. Loch figured Keening was still easily another day's ride to the south. He had two weeks to spend. He was in no hurry. Well-trodden paths began to appear in the grass. Loch took one of them and followed it to a small village. It was a snug locale, less than a league from end to end. Only a few pock-marked, cobbled stone roads striated its limits. And clusters of narrow homes and shops crowded both sides of every avenue. The buildings looked as if they'd been constructed from the same stone and with the same technique as the roads. *Maybe they had*, Loch thought. *And what maniacal architect laid out the plan for this place?* The sections of each ediface were all different sizes and piled in such a way that they were all pushing in on the other. It was as if a story might shift and find itself atop the neighboring structure. Still, it didn't feel crushed or confining like the city of Anglinore did at times. It felt like something cozy and snug . . . like an embrace.

He found an inn soon enough and followed the alley behind it. Horses, mules, and lagbeasts were already tied up in a grassy lot there, so Loch tied off Chalaren there too. "I promise to bring you a carrot before I bed," he whispered to her. She seemed not to notice, noisily gulping water from the long trough. Loch patted her on the flank and walked away.

He came back to the front of the building and looked up at the hanging sign. "The Ochre Owl," he said. "Quaint." He walked in, heard the tinkle of a little bell, and then ducked at the rush of greetings sent his way. Fifteen, maybe twenty people filled seats in the low-ceilinged common room, but Loch thought that every one of them must have called out a loud "Hallo!" as he entered the tavern. He swallowed and waved a tentative greeting back to them. To Loch's relief, they all went back to their own business just as quickly.

He chose an out-of-the-way table in the far corner near the fireplace, sat in the bench seat portion, and put his feet up on the chair. A woman in a scullery cap and apron ambled up to him and said, "Anglinore, eh? There'll be want of news here later, if you have a mind."

Loch reminded himself to change his outfit as soon as he could. Couriers, especially from Anglinore, would attract curiosity wherever he went. "Maybe," Loch replied. "I'm sore tired right now, maybe after a bit of sup."

"As you like," she replied. "Welcome to Nurn village and the Ochre Owl, best an only tavern, heh, heh. We've a bit of beef roastin' or lamb, if ye prefer. The ale here is as good as Keening's, I'm told."

"Yes and yes," Loch said. "I'll have some of all you've mentioned. Cheese and bread too, if you've got it. Oh, and I've been told there's a spicy sauce made in these parts, or is that just in Keening?"

"You mean the bonnet-pesto," she said with a laugh. "Brave lad, you are. Olive oil, crushed bonnet peppers, garlic, and basil."

"Sounds Allhavenly," Loch said. "Yes, please." She left, and Loch let his head rest against the wall. He closed his eyes and exhaled . . . and listened. It wasn't any particular conversation that caught his attention, and he wasn't eavesdropping. It was the glad mix of all the colorful voices together that made the errant king smile.

The matron returned and placed a wide platter of food on the table. She followed it with a massive mug that sloshed when she put it down. "There ye go, sweetie," she said. "If ye be needin' anything else, call for Helga."

"You are a blessing, Helga," Loch said, gazing at the delicious spread in front of him. "I do need a room for the night, if you have one."

"We do," Helga said. "Talk to Lloyd behind the bar. He'll fix ye up. He's the one to square your coppers as well."

Loch nodded and, when she left, he tore into the meal. The beef was glorious, rich with garlic and salt and juicy. The lamb was succulent and just a bit pink, the way Loch liked it. The cheese was mild with a subtle herby tang to it. And the bread was fresh-baked, crust smooth and hard, but hot, flaky, and tender within. Loch looked at the inch-high tin of sauce and wondered. Its color was deep red, and a frightful number of pale seeds were suspended within it. "Can't be that bad," he whispered. Then, he tore off a chunk of bread and dabbed it in the bonnet sauce. He held it to his nose, sniffed it, and then plopped it into his mouth.

The first taste to hit his tongue was rich with the basil and garlic, richly strewn throughout the texture of the bread. But then came the heat. Loch cleared his throat audibly, caught his breath, and at last managed to swallow. It felt as if someone had cut off the tip of his tongue with a pair of garden sheers and then pinched the rest of it with red-hot tongs. Loch poured half the mug of ale down both sides of his face as he tried to quench the heat.

"Eat another hunk of bread!" a gruff voice called from the bar. Lloyd, apparently.

Loch did as he was told and stuffed a third of what remained of the loaf in his mouth. It helped . . . a little. Loch pushed the tin of bonnet sauce to the farthest edge of the table and thoughtfully finished his meal.

What will it be? Loch wondered as he lay on his side on a low bed in his room. He faced the window looking south and had left it open to get more of the fresh cool air. Keening lay many leagues away. But just knowing it was out there and knowing he would soon see it . . . and live in it, filled his heart near to bursting. "But what will I do there?" he whispered. Baker, locksmith, cooper, minstrel, leatherworker—I can do it all. But which one? He stared at his bulging pack, propped up between the dresser and the wall. He'd brought most of what he needed. And he could buy the rest.

Okay, he admitted to himself. *So I don't have to work to survive, really.* He thought he'd probably brought enough gold to purchase the whole village of Nurn. Best to be prepared. On the outside of the big, bulging bag he'd hooked a frying pan and a lute.

Minstrel? Loch loved to play, and he loved even more to play for others to listen and enjoy. But maybe that would be too exposed, draw too much attention for the first journey.

Cook? Not if I have to mess with bonnet peppers, that's for sure.

Blacksmith? Maybe. Loch had recently acquired a fantastic new set of smithy tools and thought it might be fun to try them out. Of course, passing all those windmills on the way into Nurn, made Loch wonder if he shouldn't just be a miller. He decided to sleep on it and maybe talk to Lloyd about it in the morning.

17 SOLMONATH 2238

The breakfast at the Ochre Owl was as good as the supper. And afterwards, he tipped Lloyd a gold piece and got nearly half an hour's worth of opinion about which jobs might be in demand in Keening. After all the verbal exploration, it turned out that Lloyd really didn't know. But one thing Lloyd did know was directions. Loch had spread a map on the table, and Lloyd traced out the best route to Keening.

Loch thanked him and turned to leave.

"But you're a courier," Lloyd said. "Thought you'da know the best roads an' all."

Loch winced inwardly. *I need to think these things through a little better.* "I know the way," Loch said. "But I'm new at this and would rather hear from a local. Thanks again."

Loch delivered another carrot to Chalaren, harnessed her saddle, and strapped in his packs. *Blacksmith,* he thought. *After all the food I've eaten, I need something to tax my muscles.* He kicked Chalaren to a trot and steered her south. *Blacksmith it is.*

"Is he gone then?" came a weak voice from Sebastian's chamber door high in the castle of Anglinore City.

"Maren?" Sebastian got up. "You shouldn't have climbed all those stairs."

"Sebastian," the queen said with a wave of her hand. "I am not yet so frail that I cannot climb to your tower. Nor am I such a dotard that I would not notice you avoiding my question."

The Shepherd laughed quietly, but his face remained grim. "I think you neither frail of heart nor weak of mind. And I would see you gain in body the strength you ought to have at your age." He took her hands. "But yes, he is gone."

"To Keening?"

"Yes."

"What do you think he will find there?" she asked.

"Peace, I hope," Sebastian replied. "All men are full of holes that—"

"That cannot be filled by clutching, grasping, or taking—yes, I know the proverb, Sebastian."

Sebastian nodded. "It is more true for Lochlan than for most others."

"Why say this?" Maren asked. "Do you seek to grieve me?"

"No, my queen. You know that I do not. But your son is grieved also, and the holes he seeks to fill are deep indeed. He's known no father nor had any father figure but for a crotchety, old Shepherd and an ex-assassin. But beyond that, he's had naught but military brats for friends; he's been driven hard to excel in everything from grappling to bass viol; and, with all due respect, Maren, he's spent the last three years of his life attempting to rule an entire world while watching his mother wither before his eyes."

Tears beaded on Queen Maren's lower eyelids, but she blinked them away. "I suppose I had that coming," she said, "for being so terse. But Sebastian . . . it . . . it's so hard."

"I cannot presume to know how you must feel," Sebastian said. ". . . the tortured thoughts you must endure. But I do know this: you should not die prematurely. The First One decides when you are born and when you should pass from this world. For any to hasten that passing is nothing short of a Sabrynite plot! The boy needs you, Maren. His wife and children will need you!"

Queen Maren could not restrain the deluge any longer. She poured hot tears into the shoulder of Sebastian's robe and shook as if cold. The Shepherd held her, feeling a bit awkward but knowing full well that he would continue to hold her as long as she needed it. It turned out not to be very long. Maren pulled away and blotted her face with a linen cloth.

"I . . . I will try," she said.

"Promise me."

"I just did, Sebastian," she growled. "I am High Queen of Myriad. My word is my promise. I will try . . . try to live."

"Thank you, High Queen."

Maren went to his chamber window. "Do you think . . . he might find a wife out there?"

Sebastian laughed and joined her. "It is possible, you know. He is a handsome lad with his father's charm."

Maren's fingers went to her lips and she laughed too. "I hope he finds a wife soon, for he also has his father's appetite."

"So I have observed also. But I blame Daribel."

"So did Aravel." The queen was silent for many moments, but then said, "I . . . I would like to see children."

"Keep yourself hale and strong, my queen," he said. "And I am certain you will."

Queen Maren leaned forward to see more of the star-studded southern horizon. "I hope we have made the right choice."

"I feel in my heart that we have. Lochlan needs to know the people he will govern . . . before he truly can govern them." The Shepherd listened for voices on the wind but heard nothing.

CHAPTER 17

THE ARCHER'S GUILD

*Like broken branches caught in a whirlpool, evil from every corner of
the world will be drawn in upon Myriad, rule over her, and suffocate
her. The world and time itself will teeter on a blade's edge. For good
or ill . . . all things must come to an end.*

—Shepherd Jaavere Amberstill, Canticles LCIX.vii,
Book of End Things

18 SOLMONATH 2238

"There are more women here than men, you know," I said, feeling
like a child on Advent morning.

"It was your chore shifting idea that done it," Millard the
Mark replied. "Long as all the cleanin' gets done, the Elders can't
say nuthin'."

I scanned the ranges of the new Archers Guild. Months of
work, I thought. But had it taken ten years it would have been
worth it.

At Mill's urging, I came out of my dreary house of self pity
and finally agreed to join him in his subversive new guild. After
the spectacle at the Huntmeet, Mill had very little trouble finding recruits to join, many of them peasant men deemed too

common to join the Hunters Guild. But still more, there were women like me, women who had been told all their lives they could do this and not that, that they might come so far but no farther than the line the Elders gouged through the center of the Wetlands Village.

We decided to keep the Archers Guild as subtle and furtive as possible, keeping out of the Elders' way, making no problems in the Wetlands Village. To that end, we chose a territory deep in the Amethyst Wood. The deeply forested valley was partially enclosed like a canyon by a blue-gray moss covered claw of stone. It had once been the Hunting Guild's favorite territory, offering adventure and plentiful game—until the deer and scintelope were displaced by packs of long-toothed guerrin. The Hunters had tried to hunt the guerrin, of course, but the massive tough-skinned cats offered no reward. Their pelts were prickly and smelled like dead fish no matter how many times they were scrubbed and washed. And their meat was rancid tasting, impossible to chew, and even harder to swallow.

I laughed at the thought of the Elders at that fateful feast. They had been so proud of the dozen or so guerrin slain on the hunt, and each had a steaming bowl of guerrin stew. Smiling with pride, they each raised a spoon and slurped in a mouthful. Smiles vanished, replaced by hideous, twisting scowls. And the chewing went on and on and on. That feast had been a grand mess, and ever since then, the Hunters Guild had, for the most part, abandoned the Amethyst Wood.

Just a morning's walk from the village, the Amethyst Wood was the perfect, secluded place to train new hunters. It was also something extraordinary to look at, full of all shades of deep blue, green, and purple. From the ever-swaying midnight willows to the tall, leaning violet oaks and mighty barrel evergreens—the wood was alive with color . . . and scent. Ice-kissed honey suckle climbed all around the tree trunks, and wild lavender grew thick in every cleft and hollow. I breathed in deeply. I couldn't remember the last time I'd felt so relaxed.

"That Navvi on the far range is a right clever shot," Mill said. "I've been noticin' that."

I watched the young woman with three dark braids tied back at the nape of her neck. She'd plunged dozens of shafts in and around her target's bull's-eye. "She's amazing," I said. "Only her third week with a bow in her hand."

"Maybe a little more'n that," Mill said. "Some of 'em been practicin' on their own."

I nodded. "What about Starke Finn?" I asked.

"Ah, he's a moose!" Mill crowed. "Never seen a pull like that one. Hard t'find a bow stiff enough."

"We've put a dozen more straw bails behind his target," I said, "but he puts the shafts right through into the trees."

"Work on him with his aim," Mill said. "Every time I try I think the lad just wants t'show he's stronger than me."

"Again?" I asked. "Poor kid has it bad for me, and you know it. I've told him he's too young, but he keeps trying."

"Who can blame him?" Mill asked with a wink. "Come on, Ariana, just give him a few pointers. The lad does whatever you tell him to do."

I blew out a harsh sigh. "For all the wrong reasons, Mill. He's a good lad, but he's just fifteen."

"Imagine how strong he'll be when he's twenty. C'mon, Ariana, just give him a few pointers."

I shrugged. "Alright. I'll give him some tips. But if he tries to kiss me . . ."

"Don't you worry about that," Mill said. "If he tries to kiss you, I'll show him he's got a ways to go 'fore he'll be strong as Millard the Mark."

Good old Mill. I laughed and said, "I suppose we best get started."

"After you, then," Mill replied.

We descended from the grassy hillock and split up. Mill went to the two ranges on the right. I took the two on the left.

Each range was a cleared field, fifty yards long and thirty wide, angled so that the targets were backed up to trees. The colorful canopy hanging high overhead filtered the sunlight into an ever changing, ever blending curtain of blues and purples. I walked slowly behind the first range where seven archers ran through their forms. They varied in skill from dangerously poor to dangerously accurate, but everyone needed work. It was easy to spot. I walked to and fro among the archers making suggestions, altering stances, and in some cases, redirecting aim.

"Lift that elbow," I said to one. "Draw back to the corner of your jaw," I said to another. More often than not, my advice was one word: "Slowly." Why were they all in a rush to fire off an arrow? A bow is meant to be a quiet weapon, and that means quieting your body, pulling slowly back, and waiting until the string is ready to be released.

If I remembered truly, speed was one of the things Starke needed to work on.

I crept up behind him, trying to keep out of his field of view. No use distracting him with my decidedly plain looks.

Standing in the lad's shadow, I had to admit Mill was right. Stark was a moose. At fifteen years, he stood a hand and a half over six foot. He still bore some of the awkward signs of his age: shoulders not spread as wide as they would be, arms and legs looking a little too long for his torso, and a little knobby at the joints. But he was thick with muscle and seemingly thickening with more every day we saw him. If mountain rock and tree trunks could marry and give birth, Starke would be the result.

I watched him pull an arrow from the stand near his right heel. His hand was so massive and thick that the fletching all but disappeared as he lifted the shaft to the bowstring. Amethyst Wood was rather cool on this day, but Starke was sweating profusely. Beads appeared at the hairline of his upturned-brush, spiky hair and dribbled down the tanned skin of his neck. A spreading, dark line stained the middle back of his tunic, and the skin on his arms glistened. I looked past him to his target and thought I understood. This was frustration sweat. The lad had fired nine arrows deep into the target, but none within a sniff of the bull's-eye. And this while maids on either side of him had several bull's-eyes each.

I watched Starke pull. His strength was impressive. He looked like he could draw the bowstring all the way back with one finger, but I saw several flaws in his form. Starke released the arrow. The shaft raced away and then, faster than a striking snake, plunged into the target. But once more, the arrow had found only the outer ring. Starke's head fell and he pinched the bridge of his nose.

"Hey there, Starke Finn," I said.

"Oh, uh, hey, Ariana," he replied, high cheeks reddening. There was an awkward pause. Then he said, "I just don't think I'm cut out fer this."

"Nonsense, lad," I said, doing my best to keep the I'm-too-old-for-you tone of voice. "I suppose it's possible that the sword's more your thing. Or maybe, given how strong you are, maybe a war hammer or axe like my father. Still, I believe you'll be able to shoot well enough. Wasn't it just the other day, I saw you hit three bull's-eyes in a row?"

Starke nodded and raised his chin up a bit. "I suppose yer right. I did hit three in a row, didn't I?"

"I'm your witness," I said. "Now, let's see you do it again, then. Go ahead then, nock up an arrow, but don't fire for a moment. I have a few, uh, suggestions."

Starke put an arrow to the string and began to pull.

"Okay," I said, "hold on a second. Your feet are too spread. Keep a narrow stance, feet maybe as wide as your hips." He adjusted. "Okay, that's better. Out in the deep woods, you won't have even ground for a wide stance. Go ahead and draw back, elbow nice and high. Pull with your back muscle, not your arms. There's a little bend in your left arm. You might be strong enough to hold the bow still that way, but it's much better to just straighten out that arm."

"Like this?" Starke asked.

I nodded. "Good, good form now. Anchor the bowstring at the jawline. Put a little more weight on your front foot. Now, find your aim."

Starke went very still. Sweat continued to trickle down the side of his face. He held the arrow there for a long time, a lot longer than I could have, especially with a bow as stiff as his. I stared at the tip of his arrow and then past it to the bull's-eye. *Let go, lad, let go,* I thought. Starke looked so nervous. Poor lad. He wanted to impress me. I found myself wanting him to succeed, willing him to succeed.

He let go.

Whap!

Starke let out a whoop. "I did it! Look at that, would ya? Bull's-eye, as true as ya like!"

I gave him a pat on the back and said, "That is terrific shooting, I deem. Now then, let's see you do it again."

Starke grabbed another arrow and nocked it in a hurry. Too much of a hurry, I thought, but his form looked good. Again, I wanted so badly for him to nail the bull's-eye. The confidence would do him a world of good. He focused. I focused. He released.

I cheered. "That's two, lad! Two in a row. Well done now! Get three lad. Nock it up and get three."

Starke went through his progression. I could almost feel his motions in my own muscles.

He fired and we both leaped in the air. He'd done it. Three bull's-eyes in a row. Before I knew it, Starke had grabbed me by the waist and threw me up into a hug.

"Uh, Starke," I said, "put me down."

"Sorry," he said. "I just can't believe it." He turned to look at the target. "Funny though . . . seems like I can only do it when you're around."

"I help you with your form, that's all. You remember what I told you and do it, you'll shoot like that all the time."

"I dunno," he said. "It's hard, and I get nervous."

"Try shooting a target two hundred feet away from a bush," I said. "Or between an Elder's legs as he walks by."

A large hand fell on my shoulder and I spun. It was Mill.

"We've got trouble," he said, and pointed to the hillock overlooking the valley.

I gazed upward and felt ice forming in the pit of my stomach. The Elders and what looked like the entire Hunt Guild were there, spilling down each side and taking up threatening positions. They were armed to the teeth.

"Millard Key!" Plebian Scandeer cried out. "You have gone too far!"

"I can't believe it!" Mill growled. He grabbed the bow away from Starke and nocked an arrow.

"Mill, don't!" I put my hand on his forearm.

"I'll not shy away from a fight, Ariana," he said, "not from that tyrant!" He stormed toward the Elders at the top of the hollow. I hurried after him. The other archers, the men and women of our guild, followed in thickening groups.

At the base of the hill, Mill stopped, pointed to the High Elder, and yelled, "What brings ya here to the Archer's Guild? Your lads want to join?"

The skin in the corner of Scandeer's eye twitched. "After your mockery of the Huntmeet, after you were cast out of the Hunt Guild, I assumed your threats were hollow. But no, you actually do have the temerity to start your own guild."

"And why not?" Mill asked. "Why shouldn't a man like me be able t'start a group? It's a gatherin' of friends? Is that so bad, Scandeer?"

"In this case, it is an insurrection!" the Elder cried. "You have defied my authority and scoffed at Wetlands traditions that go back more than a thousand years. I hereby dissolve your assembly!"

I saw Mill's grip on the bow tighten.

"Why do ya have t' meddle here?" Mill demanded. "We're not hurting anyone. We've seen to it that all the village work still gets done. Look a' these folk—your folk. All they want t'do is learn t'shoot!"

"We already have a guild for archers," Scandeer said. "Any man here is free to attempt the rigors of the real Hunt Guild."

"They already have!" Mill fired back. "Or didn't ya know that? These are the men ya spat on . . . to say nothing a' the women."

"I'll speak for the women!" I yelled.

"Ariana Kurtz." Scandeer chewed on my name like he would an unpleasant bit of food. "I might have known you'd put Millard Key up to this."

"I did no such thing," I said. "But I'm glad to be a part of it, High Elder. Have you such disdain for women that you cannot even remember what some women did to save Chapparel in the Gorrack War? My mother was an archer in that battle. By her bow, she ended many a Gorrack's life and saved many of our own. What of that? Who's to say that women cannot learn to shoot, if not to fight, just to hunt and support our village?"

Scandeer's face looked pinched and was very red. When he spoke next, his words spilled out low and menacing . . . like volcanic steam. "There will NEVER be a woman in the Hunt Guild, not so long as I am High Elder!"

"Yeah, well maybe it's time for us to have a new High Elder!" Starke yelled, his voice deeper than I had ever heard it. I don't know whose bow he had taken. But he had an arrow nocked and raised it to the High Elder. The hunters surrounding us had their bows up in a heartbeat. There were probably six arrows aimed at each one of us.

"Starke no!" I yelled.

"Put that down, lad!" Mill commanded. "Believe me, I thought about it. But not this way. Put the bow down."

"Raise a bow to me?" Scandeer seethed. "To me? Insolent mongrel! Someone put this whelp down!"

"No!" I screamed, moving swiftly to stand and cover Starke's left side. Mill shielded his right.

Starke didn't lower his bow. He had the left arm straight, the bowstring pulled back to his chin. The hunters had drawn as one, more than thirty shafts aimed for us now. Amethyst Wood went silent. Nothing moved. I could barely breathe or swallow. One twitch. One small move was all it would take, and someone would fire. The longer the standoff continued the more dangerous it became. Muscles would grow weak, perhaps even spasm. Fingers would become sweaty. This had to stop.

"Tell your hunters to lower their bows!" I called out. "This is a mistake. A misunderstanding. Tell them, High Elder! We are all Wetlanders here."

"I will do no such thing," Scandeer said, "unless your miscreant lowers his weapon."

"Starke," I whispered urgently, "lower your bow. This accomplishes nothing."

"Nothing? Nothing will change if I do," Starke said. "He lets half the village eat high on the hog and puts the rest of us under his thumb."

"I know, Starke," I said. "I know. But we can't win . . . not this way." I turned my head to meet his eyes. I lifted my arm and laid my hand gently on his bow arm. "Not this way," I said again. I felt his arm begin to descend and—

Starke groaned. His eyes bulged. I stepped back, saw the shaft plunged deep into Starke's side. "No! Nooo!"

Starke's arrow fell from his bow and he slid from my arms to the ground.

Mill stormed up the hill. "Who fired that shot?! WHO?"

"I did, Millard Key. He was threatening the life of our village High Elder!"

I could not look up, but I knew the voice was Choiros Greenshambles. I couldn't take my eyes off Starke.

He wheezed out a breath and said, "I'm sorry, Ariana . . ." His eyelids fluttered closed.

"No, no, no, Starke!" I whispered. "You open those eyes, you hear me. Please, Starke . . . please." But Choiros' blasted aim had been wickedly true. If Starke opened his eyes again, I knew it wouldn't be for long.

Starke coughed and lurched upward a few inches. And blood trickled from the corner of his mouth which, to my heartbreaking surprise, was turned upward in a lopsided kind of smile. "You . . . you know, Ariana," he said, his eyes open but rolling loosely. "Even this close . . . I'd have probably missed anyway." With that, the last of his breath seeped away.

"Starke!" I cried, shaking him. "Starke, no!" I felt his neck and his wrist, but there was nothing.

I leaped to my feet and glared at Choiros. "He was putting his bow down, you wretch! And now, you've killed him. Just fifteen and you killed him."

Some of the other hunters were glaring at Choiros as well. "What?" he squealed. "He was threatening our High Elder! Any of you would've done the same."

"No, no they wouldn't!" Mill exclaimed.

Tears stinging my eyes and streaming down my cheeks, I turned on Scandeer. "High Elder, and all the Council of Elders, look what you've done!"

"What we've done—"

"Don't!" I yelled, pointing my shaking finger at him. "You brought enough of the Hunt Guild here to slay a hundred Gorracks! You had them bristling for a fight, surrounding us, preparing to shoot us down like pigs in a pit. And for what? Because we wanted our people—all our people—to feel just a little bit better about their lot in life. You're robbing them of something vital." I pointed my finger at some of the hunters. "Husbands, some of your wives are here, or might have been on a different day . . . and yet you came here bearing arms? Have you all lost your minds?"

I dropped to my knees and softly brushed Starke's hair. I looked up at Plebian Scandeer. Through my tears, he was a blurry phantom, but I looked at him. And I said, "Don't worry about telling Starke's parents. I'll do it."

CHAPTER 18

RITE OF PASSAGE

Demion was the first Spriggan to ever survive the Red Queen's "Prava sin Saengue," the Bloodtrials infamous throughout the Hinterlands during her reign. In single combat, Demion slew six Stonehands, four Spriggans, seven humans, a gray bear, a snow drake, and a three-hundred pound mortalon. After he'd been washed and his wounds tended, Demion answered a summons to the Red Queen's private chamber. He was never heard from again.

—Arjen Skevack, Royal Historian under Quevara,
the Red Queen

22 SOLMONATH 2238

"Meli, wake up!" Tango growled, giving a little shove to the lump under the covers. "How can ya sleep at a time like this?"

"I dunno, Tango," mumbled Meli, peeking out from the blanket. "Maybe cuz the sun went down."

"Yeah, but Da's gone."

"I know that, Tango. So?" She closed her eyes again and ducked under the blanket.

Tango yanked the blanket completely off. "Tango, you nerf! Don'na ya know it's cold!"

"Meli, listen to me," Tango said. "Da's been gone too long. And . . . and I know where he's gone."

Meli sat up. "Where?"

"He went a'spyin' on that Cythraul man."

"Aww, no, Tango. Why'd he do that?" She hopped down out of the bunk and started putting her hiking gear on.

"I don't know why, but I can guess, can't I? I think he went to kill that Cythraul for what he done." He tilted his head. "Meli, what are ya doin'?"

"Putting on my gear. We're goin' after him, aren't we?"

"Well, yeah, but I thought you'd fight me on it."

"Nope, besides, I'm better with a bow than you."

"Hey!" Tango started to complain. "No, yer right there. Grab yer pack too."

"Why? It'll weigh me down."

"Just grab it. You never know."

Tango threw a bucket of sand on the still glowing embers. He scuttled from oil lamp to oil lamp, turning down the wicks.

"Tango, Da forgot his hatchet."

"That's not like him at all," Tango said. He picked up the hatchet and shoved its handle through a loop in his belt. "We'll bring it to him." He turned out the last lantern and kindled a flickerstick.

"I'll go first," Meli said. "Case there's spiders."

"Yer gonna wear that one out, Meli."

The two Spriggans crawled through the tunnel swiftly but had to work together to unscrew the heavy cap. They emerged in a very dark forest with the moon threatening to vanish far to the west.

"How we gonna find him?" Meli asked.

"Should'na be too hard to get back to that hill. That's where Da would start his trackin'. I bet I can follow the trail too. Da's taught me a bit of what he knows."

"Tango," Meli said, a quiver in her voice, "do ya think Da's alright?"

"I dunno, Meli. I dunno." He blinked. "We'd better go. C'mon."

Tango led, holding the flickerstick high. Meli kept close. They traversed the forest rapidly, Tango following his sense of direction until he felt the slope begin to rise. He slowed down, trying to recognize the area through the shadows. He tromped along a few dozen yards and then stepped in something wet.

He halted immediately and Meli ran into his backpack. "Ow," he whispered harshly. "Watch it, Meli."

"Why'd you stop?"

"This." He lifted one foot and held up the flickerstick so Meli could see. "Blood."

"This is where the wolves were?"

"Yeah," he said. "Stay still a minute. I've gotta find a sign of where they went next." He worked his way around the area in a kind of crouching waddle and he kept the flickerstick just over the ground.

"Ah, here's something." He bent over a little closer. "Aye, this is it."

"How can ya tell?" Meli joined him.

"See there?" Tango pointed down. "That's Da's foot, or I'm a gourd."

"It's Da's foot alright, but you might still be a gourd. Nerfa-boy."

"Thanks." Tango had the urge to stick his tongue out or roll his eyes, but he resisted. Growing up meant not doing that kind of thing so much. "Now, we'd better keep it quiet from here out. No tellin' where they might be."

The Spriggans moved carefully and Meli shadowed Tango, staying close but trying not to foul up any evidence of the trail. Tango got himself tied up several times, losing any sign of a trail, then doubling back until he found it. Once, he got so crossed up that he ended up following his own footprints.

"We've been this way already, Tango," Meli said.

"Don't I know it, Meli?" Tango hunted for several minutes. "Ah, here! Feet bigger than mine."

They prowled onward, making slow but steady pace east. "What's the black wall up there?" Meli asked.

"The mountain," Tango replied. "The great mountain."

"It's like night," Meli said. "Night with no stars. I don'na like it."

"I don't like it either, but that's the way we've gotta go."

The face of the mountains looked grayer as they approached. Somewhere, far beyond the range, the sun was passing the horizon and casting dawn gold on the side of the mountain the Spriggans had never seen.

The Hinterlands were bathed in somber twilight blue when Tango stopped. "There was a campsite here. Lots of footprints too. Aw, no!" He snatched up something from the dirt.

"What, Tango?"

"It's one of Da's arrowheads, I think."

Meli screamed.

Tango drew his dagger and stared. The flickerstick and the half light made it so he couldn't see much. Meli raced away from him. "Meli, what're ya doin?"

Visions of wolves and blood sliced through his mind as sprinted after her. Twenty yards away, she fell to the ground, and there was something there beside her.

"Da, oh, my da!" she shrieked.

Tango dropped beside her and found his father there, stricken and bleeding. "Ah, no, Da! No! I told you not to go! Ah, no!"

Meli fell upon him and wept, but when she did, he groaned. "There's a girl, Meli. But leave me be a spell. So . . . tired."

"You're alive!" Tango took his hand, but it was cold and wet. "Da, what happened?"

Their father's eyes closed a moment and then sprang open. He looked in turn from daughter to son. "Ah, my littlins, what are ya doin' here?" A cough wracked his body, and he clutched his side. "Get ya back to the Thicket. Not safe here. Not safe."

"You're comin' with us, Da," Tango cried.

Tanner grit his teeth and cried out. "No . . ." He panted through the words and between the words. "No . . . no . . . no. I can'na . . . not this time."

"What happened to ya, Da?" Meli wailed.

"I tried to shoot him, but my shafts broke like they were made of glass." He groaned, and tears escaped, mingling with blood on his cheeks. He looked away, his eyes focusing somewhere high in the treetops. "Nothin' can'na pierce him. But I tried . . . Da, I tried."

Meli looked up through the tears and whispered, "Tango, who's he talkin' to now?"

Tango shook the question away and used the increasing light to try to find the source of the bleeding. "Where are ya, hurt, Da?"

"Don'na ya worry about that." His eyes clouded for a moment. He seemed to awaken in mid sentence. ". . . another world out there. That's where he came from, the scoundrel, and he's not content killin' here. He's . . . he's going t'take the Red Queen back there."

"What, Da?" Tango asked. "Da, I don'na understand."

". . . a tunnel, lad . . . a tunnel through the mountains. Cythraul and some tribe a' Stonehands, the likes I've not seen before. Another world . . ." He coughed repeatedly, the last one somehow cut off as he gasped for a breath. ". . . That's where they came from . . . and that's where they went."

Tango didn't know what to do, didn't know what to say. "Da, I brought ya your hatchet back," he said, handing it to him.

Tanner held it a moment and handed it back. "It's yours now, lad. And . . . I have no doubt the man yer gonna be." He reached out and took Meli's hand. "Ah, Meli, you're my breath of sunshine. You warm me even now. It's your gift, I deem. The

Starmaker Himself took down a bit of starlight and wove it into you. Shine, my daughter . . . shine."

Tango watched his father's grip of Meli's hand loosen and, because of the blood, his hand slid free and fell at his side. Meli looked down at her bloodstained hand and back to her father. Tango went to her and knelt at her side. They held each other while morning came on and the last of the stars disappeared.

23 Solmonath 2238

The days of a Spriggan lad are filled with all manner of digging: trenches, wells, channels, and furrows. But, in all of his short life, Tango never once thought he'd have to delve out a grave . . . for his father.

Brother and sister, they worked tirelessly . . . wordlessly until the shallow pit was done. With the greatest care, they dragged their father's body and let it slide down the incline until he rested four feet beneath the surface. Tango was about to push in a mound of soil when Meli said, "Wait." She disappeared into the trees a moment and returned with an armful of leaves.

Meli walked around the grave, sprinkling the colorful leaves as she went. They fell, some in arcs, some spinning, and others wafting back and forth; and they came to rest upon Tanner Goliant, wreathing him in natural majesty. "I think he'd like that," Meli said.

"He would," Tango said. "He always loved the trees."

They filled in the grave, patting down the soil a layer at a time. And then, they built a kind of cairn with such mossy stones as they could find. When they were finished, the sun had broken free of the mountain and shone down on them.

Meli fell against her brother. "What are we gonna do now?"

It was the very question Tango had been dueling for hours as they worked. Tango looked west. There lay the Thicket, an emergency home that his family had planned for and labored for over decades. South of that was their old delshroom home in Hammer's Gap. Walk from there a league in any direction and there would be other Spriggan villages set up upon the spokes of an invisible wheel with Cragheath Tor in the center. And then, there was the east. Cythraul had gone that way. An ember of rage flared in Tango's stomach, and he fingered his father's hatchet. *My hatchet now.*

"I don'na feel mutch like hidin'," he said at last.

Meli stepped away from him. "Yer not goin' after that villain. Tango, yer no match for the like a' him."

"I'm not so much a fool as that, Meli. If Da could'na taken Cythraul down, I'll not put a scratch on him. We need help. That's what we need."

"But help from where?" she asked. "We got no family left. No place is safe anymore. Da would'na taken us from Hammer's Gap if it was."

"The Red Queen's sittin' on the throne again," Tango said, hearing his father's words in his own. "The river's runnin' red with blood. This land is cursed . . . and dying." His fists opened and clenched repeatedly.

"The tunnel," Meli whispered. "Yer thinkin' of goin thru that tunnel. Are ya mad? Tango, that's where he went. We don'na know anything about that other place."

"Yes, we do, Meli. We know that Cythraul's plannin' t'bring tha' beastly dragon queen to wreak bloody death over there." He pointed east. "Maybe we can'na stop Cythraul, but maybe we can bring back some help from over there, kill off the Red Queen before it does t'them what she did to us. If not, maybe at least we can warn them."

Meli put her hands on her hips. "But we don'na know the first thing about killin' such a beast as tha' dragon."

"That we do," he said. "Cythraul himself showed us. Remember? He swung up, straddled her neck, and put a thin blade in that long ear tube a' hers. She fair rolled on her back like a heeled puppy."

Meli shivered but not from cold. "I want to tell ya yer wrong. I want to go back to that comfy Thicket and put my head under the covers and never come up. But . . . but it feels somehow like . . . well like treason. I think we should go."

"Right," Tango said. "East we'll go, then."

Meli grabbed his arm. "But promise me, Tango. Promise me, if we run into that Cythraul you won't try to take him."

"I . . . Meli, he—"

"Promise me!"

"Okay! I promise." Tango shook his head. "Now, let's go."

Tango's first few steps east were among the hardest of his life. He looked back at Meli and then to his father's grave. There was an overwhelming sense of gravity pulling at him, like being caught in a current and dragged backward. But Tango stepped out of it, and as they walked farther from that fateful campsite, the pull grew less potent. But it did not disappear. Tango wondered if it ever would.

In the dappled sunlight, the trail was easy to follow. Cythraul and the Stonehands hadn't seemed too concerned about covering their tracks. The mountain had been there the whole time they walked, of course, obscured in their view by the forest canopy. But when Tango and Meli emerged from the trees, they both gasped.

There were no foothills, no gradual upslope. The stone simply thrust up before them, ten thousand variations of gray, rising and rising, hundreds of feet, maybe thousands for all Tango knew. He felt himself wobble as he stared up the mountain. Sunlight glimmered off the rock in places, and with the clouds drifting slowly overhead, the mountain wall seemed to be moving, as if it were about to tip over and crush anyone foolish enough to stand there.

"Woo," Tango said. "Can't stare at it for long."

"It just goes on and on and on and—"

"I get it, Meli. Come on."

The footprints—and paw prints—traced a path from the forest edge almost directly into the mountain. There it turned north for a bit, skirting some massive fallen boulders, before returning to the east. Tango and Meli followed the trail and came to a place where the footprints seemed to lead directly into the stone.

"Somethin' funny here," mumbled Tango as he put his hands up on the stone of the mountain and began to feel around. Suddenly, his left hand felt nothing but air. It looked as if his hand was touching cold, hard stone. But it wasn't. Tango stepped around a corner that didn't appear to be there, but was.

"Is it magic?" Meli asked.

"Nay," Tango said. "Illusion. Clever stone cutting though. Never seen our Stonehands do anything like it."

Beyond the deceptive corner, the trail turned due south and led the two Spriggans into a fold of the mountain. And when the trail came to an end, a great black mouth opened wide before them: the tunnel's entrance.

"You'd never a' known," Meli said.

"Guess that's the idea," Tango said. He scraped a flickerstick on the wall. It flashed to light and they walked cautiously into the tunnel.

It was reminiscent of the Haunted Cave, but not natural. It was vast and high with few stalagmites or stalactites. The path had been clearly delved as had the vaulted ceiling. But there was no artistry or concern for appearances. It had been the work of many hand, many tools, and many years. Every stroke measured and precise, accomplishing the task but nothing more.

How long they had walked under the mountain, Tango couldn't figure. His feet were sore, which said something. It took a lot of walking for Tango's feet to hurt. Aside of that, the journey seemed measured in grief. They walked apart or held hands, but every so often, one of them would weep quietly. And the other would draw close. They'd walk for a time in a kind of mobile embrace.

They stopped only once for a bit of smoked meat and a hunk of bread from their packs. And then, after enough walking to burn out three flickersticks, Tango saw a curtain of ethereal gray up ahead.

"We've come to the other side, Meli," he whispered.

"What'll we find?" she asked.

He didn't answer. He had none to give. But he strode on ahead. They found another fold in the rock, and squinted in the light.

"Don't bother ye, hiding!" came a gruff voice.

"We seeing you even widout d'torch!" growled another.

"Stonehands," Tango whispered, seeing them now, standing in a squat group, barring their exit.

"Crossbows being straight at ya!" the first voice yelled. "Come on, come on. Let's seeing who you be."

Tango and Meli crept forward. A formidable group of Stonehands stood in their way. Each one bore a red sash tied tight on his upper arm. And they were clean shaven to boot.

"Who giving you leave to travel this way?" asked a Stonehand with bushy gray eyebrows.

Meli squeezed the back of Tango's tunic to the point of pinching his skin. He winced and wondered what he should say. He thought about lying, maybe saying that Cythraul had called for them. But then, he saw the picks, hammers, chisels, augers and axes the Stonehands wore on their belts and thought better of dishonesty.

"We're Spriggans," Tango said. "We're trying to escape calamity in our lands. May we pass?"

The Stonehands laughed, and their version of levity somehow sounded like rocks scraping together. "May you pass? Huck, huck. May you pass?" the gray brow laughed.

"Well, that depending," said a wall of muscle stepping forward. He had deeply tanned or dirty skin and the whitest teeth. "Having gold?"

Tango and Meli both shook their head.

"Jewels then?"

"No."

"What having you?" The gray brow put his meaty fists on his hips.

Tango slung his pack to the ground. "Uh, some smoked meats. Cheese. Uhm . . . bread. Clothes. Wait, wait—a fishing line and some hooks. Uhm . . ."

"Bah, no," said the toothy one. "But that being good." He pointed at Tango's belt.

"My belt?"

"No, nerfa boy! The little axe."

Tango cringed inwardly. The hatchet. They meant his father's hatchet. "I have a dagger," Tango suggested. "It's just as good?"

Metal rang out and the toothy one held up a jeweled dagger whose polished blade was more than a foot long. "Got a dagger."

"We have good bows," Meli tried.

"Spriggans having wax balls in yer ears? See, we've each slinging crossbows." The white-toothed goon pointed again. "Little axe."

"I'd give it to you," Tango said, feeling a quiver in his gut. "But it was my Da's. It is precious . . . I can'na give it up."

"Giving the little axe, and you can pass," the graybrow said.

Tango felt as if the gravity had kicked up a notch. It was wrong. It was all wrong. They never should have come. He turned and looked at Meli. Her blue eyes were wide with uncertainty. He took her arm and said, "I'm sorry."

They started to walk back into the tunnel. "Waiting, Spriggan cubs!" called the Stonehand with the gleaming teeth. "We having wagons, gettin' ready for leavin'. Amara, Fen, Ellador, whatever wanting you."

Meli clutched his tunic again, but it felt somehow more hopeful than scared.

Tango took a tentative step back toward them. "Do I still have t'give ya the hatchet?"

More rocks scraping together. "Huck, huck, course!" White-tooth said. "C'mon . . . you saying yes?"

Tango slid the tool from his belt, and stared down at it. His father had worn it for many long years, as long as Tango could remember. But that was over now. Everything was broken. *I guess it doesn't really matter now,* he thought. With Meli's hand warm on his shoulder, he handed the hatchet to the Stonehand.

"Huck, hoo, ha!" The Stonehand bounced, turning in a circle. He stopped, smiling so wide that his teeth seemed blinding. He ran a thick finger across the blade. "Oh, ow! Sharp!" he said, plopping it into his mouth. "Liking it!"

The graybrow rolled his eyes and gestured. "Come."

Tango and Meli followed. They walked around the fold in the mountain and stepped out into the waning sunlight of early evening . . . and into a world they had never seen before.

Rolling green lands spread in all directions, and from their vantage, it was all a magnificent intricate patchwork of features: forest, water, plains, grassland, foothills, and even more mountains. It was stunning and strange, and yet, not wholly unfamiliar. The sky was still blue, the clouds still pristine white. It was, Tango realized, still the same world. Just another vast part. "Who knows, Meli," he said. "We might be the first Spriggans t'ever see it."

"We being the Tribe of the Crimson Sash," said the graybrow. "Rendage, giving my name."

"Osi!" grunted the Stonehand with bright teeth.

"Where you wanting?" Rendage asked, gesturing to the big covered carts and the massive-limbed horses. "Wagons to Amara, Fen, Ellador . . . tomorrow leaving for Gorrack Nation, Chapparel, and Tryllium."

"No, I don'na want to wait til tomorrow," Tango said. "What do you think, Meli? Amara?"

"I dunno. No, not that one. It sounds stuffy."

Tango shrugged. "Fen?"

"Ewww, sounds like a mucky bog."

"Uh, kay. El . . . Ellador?"

"That sounds nice," Meli said. "Ellador."

"You liking there," said Osi. A couple of the other Stonehands laughed behind the Spriggans. "No, no. Villages being many. You liking."

Osi led them to one of the wagons. "You two climbing in. Ready to go."

Tango and Meli clambered up into the back of the wagon. They heard the Stonehands talking and laughing. Mostly laughing. And then, the wagon lurched forward.

"Tango, look." She pointed at the fold in the mountain. "That's everything we've ever known. And we're leaving it."

Tango buried his head in a sack of some kind of grain. He didn't want to look back. "I know, Meli," he muttered. "I know."

CHAPTER 19

PURELINE

*The tall gray rider on his tall gray steed
has come to claim his own.
The tall gray rider on his tall gray steed
has come to carry you home.*

—The Chorus of The Lay of the Gray Rider,
a popular folk song in Amara

21 DRINNAS 2238

"No!" King Ealden pleaded at the altar in the heart of Jurisduro Hall. "No, it cannot be." Sweat poured down his forehead and stung his eyes. He stared up at the avain, ancient key-shaped symbol of the First One. It hung on the wall, high above the altar between two small braziers burning with white flame. The ruler of the Prydian Wayfolk had knelt there for uncounted hours after the sun slipped behind the western forests. His knees were callused, for Ealden spent time each morning in prayer . . . but not like this. Now they were sore, his back ached, and his head pounded.

Since Alastair's visit two weeks before, Ealden had tasted very little sleep. All day and all night, he had traced lines of logic and speculation through every historical record in the substantial

Prydian archive. And every shred of evidence led to the conclusion he could not deny but couldn't bear to admit.

He suddenly arched his back and held out his arms in supplication. "Why?" he asked. "Why, Lord? I have kept your commands. I have obeyed you at every turn and rid my life of impurity. I have sought to cut through the deceptions of this world to teach others to follow you completely. Why?"

The room was as silent as a tomb. Nothing stirred outside or within. Ealden remained in that posture, listening . . . waiting. His shoulders and arms began to burn with strain, but he forced himself. At last, he could bear it no longer. He collapsed to the altar and let his neck rest. He was exhausted, emotionally spent, but still his mind raced.

A sigh, more than a hundred years in the making, issued from the Prydian king like hot steam. He looked up at the avain once more and spoke his thoughts aloud. "Morlan Stormgarden," he said, "how did you know where High King Aravel's armies would be at any given moment? How did you know when they had at last pounded the Gorracks into submission? How . . . did . . . you . . . know when Aravel's armies would be at their weakest? It wasn't any of that nonsense about twin brothers intuiting each other's actions, was it?" Ealden shook his head, leaped to his feet, and began to pace the seven-sided room.

"Nor was it some latent Shepherd ability to listen to the wind. Mosteryn the Old, Sebastian Sternbough, and a few others can hear voices on the wind and perceive far away things with some accuracy, but it takes many years to develop. No, you had a hidden advantage, didn't you? A vaskerstone table, was it? Could it be that the Eye of the North came into your possession? I think that it was. But . . . you were not the thief."

The Eye of the North, Ealden thought, staring at the center of the floor where the seven channels converged. The narrow channels cut into the stone at each window and plummeted down the wall and across the floor to the center. For many ages, the great table, the Eye of the North, had stood in this place. Ealden remembered using it himself at whiles. It had shown him amazing things. The Prydian Council used the table to explore and to protect the world of Myriad. But the table had vanished. But for the Shepherds listening to the vagaries of the wind, the Prydian Council had remained blind ever since.

Ealden shook his head, remembering the pain. "Xanalos," he whispered, dropping to his knees at the altar once more. "My apprentice . . . my friend . . . you believed, you learned, and you threw it all away."

There was no asking 'why?', for Ealden knew all too well. "I pushed you too hard, and truth became a stumbling block. You could not accept it, so you fought it instead."

Though it was so long ago, Ealden's pain was still very raw. Xanalos, his student and great friend, stood accused of stealing the Eye of the North. Though the table had never been recovered, Ealden was not convinced of Xanalos's innocence. There were far too many questions, and Ealden, at last, had refused to defend Xanalos. The young Prydian had been condemned to death.

How foolish I was, Ealden remembered. *I should have seen it . . . should have realized.*

If Ealden had had a choice, he wouldn't have attended the execution, but as the Prydian King and head of the Council, it was expected. He'd stood, stoic and impassive as always, but he'd seen the grief in Xanalos's eyes. And then, just before the death blows had been dealt, Xanalos's expression changed to utter defiance. The Prydian Trivius, the three executioners, turned loose their razor sharp blades—one at Xanalos's neck, and one on each wrist. The entire judiciary had watched as his blood drained away, and Xanalos breathed his last.

So they all thought.

Xanalos had been buried in a criminal's tomb. But just days later, Ealden had discovered the tomb empty. That was when

Ealden knew that his apprentice had been much, much more than an able student with a keen mind. Xanalos was Pureline, a being born once in a dozen generations to the Great Races of Myriad. Xanalos was an immortal.

But now, I know the rest of the story, Ealden thought. *Xanalos, you fled Llanfair, even Amara, and fell into the deeper shadows of Fen. Morlan was only to happy to welcome you in. And in that dark fortress, you shed Xanalos and became Cythraul.*

Ealden closed his eyes, the enormity of the implications weighing like millstones on his back. Who could say what horrors Cythraul has inflicted for Morlan over these many years? As Pureline, he was virtually unstoppable. He would live forever, unless . . . unless someone knew the ancient lore well enough to deliver his deathblow. King Ealden knew how.

Fire. Cythraul's heart must be burned from his chest . . . burned black to ashes. There was no other way.

Tears burning down his cheeks, King Ealden stared up at the avain. "I need to warn Alastair," he whispered. "But, First One, what . . . what if there is a chance that Xanalos might repent? No one wields a sword like Alastair Coldhollow." An image flashed into the king's mind: Alastair spinning and thrusting, driving his Star Sword straight through Xanalos's heart, and then, with the fallen warrior's chest splayed open, Alastair shoved a burning brand inside . . . "No!" Ealden caught his breath. If Alastair knew how . . . if he knew the secret, he would find Xanalos, and he would kill him.

"What . . . what am I thinking? What madness is upon me?" The chamber had never seemed so silent. "No, he may have once been Xanalos, but not anymore. He is Cythraul. I cannot let Alastair face a Pureline without knowing how to defeat him." King Ealden bowed his head. "Thank you, First One, for cutting through my muddled thoughts with wisdom."

King Ealden raced out of the chamber and jogged from Jurisduro Hall across the courtyard to the aviary. "Where are the Windborne?" he demanded of the nightward.

"On errand, Sir," the ward replied. "Should be back in two hours."

Ealden did the math in his mind. *Even if I rode the swiftest horse in our stables, waiting for the Windborne would likely prove faster.* "Very well," King Ealden said. "The very first Windborne who returns, send him to my quarters."

"Yes, my lord."

Hours passed, and still the Windborne did not return. King Ealden summoned the Prydian Council and told them rather cryptically that he must travel to the western border of Llanfair to see General Alastair Coldhollow. There was a threat to the general and his family, so Ealden would lead a *caste* of thirty-three scouts to protect Coldhollow's property. It was a matter of utmost urgency, and no messenger could go in place of the king. He left his nephew Veior Moonglaive in charge of the Council, effective for the duration of the king's absence. The Council agreed with no reservations. Veior was a well known scholar with a quick wit and decisive manner. But Veior himself was uncertain.

"Uncle, are you sure you cannot speak of this?" Veior asked. "Even to me?"

"Vei," the king replied. "This is a personal matter." He lowered his voice to a whisper. "I must right a wrong I committed long ago, and only I can do it."

"By the First One's will, you mean."

Ealden looked in the mirror on the chamber wall and gave himself a withering glance. "Yes, of course, by the First One's will." He turned, but Veior grabbed the shoulder of his tunic.

"Are you certain you want me in charge?" he asked. "You might not recognize the place when you return."

That made Ealden laugh for the first time in several days. "Do what you will," King Ealden said. "I trust you. Besides, one day the throne will be yours."

23 DRINNAS 2238

"You believe me?" Abbagael asked. "You believe Cythraul's still out there?"

Alastair stood directly in front of the crackling fireplace. "I trust you, my lady," he said. "You are sincere, of that, I have no doubt. You have sensed some kind of presence. And the villain continues to haunt your dreams, so perhaps you are right." Alastair wiped strings of black hair off his brow. "I hope you are wrong. I hope he is dead. But in any case I must find out . . . I must make sure."

"This Cythraul," Uncle Jak said, "he's already survived my best hammer strike, t'say nuthin' of the fall from Anglinore Castle. Alastair, he'll be no easy quarry."

"Of all people," Alastair said, "I know it well. If he's alive, he is a dangerous, dangerous man. To attempt to track him alone would be foolish. I'm taking Telwyn with me."

"Tel?" Abbagael exclaimed. "But . . . he . . . he's just—"

"Look at him, Abbagael," Alastair said. "He's more a man at twenty-seven than most are at fifty. He's nearly my equal with a blade, and his woodcraft is better. And his . . . his unusual skills—"

"I have no doubt of Tel's abilities," she said, her voice cracking. "But what if . . . what if Cythraul . . . ah! I couldn't bear it."

"I have to do this," Telwyn said, taking Abbagael's hand. "Mi Ma, if Cythraul lives and poses a threat to you, or to any of us, I have to act. Do you understand?"

She nodded, and tears bounced off of her cheeks to the floor.

"Besides," Tel said, "Mi Da will take care of us."

"Uncle Jak will stay here with you," Alastair said. "I assume you can still swing that hammer?"

"Well enough," he replied, balling his fist and contracting the thick knot of muscle in his upper arm.

"Good," Alastair said. "I've also arranged for a little extra help around the property."

"What do you mean?" Abbagael asked.

"King Ealden is sending a caste of scouts to watch our borders."

"A whole caste?" Uncle Jak exclaimed. "That's a bit of over-kill, isn't it, now?"

"I certainly hope so," Alastair said.

"When will you go?" Abbagael's eyes still glistened.

"Before sundown," he replied.

She nodded slowly and pushed out a breath through trembling lips. "I . . . maybe you shouldn't go at all. I can live with the dreams."

Alastair embraced her. "Your words say that you can, but your eyes speak a different tale." He held her against his chest for a long time. Then, he held her at arm's length. "Pray often for us, and do not fear. For it is Cythraul now who has aught to fear."

"How will we find him?" Telwyn asked, climbing into his saddle upon his gray steed.

"We will circle our property," Alastair replied, giving his dark stallion a kick to ride up beside Tel. "Round and round and out-ward we will go until we are certain that he is not here just wait-ing for us to leave."

"Where then?"

"Then, we look for rumor of him. We look for death and mis-ery. Cythraul won't be far away."

"You mean Fen?" asked Telwyn. "Vulmarrow?"

"Yes," he replied. "And . . . in particular, the Bone Chapel."

CHAPTER 20

KEENING ON THE NAÏTHE

The folk of Keening on the Naïthe make one thing well: everything.

—Teura, Regent of Keening, (2219 - 2240)

18 SOLMONATH 2238

A mountain of flesh sat on an all but invisible stool and brought his hammer crashing down upon white hot metal. Sparks, nuggets of fire, scattered in every direction. Some landed atop Loch's boot, but he didn't flinch. Even if it burned through the thick leather and simmered on Loch's big toe, he wouldn't flinch. When Loch arrived in town, everyone he'd asked agreed: Paulkin was the Master Blacksmith in Keening.

"Lemme see yer hands, boyee," Paulkin said, dropping his hammer into a slotted shelf on the wall where it hung beside more than a dozen other hammers of various makes and sizes.

Loch held out his hands, palms up. Paulkin held his hands beneath Loch's, and the contrast couldn't have been greater. Paulkin's were massive, meaty things, thick with calluses and burn scars, and as tough as saddle leather. Loch's hands were not of the same species. Long, slender fingers, sharp knuckles, and narrow palms—Loch suddenly felt like a toddler trying on a man's heavy coat.

Paulkin grunted, turning Loch's hands this way and that. "You've got calluses, a'right," he muttered. "But most a' the thickness be swordsman not smithy." He mumbled something Loch didn't completely hear . . . some numbers, like maybe Paulkin was trying to add something and it wasn't working out.

He practically threw Loch's hands back. "So ye think ye can be a black-smiter, do ye?"

"Uh, don't you mean blacksmith, sir?" Loch instantly wished he hadn't spoken.

Paulkin's bushy black eyebrows rose, and Loch could now see the full whites of the huge man's eyes. "Listen, pup, ye might have taken a hammer up a few times. But ye won't make much, lest ye be knowin' yer history. Black-smiter's what ye' want t'be. A smiter of black metals, got it?"

"Yes, sir." Loch almost saluted, which made him smile at a most inopportune time.

"Quit smilin' like a dumpling!" Paulkin growled. He pointed a thick finger to the rear of the shop. "Get over to the forge and make such a blade as worth a month of a man's wages. Three hours, boyee!"

This time, Loch actually did salute. He grabbed his satchel and, ducking the jangling tongs and hammers hanging above, strode over to the anvil nearest the forge. The flat surface, or table, of this anvil wasn't as broad as the one Loch was used to back in Anglinore, but he thought it would do. He reached into his satchel and withdrew his leather apron. With a sharp snap, he shook it loose and then slung it over his neck. This earned Loch a look from Paulkin that was somewhere between curiosity and approval. Lock went back to his satchel and withdrew a large roll of heavy cloth. He spread it out on a nearby table and surveyed his newest set of tools: hammers—flat and ball peen, various hardies and other chisels, tongs, punches, drifts, and files. I'm ready, he thought. But three hours—that's quick.

Loch had already planned out the blade in his mind and sorted through the long pieces of iron and steel for just the right combination of metals. He found four pieces and, with blasting heat washing over his hands and forearms, he shoved them one by one into the forge. This was the hard part for Loch: waiting. Most of his three hours would be eaten up by the heating and the reheating of the metals. Depending on the temperature of the forge, it could take several minutes to warm the pieces to that beautiful orange-white glow. Loch rocked on his heels and alternately tapped his feet while blinking at the forge.

Finally, he thought the metals would be ready, and one by one, he drew them out of the forge. "Hmph, hot forge," he muttered. The metals were nearly full-on white, about a few minutes from molten. Loch would be more careful with the next heating. He went to work with the hammer next, slamming down full face blows to break loose the scales, the flakes of impurities that can threaten the integrity of a blade. Ah, this is the life, Loch thought, reveling in the work. The exertion brought a familiar pump of blood to the muscles in his arms as he pounded away.

Holstering the hammer in one of the slots on the anvil, Loch grabbed a wire brush as thick as a hedgehog. He tore into each piece of metal, scouring until every last flake was gone. Then, it was back to the forge for the metals . . . and more dreadful waiting. He sighed, growled, and tapped his feet some more. He pulled out the metal, hammered each strip—side, side, side, then on the flat. He saved himself some time by drawing out the metal, thinning and lengthening it, even as he pounded the scales free. He plunged the strips of metal into the water barrel and laughed at the satisfying hiss of steam. Now, he shoved the other end of the metal into the forge and repeated the process.

Once he was convinced that he'd broken the metal of its largest impurities, he heated them once more. Then, he looked about for the flux. He found a covered barrel of sand, shrugged, and grabbed up a handful. This time, when the metals came out, he sprinkled each strip with sand and then stacked them one atop the other and carefully mated the edges. He gave the stacked metals a few light strokes of the hammer and then, thrust it into the forge.

"Almost done?" Paulkin asked. The sweat running down the center of Loch's back turned icy cold until he heard Paulkin's rumbly laugh and realized that the big man had been teasing.

Loch withdrew the stack of metals and began pounding it for all he was worth. He started slamming the hammer onto the center to start the weld and then pummeled outward. As the strips of metal were joined and compressed, all the tiniest bits of scale were squeezed out until nothing but the purest combination of metals remained.

After another trip to the forge, the real crafting began. Loch was a whirl with the hammers and chisels, banging away until the tang was long and round and about as thick as a finger—Loch's not Paulkin's. Later, he'd slip the tang into the wooden grip, wrap it in cords of heavy twine, and then cap it with a sturdy pommel. Back to the forge, again and again, he went. Sparks flew, and soon, a long, wickedly sharp blade took shape.

By this time, Paulkin had ambled over to watch Loch work. He didn't say anything, but grunted and mumbled continuously. Loch tried not to be too conscious of the big man standing there, lest it affect his craft. But it was hard. Loch kept expecting Paulkin to slap him in the back of the neck and bellow, "NO NO NO, that's not how it's done, boyee! Get away from that anvil!" But he never said any such thing. Only grumbles and mutters.

Finally, after all the filing and grinding, the blade had a keen edge on both sides. Loch slid the cross guard onto the tang, then the wooden grip, and last the pommel. He tested the weight of the weapon, decided he didn't like it much, and replaced the pommel with a heavier piece. Convinced the sword was as balanced as he could get it, Loch turned around and found Paulkin standing right next to him. And he did not look happy.

"What ya think yer doin' here, boyee?" he demanded. "Slake put you up to this, did he?"

Loch blinked. "Wuh-what?"

Paulkin snatched the sword from Loch's hands. "Think yer wise, then? Funnin' old Paulkin in his own shop?"

"I . . . I don't understand," Loch said. "Is there something wrong with the sword?"

Paulkin shifted his jaw six inches to the right and spoke out of the corner of his mouth. "That's just it, ye bloomin' scammer. This here sword is almost—almost, mind ye—better than one of me own. C'mon now, out with it. Who put ye up to this?"

"N-no one," Loch answered.

"Ye forge-welded wrought iron and three kinds of steel, and ye had the arm strength to flatten it, draw it out like this? It was Slake, weren't it?"

"No, sir," Loch said. "I learned my craft in Anglinore." That much was true. "I'm just looking for a little work before I'm on my way."

Paulkin looked Loch up and down and back at the sword. He frowned and narrowed his eyes. But then, a little grin formed. Then it widened until it consumed the bottom half of his face. And Paulkin laughed so hard that every part of his body bounced. "Well," he said, "heh, heh, heh, what's yer name lad?"

Loch hesitated. *Ah, why don't I think of these things ahead of time?* Then, not knowing what else to do, he said, "Lochlan." His mind spun rapidly. "Lochlan . . . Wandermill." *Wandermill? Really, Lochlan, that's the best you can do?*

"Well, Lochlan Wandermill, ye've come to the right shop in Keening." Paulkin patted Loch on the back. He pointed back to the forge. "We've got a long day's work ahead. Three more blades like this one to start. Come nightfall, we'll sup at the Brickstore and discuss yer terms."

"The Brickstore?"

"Best tavern in Keening, lad," Paulkin said. "And Matilda's there. Food ye wouldn't believe. And after, the place'll be ripe fer a game a darts if ye fancy it."

Loch nodded repeatedly. *Just like that,* he thought. *I'm one of them. Why didn't I think of this years ago?* A smile on his face and a spring in his step, Loch went back to the forge.

L och pushed his bowl toward the center of the table and fought the urge to release the gargantuan burp that was inflating in his chest. Wait, he thought. I'm in a local tavern, not the royal dining chamber. So, with great trepidation, he turned it loose.

Paulkin and everyone else at the table stopped talking and stared. Most of the townies at the bar turned as well. In fact, the minstrels lowered their lutes and fiddles and looked for the source of the explosion.

A split-second later, the room erupted in cheers. Paulkin whacked Loch on the back. Complete and total strangers nodded at him with approval. A stunning blond Elladorian woman, her feathery hair in pigtails so long that they lay down her shoulders and across her chest, gave Lochlan a smile of such blinding beauty that he had to turn away. His cheeks had already been reddening from embarrassment. Now, they flushed for other reasons.

"Now that, lad, was done with relish!" Paulkin said, whacking Loch on the back again. "Ye fancied Matilda's stew, ye did."

Loch looked at the remnants in his bowl. He'd eaten all the beef, but a few boulder-sized hunks of potato, chunks of carrot, and slivers of onion remained. "Beyond delectable," he said. "It was somehow . . . just perfect after such a day of work as today. Wholesome, savory, and filling." Loch patted his stomach. He couldn't fathom attempting another bite. If I did, there really would be an explosion. "I'd like to thank Matilda. Where is she?"

"Ah, no," Paulkin said. "Ye won't be seein' her 'til the last meal is cooked. Dedicated to her craft, she is."

An Elladorian friend of Paulkin's named Alun Bryce returned to their table with two fistfuls of tankards. Without a word, he slid a mug to Lochlan and each of the others. No one said thank you, and Alun smiled all the way back to his chair. He hadn't been looking for thanks. It was expected. That's what friends did.

Loch sipped his mug thoughtfully. Paulkin and the others fell into a thousand conversations: future hunts, the gardens, local mysteries, and the such. Wives and children dominated the discussions. And while there were just men at his table, Loch noted that their were plenty of women and children scattered around the pub. It really was a public house in the truest sense, Loch thought. As he listened, he heard proud fathers raving about their undoubtedly precocious children and husbands speaking lovingly about their wives. Well, mostly, Loch thought. That Cadmon fellow seemed a little vexed about his bride. Something about moving the furniture around his cottage for the eighteenth time—this week.

Lochlan scanned the room and drank it all in. A cozy fire burning at either end of the room; warm, golden light from hanging oil lanterns washing over many glad faces—these were exhausted, hard-working people in great need of washing and bed. And yet, here they were rubbing elbows with other sweaty, dirty folk just like themselves. It was a curious, amazing sight. Lochlan wondered at how they seemed to just want to be together. They were sharing life.

For Loch, it was a kind of nourishment he'd never had consistently in Anglinore. Not that their weren't good folk in the capital city. There were, and plenty of them. But Loch spent such precious little time with them that he'd become too accustomed to politics, private ambitions, and self-seeking personal agendas. But not now. Now in the back corner of the Brickstore, in the heart of Keening on the Naïthe, Loch felt himself content, filling up on shared experience and kinship.

"Unhand me, ruffians!" yowled a gruff voice from the other side of the room.

So much for kinship, thought Loch as he stood for a better look. Three stout men and a woman with upper arm muscle as big as her male counterparts were escorting a spindly looking man toward the door. He wore a black, hooded cloak, but the cloak was thrown back and his greasy hair tossed as he turned his head this way and that. The poor guy thrashed about as if he thought he had a prayer of escape. He didn't.

"Leave me be!" he shouted. "I . . . am . . . ungh . . . a paying customer . . . just like the lot!"

His escorts paid him no head and rushed him inexorably toward the front of the tavern. One of the nearby patrons opened the door, and the man flew bodily out into the night. "Don't come back!" yelled the strong maiden, wiping her hands on each other dismissively.

"That," Paulkin said, "is Matilda."

Loch watched her stride purposefully to the back of the tavern. She disappeared into a door at the far side of the fireplace. "What was that all about?" Loch asked as he took his seat.

"Witchdrale, no doubt," Alun Bryce said with a snort. "And good riddance."

Paulkin clinked tankards with Alun Bryce and said, "They ought t'know better by now not to mess with Matilda's place. She lost 'er father to that wicked ale."

A thought of Alastair blinked in Loch's mind. How long had Witchdrale held Alastair captive? Loch couldn't remember. And how did he ever get free of it? Loch couldn't remember that either. He suspected it was the virtues of Lady Abbagael that had turned the man back. Though, from what Lochlan had learned of Witchdrale, it was diabolically hard to leave it behind.

"If he knows what's good fer 'im," Alun Bryce said, "he'll get on his horse and ride far away from here. If I know Matilda, she'll go out lookin' fer 'im after she shuts down the Brick."

Paulkin laughed mischievously. A few quiet moments passed, and then Paulkin looked up from the table sharply. "Ah, ye' ready, Lochlan?"

"Uh . . . for what?"

"Darts, lad," he replied. "A board just opened up."

Because of his size, Paulkin wasn't as mobile as some, but he could throw a mean game of darts. He stood exactly nine feet, seven inches from the board—the Elladorian standard—and lined up his shot. He had good form, Loch thought. For the most part. Like most so-called experts, Paulkin kept his elbow too still. General Adelbard had taught Loch better than that.

Paulkin's forearm levered forward. The dart flew on a gentle arc and plunged into the blue slot inside the third ring. "Ha!" he crowed. "That closes out the 20's! Lessee ye' catch me now."

Loch took his place on the line. They'd been playing a round of "Plunder," a favorite of the locals and, fortunately for Loch, a variation of the game "Treble" that he'd played since he was a kid. Paulkin's recent throw had indeed made things difficult for Loch. To best Paulkin, Loch knew he'd need two outer purple 15's and then the last gold 21. Tiny targets to be sure. But Loch felt good, especially since a crowd had gathered to watch. Paulkin was something of a dart-throwing legend in Keening, it seemed. Not tonight, Loch thought.

He lined everything up, his eye, the dart, the purple 15 space. His body perfectly still, Loch's hand flew forward. His elbow rose a few inches, even as he flipped his wrist and followed through toward the target. Thump. His dart skewered the purple 15, dead center. A perfect shot. And the patrons of the Brickstore knew it well. They cheered, hooted and hollered. Several lads— and lasses—gave Paulkin a friendly ribbing.

"He's gonna take ye!" one man said.

"What's this?" asked a man whose hair looked like a thatch of straw. "Yer not gonna let this here calf put ye off, are ye, Paulkin."

The big man grumbled a few things and stared at the dart board.

The blond Elladorian in pigtails put a gentle hand on his shoulder and said, "Don't ye, worry, Paulkin. He's good, but he's not Paulkin-good."

Paulkin-good? Loch thought. What about Lochlan-good? He lined up for the second shot, a simple matter of repeating the same mechanic along the same trajectory. The elbow move really was the secret. Loch knew it was counterintuitive. Everyone reasoned, the fewer moving parts, the simpler the shot. But not so with the elbow. Keeping the elbow fixed forces too early a release. It had to come up just a little to allow the perfect release and the most accurate path of flight. He glanced at Paulkin and then zeroed in on the target once more. He let fly, and the dart followed its intended course. Thump. Loch closed off the purple 15's.

More cheers, more ribbing, more anxious glances. Loch noted that the minstrels had stopped playing, and everyone, who could be seen by fire or lantern light, had turned to watch the match unfold. Loch took a deep breath and exhaled at almost the precise time that Paulkin had. He looked at the big man sitting on the bench a few strides away. Sweat trickled down his forehead and stained his tunic. The man looked stiff with . . . fear?

But it's just a game, Loch thought. He turned back to the dartboard. The gold 21 was no easy shot. Paulkin and he had each hit it once earlier in the game. His hit had been an accident. He'd been aiming to close out the blue 25, rocked forward on his toes a little, and fired low. He thought sure Paulkin's 21 had been a happy miss as well. But now, he had to hit it. It was everything, the last space on the board worth enough points to beat Paulkin. He took careful aim, brought the dart back nearly to his chin, and—

Everything. The thought hit a sour note. It's not just a game, not to Paulkin. Loch closed his eyes, internally blasting himself for the colossal mistake he had been about to make. Here I am, just washed into town . . . a stranger . . . an upstart youngling. Paulkin's been here his entire life. This place . . . this tavern even . . . is a huge part of who Paulkin is. Lochlan considered the man's size. Sure, most of that may have been his own fault. Loch had seen Paulkin put away three times Loch's portion of stew and still have room for pie. Nonetheless, Paulkin seemed a good man. Good enough to hire a drifter out of the wild, pay him a decent wage, and give him a seat at his table.

Loch rolled the dart between his thumb and forefinger. Idiot, he called himself. There probably aren't too many things Paulkin can call himself champion of, and here I am about to take one of those away. Loch knew what he had to do.

He renewed his aim. And as he released the dart, he kept his elbow perfectly still. His shot followed a beautiful arc and settled dead center of the gold . . . the gold 9, that is. The room erupted. Paulkin . . . their champion, had won.

"**W**here ye stayin' the night?" Paulkin asked, as they left the Brickstore behind them and meandered the cobblestone.

Loch shrugged. "Figured I'd find an inn. Turns out Brickstore's just a tavern or I'd have gladly stayed there."

Paulkin laughed, his eyes gleaming in the falling moon's light. "Matilda's been talking fer years about expanding. Guess it'll come when she's ready. Stars, but she's a good cook."

"True."

"She opens early fer breakfast," Paulkin said, scratching one hemisphere of his belly. "Garlic sausage . . . worth every pence."

"I'm sure it is," Loch said. "So . . . can you recommend a decent inn?"

Paulkin nodded. "I know just the place fer a pup like you."

They walked along in amiable silence, passing the doors of many a quaint home. A hanging sign protruded on the right. Marley's Inn it read. "This the place?" asked Loch.

"Nah, no," Paulkin replied. "Marley's a decent man, but truth be told, his wife does all the work 'round there. I don't support lazy, and I sure as Stars don't support a man what takes advantage of the woman he's been blessed with."

"What about you?" Loch asked.

"Unh?"

"A woman?" Loch slowed his pace a bit. "Alun Bryce, the others, they were talking constantly about family. You didn't say anything about your own—though you did seem to know a great deal about the others."

"Ah," he said and shrugged. "I think I'm meant to be everyone's uncle, heh."

"Oh c'mon, Paulkin. What about that pretty blond Elladorian, the one with the pigtails? She was definitely in your corner."

A careful smile spread in his ocean of stubble. "You mean Rhian, she's sweet."

"What's that mean?" Loch laughed. "Sweet's all the better. And she's quite the beauty."

"Heh, heh, yeah, well that's the problem." He stared at the road. "Woman like that . . . she won't settle fer such as me. She's Elladorian, case ye missed it."

"No," Loch said. "That'd be hard to miss. She's as close to Queen Briawynn as I've ever seen."

Paulkin stopped walking. "The queen? You've seen her? Up close?"

Lochlan mentally slapped himself with tree trunk. "I, uh . . . was in the crowd at the Ceremony of Crowns. I had a pretty good view of her when she sang the Invocation."

"Lucky dog," Paulkin said. He started walking again. Then he whispered, "Still, I'd wager Rhian's got her beat. I don't go in much for royal folk. Noses too high in the air."

Loch caught that blow just below his ribs. "Kings and queens, yeah, they can be royal pains."

Paulkin laughed. He turned down an alley, and Loch followed, recognizing the buildings somewhat. They ducked between a few buildings and emerged at a fenced-in stable. Chalaren was there, drinking quietly from the trough.

"Welcome to the inn!" Paulkin announced.

"You want me to sleep in a stable?"

"No, ye idjit." He boxed Loch on the ear.

"Ow!" Loch protested. Men have been beheaded for less.

"Serves ye, right. As if I might have ye sleep in the hay—the very notion!" Paulkin shook his head and waddled in front of Loch. He went round the corner of his smithy shop to the little cottage a few yards away. He opened the door and strode inside. Loch followed and came in just as Paulkin turned up a few oil lamps.

"It's gettin' late," Paulkin said. "And there's work t'be done in the mornin'." He gestured into the adjoining room. "That couch is just shy of a cloud in Allhaven. There are blankets in the box there." He stepped up on the stair. "I'd uh . . . give ye the bed, but it's . . . well, it's the only thing big enough . . ." He didn't finish the thought.

Loch knew what he'd meant. Poor guy, he thought as he dropped to the couch. "Good for me," he said. "Paulkin, thanks."

Paulkin nodded, climbed a few creaky steps, and stopped. "I know what ye' did."

Loch's blood froze. He hadn't been careful enough around Paulkin. Too many slips of the tongue. "I can explain."

"No need." Paulkin held up his hand. "I saw yer form. Ye didn't move yer elbow on that last throw. But ye had on all the others. You missed that shot a'purpose."

Loch sighed. "I'm sorry."

"Sorry, lad?" Paulkin made a growling noise. "No, I know why ye did it. And . . . thanks. But next time, give me yer best game. I think I'll try that elbow move that ye' do. How long ye' gonna be in town?"

Loch reclined on the couch. "A week."

"A week, huh. Well, I best get all the work outta ye' as I can."

Loch smiled and lay his head down on the armrest. I sure hope so.

CHAPTER 21

STOWAWAYS

"They all said the old coot was mad. Mountains don't just walk away. But Haban Zook just kept quoting that old Canticles verse about a faith that could move mountains."

—From Greenshire Tales, Hans Fablemeister

8 SOLMAS 2238

An especially harsh bump jolted Meli out of sleep. She might have nodded off again, but seconds later, the wagon jounced even harder. Meli was thrown a foot into the air, came down, and bonked her head on the edge of a barrel.

"That's it!" Meli growled. "Tango! Tango!" She stared at her brother who was still sleeping soundly. She had half a mind to flick his ear. *Probably still wouldn't wake him,* she thought. "Guess I'll have t'tell the Stonehands myself."

None of the trip from the mountains had been exactly smooth and comfortable. Days and nights had gone by in a dizzying blur of strange lands, strange villages, and even stranger peoples. But at least there had been trails and roads. Now it seemed the Stonehands were cutting across country. A country made mostly of jagged rock, apparently.

The wagon rolled along now at a pretty good clip, and Meli found the nine-foot crawl to the front to be extremely challenging. Bounced, bumped, and tossed, she clambered as well as she could, building up a nice, steaming fit of rage to expel at the Stonehands. She toppled over onto her back, growled, and righted herself. Then she rolled down a slope of grain bags and wedged herself between two crates.

"Cruel," Osi said, but he laughed through the word. "Gorracks eating them like toastcorn!"

"What caring you fer that, then?" asked the other. "Gold's always right. Hu-huck, hu-huck!"

Meli started to interrupt, but felt her own giggles bubble up inside. These red ribbon Stonehands or whatever they called themselves sure had a funny laugh.

"They will fetching good price in Fen anywho." It sounded like Osi smacked the other Stonehand's shoulder. "Kurda Bostwich liking the younger ones. Good for breaking, breaking, slave making! Huck-hoo-huck!"

Meli froze. The wheels in her mind spun faster than the wagon wheels. She bounced to the rear of the wagon but went too far. She skipped off of a barrel and scraped half way across the tailgate before clawing at Tango's leg.

"Ahhh!" Tango screamed. "Wha-owww! What's goin' on? Leggo, let go!"

"I can'na let go, Tango! Help me!"

Tango woke fully at last, saw his sister sliding over the gate. He curled like a pill bug and lunged for her, snagging her hand just before she would have been gone. Tango moved fast, scrambled to grab her other hand, and then hauled her back on board the wagon. "Tha' was close, Meli. What were ya doin?"

"Just tryin' t'get to you. I'm sorry about the blood. But I had to tell—"

"Near cut my leg t'ribbons," he complained, rubbing his calve. "What's this about, then?"

She told him about the Stonehands troubling conversation. Tango growled. "To think I gave 'em the hatchet! Slaves, is it? No, Meli, not for us."

"What'll we do?"

Tango thought for several moments, staring out of the wagon at the shadowy predawn world. Meli couldn't tell if he was nodding or if it was just the jounce of the wagon on the terrain. "What are ya thinkin'?"

He blinked. "I'm not much fer plannin'," he said. "But seems to me we've got to be gettin' close to wherever this Fen place is. How many days is it now? Eight? Ten?"

"Yeah, so?"

"So, we don'na have much time to get free of these scoundrels." He stole a glance at the front of the wagon. "Next time we stop, we make a run for it."

"Run? Run where?"

"I dunno, Meli. Most a' these villages have had other wagons comin' and goin'. Maybe we can duck into one of those before the Stonehands are any the wiser."

"Maybe," Meli whispered. "But we might be jumpin' from the fry pan into the fire."

"Anything's got to be better than slavery," Tango muttered. "Besides we're littlins, right? One thing littlins can do well is hide."

12 SOLMAS 2238

The next stop came just after sun up. It didn't look like a village at all. Tango thought it might be some rich baron's manor house. The stone edifice was tall and narrow with lots of windows and a steepled kind of roof. A castle turret stood on either side and each was topped with a pointed conical cap of dark shingles. Tango swallowed. The place looked ominous . . . haunted even.

"You'ins staying in the wagon," Osi grumbled, appearing suddenly at the back of the wagon and startling Tango and Meli. "Short stop this time to paying a visit."

When the Stonehand joined a group of robed men about forty yards from the wagon, Tango said, "Did ya see that, Meli?"

"What?"

"He did'na have the hatchet with him."

"So."

"Ah, you are a dense one, aren't ya?" Tango mussed her hair. "Means he left it up front. Probably doesn't want any of these others to see it. Just as greedy as he is, I bet. C'mon."

Meli held back the canvas flap. "There's only three other wagons here. Which one?"

"The one farthest away from that wicked old house," Tango said, smiling inwardly. It made a kind of sense that the wagon farthest away would be the first one to leave.

Keeping their eyes riveted to Osi, the Spriggans eased over the tailgate and slithered around to the side of the wagon. It was maybe thirty paces to the other wagon, but it was open ground. Not so much as a bush to hide behind.

"What doing is Osi?" asked one of the Stonehands dropping to the ground from the front.

Tango dragged Meli beneath the wagon, and they cowered behind the front wheel.

"Can't saying for certain," the third Stonehand said. "Buying Witchdrale is my guess. He will keeping it all to his self too."

"No he won't," said the other. "I will getting some too."

The pair of Stonehands wandered by the wagon wheel without so much as a glance at the Spriggans crouching there. "Now," whispered Tango. He led his sister in a kind of rapid crabwalk to the other wagon. It was a little higher from the ground than the Stonehand wagon, so Tango and Meli slipped easily underneath. Once more, they found refuge behind the spokes of a wagon's wheel.

Meli started to say something, but Tango put his fingers to her lips. They heard voices near the front of the wagon, a woman and probably a man, though his voice was high and scratchy.

"... not interested," she said. "The salt-venison, and I'll be on my way."

"You won't find a better vintage," said the man. Tango thought he sounded very old, or maybe ill. The man chuckled, a creepy rasping kind of laugh. "You won't find any vintage, once you cross into Ellador."

"Good," the woman said. "I don't want any vintage of that poison. Just the meat. Thank you."

The Spriggans heard the clink of coins changing hands. The wagon rocked a little above them.

"She's gettin' ready to leave," Tango whispered. "Now for it."

They shot out from under the wagon and found the tailgate too high for an easy climb. Just then, the wagon lurched forward. "Hurry, Meli, up on my shoulders."

Tango bent at the waist. His sister bounced up upon him and came to a wobbly stand. Tango waddled forward after the wagon. "Jump in, and then pull me up!"

Meli obeyed, leaping from her brother's shoulders. She landed awkwardly, almost sideways, on the tailgate. She coughed out a cry and then stuck out her arms for her brother.

"H'ya!" came the woman's voice. The crack of a whip. The wagon began to pick up speed. Tango raced after it, leaped up, and grabbed Meli's forearms. She started to swing him, to pull him up. But then, suddenly, he let go and dropped to the ground.

"Tango, what are ya doin'?" Meli whisper-shouted.

But Tango didn't answer. He raced away, and Meli finally understood. The woman's wagon was crossing directly in front of the Stonehand's wagon. The hatchet. It had to be. Meli swallowed. The wagon she was in was picking up speed. If he didn't hurry, he'd never make it back.

Meli watched Tango clamber up into the driver's seat of the Stonehand's wagon. He rooted around frantically. Meli's stomach nearly tied itself in a knot.

The Stonehands were coming back to their wagon.

They lumbered along the left side of the wagon and were almost to the driver's seat. Tango didn't seem to see them, but somehow, he leaped down the other side a split second before they clambered up. He sprinted toward Meli, but the horses drawing the woman's wagon were hitting their stride, and Tango was falling behind. "Come on," she whispered urgently. She wanted to yell but couldn't risk alerting the driver or anyone else who might be at the front of the wagon.

"Come on, Tango," she said again. *What was wrong with him?* He was usually much faster—reckoned speedy even among the fleet-footed Spriggans. The wagon came out of a slight turn and, now that it was headed virtually straight, accelerated rapidly. Tango seemed to be fiddling with something as he ran, but when he looked up, his eyes went wide. He started pumping his arms and blasted up the road, closing the distance rapidly.

"That's it, Tango," Meli whispered. "C'mon." He was getting close, but seemed to have no more acceleration. He huffed and panted, trying to coax more speed out of his legs, but instead, the wagon moved a little more out of reach. Meli hung her arms over the tailgate. "Grab my arms!" she urged.

What're ya doin', Tango? Meli wondered. He wore the oddest frown and seemed to be trying to wave her off. Just then, Tango thrust down his legs and lunged for the wagon. Meli had her arms outstretched for him, but caught just the slightest glint of metal. She drew her hands back in just as Tango's hatchet bit into the tailgate. It held the wood, and Tango held onto the handle for dear life. Meli was there in a heartbeat, helping Tango clamber up. He collapsed on his back in the bottom of the wagon.

"I . . . I got the hatchet," he panted. He held it up to show her but cut the seam of a sack. A cloud of flour spilled out, making Tango look very much like a ghost. A laughing ghost.

18 Solmas 2238

"What 'ave we here?" a deep womanly voice asked. "A stowaway?"

Uh oh, thought Tango, snapping awake.

"Two stowaways, looks like," the woman said. "Grindle, fetch my blade!"

Double uh, oh. Tango sat bolt upright to face a woman standing at the back of the wagon. "I can explain."

"I am sure you can explain," she said, as an enormous shadow appeared behind her. "Stowaways are usually good with stories." She turned and received a sheath about ten inches long from which she drew a dagger with a thin, oddly curved blade.

Tango thought it looked like a boning knife. *Triple uh, oh with a twist.* Tango readied his hatchet but he wasn't fast enough. The dagger flashed, and Tango felt a fine misting spray across his cheek and chin . . .

. . . And two halves of a nerfa gourd fell into his lap.

"Eat up, youngling," said the woman. "Wake your girlfriend and give her some." She laughed and strode around the side of the wagon.

"She's my sister!" Tango grumbled. But the massive shadow was still there.

Tango stared up and felt dizzy. A huge, barrel-chested man stood there, gazing down a beakish nose with fierce, thundercloud-gray eyes. He crossed thick arms across his chest, and something spread out behind him . . . like wings. Tango nearly choked on a swallow of gourd pulp. "You . . . you've got wings!"

"Very observant," said the winged man, his laugh a canyon roll of thunder. He grabbed a huge crate from the back of the wagon.

Meli woke up. And screamed.

"Meli, no! Shhhh!" Tango put an arm around her. "It's okay. They're . . . they're friends. I think."

The winged man strode away laughing. Tango leaned out of the wagon, watching the man until he disappeared from view. And what a view it was. A fiery sunset sky burned behind a horseshoe shaped town. Gables, steeples, arches, turrets, and parapets curled up one side and down the other of the bustling marketplace. Street lamps glowed, and here and there, people with long poles were lighting more. People wheeled carts hither and thither, and smoke curled into the sky from open kettle grills. Savory aromas of roasted meat wafted beneath Tango's nose.

"Where are we?" Meli asked.

"Dunno, Meli," he replied, handing her the other half of the gourd. "Let's find out." He vaulted over the tailgate and landed in the road with a dusty flourish. Meli followed, slurping noisily on the gourd.

The woman appeared beside them. She was tall, all ropey muscle beneath a leather vest and a dark blue tunic. Tango couldn't help but notice she was quite pretty. Raven-black hair, dark brows that were thick but didn't look manly at all, and clever eyes of deep, midnight blue. She held out a hand, and Tango gladly shook it, feeling a nervous tingle as he did so.

"Well my little stowaways," she said, "I am Clarisse Graymane, treasure-hunter, explorer, and all around sojourner of this great land. And who might you be?"

Tango looked sheepishly to Meli and back. He shrugged. What could it hurt? "I'm Tanneth Goliant. My friends call me Tango. And this is my sister, Meli."

"Sister?" The woman raised both eyebrows. "Oh, I misspoke, didn't I? Goliant, eh? Can't say I recognize the name. Can't say I recognize the breed either. You're little, but not quite as children of my kind are little."

"We're Spriggans," Meli said. "We don't get much bigger than Tango."

"Ah," Clarisse Graymane replied. "Love it! How long have I been traveling in this world, and yet I've not met your kind before."

"That's because—"

Tango cut Meli off. "Please Lady Graymane, can'na you tell us where we are?"

"Why, you're in the town of Ravensgate on the western border of Ellador."

"Ellador," Tango enchoed. "The Stonehands mentioned that."

"Stonehands," Clarisse Graymane muttered. "Ah, so things become a little more clear now. You were there at Krickhallow in Fen, weren't you?"

"I don'na rightly know," Tango said. "But the Stonehands were gonna make slaves of us. We escaped their wagon . . . and, uh . . ."

"Stowed away in ours," she finished. "That was fortunate for you." She laughed and clapped the winged man on the shoulder as he went to the wagon for another crate. "Ah, and this muscular fellow is Grindle Freeman. As fine a Windborne as you'll ever meet."

He bowed slightly. "Flattery, bah!"

"You've traveled with us for near one hundred leagues," Clarisse said. "Now you must earn your keep—not to mention making recompense for the flour you spilled all over." She gestured to the back of the wagon. "We need to unload. Take any of the sacks and crates you can carry and bring them in there." She pointed around the wagon to a many-windowed building with a lazy, sloping roof and an arched doorway big enough for ten Spriggans to walk through side-by-side.

Tango went to work at once, grabbing a crate a little too big for him and waddling toward the building.

"Show off," Meli whispered from behind. "You're smitten, you are."

"Am not," growled Tango. "Just tryin' t'help. That's all."

"Right, Tango. Right."

Tango struggled a moment and adjusted his grip on the crate. He continued on, noticing a heavy wooden sign hanging down from a black wrought iron hook. The sign swayed slightly in the whispering breeze. "The Venture Inn," Tango muttered before he disappeared beneath the sign and entered the building.

Inside, he found a network of catacombs and roundish chambers filled with tables. He waddled quickly to a table and started to put down his load.

"Ah, not there, lad!" came a disembodied female voice. "That there's for the customers that'll be swarmin' in soonish. Put the crate back here in the kitchen."

Tango didn't see anyone, but a light shone out from a door behind a tall counter. *How'd she know I had a crate?* Tango wondered as he made his way behind the bar. *How'd she know where I was gon'na put it? For all that, how'd she know I was a lad?*

"Ah, there's a good lad," said a woman, bent over and very focused on the contents of a great oak chest. "On the floor there by the others."

Tango was glad to put his load down. His arms burned; something in his back throbbed; and his fingers cramped from clamping onto the bottom of the heavy crate.

Meli came in behind Tango. "Where do I put this sack of—"

"Rice, hon," said the woman, still completely bent over. "In the pantry to yer left. Rice bags in back right corner, if ye please."

Meli dutifully disappeared into the pantry. Before she returned, the woman stood up and turned around at last. "Ah, there he is, then," she said, a broad white smile gleaming out from full rosy cheeks. She bustled over to Tango and, before he could protest, she tied a well-used, many-pocketed apron around his waist.

"I . . . uh . . . but . . . ?" Tango barely uttered a few more stupefied mumbles as he watched the woman snare Meli with a similar apron.

"Uh . . . thank you?" Meli couldn't manage any better.

"No, thank you, dears!" the woman said. She was roughly pear shaped. Her hair was silky gray and tied up in a three-tiered bun. Crisp blue eyes gazed out from behind spectacles that threatened to slide down her bulbous nose. "You couldn't have come at a better time, really. Shorthanded, I am, and on the eve of the Tradegather too."

Tango blinked. "But . . ."

"Now, now, don't ye worry about a thing," the woman said, patting the two Spriggans on the head. "Learn on the job . . . least ways, ye better!"

Meli whirled in her apron. "I like it," she said. "But . . ."

"Oh, where are me manners, my dears? I'm Matron Tess, and I'm the sole proprietor of the Venture Inn. You can call me Matron or Tess or Mattie or Miss Tess or—"

"I like Mattie," Meli said. "But, uh what are we—"

"Time's a wastin' me Spri—me dearies." She scuttled into the pantry. "There's a pair of great pails behind the counter. Fill 'em with water from the well out back. Then, there's a heap a' mugs from supper that need washin'."

Tango took a tentative step toward the pantry. "But, Matron, we did'na come here for wor—"

"Room and board, of course," Matron Tess said. "And a few coppers to keep yer sweet tooth happy. More if ye do good work. Now, fetch the pails."

Tango and Meli fetched the pails.

CHAPTER 22

NEW LIFE

*"And behold, the Caller must fade for my Halfainin to rise.
Under the chilling moon, a single bright star will fall from the sky."*

—From Canticles (IX.ii), Barde Fane (r. 846 AO)

27 SOLMONATH 2238

Sebastian sat in silence as long as he could. He drummed his fingers on his desk and thought, *How ironic. I am High Shepherd, leader of an order known for keeping secrets, defying the curiosity of outsiders for ages. And I cannot bear the suspense myself! So be it.* "Lochlan Stormgarden, if you don't tell us this moment . . . I'll . . . I'll command poison ivy plants to root themselves beneath your bedspread."

Loch frowned. "You can do that?"

Queen Maren stifled a laugh.

"Believe it," Sebastian said, grabbing his gnarled staff from the corner.

"Okay, okay!" Loch stood up and paced to the window. He turned around, gesturing wildly. "It was . . . it was . . . magnificent!

That falls far short. Ah, how do I describe it? I met so many good people—Paulkin, Alun Bryce, Rhian, and Matilda." Lochlan's eyes grew misty. "Mother, it was . . . life giving."

"You are life giving, my son," she said. "To see you so happy, so animated . . . it makes me glad."

"You must tell us more," Sebastian said. "Who are these people? What trade did you perform?"

"Yes, Loch, especially about Rhian and Matilda. Don't, uh—" Queen Maren cleared her throat, "Leave out any detail."

So Loch told them all that he could remember. When he finished, the moon was high, and the candles in Sebastian's tower chamber had burned low. "Whew," Loch said. "I am exhausted from just the retelling in brief. My mind swims in the memories, and I already miss my new friends."

"You plan to go errant again, then?" Sebastian asked.

Loch made a sour face. "Of course I want to go errant again. Uh . . . so long as the kingdom can spare me. Not right away, of course. I understand that."

"I have already explored that possibility," Sebastian said. "I believe you could get away as soon as the end of Avrill."

"Really?" Loch looked to his mother. She nodded.

"Will you go back to Keening?" she asked.

Loch looked pained. "As much as I would like to go back . . . I don't think I can. Not yet. I think I'll go a little farther out. Amara, maybe."

"Not near Llanfair," Sebastian cautioned. "King Ealden and his folk would know you right away. He probably has your portrait hanging in Jurisduro Hall."

Loch shook his head. "No, you're right. Maybe just Bright-castle, then. Or . . . I've always wanted to visit the Stormsheer Mountains."

"What?" Maren exclaimed.

"Not the Gorrack side, mother," Loch said, laughing. "I like adventure, but not that much adventure. I was thinking, perhaps,

Silverglen—oh, and the Crimson Way—Sebastian, you once told me that every king of Myriad should walk that path."

"And every king should," Sebastian replied. "Like venturing into the Felhaunt, there is much to be learned from that sober journey. Maren, have you been?"

"The Crimson Way?" Her expression tightened. "Once . . . long ago. I will never forget . . . I don't think."

"It's settled then," Loch said. "Unless something comes up and Myriad needs me on the throne, I will plan to depart for the Stormsheer Mountains in one month's time."

"Ah, there is one more matter," Sebastian said.

Queen Maren sighed, crossed her arms, and glared at the chamber window.

"What?" Loch asked.

"Your cousin, Baron Cardiff," Sebastian said, "He was here in Anglinore almost as soon as you left."

Lochlan suddenly remembered the eleven-horse-team drawing his cousin's coach. "Is that a concern?" Loch asked, trying to sound brave, but feeling rather nervous about the answer to come.

"Baron Cardiff Strengle is always a concern . . . when he smells power," Sebastian said. "He spent half of his time here mucking about the castle looking for you. He was quite like a bloodhound . . . very difficult to divert."

"The other half of his time," Maren chimed in, "he spent in the vaults, specifically in the archives."

Loch frowned. "What of it?" he asked. "Perhaps he did overhear us that night we found him outside this very chamber. Maybe he knows I went errant. He could spread word of it and ruin my future trips, I suppose. But that is damage only to me."

"Damage to the throne, my son," Maren said. "You are well-loved in Myriad and especially in this city, but there are those in all places who deem you too young to wield such power. To learn that you have vacated the throne to seek your own pleasures, might give those grumblers enough voice to gain followers."

Loch scratched at the whiskers on his jawline. Cardiff might indeed do such a thing.

"There is also something more serious," Sebastian explained. "Among the statutes, laws, and policies of Anglinore from ancient times, few decrees have survived to our time without some reworking or even complete rewriting. But there is one troubling statute that remains. It was written and codified in 3701 of the Age of Origin. Tomarind and Ciela's hot-blooded son, Elorvorn left his throne for a secret marriage to a Vespal Wayfolk princess by the name of Alinya. As it happened, Elorvorn was needed for several important decisions—not least of which was what to do about a deadly flood on the Naïthe."

"I don't understand how this affects me," Loch said. "So long as we make certain I don't go errant when I am needed here. And, Mother, you have power of rule if I am absent."

Queen Maren shook her head. Shepherd Sebastian said, "If only it were that simple. You see, the law that was written as a response to Elorvorn's ill-timed romance states that if it can be proven that any High King or Queen of Myriad departs the throne on personal whims—without the Council's prior approval—that king of queen shall be deemed unfit to rule."

"Unfit? How can this be?" Loch asked. "Cardiff doesn't have authority—"

"To draw attention to your absence?" Sebastian countered. "He all but did that while you were in Keening. He could lodge a formal inquiry. If Cardiff pulls that string, who can say when it all will cease to unravel?"

Loch was quiet and still for many moments. "Bah," he said at last, "I'm not going to let my meddling cousin steal my newfound joy. Now, I'm going to retire, I think. Council in the morning. I want to be ready. Important things to discuss."

He departed Sebastian's chamber, leaving a Shepherd and a queen speechless and staring at one another.

28 SOLMONATH 2238

"I believe you fail to see the implications of such delays, Lord Waeybil." Loch leaned forward. He scanned the tradesmen and dignitaries gathered in the Council Chamber. "The only commodity produced start to finish by the cities and villages of the Naïthe is grain. Foodstuffs are plentiful. Everything else, they need. Lumber from the Verdant Mountains, pelts and skins from Silverglen and Chapparel, and perhaps, most importantly raw ore from Tryllium."

Shepherd Sebastian nodded and turned to Lord Waeybil, Stonehand Guild leader of Carrack Vale.

The stout businessman scribbled something on a sheet of parchment and slid it over to his lieutenant, a shrewd Stonehand maiden named Fianna Induress. She smiled and whispered something back. Waeybil's bushy gray eyebrows bounced once, and he said, "The demand for our ore is universal, High King. We've had increased orders from Amara, Fen, everywhere really. Even Anglinore."

"So is the problem raw materials?" Loch asked.

"No, no," Waeybil replied. "It isn't, is it, Fianna?"

She arched a dark eyebrow. "Not in the least. We've all the ore Myriad might ever need. Labor and transportation, however, are what vex us now. Hence the projected delays."

"If Anglinore could reduce its own requisitions," Lord Waeybil suggested. "Perhaps by one quarter . . ."

"Alright," Loch said, the edge on his words sharpened by tone and confidence. "Anglinore shall reduce its order by a fourth, leaving our military short of arms and armor. But no sense sending poorly outfitted warriors to die in battle, so we would need to reduce our standing army by a quarter as well. Alas, should war arise, Tryllium might need to defend its own borders without Anglinore's aid."

Mouth's gaping across the table, slapped shut audibly. "No need for such . . . decisive . . . measures, High King Lochlan," Lord Waeybil said, pronouncing each word carefully. "We did not mean to suggest that Anglinore places unnecessary burden upon the mining clans of Tryllium. As Guildmaster of Carrack Vale, I believe I can speak for all the clans, when I say we are ever grateful for Anglinore's powerful right hand."

Anxious nods rippled around the table. "Even so," Waeybil continued, "we simply cannot meet all the new demands under the old timetable. We must negotiate a new schedule of deliveries."

"That," Lochlan said, "is what we must not do. The increasing demands for ore mean only that our current delivery schedules are even more important than before. Prithee, Lord Waeybil, what might enable the mining clans to train new recruits or better motivate your current workforces to meet the kingdom's increasing needs?"

Sebastian felt as if he were watching a heated game of Jacksprite ball, and Loch had just returned serve rather well. If the issue truly was about labor, Loch had given Waeybil an opportunity to discuss increases in manpower. If, on the other hand, Waeybil took the bait and requested an increase in price, it would be just the same as an admission that labor and transportation were never the issue to begin with. Profit was usually the name of their game. Loch had forced the negotiation into a question of integrity. *Well done, lad.* He glanced at Maren who was beaming with pride.

Fianna whispered something to her leader. Lord Waeybil frowned, nodded once, and said, "It is, as I have said, High King: we have ore in plenty, but we need one of two things: more miners or more mining shifts. Either would be costly."

"But no more costly by percentage than your current situation," Loch volleyed back. "Certainly you will pay more for the extra workers or extra hours, but you also receive more in payment for the increased orders. If training new miners is too costly for your clans to bear, perhaps it would be time to invite other skilled miners from around the realm? The Stonehands in Fen are quite capable, as are the Wayfolk."

Lord Waeybil appeared stricken, and the other clan leaders murmured. Fianna spoke up. "High King, as you know, the mining clans of Tryllium are as much about family and tradition as we are about business. To bring in outsiders, no matter how skilled, would be a smack in the face to the families who have delved for ages on Myriad's behalf."

"No," Lord Waeybil said, his voice shaky, "no, we cannot do what you suggest. We will take care of our own. We will find a way. We will fill the ever-increasing orders, and we will meet our agreed upon delivery schedules. You do understand—"

Loch interrupted, "I understand that changing times require all of us to change. Anglinore must also do its share. I propose that the mining clans of Tryllium are entitled to increase their prices for raw materials, labor, and transportation by five percent."

"Five percent!" Lord Waeybil looked as if he had died and gone to Allhaven.

Sebastian leaned over to the High King and whispered, "Lochlan, five percent is too much. We—"

"I do not want to overburden the realm of Myriad," Loch said. "Let an increase of two percent be paid by each ore-consuming nation. The extra three percent will be absorbed by Anglinore. We are by far the richest nation in the land. Our coffers grow ever deeper from the realm's taxes and, of late, we have experienced unprecedented surplus. In short, we can afford what the rest of the realm cannot. Do you agree to these terms?"

"We do heartily," Waeybil said.

"Good then." Loch pounded the table with his palm. "Have the contracts drawn up. See them to Paige Martin. We will dispatch couriers across the realm to announce the new arrangement."

"Did you see my son?" Maren asked. She picked up a stalk of celery and gave it a satisfying crunch. "The way he took control of the negotiations . . . reminded me—"

"Of Aravel," Sebastian answered. "Yes, I thought so as well." They sat in the shade of a swaying maple in Maren's private garden courtyard. She hasn't come here in an age, the Shepherd thought. And . . . she's eating!

"But he didn't try to strong arm them like Aravel might have," Maren said. "He could have, you know. Those Stonehands were making excuses for their lack of efficiency. Lochlan could have forced the issue."

"Ah, but that was the genius of it," the Shepherd said. He nonchalantly slid a plate of cheese a little closer to the queen. "Lochlan is High King of Myriad. He didn't need to come down hard. He didn't need to hammer them. He merely suggested it. I think it was all the more devastating for Waeybil and the others to draw their own conclusions. Curious . . . Lochlan didn't send them back to Tryllium empty handed."

"Far from it," the queen said as she reached for a piece of smoked cheddar.

Sebastian smiled and said, "Lochlan could have let them stew in their own greed, but he didn't. He probably gave them more than they were going to demand. And to make it happen, he let Anglinore bear the burden. He is growing into the crown . . . becoming a good king."

"Not only a good king," Maren said. "But a good man."

Shepherd Sebastian nodded. "I had my worries about Loch venturing out into the world alone . . . going errant. And Cardiff is a concern. But it seems to have worked wonders upon the young High King."

"I wish we had thought of it sooner."

The Shepherd laughed quietly. "Everything in its season, Maren."

"Next time he goes, however, I hope he finds a woman."

CHAPTER 23

HUNTERS AND HUNTED

"There comes a moment in every hunter's life when, with chills and cold sweat, he fears that he has been tracking a superior hunter . . . and walked right into his trap."

—Avis Grayling in a letter to his youngest son, on the occasion of his earning a place in the Hunt Guild.

24 DRINNAS 2238

"How long has he been gone?" King Ealden asked.

"Left just after sundown, the day before yesterday," Uncle Jak said.

"Why?" asked Abbagael. "Is something wrong?"

King Ealden tried to keep his face impassive as he spoke to her. "I am afraid, afraid Alastair will find Cythraul. I have . . . insights . . . that will help him."

"You believe Cythraul is alive, then?" she asked.

King Ealden nodded. "I am nearly certain, though I wish that I was not."

"He didn't go it alone," Jak said. "He's got Tel with him, he does. Lad's as good a tracker as they come, and more than fair in a scrap, I can tell ye."

"Not alone?" Ealden nodded. "That gladdens my heart. Alastair by himself is as formidable as any single warrior in Myriad, but if Telwyn is with him . . . they should be safe. Do you know where they were headed first?"

"No," Abbagael replied. "But if I know my husband, he won't stop until he's sure."

"He is . . . somewhat determined, isn't he?" King Ealden almost smiled. "Very well then. I've brought a caste of our finest scouts to watch your property. You will not see them, but they are there. And they are . . . effective. Still, be vigilant."

"We will," Abbagael said, patting the long dagger on her belt. "Are you sure you won't stay a moment, your majesty? A bit of tea will warm the heart for a long journey."

Ealden bowed. "You are very kind, but time is critical to me. I must bid you good day."

Abbagael and Jak bowed, and King Ealden left their cottage. He'd barely gotten into his saddle when Jak appeared at his side. "They're circling the stead first," he said. "Alastair told me . . . just in case. They was going t'make sure Abbs was safe here first. Then they were headin' for Fen, Vulmarrow ruins."

"Jak, thank you," King Ealden said. "First One bless you." Ealden spurred his horse and rode a tight circle around the cottage. He nodded to the seven scouts positioned upon the eaves of the building, in the trees, and other less visible places. He turned south and cried out to the trees, "Calivere, Faero, Jenwa . . . it is time!"

There was some rustling in the treetops, but nothing more than a spritely breeze might cause. A few moments later three Prydian scouts rode up.

"You were faster than we expected," Calivere said, tightening a belt on his saddle.

"I'd only just found concealment for young Maena, here." Faero patted his horse's sleek, amber neck.

"Urgency is called for," Ealden said. "If we are swift, we may yet have time to avert a tragedy."

The four riders sped south with all the haste their steeds could muster.

Alastair knelt by the hooves of his stallion, appraised the shallow impressions in the dark soil, and weighed those with the trail of low broken limbs and crushed saplings that wound into the trees before him.

"Cave delk?" Telwyn asked.

"You are good," Alastair said with a laugh. "Six or seven of them, I should think. Geldberry ferns are thick in here. Probably a regular feeding spot for them."

"I hope Icy doesn't find them," Tel said. "This isn't too far out of his range."

"For the delks' sake, I hope that snow drake of yours doesn't come out this far."

Telwyn walked his gray steed forward and then, he dropped lightly to the ground beside Alastair. "Are you satisfied then, MiDa?" he asked.

Alastair expelled a deep breath. "He has not been here," he said. "No one has but wilderland beasts. Thank the First One."

"Yes," Telwyn said. "I have been."

"Mount up, Tel," Alastair commanded. "We've a long ride before us."

32 DRINNAS 2238

Ealden had seen the mountains ahead of him growing steadily larger for many hours, ever since the sun peaked over the horizon. But now, in their midst, the Windbyrne Eyries were a dizzying spectacle. Towering fingers of stone, these mountains burst up out of the Myridian crust, stabbed up through the clouds, and flirted with the ceiling of the sky itself. Ealden wondered at the smooth surface of the dark blue-gray stone. How long had they toiled over its surface, hammering out the ridges and clefts until there was nothing for a climber to reach for or gain purchase? There was now, of course, no way to climb the Windbyrne Eyries. No pick or grappling device would penetrate this stone. There was no way in and no way up. Unless of course, you could fly.

King Ealden led his team to the centermost peak feeling much more than the monolithic shadows falling over him.

"How many are watching me?" Jenwa asked.

"Impossible to know," Ealden said. "Many, I would think." He dropped to the ground, trudged through the strange plum-colored leaves that lined his path ankle deep. There was an enormous golden platter strung up between two black pillars. Latched to its side was a massive hammer. Ealden laughed as he removed the hammer. He knew full well that he wouldn't need the gong to get their attention. He went through the motions anyway, hefted the hammer, and drew it back for a massive swing. And then, just as he swung it forward, the hammer simply disappeared from his grasp.

New flickering shadows were there. "No need to ring the bell," said a Windborne Sky Captain.

"We saw you coming long ago," said another.

They both dropped to the ground a few feet from Ealden. "I am Baragund, Skycaptain of Alpha Peak." He nodded and made a half bow that seemed more sweeping due to the breadth of his iron-blue wings.

"And I am Kane, First Wing-guard of Alpha Peak. He drew his rust-colored wings tight behind him and bowed also. "What brings the esteemed ruler of the Prydian Wayfolk to *our* door?"

"Just passing through," Ealden said.

"With so few?" Baragund asked. "No official delegation here?"

Ealden frowned. "Just as your own lord, Drüst ever hale, will a' times venture forth from his throne on personal errands, so too must I on occasion."

"Well spoken," Kane said. "How can we be of service, King Ealden?"

"Our path takes us through the Felhaunt," Ealden said.

"Ah," Baragund said. "You wish to know if there is Gorrack activity. There is none. They have all but abandoned any scouting ventures into those dark woods. Perhaps too full of painful memory, eh?"

Ealden smiled thinly. He remembered all too well the loss of life on both sides in the Felhaunt. Of course, the Gorracks bore the worst of it, being driven like cattle into the Nightwash where the waiting Marinaens completed the slaughter. "I am glad that the Gorrack Nation lingers within its own borders. Better that way for all concerned."

"They do more than linger," Kane said. "They've completely rebuilt since the war. Razeen Ghash has proven to be a resourceful, if not ruthless, new king for the Gorrack Nation. Their border cities are now fortified like the Skellery in its prime."

"That is noteworthy," Ealden said. "You've no doubt sent word to King Lochlan?"

"Of course," Baragund replied.

"There is one other thing I would inquire of you," said Ealden.

"Yes?" Kane said.

"The Windborne are ever vigilant," Ealden began. "Nothing escapes your eyes, so I wonder if, over the past two days, you have witnessed a pair of riders. Two names you have heard: Alastair Coldhollow and his son Telwyn. And they would have been in great haste."

"General Coldhollow?" Baragund echoed. "And Telwyn, no, they have not passed this way. Even if they came through when I was not on duty, the other Skycaptains would have sent word of such eminent travelers."

"Thank you, Baragund, Kane." He nodded to both of them and turned his horse. "Please give King Drüst my highest regards."

"We will," Baragund said. With seemingly no effort, he flexed his wings and rose into the sky.

King Ealden crouched low to his horses neck, coaxing as much speed from her as he could. *I am ahead of them, he thought. I might possibly find Xana—Cythraul first.*

The Prydian king offered a silent prayer. At some deep level, he knew that Cythraul would not repent. But Ealden would confront him and at least give him a chance. *His last chance,* Ealden thought. He felt the weight of the sealed packets tucked within the outer pockets of his breeches. Incendiary powder . . . enough in each packet to flash-burn a mature tree to ashes.

37 DRINNAS 2238

"We'll need to rest the horses, MiDa," Telwyn said. "They are near exhaustion."

Alastair pulled up on the reins. "Ah, I know it, I know it. It seems a shame. The land is flat. We are making very good time."

"Where are we . . . do you know?"

Alastair made a show of looking around and checking the sun's location. "Twelve or thirteen leagues west of the Bay of Taranaar, give or take. I can smell the water."

"That far east?" Telwyn shrugged. "Are you steering away from the Windbyrne Eyries on purpose?"

Alastair laughed. "I am not trying to get by them unseen," he said. "That is virtually impossible. Look up." Tel did. "You won't see them, but their Skyflights are always there, and they can see us. But the closer we get to the Eyries, the more sets of eyes we invite. And they are a curious people. I do not want to be delayed with questions." Alastair slid off his horse and searched through one of the saddlebags. He found the flints and began casting about the grass for stones of decent size. "We'll make camp for three hours. I'll see to the fire and something to eat. Will you feed and water the horses?"

"I will," Tel replied. He dropped to the ground as well and took both horses' reins. "We'll be going through the Felhaunt, won't we?"

Alastair nodded and kicked a few more stones into the circle he'd constructed. "No other way," he said. He knelt to his circle and tossed in a few pieces of kindling. Then, he started scraping the flint on a stone. "I suppose we could have sailed, but Dagspaddle's out of town. Or maybe we could have visited the Gorracks."

"No, no," Tel said, laughing and then raising a hand as if to ward off a blow. "I'd rather not trouble the Gorrack Nation. We'd probably start another war."

"Most likely," Alastair said with a chortle-grunt.

"You know," Telwyn said, "in spite of our purpose . . . it's kind of nice to be out, just the two of us."

"All the same," Alastair said, back to the flint. "I'd rather us be fishing,"

39 DRINNAS 2238

King Ealden knew the kingdom of Myriad as well as anyone. He'd spent many an hour poring over the best maps in the archive, but traveling across it all on horseback was something altogether eye-opening . . . and confounding. He and his team had been traveling now for a week and one day. They'd traversed the Felhaunt, thankfully by day, crossed the Nightwash, and meandered east of Stonecrest's mountains deep into the heart of Tryllium. At just after sunup, he'd crossed the border into Fen.

"You realize, King Ealden," Calivere said, "our timing will put us in the Ruins of Vulmarrow in darkness."

"Not ideal," Ealden replied. "But we cannot wait."

Still, Ealden led his team onward. Blackwolves and other beasts of the night were the least of his worries.

King Ealden and the Prydian scouts had finally driven off a third pack of Blackwolves, but this pack had taken the last of their horses down. But now, battered and bleeding, and as determined as ever, they emerged from the thick woods and stood before the city of Vulmarrow. Or, at least, its remains.

The high tower that had once pierced the forest canopy had fallen. The nearly full moon climbed slowly behind what was left: a hollow turret with a jagged crown of stone. Vulmarrow Keep itself was still structurally intact, owing that to the mighty stone bulwarks that secured its walls. But all of its detail was destroyed. Parapets, balconies, towers—and any of the wooden structures had collapsed or been thrown down. Away from the boxy keep, however, the destruction was more complete. All that remained of the city were irregular foundations and toppled stone. And the protective walls were but a memory, scarcely one stone left standing upon another along its entire circumference.

"Fitting," Ealden whispered as he trod toward the nearest rampart. For it was clear that the damage wrought upon Vulmarrow in the last twenty years had not been solely from weather.

Faero nodded and said, "After the horrors Morlan visited upon them, it would seem the surrounding peoples have had their measure of revenge."

Calivere added, "As have the relentless hands of time."

As they picked their way through the rubble and broken timber spread over the rampart, they saw the gaping mouth of Vulmarrow's main gate. Its crisscrossing, wrought-iron portcullis had been torn from its track. It now lay akimbo against the arched stone. Ealden carefully skirted its sharp metal edges and stepped out of the moonlight into the fortress that had, for ages, housed everything from madmen to murderers and worse. Ealden drew his glaive; his team followed suit. They trod as far as they could until night vision utterly failed.

It was some comfort to bear his familiar weapon, a three foot shaft with a hand-fitted grip in the center and a curving scythe-like blade on either end. All the Wayfolk used them in battle, and Ealden had dealt his share of damage with his. But weapons did no good, Ealden reminded himself, if one could not see the enemy that approached.

The Prydian king reached into a pouch on his belt and removed two gems. They were not precious jewels by any means, but they were precious to Ealden. Emberstones were actually immature vaskerstones that had not yet been brought to full potency by the years and pressures of Myriad's deep places. While not as powerful in its immature state, each emberstone possessed some uncanny virtue. Green emberstones would speed the healing process on a nonlethal wound. Blue would purify drinking water. Red—well, Ealden had never seen red emberstones before. He'd heard things about them that made him glad he hadn't. But yellow emberstones were most useful in dark places. Move them around a bit, jiggle them, even bounce them off the ground, and they will flare to life with light. Ealden had a very talented gem cutter set these yellow emberstones in threaded caps that he could screw into either end of his glaive. He did this now, screwed them in tight, and then began whirling his glaive through some basic combat forms.

Soon a faint glow traced through the movements. Then brighter . . . and brighter. It was as if Ealden were whirling torches round and round, tracing searing golden arcs through the darkness. Ealden stilled his glaive. "There," he whispered. "That ought to give us light for quite a while."

"That—is very, very interesting," Jenwa said. "When we return to Llanfair, I want to do that too."

Calivere and Faero laughed.

It was enough light to see what was above them: a vaulted ceiling cut through with curving stone ridges like the ribs of some giant. Mangled black chains, from which chandeliers had once hung, dangled down. The emberstone light cast odd flickering shadows, and the way the plaster above had cracked, there seemed to be a horde of hideous, hateful faces leering down at the Wayfolk. The Prydian King was not prone to wandering imaginations, but those faces troubled him. They seemed dead, dead and decomposing. But, of course, the faces weren't there. Not really.

Perhaps that is what this place does, Ealden thought. *It rots you from the inside.* Vulmarrow was a city that seemingly could not endure purity or goodness for any length of time. Beginning long ago with Duke Ichollor, who murdered his entire family before setting himself on fire and leaping from the parapets, the history of Vulmarrow Keep was dotted with horrors. Bloody Kalex, Tosque the Cruel, King Samman, Mistress Bordon . . . and more recently, Mendeleev and Morlan—monsters. Even the ones who began with noble intentions spiraled into infamy.

Queen Maren was right, Ealden thought, *moving Fen's capital to Sennec.* But that didn't make any difference to Ealden now. He had to lead his team deep into Vulmarrow Keep. There were two places within where he thought Cythraul might be hiding: Morlan's throne room . . . and the Bone Chapel.

The emberstones illuminated a cavernous chamber that was divided by a half-dozen walled rooms and several narrow stairwells that weren't quite spiral stair, but wound this way and that, disappearing into the unknown heights. Ealden spun. He'd heard something. A scrape? A hinge? Maybe a night bird? He scanned the shadows and saw no movement. *Wait,* he thought suddenly. One of the chains up in the vaulted ceiling was swaying.

Faero started to whisper, "What was—"

Something behind him. He didn't turn fast enough. It hit him like hammer and tore a chunk from his neck. In a spray of blood, Faero went down.

Jenwa moved faster, but not fast enough. Something took her by the arm and dragged her bodily into the air. She fought the thing and slashed with her glaive, but it took her straight up. Then it let her go. She screamed, plummeting in the darkness and then was silent.

Ealden was thrown off of his feet, ten yards in the air, and sprawled hard on the stone floor. His glaive and its light clattered away. Ealden rose to a crouch but collapsed back to the ground, tasting something warm and coppery on his lips.

"Get up, my lord," Calivere hissed at him.

Ealden rose up again, stronger this time, and ran for his glaive. There was another scraping sound from behind. Instinctively, Ealden ducked. He felt something swoop down overhead and saw a darker shadow briefly in the light of his glaive.

Ealden dove for his weapon, fell short of it, but slid the rest of the way. He grabbed it up, spun backward to one knee, and whirled the weapon just as the thing came on again. A glaive blade struck solidly on a tough hide, but bit through it. Something cold spattered Ealden's forearm, and an ear drum shattering shriek blasted right next to his ear. Ealden took a hard shot to the chin, and his thoughts swam for a moment. He snapped to focus and held up his glaive defensively. The ember-light shown upon something hovering several yards away. It was all gray, scaly flesh, ropey muscle and coltish joints.

The shape of its face with triangular, external ears and high cheekbones, was feline. But its facial features and expression were distinctively reptilian: slanted globe eyes, glimmering red and orange with vertical pupils; pugged, adder-like nostrils, and perpetually grinning jaws full of needlish teeth. Its broad wings seemed to beat slowly and yet it hung, suspended in the air. It clawed at its chest, where pale blue blood trickled in several wandering streams from a deep wound. It was as if it were trying to scrape the wound away, but could not.

That was when Calivere appeared in the shadow behind it and plunged his glaive through the creature's back. It shrieked and mewled and then fell suddenly to the ground. It flopped for a moment, wings slapping awkwardly to the stone. And then, it curled up from the ground, arching its back severely and throwing its head skyward—to release a splintering scream.

There was a leathery slap. Ealden yelled, "Calivere, get down!"

But it was too late. A second creature swooped out of the darkness, using its hind claws to take Calivere by the head. He struggled, and Ealden leaped at the beast. He drove his glaive into the creature's left eye. Its cry was cut short and it dropped to the ground. But as it did, there was a hideous crack. Ealden stumbled to Calivere and wrenched the creature's claws loose. But the brave scout was gone, his neck broken.

The sound careened through the vaulted space and into the stair chamber. Seconds later there came a distant, answering cry. Then another. Then a horrible wailing chorus. Ealden leaped to his feet. But he did not run away, fleeing Vulmarrow keep as so many others might. He charged toward the sounds, the emberstones glowing white-hot as he whirled the glaive and stormed ahead.

39 FEFTIN 2238

"There is something unnatural about this place," Telwyn said, frowning up at the eaves of the trees. "It is unwholesome."

"You speak rightly," Alastair said. "The roots of the Felhaunt have fed on generations of blood." He shuddered. The serpent-wood trees that far outnumbered the black oaks, skagmaple, hemlocks, and firs seemed to have become more numerous and dense, strengthening their stranglehold on the forest. Their thick roots, from which the trees earned their name, slithered far from their gnarled and twisted trunks. They plunged into the ground only to surface again and dive once more. It was treacherous footing for a man walking. For the horses it was perilous.

"What is it, the trunks and boughs are shrouded . . . in some kind of shredded moss?" Telwyn stared at the ragged, blue-gray tatters that striated the black trunks and hung down from the boughs.

"Lichen," Alastair confirmed. "Not of the trees itself, but its own living thing, full of tiny sharp thorns. It'll kill the trees if the trees don't consume it first."

"What do you mean?"

"Insects," Alastair replied. "They devour the tree's bark as fast as they can, secreting the lichen and nesting within it. But with every strip of the tree's flesh they feast upon, the tree unleashes a torrent of burning sap which will capture, suffocate, and eventually dissolve the insects."

Telwyn's hand dropped to the hilt of his sword. "You mean . . . all they do, day after day, age after age, is slowly kill each other?"

Alastair nodded. "Aren't you glad you came?"

Telwyn laughed but not merrily. A dagger-shaped leaf the color of a fresh bruise drifted down from the canopy, floating past Tel's face with eerie slowness.

"Mind the vines," Alastair cautioned. "You don't want to tangle in them—or get any of that lichen on your flesh."

Telwyn blinked and ducked under a low-hanging cord. "I really do not like this place," Tel said. "The sooner we see the Nightwash, the happier I'll be."

They rode on in wary silence for many hours. Alastair had been in the Felhaunt many times, but it still amazed him how the treetops managed to veil even the midday strength of the sun. The entire wood was cast in an ethereal twilight. Still, it was much, much better than traveling the forest at night.

As time passed, the floor of root, moss, and scraggly grass gave way to more and more stone. They walked the horses forward with even more trepidation. The hollow clops of their hooves made their passing all the more forlorn and lonely. Alastair looked up at whiles, just to make sure Telwyn was still there. Many times, he caught Telwyn looking back. *Yes,* Alastair would nod. *I'm still here.*

A mournful cry arose like a moaning wind, but the trees were still. Telwyn's sword flashed out in an instant. "What was that?"

"Easy, Son," Alastair said. "It's no threat, least not to us. A graystrider, looking for its mate . . . nothing more."

Telwyn shook his head. "The graystriders near home don't sound like that."

"No," Alastair replied. "No, they don't."

On they rode, and to Alastair it seemed they should have been farther along. "We've wandered from our course, I think," he said, looking skyward at the canopy roof. "It is near dusk. We should have come to—wait, there!" He pointed.

"Is that it?" Telwyn asked, a tentative smile on his lips. "The banks of the Nightwash? Are we through?"

"Nay, lad. We have but come to the Barrow Field." He pointed again. The trees thinned out ahead, and a rolling sea of grassy mounds loomed in the dusk. "Hmm, I had hoped to strike just the western edge or skirt it altogether. Not sure how we ended up this far east."

As the horses picked their way through the last few trees and trod onto the patchy turf, Telwyn stared at the peculiar clearing. The trees were thick all around, but not so much as a sapling grew among the undulating hillocks. "Barrows . . . as in—"

"Ancient graves," Alastair confirmed, "overgrown by the grass . . . part of the landscape now." Alastair gave his horse a gentle kick to pick up the pace a bit. He'd passed through the Barrow Fields once before, during broad daylight, and found it disquieting then. Now, in the shadows of dusk, it was far worse, and Alastair felt every nerve on edge.

"Mi Da?"

Tel's voice made Alastair bounce in his saddle. "What?" he answered, his voice a little more shrill than he'd have liked.

"Why are you so tense?"

"The last time I was here," he said, "I saw something."

"What was it?" Tel asked, his eyes widening.

"No, not here. Wait until we get out of this wretched forest."

They rode on in silence, Alastair, giving his horse little nudges to keep the pace up. The mounds grew more numerous in the center of the field, and some of them rose up too high to see over. Alastair tried to think of Abbagael, tried to pray, tried to do anything but think about that experience where he'd seen . . . he'd seen. *No*, he commanded himself. *Do not think of it!*

"Mi Da," Telwyn said, "I see something."

Alastair had the Star Sword out in a heartbeat. He looked past Telwyn, across the mounds, and saw . . . nothing.

At first.

But as he stared, the shadows between distant mounds began to shift and move, and the movements, though strangely slow and deliberate, were familiar. A moment later and Alastair could see their shapes more clearly. Tall figures, vaguely humanoid, but shifting and ethereal—there were several, more than a dozen—and they seemed to be marching, drawing closer.

"What are they, Mi Da?"

"I . . . I do not know." Alastair swallowed back the frozen bile in his throat. Something about these shade beings shook Alastair in ways that even Morlan did not.

"They're in front of us too," Telwyn said, drawing his blade.

Alastair twisted at the waist and saw them. Definitely the shapes of men, but also Stonehands, and even Wayfolk. And they were armed with all manner of weapon: sword, cudgel, ax, pike, spear, and flail. They seemed to be coming out of the treeline, but no . . . Alastair gasped. They were rising up out of the ground, clawing up from the mounds, standing awkwardly, and then moving forward. Alastair's wasn't sure any of his senses were working correctly, but he thought now he could actually hear them. Whispering and rustling and a very faint rattling sound . . . but the longer he listened, the more Alastair realized something wasn't right. The sounds weren't coming from those apparitions ahead.

Alastair whipped around to look behind him, and he did something he hadn't done in all his years as a swordsman: he dropped his sword. A great horde of shadowy figures was almost upon them, only fifteen, twenty yards away. Gasping, Alastair leaped down from his steed to snatch the sword off the grass.

"Mi Da!" Telwyn yelled.

"Don't watch me!" Alastair called. "Watch them!" But the moment Alastair's fingers were on the hilt of his fallen sword, a transluscent hand burst up from the grass and seized Alastair's wrist.

THE VENTURE INN

There are seven days in a Myridian week. They are:
Soliday
Halfinday (also called Halfiday)
Asterday
Triviel
Celester
Thestiday (also called Thesty)
Sennett

—Letti's Almanac, 2085, AS

18 SOLMAS 2238

After some four hundred mug washings, Tango and Meli's hands were as dimpled and pruned as they could be. The Venture Inn was filled to bursting now, dozens and dozens of tradesmen and merchants from all over and more than a few warrior types as well. And apparently they had all come from desert regions where there was nothing to drink because they were all insanely thirsty. No sooner did Tango and Meli finish washing one set of dirty mugs than another set arrived.

Matron Tess whooshed by from time to time, uttering a hasty, "Yer doin' fine!" or "You've got the hang of it now!" or, most often "More clean mugs please!" The Spriggans had tried to stop their new employer to ask questions, but she always seemed to scoot by just out of reach.

It was driving Tango crazy. Every so often, he'd heard the pronounced ringing of a bell. It sounded like a tall ship's bell, and each time it rang, all the patrons of the Venture Inn raised a tremendous shout. Hoo-rahs! Huzzahs! Woo hoos!—mingled with all manner of exultant cheers and shrieks of pure excitement. Tango wanted to know what it all was about, but he dare not leave his post behind the counter.

Had they been at home in Hammer's Gap, Tango and Meli would have complained fervently for all the work. But not here, and not now. The Venture Inn's patronage was simply too interesting and peculiar to worry much about the job. The winged man Grindle Freeman had taken a booth with Clarisse Graymane in a shadowy corner. Tango could barely keep his eyes off both of them, but for very different reasons.

A sortie of Stonehands had come in as well. But these were very bearded and very tattooed—and thankfully not into slavery like the Crimson Sash tribes. Then, in just the last half-hour, a man and woman came in, arm in arm. The man had deeply bronzed, almost golden skin. The woman was as pale-white as cream. But aside of the skin color, they were alike. Each had unnaturally large, dark eyes and an arrowhead shape of strange, feathery hair that swept from just above the bridge of the nose up over the head and falling into a smooth, shoulder-length mane. The luminous pair was only the first of many of this kind. In fact, they seemed the most numerous race represented in the vast common room. Elladorians, they'd learned, numerous but each one captivating in his own way.

The early evening clientele might have been distracting, but that was nothing compared to the late comers.

"Look a' that one," Meli said as a woman with deep blue skin walked by. "I think she had gills."

"It's not polite to stare," Tango admonished. But it wasn't a heartbeat before it was his turn to gawk. A very little person with a very little mug flew up to one of the great kegs along the west wall of the tavern and proceeded to fill up. "Why . . . why, it's a pixie," whispered Tango.

"Tango, fetch me a wheel of cheddar, would you?" called Matron Tess from a crowd near the crackling fireplace.

"Wheel of cheddar," Tango echoed. "I don't even know where the cheese—"

"The cheese is in the deep cellar," Matron called out. "Look for a trapdoor near the barley sacks!"

"How does she do that?" Tango asked. Meli shrugged.

Above the clamor of the crowded room, the bell rang out once again. The patrons roared and cheered and raised their mugs. "What is that?" Tango blurted out. Meli shrugged again. "Bah, some help you are."

Tango ducked out from behind the counter, turned the corner for the pantry, and ran smack into an oak tree. Or, at least that's what it felt like to Tango. He stumbled backward a step, blinked a few times, and stared up at a being so tall and broad-shouldered, he seemed to fill up the room all by himself.

"So sorry lad," he said, but Tango didn't see his lips move. In fact, he didn't see that the man had any lips at all. There were eyes, big brown eyes with the raised brows and creases of some-one who laughed often. He had a nose, a great gourd-shaped nose as ruddy as his full cheeks. But beneath that, there was just a tre-mendous tuft of beard that hung down to the middle of his chest where it forked into two intricate braids. "Lad," the man spoke again, his lips completely hidden in the beard. "You alright?"

Tango blinked again. "I . . . I'm fine, sir. Sorry I ran into ya."

"Fault's all mine," he said. "I didn't see you there. Sturdy lad, you are. I've knocked out men twice your size with such a blow from my knee. You sure you're okay, then?"

Tango straightened up and stuck his chest out. "Ya, good. Was just gon'na fetch an apple from the roof."

The big man's eyes narrowed. "You have apples on the r—"

"Cheese—CHEESE—from the basement," Tango corrected himself, the cobwebs vanishing at last.

"That does make a bit more sense," the giant said with disarming wink. "Now then, lad. I'll be here most a' the night. You come find me later. I'll have somethin' for you."

"How will I find you?" Tango asked.

"Look behind the bar, lad. But if you don't see me, ask around for Bulwar Zanderose, wielder of the sharpest axe and the heaviest hammer in all the land." He patted Tango on the shoulder and then thundered off into the common room.

Tango at last resumed his errand. He found the trapdoor right where Matron Tess had said it would be. It was a heavy door and creaked on its two black metal hinges. A ladder led down into the darkness, and it felt like fingers of cold reached up to tickle at his chin. "Wee bit creepy down there," Tango muttered. But there was nothing for it. The matron needed the cheese. "She would'na sent me down there if there was anythin' dangerous." Besides, he could see the cheese wheels on a half-shaded shelf close to the ladder.

Tango shimmied down the ladder and plopped onto the dusty floor. It was cold down there . . . and quiet. Wasting no time, Tango grabbed the wheel closest to the ladder. He grumbled. There was no label on it. He sat that one aside and snatched up another. No label there either. In fact, none of the eight wheels he looked at had a label on it.

Tango froze. He'd heard something behind him. It was a quiet, complicated sound: kind of like a heavy sack sliding along the floor, but also a sharp scraping—like a blade on stone. Holding a cheese wheel like a shield, Tango spun around. "Sorry," he said. "Didn't know anyone was down here." There came no answer. No sound. "Hello?" he called. Still no answer. Tango shrugged. *Must've been foolin' meself,* he thought.

Then he sniffed. He held the cheese wheel closer to his nose and sniffed again. "Ah, cheddar," he whispered. "This is what I was lookin—"

A deep, thrumming growl rolled out of the darkness directly in front of Tango. Bass vibrations rumbled up through his bare feet and set him to trembling. He saw nothing at all but knew something was there. Something large.

Tango reached slowly for the ladder, but was flash paralyzed by the sliding, scraping sound. Two luminous, moon white eyes appeared, and the growl came again, ending in a concussive, *Grrrroof!*

Feeling encased in sudden ice, Tango awkwardly banged up the ladder. He leaped to the pantry floor, kicked the trapdoor shut, and slammed the heavy bolt lock home. Clutching the cheese, Tango bounced back against the pantry wall and tried to catch his breath. "I can'na believe . . . she sent me down there . . . with tha' thing." Tango puffed until his breathing slowed to normal. Then, he bolted out of the pantry and strode back into the common room.

He wove between the customers, sometimes bouncing from one to another. "I'm gon'na tell that matron what for," he grumbled. "I could'a died down—" *DING.* The crowd roared. A mug bonked Tango in the back of the head. And some ice cold liquid sloshed down on him from above. It smelled vaguely like honey but didn't feel too good dribbling down Tango's back.

With an involuntary quiver, Tango resumed his path to Matron Tess. He found her leaning on a candlelit table by the window. Two men sat at the table, both rugged, woodsman types, and both smirking as if from a recent jest.

"Here's the cheese, ya asked for," Tango said, handing her the wheel.

"What are all these little ruts?" Matron Tess asked. "It almost looks like you squeezed the thing."

"Well ya have a great big beast down there!" Tango groused. "'Bout killed me, it did."

Matron Tess giggled. "What . . . Basil?" She laughed again. "Basil's no beast, lad. Just a great big cuddly bear."

Tango was about to complain when the bell rang again. Matron Tess and the two rogues at the table cheered along with the rest of the common room. "Here now," Tango said. "There it is again. Matron, what is that bell and all the cheering?"

"That's the Glory Bell," muttered one of the men, chewing on a hunk of cheddar.

"Someone's been at the board again," said the other.

Matron Tess eyed Tango strangely. "I'll show it to ye later, lad," she said. "After hours . . . when things are a bit quieter. But you, lad, you've been workin' hard. Why don't ye take a bit of a break. You and your sister, slip outside with a plate of cheese and meat and rest up. It gets busy in here later."

Tango blinked and shook his head. *Busy later?* he thought. *I can barely walk in here as it is.* Still, a break sounded good. He picked his way back across the room, gathered up Meli and some stores from the pantry, but he decided not to go outside. Instead, they made their way over to the shadowy booth where Clarisse Graymane and Grindle Freeman sitting.

"Well, if it isn't our two stowaways," Clarisse said. "How are you liking your first night of Tradegather in Ravensgate?"

"It's fun!" Meli said.

"It certainly keeps me busy," Tango said. "Not sure if fun is the right word." Tango stared at the ground a moment but flickered a glance at Clarisse's midnight eyes. "Could we . . . uh . . . maybe sit with you a bit?"

Grindle laughed deeply, drew his coal-black wings in tight to his back, and slid over. He patted a thick hand on the bench seat for Meli.

"Course you can sit with us," Clarisse said. "But you've not quit on Tess, have ya? She'll have all our hides."

"No, no," said Tango. "She told us to take a break."

"Well, join us then," she said, making room for Tango next to her.

Tango hopped up and slid over. His shoulder brushed up against Clarisse's arm. She was so warm, and Tango felt his thoughts go to mush. The four of them sat in awkward silence for some time. Meli nibbled on cheese. Grindle sipped from a big mug.

Tango cleared his throat. "I don't understand," he said.

"Understand what?" Clarisse asked.

"Well . . . anything really. We hid in your wagon, and you weren't angry. Then you brought us to this inn here."

Clarisse smiled. "No reason to be angry. It was already done. Besides, you and your sister combined barely weigh as much as a barrel of ale."

"And we brought you here," Grindle rumbled, "because here is where we are."

"But, what is this . . . this Venture Inn?" Tango asked. "I mean, we can'na been here two minutes and ya got us room and board and a job and all."

"Matron Tess gave you all that," Clarisse said. "She can always use the help, especially at this time of year." She was quiet a moment, seemingly lost in thought. "And . . . she has a heart for runaways. She took me in the same way just eighty some odd years ago."

"That long ago, was it?" Grindle asked. He blinked and gazed into his mug. "That's a long time."

"I knew she'd open her arms for you," Clarisse said. "So tell me, young ones, where are ya runnin' from?"

Meli's eyes misted over. Tango felt his throat constrict. In all the hectic movement, he hadn't thought much about things.

"We're . . . well we were from Hammer's Gap," he said.

"Don't know that name," Clarisse said. "Where's that, up in Amara?"

Tango shook his head. "No, it's a little village near Cragheath Tor."

"Don't know that one either. You?" She glanced at Grindle who shook his head.

Tango squinted. "You've never heard of Cragheath Tor? It's the capital city of the Hinterlands."

Grindle nearly choked on his sip and took a napkin to his chin. Clarisse sat up straighter. "The . . . the Hinterlands?" She gave a nervous laugh. "You aren't . . . you aren't . . . wait, you are serious, aren't you?"

Tango and Meli nodded fiercely.

Clarisse exhaled audibly. "But how? The mountains . . . they're impenetrable."

"Even my kind cannot overfly those high peaks," Grindle said. "How then, come you?"

Tango looked at Meli. "There's a tunnel there now. Stonehands, the ones with the red arm bands, they delved it."

Clarisse made fierce eye contact with Grindle. They sipped from their mugs at exactly the same moment. "So the way is open at last," Clarisse whispered. "The Stonehands took you then? Brought you here as slaves?"

"Not exactly," Tango muttered. "It's a very long story and hard to tell. We were fleeing."

"From what, lad?" she asked.

"A dragon thing," Meli said, a tear sliding down her cheek.

"This villain, this man Cythraul did it," Tango said. "Made the dragon come out. And . . . Cythraul . . . he killed my Da." Tango couldn't stop the tears now. He couldn't stop the churning pain in his gut. He'd promised his father. He'd promised to have his father's back. But he'd let him leave the Thicket and only followed after him when it was too late.

Clarisse gathered Tango up in a warm embrace and let him weep on her shoulder. Grindle extended one wing and enfolded Meli. "You've lost much," he rumbled. "But you are safe here."

They sat in peace, if not quiet. The buzz in the common room grew louder with each passing hour, punctuated by the ringing of the bell and subsequent roar.

"More mugs and tankards!" Matron Tess called from somewhere in the writhing throng.

"I suppose that means your break is over," Clarisse said. "Best get back at it."

Grindle unfolded his wing, and Meli, smiling and glad, slid off the bench seat. Tango reluctantly parted from Clarisse Graymane and hopped down as well. He bowed and said, "Thank you for everything. I don'na know how we would've made it without you."

She nodded back and said, "Our pleasure and honor to help. We all need a helping hand at times." She winked at Grindle. "Well, my young champions, unless you are both up very early, we won't see you again for a time. Grindle and I will be off with the sun. But, should you make Ravensgate your new home, I'm sure we'll meet again. We return here thrice a year. There's no place in Myriad quite like the Venture Inn."

If the beginning of the night had been hectic and busy, the late hours had been doubly so. But, the night waned, and slowly the common room cleared. To Tango and Meli's surprise and everlasting thankfulness, the patrons of the Venture Inn didn't leave a huge mess. Sure, there were stacks of plates and platters, cups, goblets, and mugs—but the floors were relatively clean of refuse.

Matron Tess and her other more experienced employees showed Tango and Meli the intricacies of cleaning up. But when the moon was falling well below the treeline, at last, the work was completed. Tango and Meli sat at a two-seater table near the room's entrance and nibbled on crackers. "My hands, Tango . . . I can'na barely open and close 'em to hold this cracker."

"Aye," he said. "Mine too. And it feels like my hands and arms up to my elbow are still underwater." He laughed. "Funny though. It kind of feels good."

"That's right, my dears," Matron Tess said, appearing beside them. "That's what a good night's work feels like. And you've more than earned your keep tonight. Of all the nights to start, Tradegather eve." She laughed. "I suppose you'll be ready for a soft bed then, eh?"

"Yes, please," Meli said.

Tango hesitated. "Uh . . . bed's good, but I was wonderin' about—"

"That's right," Matron Tess said. "You wanted to see the Venture Board and the Glory Bell, now didn't ye?"

Tango nodded. "It drove me fair crazy half the night."

"This way," she said, bustling away into the depths of the common room. Tango and Meli followed her past the central counter, past the keg wall, past the pit roaster, and down a narrow corridor the Spriggans hadn't noticed. The passage led to an almost perfectly round chamber. It was void of seats, void of furniture of any kind save one small writing desk. But the wall was the focal point. Windowless and, unlike the common room, empty of trophy or trinket, the wall was covered by a vast leather tapestry. Whatever creature had been large enough to have such a skin, Tango didn't want to meet it.

"It's a map," Meli said.

"Quick study, you are," Matron Tess said with a wink, but she meant it kindly. "Map of the whole world of Myriad."

Tango closed in on the center of the map. "What are all these?" he asked, pointing to several irregular squares of parchment that had been tacked to the map. He gazed left and right. "They're are hundreds of 'em."

"Ah, those are open quests, lad." Matron Tess held out her arms and turned a slow circle. "This, you see, is the Venture Board. Those who have great calamity or great need travel here from thousands of leagues all around to leave notice of their plight. Then, adventurers from far and wide come to answer their call. See here." She went to the desk and upon it, mounted on a wooden headstock within a black, wrought iron wheel was a polished silver bell. It had a lever to turn the wheel and also a petite hammer in a stand next to it.

"The Glory Bell?" Tango asked.

"Right you are," Matron Tess replied. "It rings on three occasions only. Once when someone leaves a venture note, once when a hero comes and takes up a quest, and finally when the adventurer returns triumphant. And this is why we cheer, ye see? Every time this bell rings, there's good bein' done in Myriad."

"Whoa," Tango said, but it came out like a breath. He gazed from note to note, imagining what it would be like to armor up and strap on a blade to go help someone in need. "Turgaloo Farm: gots rat troubles," he said. "Ha, maybe I could do that one."

Matron Tess smiled. "You've not seen the rats in Fen," she said. "Near as big as Basil."

Tango swallowed. In truth, he hadn't actually seen Basil, but if it was as big as its growl, it was immense indeed. Tango kept reading. "Help fighting ribbon storms in Surrey, Llanfair." Tango had no idea what a ribbon storm might be . . . or how anyone fights a storm.

"What's an ogray?" Meli asked, looking at a note posted near the border of the Hinterlands.

"Ogre, dear," Matron Tess said. "Big mutt-faced beasties, they are. Devilish taste for sheep too."

"Oh."

Tango laughed but couldn't take his eyes off the notes. *Gorracks stealing my chickens, Dolf Ganderhorn from Stonecrest*—read one. *Missing family heirloom: Enchanted Brooch*—read another. *Spirax infestation in Ardon, Gremlings assaulting a keep in the Verdant Mountains, a grandmother abducted by trolls near the Muskycopse Forest*—Tango shook his head at the strange and wondrous adventures out there waiting.

The bell sounded a clear note that held for many heartbeats. Her cheeks reddening by the moment, Meli stood next to the bell. She held the small mallet in her hand. "Oops," she said.

"Don't you fib, young lady," Matron Tess said, mussing Meli's golden locks. "That mallet didn't get into your hand by accident, now did it?"

Tango laughed. He wandered over to Meli and snatched the tiny hammer from her hand. "Can I ring it once?" he asked.

"Now that is the proper way to do things. Askin' first. Go ahead, Tango."

He gave the bell a swift tap with the hammer and, once more, the crystal ring filled the room. There was something exhilarating about that sound. Tango closed his eyes and shuddered.

"Alright, then," Matron Tess said. "You've had your fun. Now for bed." She turned to leave but stopped a moment, surprised to see that Meli had taken her hand. Matron Tess bit her lower lip and then smiled warmly at Meli. "How old are ye?" she asked.

"Ten summers," Meli said.

Matron Tess blinked repeatedly. "Been through a lot, haven't ye?" Meli nodded. "Well, come on then. Sleep will come easy here. No bad dreams or night creepers dare pass these walls."

She and Meli left the room, but Matron Tess called back over her shoulder. "C'mon, Tango lad!"

"Be right there!" he called back. But when he put the mallet back in its stand by the bell, he saw a stack of blank parchment squares, a fistful of charque in a can, and a little box of tacking pins. Glancing first at the doorway, then back to the vast, wall-covering map, Tango snatched out a piece of parchment and a stick of charque. Thanking Da for teaching him his letters, he scribbled a few quick lines. Then he grabbed a tacking pin and raced west along the map. There he tacked up his piece of parchment and uttered a silent prayer to the Starmaker.

CHAPTER 25

PAIN OF DEATH

"Sabryne's chains will be broken. Black words will be spoken. The Sevenfold Curse will devour peace as a voraelion strips the flesh from its prey."

—From the Book of Future Things added to Canticles
during the Council of Shepherds 1770 AO,
Barde Richter (r. 1203 AO)

40 DRINNAS 2238

First One, preserve me, Ealden prayed as he charged into the stair chamber. Gray green light from some unseen source bathed the curling stairways. And now, Ealden could see the writhing, swarming forms fly out of the upper levels and dive down. Glistening red eyes, white claws, white teeth, leather wings, tangled knobby limbs—a storm of creatures—plummeted toward Ealden. The Prydian King knew to wait would mean certain death. He had to strike on his terms. He raised his glaive and leaped for the first creature that came within reach. He impaled that beast and ripped the blade out—and straight into the face of the next creature. Shrieks rang out. Ealden fell to the ground, rolled, and darted beneath one of the stairwells.

Twittering chirps surrounded him as the creatures spiraled in on his position. Claws bit into his upper arm. Ealden spun, and the offending beast lost that arm at the elbow. In shocked bewilderment, the creature stared at its bleeding stump, but only for a moment. King Ealden whirled his glaive, and the creature's head bounced on the ground and rolled away. Ealden raced out from under the stairs and slashed at three hovering creatures. He didn't care where he hit them, just so long as the bite was deep. Either the monsters would flee in pain or they would be weakened in their attack.

The creatures continued to dive at him, and Ealden moved like a tornadic wind among them. Cold blue blood spattered and sprayed. Limbs or pieces of them flew or fell away. As he fought, Ealden tried to recall the architecture of Vulmarrow Keep. He knew one of these three stairwells led to Morlan's throneroom. But which one?

His glaive in constant motion, he circled around the front of the stairs for a better look. Dodging one creature, slashing it as it went by, and then ducking another swooping beast, Ealden darted back and forth between the staircases. He thought sure the stair on the right went to the armory. One of the other two went to the old archives directly beneath the throneroom. Ealden thought that, perhaps, there might be an internal passage from the archive to the throneroom. He drove his glaive forward into the gut of one creature and then yanked it backward as hard as he could, splitting the jaw of the beast that attacked from his right. Still he stared at the two stairways: left and center. But he stared too long.

A creature struck him between the shoulderblades, knocking him off his feet. The blow propelled Ealden into the air and he careened toward the blocky stone pillar at the middle stair's foot. The collision never happened. Claws tightened like vice grips on Ealden's upper arms; on his ankles as well, and Ealden was lifted into the air. Four of the creatures, working in unison, they slowly began to ascend. Ealden didn't want to let them gain any altitude, for being dropped thirty or forty feet would cripple him for sure.

He groaned and tried to free his limbs, tried to turn his wrist to wrench the glaive toward the creature. But it was no good; the more Ealden struggled, the farther apart the beasts flew, stretching his limbs into realms of agony Ealden had never trod.

Higher and higher they flew, rising far above the stairs. They wheeled about suddenly, caroming toward an arched black opening in the blank stone wall. The grip on Ealden's right wrist constricted viciously. He groaned and screamed, clenching his teeth and fighting the pain. But the tendons in his forearm spasmed, his fingers involuntarily opened. And Ealden's glaive fell.

39 DRINNAS 2238

Telwyn leaped from his horse, rolled across the mound, and, in one fluid motion, gained his feet and slashed his blade across the ethereal arm of the thing that held Alastair. An angry whisper, hoarse and scraping like crunch of dead leaves underfoot, erupted from the mound. A monstrous gray soldier clambered up to the surface, sending chunks of earth and sod flying and knocking Telwyn and Alastair down the slope of the mount. It, like the other shades, was translucent, its body seemingly made of vapor and constantly in motion. And yet, Alastair could discern its every detail. Tall and broad, the ghostly being wore armor over most of its form. It brandished a wide-bladed axe in one bony hand; a menacing mace dangled from the other. Its flesh seemed to be peeling away from bone, especially on its face where a gaping cavity was all that was left of its nose. Fiery green orbs blazed out from its otherwise empty sockets. The spectral warrior arched its back and unleashed another grating howl. Then, it stared down at Alastair.

"Uh, oh," Alastair muttered. He rolled backward to his feet and looked for the Star Sword, but he'd lost track of it when the thing burst through the mound. He whisked a dagger out of his belt and stood his ground. The thing took a heavy step down the slope. Then another. Worse still, the rustling and whispering grew louder all around him. The other shades were coming, closing in, tightening like hangman's noose.

"Telwyn!" Alastair screamed. "Get back to your steed! Get across! Go!"

"Leave you?" Tel's incredulous voice answered. "Not a chance, Mi Da!"

The massive axe swept down, aiming to split Alastair's skull. He stepped to one side, easily avoiding it, but the backhanded mace swing almost took his head off. He ducked just in time, lunged, and flicked his dagger but made no contact. Or at least he didn't think that he had. *What am I doing trying to stab something that isn't there?* But it was there. There was some substance to it. He'd felt the air move as the thing's axe whooshed by . . . and again with the mace.

Alastair maneuvered to the thing's side, but it turned with him and attacked. The spiked ball at the end of the flail weapon may have looked ethereal, but it came crashing to the ground with plenty of force. Alastair leaped backward and gaped at the crater in the earth where the mace head struck. Then, Alastair saw Telwyn standing on the mound behind the creature. He had the Star Sword! *Wait, what are you doing Tel?*

Alastair gasped. Telwyn reared back and threw the sword like a spear right at the creature's back. The blade plunged into center of the spectral knight's mass and burst through its chest . . . and kept going. Alastair dove out of the way, and his Star Sword stuck hard into the turf. He rolled and grabbed the hilt, but his fingers slipped off. It was coated in some kind of faintly glowing slime. "These things aren't spirits!" he yelled. He wiped the grip off on his tunic and took the blade once more into his hand. He spun in time to watch the gigantic knight crumble to its knees. And then . . . it melted.

The detailed form, from the helm that barely covered its rotting face down to its iron greaves, seemed to pour in on itself, like a fountain in reverse. And suddenly there was a slimy, writhing form oozing slowly down the hill. It still glowed with pale light, but it had much more density, like a thick snake or worm made of some murky gelatinous substance. And indeed, it had dozens and dozens of curving talon-like limbs running all along its flank. It's head was much like that of a leech with a wide round mouth ringed with teeth. Its eyes were spider-like, numerous cold black orbs, but they rested within—at least a few inches deep in the creature's slimy flesh. From it came a wet, gargling sound, and the leech-thing sagged into the turf. Glistening pale fluids ran down the hill beneath it.

"You killed it, Tel!"

"LOOK OUT!!" Telwyn yelled back.

Alastair didn't even look. He sensed the movement behind, spun and knocked away the spear thrust with the Star Sword. A ghostly figure in the shape of a Stonehand stood before him. Alastair didn't wait. He coiled and struck hard on the shaft of the spear. It split in half, and to Alastair's surprise, it bled. The thing wailed in its scraping, keening whisper. Alastair drove his blade into the thing's chest, drew it free, and then slashed its legs out from under.

Suddenly Tel was beside him. The young warrior kicked the dying Stonehand over on its side and went to work on the next creature. Alastair had two of his own to deal with: both pale misty images of decomposing Gorracks. As terrifying as they looked, the creatures lacked the fighting skills of the real Gorracks. Alastair dispatched them quickly. He turned and saw Telwyn fighting, drifting back toward the creatures coming up from behind.

"No, Tel!" he yelled. "Not that way. There are too many. We need to get out of the center—fight your way south!"

Telwyn clove one ghostly knight nearly in half, then turned and nodded. Alastair and Tel flinched at a horrific scream, not one of the creatures.

The horses.

"Tel!" Alastair screamed. "Get—"

"On it, Mi Da!"

From two wide angles, Alastair and Telwyn converged on the horses. The creatures had surrounded them and were pressing in with their weapons. To their credit, the horses were not sheep for the slaughter. They reared and kicked and slammed the ghostly invaders with bullish thrusts of head and flank. Alastair and Telwyn sprinted for them. Telwyn climbed up a hill and dove into the fray. Alastair leaped and slid into the creatures' legs.

Piles of the translucent beings went down. Alastair and Telwyn went to work, impaling the fallen and slashing those still standing until they backed away. Telwyn charged his horse and leaped over its flank to land gracefully in the saddle.

"Show off," Alastair muttered, clambering wearily into his own saddle. He gave his steed a sharp kick and they galloped south.

40 Drinnas 2238

It occurred to King Ealden that the winged creatures were not out to kill him. If that had been their aim, they could have dropped him any number of places along their high altitude flight through the cavernous Vulmarrow Keep. Other creatures flew beside the four that carried Ealden. He could hear them chittering.

In all his years as Prydian King, Ealden had only visited Morlan's stronghold on two occasions. And now, his recollection of the architecture utterly failed. He'd never even seen the vast arched entrance the creatures had taken him through. Immersed in darkness for some time, Ealden was somewhat relieved to see little blotches of gray light. There were passages and openings on either side, and a slightly brighter shade up ahead.

Suddenly they emerged into a yawning cavern of stone. The floor plummeted away, and the ceiling soared an equal distance above. Mote-flooded beams of moonlight stabbed down from six hemisphere windows high above and then diffused into the shadows far below. The swarm of creatures flew Ealden in a wide sickle-shaped turn, descending into the massive chamber. And Ealden felt he was now traveling beneath ground level. "Where are they—" His mouth shut with a snap.

Just ahead but still far below, an ominous structure rose up. It was like a castle within a castle, and Ealden wondered how everything on the inside could possibly fit within Vulmarrow Keep's outward appearance. But as he descended closer, the building appeared more like to a sanctuary than an outright castle. Built entirely of pale stone, it had one tall turret divided into three vertical sections. Three occular windows gaped blackly from layers of fine tracery on each side. A squat pyramid-shaped roof sat upon the turret, and from its tip a strange piece of wrought iron stabbed. A symbol surely, but Ealden had never seen it before.

The gabled main body of the structure, what would have been the nave of a Sanctuary, extended some sixty yards on one side of the turret, maybe thirty on the other. Its walls had high, arched lancet-windows and was buttressed by tapering slabs of stone. And sticking out from the body like a toad's squat appendages, were several round apse-like buildings. The short end of the building disappeared into the surrounding wall.

The volume of the creatures' screeching chitter increased markedly as they descended toward the the building. Ealden could not see their target. Aside of the windows, there seemed no way into the structure. But as they drew much closer, Ealden let out a shout. For now, so close that he could see the intricate detail, Ealden saw that every piece of stone, from the great blank sections of wall to the complicated arches and the turret were bordered, even striated by, pale gray segments of bone.

The Bone Chapel.

The creatures dove down another few feet, swooped so low to the ground that Ealden strained to keep his torso from scraping. Then they rose up as if on a sudden sea swell and drove right through the center of a massive round window. Ealden barely had time to register his surroundings before the creatures dropped him on his feet in front of a wide table made of some dark metal. Red candles by the hundreds lit the ghastly architecture of the chamber. And a deep voice startled Ealden.

"Now this is a riveting development," the voice said. "I knew someone would come looking for me eventually, but I expected Coldhollow or some other glory-seeking general from Anglinore . . . not you."

Ealden looked ahead and saw a figure seated behind a black stone table upon a raised dais. He couldn't see the face, but he didn't need to see him to know who it was. "The Iceman is coming for you," Ealden declared. "Any day now. He plans to kill you, Xanalos."

"Do you know me?" He rose from the table and quickly descended a few steps down from the platform. His voice lowered. "Use that name again . . . and I will gut you. I . . . am . . . Cythraul."

"Whatever name you choose," Ealden said, "you will die by Coldhollow's hand. That is why I have come . . . to offer you one last chance."

"Sanctimonious teacher," Cythraul hissed. "Spare me your chances. I have no fear of Coldhollow. Still, I suppose your being here at all speaks something of your concern. You must feel so . . . besmirched to venture into Vulmarrow, more so here in my place of worship."

"I find it . . . unpleasant." With every breath, Ealden inhaled some new stench. "But some things are more important than ceremony."

"I didn't think there was anything more important than ceremony . . . or doctrine . . . to you." Cythraul gripped the pommel of his sword as if he might crush it.

Ealden felt his hands shaking and quickly clasped them behind his back. "I . . . I failed you," he said. "And I am sorry."

He stepped forward and stood directly across the long table from Ealden. "An apology? What has come over you, Ealden?

But no, your apology is misplaced. I have you to thank for . . . for all this."

Cythraul held up his arms and gestured to the charnel-like interior. "I wield more power here than I could have dreamed of in Llanfair. And do you know what else I have, teacher? I have FREEDOM!"

The roar washed over Ealden. He blinked and turned away. "You stole the Eye of the North," he muttered at last. "I had no choice."

"Idiot," Cythraul hissed. "I'm not talking about freedom from the Wayfolk's prisons, or even my execution. I mean—freedom from you!"

The words struck Ealden like a blow. "I . . . I know. I pushed you too hard. I was harsh—"

"Harsh?" Cythraul threw his head back and laughed. "Harsh doesn't begin to cover what you put me through. I learned all I could but it was never enough because I was not perfect. And I could never—NEVER—please the First One until I was perfect, you self righteous bastard!"

"How dare—" Ealden caught himself. "Again, I am sorry, but Xanalos, it is not too late. The First One can forgive even the most egregious acts."

Cythraul's eyes narrowed. "You mean acts such as I have done these last hundred years or so. Hmm, I think not." He grew quiet a moment and ran his hand over the pristine stone surface. "Let us put your vision of the First One to the test then, shall we? I wish to show you what I've been working on these many years. Once you've seen it, should you still believe that I can attain forgiveness, I will submit to you. I will . . . surrender."

"And the Eye?"

"Back to Llanfair, of course." Cythraul did not smile, but his eyes gleamed. "Will you accept my terms?"

Ealden involuntarily backed up a step. "I have not yet heard the other side of those terms. What if—"

"What if you change your mind? What if you are so horrified that you believe I am utterly beyond salvation? What then?" Cythraul patted the hilt of his sword. "Then, Ealden, you do what you came here to do."

39 DRINNAS 2238

"What were those things?" Telwyn asked. He and Alastair sat on the bank of the Nightwash River.

"I do not know precisely," Alastair said. "I feared they were the spirits of the dead . . . I really did. In spite of all I know to be true in the word of the First One, I still thought the dead had risen. But now, we've seen their true faces."

"Big leeches, they seemed."

"Yes, but much more than that. Disturbing to ponder, but these creatures must have inhabited the barrows."

"But they appeared as dead warriors. I saw Anglish armor. I saw Stonehands and Gorracks."

Alastair scowled. "Perhaps they devour the corpses and can somehow mimic them, using the more agile bodies to capture more prey. We were fortunate even to get our horses back."

"That's disgusting," Tel said. "And what do you mean, more prey? Would those things . . . would they eat the living?"

"Who can say?" Alastair replied as he stood. "But they were coming after us for some reason. In any case, I have no desire to test the theory. What troubles me is why there are so many now. When I first saw them, during the war, there were only a few . . . and they kept their distance." Alastair strode to his horse and clambered up into the saddle.

Telwyn rose. "I sincerely hope we will not see those things again," he said. "Perhaps, when we return, we can charter a ship and avoid the Felhaunt altogether."

"Steel yourself," Alastair said.

"Why, Mi Da?"

"We are riding for Vulmarrow Keep. There we may find ourselves wishing for the pleasantries of the Felhaunt."

40 Drinnas 2238

King Ealden stood among the flickering red candles and waited. Cythraul had left the chamber, descending a stairwell behind the dais to Allhaven knew where. A few moments later, Ealden heard voices. There was a scuffle and a frail voice shouting, "No, no, no!" There came a sharp, sudden scream . . . a weak gurgling . . . and then, silence.

Cythraul emerged, dragging something across the dais.

Ealden grimaced and closed his eyes. But that did him no favors. He could hear the flopping of limp arms and the thudding of a head on the stairs.

"I apologize for the delay," Cythraul said, his voice oddly detached. "It never ceases to amaze me how, in spite of living a tortured existence, how reluctant people are to die."

King Ealden opened his eyes in time to watch Cythraul lift the body up onto the wide table. He had been a young man, maybe thirty summers, if that. He bore the frame of someone who had once been very strong, but had withered away over time. A purplish open gash marred the skin of his chest, and streaks of blood trailed his protruding rib cage. "You took his life?" Ealden asked.

"Some questions do not deserve answers," Cythraul said. He reached beneath the table. After several clicks, panels recessed in the table top flipped open. He went to work pulling a length of thick strap from each compartment.

"Who was he?" Ealden asked.

"That is another such question," Cythraul replied. "Time is precious, don't you think? Let's not waste it."

Ealden let his hand drop to his side and just a little lower to the pocket containing the weapon he needed. "That man had a name, an identity, a life. And Cythraul you took it from him."

"Formality," Cythraul replied. "Anyone can take a life."

"Wait, what are you doing?"

Cythraul ignored him and finished strapping down the corpse. "There," he said. "Arms and legs are done, but you cannot forget to immobilize the head and neck." He gave a full tug on the neck strap and stepped away from the table. "Are you ready?"

"What . . . what have you—" Ealden's throat constricted. He felt like he could barely breathe.

"As I said, anyone can take a life," Cythraul explained. "Even you, Prydian King. But I defy you to tell me of one who can give life back." Cythraul removed a glass cylinder from the inside of his jacket and held it up for Ealden to see. It was filled with a bruise-colored liquid and appeared somewhat viscous.

"Years of study, Ealden. Careful study. But in the end, all worth it. I have discovered a certain creature, a very rare creature with a singularly extraordinary ability. Over time, I have learned its secret." He began to turn the cylinder this way and that so that the liquid ran slowly from one end to the other.

"You'll be pleased to know, I've advanced in my faith, learning new rites and rituals. Intricate and demanding, yes, but Sabryne rewards the diligent." He removed the stopper from the cylinder and affixed a strange curved spout in its place.

"And last, I've discovered some aspects of being a Pureline that have gone unchronicled and unnoticed, I'll wager, even by you. My blood, for instance, when mingled that of the creature I mentioned and then transmuted by the rituals I mentioned, can have some breathtaking effects."

Then, he plunged the spout into the dead man's chest wound. The unwholesome plum-colored liquid gurgled out of the cylinder until the glass showed clear. With a flourish, Cythraul yanked it free from the body. "Watch, Ealden, watch!" his voice thundered. "And see what your apprentice has wrought!"

King Ealden stood transfixed . . . in a kind of paralysis of macabre fascination. The body began to tremble, its muscles spasmed, and its fingers and toes curled. Ealden heard sounds from its throat, like half-attempted breaths drowned out by phlegm and spittle. Ealden found himself moving inches closer to the table, his eyes locked on the spasming corpse. Suddenly its head lifted, straining against the neck strap. Its eyes found Ealden's. The look on his face—his—for Ealden could no longer think of it as a dead piece of flesh, was utter and desperate anguish. Tears streaked from his bulging eyes, and his mouth contorted, releasing a ghastly, sorrowful moan: "Nooo . . . noo . . ." Then, the head fell back to the table, and the body went still.

Ealden looked from the corpse to Cythraul. But Ealden's former apprentice still stared intently at the body. Ealden shifted his gaze back to the body and—

A shriek erupted from the corpse. And where before it had trembled and spasmed, now it bounced and thrashed and tore at the restraints. Its head came up as far as it could, and again, its eyes found Ealden's. But now there was nothing in its countenance remotely human—only a vicious animalistic rage. Its eyes still bulged with blood now pooling in the whites. Peculiar blue veins streaked away from the corners of its eyes. An entire root system of those same blue vessels spread down its chest and limbs.

"You see, Ealden?" Cythraul said. "I have given this empty shell new life!"

Ealden backed away from the table. The body grunted and spat and hissed. It fought the restraints, writhed, and jerked.

"This . . . Xanalos . . . is an abomination!" He drove his hand into his breech pocket and pulled free one of the two packets. "You are playing with forces far beyond you! Y-you make a mockery of life—and death!"

"So, you do not approve then?" Cythraul laughed. "I might have known." A sudden flash of iron—Cythraul brought an ax crashing down on the corpse's neck. It thrashed for a few moments more and went still.

Cythraul turned and took a menacing step toward Ealden. "Where is your forgiveness now, teacher?"

"Beast!" Ealden screamed. "Blaspheming, miscreant!" He tore a corner of the packet and heaved it at Cythraul. As it raced through the air, it ignited as if Ealden had thrown a small comet.

Cythraul's eyes widened, but he turned the ax blade and used it like a shield to block the flaming projectile. It left a burning resin on the ax, but the majority of its mass fell on the body. In seconds, its entire upper torso was engulfed in white hot flame.

"Fire?" Cythraul hissed, tossing the burning ax away. "Now, you're making this personal." Cythraul's eyes roamed over Ealden. "You've lost your glaive have you?"

"Perhaps your creatures would fetch it for me?" Ealden suggested.

"I think not." Cythraul drew a sword and pointed it toward Ealden. "But I'll not fight an unarmed foe." He tossed the sword, hilt first, to Ealden. But the toss had been high. Ealden kept his eyes on the blade, reached up, and grabbed it—

And suddenly, Cythraul was there, right in Ealden's face. And Ealden felt a searing pain in his abdomen.

Cythraul's low voice rumbled out in thunderous syllables. "I told you if you ever spoke the name of Xanalos again, I would gut you."

He wrenched the hand with the dagger, and Ealden groaned. "Goodbye, teacher!" Cythraul tore the dagger through Ealden's flesh and shoved him away. "If you meet the First One, please thank him for making me what I am today."

CHAPTER 26

THE RED CAMPAIGN

*"Being Swordmaster and combat trainer for the Anglish Guard, I've
trained a great many pupils and seen incredibly talented warriors come
and go. But there was once a most surprising young combatant who
quite literally took my breath away. Dark hair, skin pale as the moon,
but green eyes that flashed with intensity—this particular newcomer
insisted on training without a weapon. And, more often than not,
this warrior preferred to train against someone who was armed. After
months of training, it came time for the Guard Exam. This brave heart
told me not to hold back, so I did not. My sword flashed in the afternoon light, but I'll be a dragon's uncle if my blade got anywhere near
my opponent. Whirling, ducking, sliding, leaping, and spinning—my
challenger evaded my every attack, vexing me to no end. My final
gambit, a move that had laid many polished Anglish Guards on their
backsides, gave me the best angle of attack I'd had. But by the time I'd
drawn back my blade for the lunge, I found the hard lower palm of my
opponent slamming into my gut. It was the second of only three times I
had been knocked to the ground during an exam. That warrior was the
best unarmed combatant I have ever faced. She would have made an
excellent addition to the Anglish Guard. It's a shame she had to go and
marry that Aravel and become the High Queen."*

—Memoirs of General Alfred Adelbard,
Swordmaster of Anglinore Castle (2172 - 2238 AS)

6 SOLMONATH, 2238

Raudrim-Quevara extended a talon from her hand and sliced a thick wedge of beef from the still-smoking steer carcass. The knock at her chamber door surprised her, for she had given strict orders not to be disturbed while she fed. The only one with the gall to dare would be—

"My queen!" Vilnus Skevack called from the widening crack between the twin chamber doors. "I bear news." He closed the doors behind him, half-tip-toed up to the table, and bowed.

"Council Chairman Vilnus," the queen said quietly. "Did I not command peace while I sup? Did I not forbid any disturbance?"

Vilnus bowed again. His squinty eyes became mere slits. "It is as you say. But, my lady queen, when two of your commands are in conflict, which shall I obey? Long before your command that you be left alone was spoken, you told me to alert you immediately if the Red Campaign met any resistance. Oh!"

He gasped and stepped backward. Reptillian, fang-shaped pupils flashed yellow in the queen's eyes. Vilnus tried to back up another step but found an iron-hard length of scaled flesh behind him, barring his movements.

Raudrim-Quevara's armored tail forced Vilnus back to the table's edge. "What village?" she demanded.

"N-n-not a village," Vilnus said. "An entire province."

The transformation was not some drawn out, piece-by-piece change. It happened fast, her human flesh expanding and melting away, revealing dark, rose colored scales. Her neck collided with the ceiling, and her wings extended, knocking over furniture left and right. "Which provinsssss?" she hissed.

Her heated breath washed over Vilnus. He held up his hands and turned his head as much as he dared. "Drinaris," he said. "Steadfeld fortress in the mountains and Rel-Vigil on Lake Ioma. Stonehand, Spriggan, and Human, formidable defenses, natural— and—constructed. Strong contingents of Cragfel still loyal to the former queen stationed in both outposts. It will not be—"

"I will bathe in their blood." As Raudrim-Quevara turned, her tail knocked Vilnus to the floor. When he got back to his feet, she was gone.

7 SOMONATH, 2238

Drinaris Province lay in the extreme northwest of the Hinterlands. Inescapable mountains formed its outer border, part of the greater chain of mountains that had kept the Hinterlands sealed off from the rest of Myriad for untold generations. The climate of the region varied wildly. Sprawling farms quilted the southern third of the province while snowy mining cities and military bases ruled the north. Vast herds of range-feeding scormount roamed the lands between—as did the Stonehand tribes that hunted them.

The farmers in southern Drinaris Province often did battle with kraoaks, gigantic black birds with an appetite for corn and other staple crops. Savvy farmers would often lie in wait in their fields with loaded and cocked ballistas . . . waiting for the kraoaks to come to feed. No sooner would the great bird land but it would find itself impaled with one of the post-length shafts from the ballista. But other farmers weren't nearly as vigilant. Some, in fact, accepted the kraoaks as part of the natural farming process. They took what they took. There was always enough left to live on and more besides to trade.

That is probably why Gangel Bitwiler paid no heed to the vast black shadow that passed over his head as he plowed out the weeds between the tall rows of sweet-greens. Old Gangel kept his head down, his mind on the work. So did Baily, his mule-scormount who made light work of pulling the heavy plow-sled through the rooty soil. It wasn't until he heard his wife Gertrude screaming shrilly from their cottage behind him that he knew something was terribly wrong.

"For peak's sake, woman," Gangel grumbled, spinning on his bare heel. He saw her there on the cottage's back porch, hopping up and down like she'd just stepped in fire pit. "What's-a-matta with you . . . you?" He saw her pointing at the same time as he heard Baily bray angrily. A shadow fell over him in an instant, and Gangel thought he understood, thought a nasty freak storm had just blown up on him while he wasn't paying attention.

But when Gangel turned round, he nearly died in his tracks. Wings that seemed to stretch from one end of the field to the other obscured his view of the horizon and even the sky. An immense creature towered before him. It was almost completely covered in deep red scales so large they looked like sections of plate armor. But aside from scales, its torso looked like that of a giant human, a female human at that. It's powerful legs were as thick as ancient maple trunks, its arms full of taught, ropey muscle, and its five-fingered hands displayed long, bone-white talons. Between its massive shoulders, its long, snaking neck began, ending some thirty feet later at its horrific head. Its muzzle was long and flat; its mouth full of short needlish teeth and long, tusk-like incisors. But its features were somehow like that of a human face, stretched and contorted to fit the raptorish skull. The thing had bulky, curling horns like those of a mountain ram and a flowing crimson mane trailing down the back of its neck.

Baily was still braying away at the thing, perhaps seeing its similar horns and mistaking it for some monstrous form of its own kind. "Baily!" Gangel whispered urgently. "Shut yer yap! Shut yer—"

It was too late. The dragon struck, its jaws opening and closing in a blur and crushing the scormount in a bloody instant. The plow sled was torn right out from under Gangel and he toppled into a row of sweet-greens. His heart pounding near out of his chest, Gangel sprang to his feet and started running. *Poor Baily,* he thought. *Poor, poor Baily.*

The dragon's roar shook the ground and made Gangel's ears ring. He stumbled to a knee and realized that he'd been running toward his cottage. "No, Gangel!" he growled at himself. "Got to lead it away from my Gertie! But where? C'mon, think!" Then he knew. He peeked out of the stalks to get his bearings and then sprinted towards the Billups' farm. Old Billups had a field full of tall corn and not a few ballistas hidden around for the kraoaks.

Another roar, and then a devastating wave of heat washed over Gangel. The sweat on his back flash-dried, and Gangel found himself rolling in the soil for a moment. He leaped to his feet and saw his sweet-greens ablaze with crimson fire. But the dragon was walking through it, straight towards his cottage. Gangel ran for the open soil and started leaping as high in the air as he could. "Over here!" he yelled. "Over here, ye big fat hog! Come'n get me if ye can!" He grabbed a fist full of egg-sized stones and hurled them at the dragon. "Uh, oh!" Then, he ran for his life.

A voice rang out, its voice a dreadful combination of the peal of thunder, the ringing of great bells, and rumbling of stone in an avalanche. "Spriggan INSECT!" the dragon shrieked. "I am Raudrim-Quevara, Lord of Dragons and Queen of this world. Dare you raise your tiny fist to me?" A gout of red flame spewed from her jaws. "Cower and DIE!"

Gangel didn't care much for the whole dying idea, but he was cowering aplenty, even as he ran. He heard the deep whoosh of the dragon's broad wings as it took to the air. Gangel swallowed hard and sprinted for the wire fence ahead that marked Billups' boundary. He dove over the fence, tearing a panel out of his overalls, and then rolled back to his feet. "Blasted corn!" he yelled. He couldn't see a foot in any direction through the thickening stalks. On the other hand, that meant the monster probably couldn't see him very well either. There was a certain charm to that thought.

Heat rushed through the corn on the right like a sudden flood. Gangel veered sharply left just as fire colored the entire area red. Gangel had worked fields in direct summer sun. He'd stoked and tended bonfires of deadfall so hot and fierce that friends could see the flames from the mountains. And he'd managed forges hot enough to melt wrought iron. But he'd never felt any heat like this. *So much for not seein' me,* he thought. *Doesn't need t'see me.*

Doesn't need to get me with the flames, either. Blasted heat'll bake me if'n I get too near.

Raudrim-Quevara swooped overhead, unleashing a quaking roar. Gangel covered his ears, running awkwardly with his elbows smacking corn stalks. *Mice in the cellar*—the image popped right into his mind as he ran. Blasted nuisances zigzagging as he tried to clobber them with a piece of wood scrap—*That's what I've got to do.* Gangel slid to a sudden stop on one heel, jagged to the left and then raced back in the direction he had come. Then, he darted back to the right and sprinted back and forth through the corn. That seemed to be working. He heard the swoosh of the dragon's wings, but it was much farther away.

The next thing Gangel knew, he was flat on his back, a splitting headache blossoming within, and blood stinging his right eye. He sat up, tentatively feeling the welt rising on his forehead. Then, he saw the massive wooden wheel he'd just run right into. *Good thing I didn't run into the slider,* he thought. *Might'a brained myself.*

If there wasn't a welt on his head, Gangel would have smacked himself. A ballista. One of Billups finest anti-kraoak weapons sat in the midst of the corn. It wasn't loaded, but several post-sized bolts were stuck in the ground next to the other wheel. He stood there staring at the massive rolling crossbow. Another roar from the creature snapped him to action. With a quick, violent jerk, he hefted up one of the bolts, turned and dropped it onto the slide. Then he went to work, cranking back the lever, turning the torsion springs, and rachetting the firing cord as far back as—

The dragon's shadow fell over him. It swooped low enough for him to smell the beast before it glided away. It was no good. Gangel had barely ever shot a ballista before. He wasn't like Billups who could shoot kraoaks right out of the sky. Gangel needed the creature to be relatively still. He kicked out the wheel chocks and spun the weapon in the direction the dragon had flown. *Ah, Gertie,* he thought as he scrambled up on the ballista's frame, *this might just be the end'a me. But I gotta try.*

Careful not to get caught up in the firing mechanism, he clambered up the structure until he was head and shoulders above the corn. "Hey'a you! Rude-drip, or whatever yer name be! Ye missed me, ye did, big fat flyin' lizard!" He watched the creature wheel about, red fire spurting out in a flaming arc. "That's right! Right here, beast! Ye flew right over me, ye stupid—" *Uh, oh!* The dragon came on so fast, crashing into the corn just thirty yards ahead. Racing back down the slide, Gangel tripped over the firing cord and planted his face hard into the soil. Sensing the danger, he was on his feet and at the firing pin.

"INSECT, I have you now!"

Gangel could actually feel the creature's footfalls, low *whumps*, vibrating through the soles of his feet. "Keep a'comin'," he muttered. "Yer gonna get more than ye put in fer." He looked up, seeing the creature's full body. It was as big as a castle keep, and then the wings . . . Gangel had never seen a living creature remotely as big. It advanced slowly, putting itself directly in the ballista's line of fire.

Gangel took up the rear balance and adjusted the aim as best he could to line up the slide with the beast's chest. It was closing fast. Red scales filled Gangel's whole field of vision. "I'm not gonna get a better shot." He dove for the firing pin. It released. The torsion springs unleashed their stored forces. The firing cord whipped forward, launching the sixty pound, steel-tipped bolt with enough force to clear the corn fields and land in the foothills. But instead, all the energy of bolt drove it straight into the dragon's chest. Raudrim-Quevara roared and fell backward, crashing into the corn.

"Ha, ha!" Gangel exulted. "Got ya, I did! Overblown freak, I got . . . got ya—"

Sounding like great chains clattering over gears, a deep laugh rolled out of the corn. The dragon leaped to its feet and eclipsed all sight, even the sun, with its wings. Gangel stared at its chest. No wound. No damage at all. Not even a scratch on one of the red scales. Raudrim-Quevara flung back its head and its neck snapped back and forth like a whip.

The last thing Gangel saw was a great wave of red.

Pleased with her initial efforts, Quevara left the burning farms of southern Drinaris Province and soared northward on wind that was growing steadily colder. The snowcapped mountains loomed ever larger in the distance, but there also was a curious sight. Quevara dropped the angle of her left wing and dropped several thousand feet for a better look. Scormount, tens of thousands of them, herded on the undulating grassland below.

Obeying an impulse she didn't completely understand, she dove down until she could drop in the midst of them. Her landing pulped several scormount, but that was merely the beginning. She spread her wings to control their movements. She whipped her heavy tail onto the backs of the scormount, snapping spines and crushing bones. Her talons flashed, impaling and disemboweling the helpless scormount even as they tried to flee. Then, she took to the air and unleashed her deadly fire. Back and forth, across the herd, she swooped, spraying down streams of scarlet flame. The anguished cries of the burning scormount, the shrieks of agony, and even the quiet death-sighs were all as music to Quevara. She felt herself empowered by that macabre song, strengthened at her core and filled with a pulsing lust for more.

The scormount were not her enemy. Nor did she need them for food. But the very fact that they lived and breathed and moved about—felt like a singular act of defiance to Quevara. Talons flashing, tail slashing, and liquid fire raining down, she swept across the herd until nothing moved but the dancing flames.

A red mist settled over the valley as Quevara departed.

8 SOLMONATH, 2238

The soldiers stationed at Steadfeld Keep had not been idle. Couriers had brought word of the return of the Red Queen to Cragfel Tor, the assassination of Queen Righel and subsequent coup. They'd heard report of the Red Campaign . . . that the Red Queen had built an army of traitors who were beating down all opposition. And they'd even heard rumors that the Red Queen had somehow gained control over a monstrous dragon, a catastrophic creature that left ruin in its wake.

So for nigh on a month, the soldiers of Steadfeld Keep, buttressed by Cragfel troops who'd escaped from other already conquered provinces, had fortified the fortress' defenses.

Stevan Windcrest stood tall on the curling parapet atop the forward tower. "Suicide," he said to Ali Tobin, his squire who stood at his side.

She looked up questioningly. "Lord?"

"It would be suicide to march troops up these mountain passes for an assault." He stared down at the defenses. They'd built brick and mortar bottlenecks at the head of each path. Armies would have to squeeze to two soldiers broad to get through, and it would be slow moving and deadly. "I don't care how many thousands of soldiers this Red Queen can muster. They will perish here before they reach the front gate."

"Surely, it is as you say," Ali replied. She frowned as a lock of her curly golden hair fell from her helm. She hurriedly tucked it back up and under. The less Knight Stevan thought of her as a simple girl, the better. "What word shall I bring to Forward Commander Faust?"

"Same as always, Squire," he replied. "Tell him to stand ready."

The words were scarcely off his lips when he noted a tiny figure on horseback racing up the southernmost pass. He leaned forward over the parapet and watched the stallion kick up puffs of powdered snow as it passed one bottleneck and raced to the next.

"Who is that?" Squire Ali asked.

"Green tunic," Stevan said, thinking aloud. "The Timberguard, I would think. First line, Commander Belsen's team. He's in a dreadful hurry. Come, squire."

There was no fast path from any of the towers or bastions in Steadfeld Keep to the main gatehouse. Enemies who might somehow pass the front gates would not find advancement easy or swift. And so, when Knight-Commander Windcrest and his squire finally arrived at the central stair in the middle of the fortress, the Timberguard they'd seen from far above, met them halfway up the stair.

"Knight-Commander!" he said. "I am Timberguard Kolmorgen, and I bring word from the Palisades. I seek audience with you."

"You have it," Stevan replied. "I saw you from above. What news?"

"Quevara, the Red Queen, she is here."

"Here! But there is no army . . . I would have seen—"

"She is alone, Knight-Commander," Kolmorgen explained. "Commander Belsen has her at the Palisades. She claims she's come to parley."

"Parley?" Knight-Commander Stevan didn't laugh, though the situation did indeed seem ridiculous to him.

"And the scouts?" Ali asked. "Are they coming and going as usual?"

"By the hour," Kolmorgen said. "If the Red Queen has her army backing her, then they are invisible."

Knight-Commander Stevan, scratched the beard he'd meant to shave that morning and said, "I do not like the feel of this. But if she has indeed come alone, we cannot pass up this opportunity. Search her. Escort her forward. We'll parley in the Library Vault. But, Kolmorgen, watch her every move. If she so much as exhales a hint of treachery, behead her on the spot."

"Yes, Knight-Commander."

"My lord?" Squire Ali said. "What of the dragon? Perhaps it waits in some hidden spot to strike us. Perhaps, the Red Queen will signal the beast in some way."

Stevan nodded. "You'll make a fine knight yet, Ali," he said. "If not Knight-Commander. That's good thinking. Go and alert the tower chiefs to load every arbalest, every ballista and catapult. We cannot ignore the skies." He was quiet a moment and then said, "If she should make some signal and bring the dragon against here, at least she will not leave Steadfeld Keep alive to trouble the rest of our world."

The Library Vault was a vast octagonal room filled with towering bookcases some sixty feet high. The high shelves were accessible by an intricate network of ladders and rails that crisscrossed the face of each wall like a metallic spider's web. It was Stevan's favorite place to think when he was alone and his favorite place to hold council when he was not. He and his squire waited at the vast oaken table, and Cragfel soldiers, armed with blade and crossbow, stood ready at each ladder.

Stevan heard footsteps in the hall. Kolmorgen and a team of Timberguard warriors strode into the room, and with them, was the most captivating woman the Knight-Commander had ever seen. Rich scarlet hair flowed beneath the Crown of Cragheath Tor and spilled down her milk white neck and shoulders. Her eyes were large, emerald green, and slightly angled down toward the base of her nose. Her brows were curiously arched and she bore a playful smile on her heart-shaped face. She wore a flowing burgundy gown with open, fluted sleeves and a somewhat daring neckline. Stevan wondered that she could have borne cold for so long, wearing just that bit of cloth.

He shook thoughts of admiration from his mind and reminded himself of the history of this woman. She had not been called the Red Queen for her hair. Stevan stood and said, "Quevara, you are come to Steadfeld Keep, but unless you have come to surrender and submit yourself to trial, you are not welcome here."

"Surrender?" Quevara replied, the tone in her voice light and playful like her smile. "But I've only just arrived."

"Parley is it?" Stevan asked. "What are your terms."

"Won't you even offer a lady a seat at the table?"

Stevan looked to Kolmorgen who said, "We've searched her. She bears no weapon."

"Yes," she said. "They searched me very, very well. I am unarmed."

"Very well," said the Knight Commander. "Then take your seat and state your terms."

Quevara snuggled down into the high-backed chair and leaned seductively to one side. "Terms . . . parley, they sound so formal and negative. I prefer to speak as colleagues. Knight-Commander, is it? A very high rank, and well earned, I am sure. My scouts report that you've refused my advances, turned me down flat . . . cold. I wondered if you were even truly aware of what I offer."

"To know that rightful Queen Righel is dead by your hand is enough. You have nothing you can offer me but your head for a noose."

"Nasty, nasty boy," she said, arching her back. "Why such a rush for death and vengeance? Was Queen Righel really such a fine ruler? I'd be willing to wager that she never came to call upon you out here . . . so far away in these cold, cold mountains. Did she?"

"That is irrelevant," Stevan replied. "She was not perfect, but she was just. And I swore an oath that I will never rescind."

"I thought you might say that," Quevara said, her smile turning somewhat sad . . . almost forlorn. "I really hoped I could persuade you somehow. Military overthrows are not so uncommon. And, historically speaking, the throne of Cragheath Tor has been taken many times through bloodshed. When I departed the first time, I believe you know who assumed the throne and how she took it. Listen to my offer, Knight-Commander . . . Stevan Windcrest. I won't repeat it. Vow to serve me. Bear the red standard on the towers of Steadfeld Keep. Defend me when I am attacked and march to war with me when I must fight for our land. Do these . . . and I will make Drinaris Province a royal holding . . . a duchy. And you shall be its Duke."

The Timberguards shifted in their stance. The Cragfel exchanged nervous glances.

"I refuse," Stevan answered. "I refuse utterly. You are a criminal . . . an assassin . . . and an enemy of all who call the Hinterlands home."

"Well, that doesn't leave much room for discussion, does it?" She laughed. "As you wish. Time to die."

"Guards!" he called. "Arrest her and throw her in the dun—" His words choked off. Indeed all the breath in his lungs was forced out. He fought at something beneath the tabletop. His face turned brilliant red, then purple, and his eyes bulged. The guards rushed to his aid and others attacked the Queen, but it was too late. There came a horrific crack, and the Knight-Commander slumped to the floor. Quevara's tail slammed the massive table into several of the Cragfel. And her skin melted away to scales.

Fire kindled in the Library Vault, and everything within it . . . burned.

CHAPTER 27

SILVERGLEN

Myridians follow a simple fourteen month calendar. Seven months have 55 days; seven have 56.

1. Alpheus (Full Winter)
2. Wenvier (The White Month)
3. Avrill
4. Sedwyn (Full Spring)
5. Feftin
6. Solmonath
7. Solmas (Full Summer)
8. Celesandur
9. Drinnas
10. Octale
11. Marne (Full Autumn)
12. Atervast
13. Muertanas (The Dead Month)
14. Advent (Month of Anticipation)

—Letti's Almanac, 2085, AS

11 SOLMAS 2238

This time, Loch would leave Anglinore City by the docks. He saw Captain Dagspaddle's Mynx moored there, and smiled. He wouldn't take that ship, but finding alternate passage to Brightcastle was easy enough. He found a swift tri-masted barq called *Windmaiden*, paid a hefty sum to board at the last minute, and then grinned as he watched the Cliffs of Anglinore fade away.

12 SOLMAS 2238

Lochlan wore a plain, slate-gray tunic, leather breeches dyed dark blue, and black boots. He appraised himself in the mirror of his cabin. "There," he said, hoisting his pack onto his shoulder. "I look every bit the average tradesman." He'd spent the entire sea voyage wondering which trade to assume once he got to Silverglen. They were known for their hunting prowess, hunting and trapping. Loch didn't care much for trapping. *Not much skill involved there,* he thought. His mother had suggested being a baker or confectionary . . . meet more young ladies that way, she'd claimed. So, hunting it would be. Loch laughed to himself. He'd brought his whole pack of trade supplies just in case, everything except for his blacksmith tools. So, with cook pans and lute bouncing around on his back and bow hung over his shoulder, Lochlan left his cabin and went to fetch Chalaren from the holds.

13 SOLMAS 2238

In Brightcastle, Lochlan grabbed a hot breakfast of biscuits and savory sausage gravy and was soon on his way. The journey west across Amara was swift and relatively brief. Loch decided to ride well south of Llanfair. He didn't want to run into any of Ealden's folk. When he had passed far enough west, he drove immediately north and was gratified to find that at least a league of his journey was through the seemingly endless fields of flowers. Alastair, Abbagael, and Telwyn had told him of their beauty, but their words were far from sufficient. He slowed Chalaren just a little so that he could watch the waves of scarlet, violet, gold, red, blue, and white undulate in the ever present breeze. *If ever I find a maiden to be my wife,* he thought. *I will bring her here to propose.*

The flowers left far behind now, he made camp at nightfall. On the morrow he would set forth for The Crimson Way.

14 Solmas 2238

It was the wrong time of year to visit The Crimson Way, Loch knew. The silver oaks would be in the grandeur of bloom, leaves silver gray and smooth as suede, clusters of soft purple flowers dotting the lush foliage. It would still be pretty enough and still a worthy visit, but not like in the fall. Still, there was plenty to see and enjoy. The Stormsheer Mountain range stretched from well inside the Gorrack nation all the way to the north-eastern tip of Amara. And in between, two arms of the impassible mountains created a very long, narrow valley. The massive silver oaks pressing in from the mountains' roots made the way more narrow still.

Lochlan slowed Chalaren to a trot and found himself awed. Just a matter of traversing a few hundred paces, from the passage's opening to the first silver oaks, was enough for palpable change. The mountains and the trees seemed to muffle all ambient sound, so that silence itself took on its own audible texture. It seemed to Loch that it was like holding sea shells to both ears. And though he'd had it described to him many times, it was nothing like experiencing it in person. The silver oaks towered high on either side of a passage that was maybe sixty paces wide. But the uncanny thing was that the trees had grown up naturally and yet they created a perfectly bordered corridor. No trunk strayed into the path so much as a foot. They looked as if some particular army of gardeners had measure plots and planted thousands of saplings just so.

As Chalaren clopped slowly forward, Loch looked past the eerie symmetry and thought also the history of The Crimson Way. And for that, he felt a sense of heavy reverence. Loch shuddered, but it was not cold. On he rode, his eyes roaming into the thickening silver oaks and into the foothills of the mountains on either side. Then just at the edge of sight, there was a slight bend in the perfect path. And on the outside of that bend was a pillar of dark bronze.

Lochlan slid down from the saddle and stood before the monument. It commemorated an event from Anglish lore that would be found in every military journal or tactics class. Somehow, seeing the tale written in bronze, brought the reality of the account. The feeling of reverence he'd had before became something of supernatural impact. It wasn't often that someone could stand where 10,000 people had been slaughtered.

Loch read the monument:

In the waning days of summer in the year 2408 D, Gaelan Keenblade emptied Manticore Keep
Of the Great Northern Host for the long journey to their new home in Graymere.
Ten Thousand souls marched this path between the silver oaks: soldiers, women, children, old ones,
They were glad of heart to escape the reach of the tempestuous sea.
It was here on this very spot where Gaelan and the others first knew something was wrong.
War horns, deep and sonorous, rang out from the mountains.
Ingvell Kur, Warlord of the Gorrack Nation, drove his bands down from the cliffs and ledges
and in from both entryways, cutting off all escape. In the largest unprovoked attack in Myridian history,

The Gorracks routed Gaelan Keenblade and the Manticore remnant. Thus began the First Gorrack Invasion.
There were no survivors, save one. Lucius Farfallon,
volatile Shepherd of Manticore Keep lived
To tell this tale. For it was from his own deathbed confession, wasted by plague, and shriveled by guilt
Shepherd Lucius revealed the price he'd been paid to
betray his own.

Lochlan shivered, turned away from the monument, and
clambered back into his saddle. He didn't need to read the rest of
what had been inscribed there. He knew it well. The leaves of the
silver oaks in all the rest of the world turned a shimmery silver-
blue in fall. But not here. The leaves along this long, forlorn trail
turn deep crimson.

In some ways, now that he was here, now that he was traveling the path for himself, he was glad he'd come at this time of
years. To see the blood-red leaves would be a burden, one Loch
wasn't sure he was ready to bear.

Dozens of gabled roofs poked up above Silverglen's stout city
walls. Lochlan had always heard that Silverglen was a simple
village of miners and hunters, not so well fortified as all this.

*A function of being a mere handful of leagues from the Gor-
rack Nation,* thought Loch. He rode up to the main gates, tall
arched doors, stained near to black, and saw no sign of movement.
Loch fought down an inexplicable fear that the village had been
raided, and no one left alive. Remnant visions of the Crimson
Way, he thought, shaking his head free of such images. He gave
the door a good pounding.

A panel of wood slid away, revealing a grated window on the
left hand door. "Welcome to Silverglen!"

An identical panel withdrew on the right. "An ideal place to
live and work . . . where silver flows down from the mountains to
line your pockets!" Both guards laughed heartily.

"Uh, well I am looking for a place to live and work . . . for a time," Loch said. "Might I gain entry?"

The gate guard on the left looked through the grate and said, "Nice hair."

"Uh . . . thanks," Loch replied, feeling more than a little awkward.

"Do you play?" asked the gate guard on the right.

"Play what?" asked Loch.

"The lute, ya baffoon," he said. "I see it peekin' over yer shoulder there."

"Oh," Loch replied. "Yes, I play a little."

"Welcome and well met," the guard on the left said, and the doors swung open.

The guard on the right dropped down from his post and came round the door. He was a Stonehand and not more than three and half feet tall. "You must go to the Pipe and Tabor. It's our local inn. We compete in the common room every Halfinday just after sundown."

The guard on the left hopped down as well. He was nearly as tall as Loch, and given his narrow features and pointed, slanting ears, he was Vespal Wayfolk by birth. "Yes, yes," he said. "You must compete. First prize is a gold piece!"

Ooooh, thought Lochlan. *A whole gold piece.*

"Yes, yes, you must go," said the right hand guard.

"Well," Loch said, "I was looking for work."

"Most excellent!" said the left hand guard. "If you're any good, Ole Bartles is sure to give ye a job, y'know, just playin' for atmosphere music and like that."

"I'll look into it," Loch said.

"Just go down the road a'piece," the right hand guard said, pointing. "The road splits at the clock tower. The Pipe and Tabor is about ten doors down on the left. If you get to the old Sanctuary, you've gone too far."

"Thank you, gentleman," Loch said and he started Chalaren to a slow walk.

"A moment," the left hand guard called.

Loch stopped Chalaren and turned.

"I was wonderin' how do you get your hair to wave like that? I mean—"

"Shhh, shh, shh!" the right hand guard took the other by the shoulder. "Don't be rude!"

"Sorry, sorry, Sir! I was meanin' no offense."

Loch nodded warily, turned, and rode away. *What's with the hair?* He wondered. Both of the guards had very long, very full hair. The left hand guard had dark hair, drawn back behind his head in several sweeping tails. The right hand guard had burnished brown hair worn in intricate braids that were woven this way and that behind his neck. Lochlan shrugged and followed the guards directions. Until the fork in the road, he found Silverglen largely unpopulated. But just past the clock tower, there were bustling shops, selling carts, and vendors. And . . . there was music. Minstrels sat in windowsills or lounged on balconies playing everything from flutes and lutes to guitars and harpsichords. And by the skill of the musicians, it all blended together.

Loch felt his spirit lightened immediately. He felt quite merry. The villagers noticed Loch immediately as he passed them. And Loch noticed them as well. The men, like the guards, had amazingly long and lush hair. And they wore it in styles and designs Loch had never seen before. The women also wore their hair long, but generally with a decorative scarf or wrap hiding some of their locks. And their gowns! Lavish, opulent evening gowns fit for a royal ball. Silks, cashmere, cannessett wool, handmade lace, and some of the finest embroidery Loch had ever seen. Surely, Silverglen was flowing in riches . . . if women went about daily shopping in such finery.

Distracted by the people, Loch continued to wander until he found himself facing the town's Sanctuary. He paused there, staring at the structure. It was in a sad state. The stonework hadn't been washed in ages. Shutters hung loose or were missing altogether. The high, slanting roof was in sore need of repair. And the walk was cracked and overgrown with weeds. Loch noted too that there wasn't much left of the avain, high on the bell tower. The place looked deserted, which, on Soliday, just twenty-four hours from Halfinday, the day of worship, was unheard of. There should have been clerics and volunteers all about the place, getting ready for the morrow. But it was empty.

Loch frowned and turned back the way he had come. This time he didn't miss the Pipe and Tabor. From the road, it appeared to be a narrow structure, maybe ten paces on either side of the door. There was a horse tie on the other side of the road, so Loch left Chalaren there. Once inside, Loch realized there was much more to the tavern. The narrow hall was freshly plastered and lined with long bench seats of rich dark wood. Brass coat hooks above the seats ran the length of both sides of the hall, and then the room ballooned out into a vast bulb of a chamber.

There were at least a dozen booth-styled tables on the left and right, the seats high backed and made of the same dark wood as those in the hall. More of the same lined the near wall, and Loch noted a little access way on the far side, presumably to a kitchen. But the obvious center of attention was the low stage built out from the center of the far wall. It looked empty for now, a few chairs scattered about. Loch could imagine the chairs filled with ghosts of past minstrels: bowing the tall viols, tip-tapping the dulcimers, strumming the lute and guitars, fingers dancing on the flutes and pipes, and maybe even the tom-tomming of drums. It quickened his heart, and he thought, *Yes, I would like to play.*

Someone cleared his throat deeply to Loch's left. "Help you?" asked a living square of a man. He was Stonehand, Loch assumed. But he was literally as wide as he was tall. Bare, rock-hard shoulders burst from the sleeveless tunic he wore. His thick and ample belly bulged beneath his apron, but didn't look overly fat. Loch ventured a guess that the man could take a Gorrack punch in the gut and not so much as flinch. His legs too, set in a wide stance as if he was ready to defend his turf, were very, very thick with muscle. They made his tiny feet look comical.

Loch said, "I'm looking for Bartles."

"Found 'im," the man said. "What'cha need, then?"

"A job, for one," Loch said. "Need a room for about a week for the other."

Bartles snorted once. His broad nose flattened out. He raised a black eyebrow and, with heavily-lidded brown eyes, looked Loch up and down. "Rooms we got," he said. "Fee's reasonable, off season, ye know. Work's plenty too. What can ye do?"

"The gentlemen at the gate said you sometimes hired minstrels . . . just to play for customers." Loch swallowed. "I play . . . and sing, a little."

"We got a lotta music in Silverglen," he said. His pinky fingernail somehow found a path through his bristly thick mustache and beard. He picked at his teeth a bit and said, "Maybe ye should just wait 'til tomorra night. Take yer chances with the locals."

"I plan to," Loch said. "But I do need a job."

"Hmph," Bartles muttered, more than a little skepticism in his tone. "Get ye up there and start playin.' It's slow hour here. Always is between two and four strokes. You get me a dozen payin' customers or more, make 'em stay with yer music, and yer hired. Left a' the stage is the back door. The locals can get pretty upset if yer no good." Bartles walked off without a second glance.

Loch shrugged. *Interesting man,* he thought. *Wouldn't want to cross him, that's for sure.* Loch could easily picture Bartles atop the city walls swinging a heavy hammer against invading foes. He smiled, went up to the stage, and took the center chair. He plopped down his backpack and carefully removed his lute. The pear-shaped instrument had once belonged to his great cousin, an accomplished minstrel who played in Anglinore City for over a hundred years. It had a longer neck and more frets than the modern nine-fret varieties. Fourteen strings set in seven courses spanned the neck to its bent headstock. The face, or soundboard, of the instrument was a thin, flat plate of well-aged spruce carved in an decorative knot of design over the sound hole. Loch glanced up at the kitchen window as he tuned. Bartles was nowhere to be seen.

So Loch began to play. His fingers moved clumsily over the fretboard at first as he plucked and strummed the introductory notes to an Elladorian hymn he'd learned when he was seven. His gentle notes soon filled the room, and Loch realized that the contours of the entire chamber had been designed and built for that very purpose. He closed his eyes and got lost in the song, adding trills and flourishes the original composer hadn't imagined. Soon the hymn reached its crescendo, and Loch's thumb stretched impossibly to hit the bass courses even as his pinky and ring fingers peppered the melody on the treble courses.

When he opened his eyes and the final notes rang, Loch noticed two couples had come in. They must have tiptoed to their seats, for Loch hadn't heard a sound. They stared back at Loch with open admiration. "Bravo, sirrah!" one man said. "Play on, play on, if you please."

The woman at the same table held up two fingers. Bartles took the order and in moments hurried out with two over-full tankards. One of the other pair got up and left in a hurry. Loch worried he'd offended the man, though the woman he left behind looked anything but offended.

Loch picked a new song from memory, a short and lively prelude from Maiocco, Anglinore's most accomplished composer. It was one of Loch's favorites, but it required sword-point focus. He closed his eyes once more and unleashed the song. Full of trills and sweeping legato, the piece challenged Loch more than he'd anticipated but, though the muscles in his hand complained, he didn't miss a note. Prior to coming to Silverglen, Loch had fully intended to be a cook or a baker, or maybe even a tavernkeep, but now that he was playing, he felt there was nothing he'd rather be doing. He finished the furious outro by hammering the strings with his left hand while tapping higher frets with his right hand fingertips. He heard the applause even before he opened his eyes to find a half dozen other tables filled.

By four o'clock, the great room at the Pipe and Tabor was packed. Bartles, sweaty and out of breath from waiting on all the orders, approached the stage, patted Loch on the shoulder, and said, "Lemme show you to your room."

It was dusk, and Loch had a delightfully full stomach. He left the Pipe and Tabor, checked on Chalaren, and then set out to see the rest of Silverglen. The shops stayed open later than in Anglinore, so Loch took his time and explored. What he found amazed him. There were far more jewelry shops and clothiers than he'd seen in many towns this size. And the wares they sold were as luxurious as anyone could want. *No wonder they're all about in such gowns,* he thought. *That's all they sell around here.* And the prices were absurdly low for such rich trappings. *If the women of Anglinore knew of these shops, they'd wear a path to Silverglen.* Three of the stores had whole sections of shelf space devoted to brushes, combs, picks, as well as, various hair bands and wraps, tails, and ribbons. There was even a local barber whose shop was packed out with men, not getting their hair cut—not much hair cut, that is—but rather getting it styled. Loch shrugged at the apparent vanity of it all. *All this for hair?*

Out of the shops now, Loch ventured up the road to the clock tower. It chimed out seven as Loch passed by, and he turned down the right hand fork. This side of town was a little less festive. The few minstrels seemed to languish on crooked front porches, and their songs were mournful and slow. There were at least four inns, Loch noted. They were not well lit, but people were inside or milling about outside, bottles and tankards close at hand. Loch felt oddly nervous and glanced up at the buildings. Darkened windows gaped back at him. It felt as if there were people in that darkness, watching this newcomer on their streets. Any moment a crossbow dart might whistle forth and take him down.

Just as Loch shook that thought away, someone grabbed his left arm. "Silver for black," he said, and his breath reeked of something acrid and strong.

"No," Loch said firmly. "Nothing for me."

"You sure," he asked. "Fine bloke like you with a head of silky hair like that, ye've got plenty of coin, am I right? See there." He pointed to a cart where several dark bottles rested. "Finest black imported all the way from Fen. Free sample if ye like."

The smell got to Loch, and he pushed the man away. "I told you, no," he said, his voice edged with steel. "Let my first refusal be final . . . and keep your distance."

The man practically sneered. "Fine, fine," he said. "But ye won't get it any cheaper than east side, hear?"

Loch picked up his pace down a hill. *Witchdrale in the streets, out in the open? In Amara? If King Ealden got word of this, there'd be a Wayfolk invasion.*

Commotion on his right, drew Loch's attention. He found two men harassing a third. The two men were brutes decked out in dark leather armor, tall with lean, stringy muscle, mops of black hair and full beards. The man on the ground wore a plain blue tunic and threadbare breeches. And he had no hair at all.

One of the ruffians planted a boot on the stricken man's backside and shoved him ruthlessly down the hill. "Get you gone, shine-head!" he growled, pursuing his prey.

The other long-haired brute chased after and gave a kick into the bald man's stomach. Loch heard the man groan, and he'd seen enough. "Here now!" he shouted as he ran. "Leave that poor fellow alone!"

The two scoundrels wheeled on Loch. The bald man clutched his stomach but looked up. Loch caught a glint of bright blue eyes. "Poor fellow?" one of the rogues said. "Why he's no man at all, not with that gleaming pate of his."

"Didn't you notice?" asked the other man. "A right disgrace, he is. Now leave us to our fun."

"Fun?" Loch exclaimed. "What sort of man takes pleasure at another man's anguish?"

They both laughed. "Why we do, of course," said the taller of the two. "Now, take your clean self back over to west side before I kick you all the way there."

"Lift a fist to me?" Loch's eyes narrowed. "Take your best shot."

They moved quicker than Loch expected. The shorter man attempted to flank him and swung for his ear while the tall rogue bull-rushed straight at him. Loch spun to a crouch and swept his leg out. The tall man tripped and buried his chin in the road. The flanker stumbled over his comrade and ate a bit of road himself. Both men were up in a hurry. Blood trickled from their yellowed teeth. "Your last mistake, boy!" the tall man growled. He threw a heavy forearm that Loch barely ducked, but it had been a ploy. The second man had drawn a blade and darted in behind the other's rush. Loch slipped it, but just barely. The blade cut a hole in his tunic.

Loch rounded on the second man slamming the bony heel of his hand into the back of the man's shoulder joint. There was a sharp pop. He dropped the blade and fell to his knees clutching at his shoulder. The taller man stood gaping until Loch unleashed a devastating uppercut under the man's jaw. He flew backward, sprawling to the road. He didn't get up.

Loch turned and helped the bald man to his feet. "Here, up you go."

"Thank you, stranger," he said, and he held out a hand. "I am Flynn."

"Loch." They shook. "It's none of my business, but why were those men accosting you?"

Flynn laughed, and his blue eyes gleamed even in the dusky twilight. "I'm glad you made it your business," he said. "I don't think my backside could take much more of that." He brushed himself off, frowning at the tears in his own tunic. "Ah, that's Fergus and Leery for you. They didn't much like what I was telling them, especially because it came from the likes of me."

"What did you do, insult their mothers?"

Flynn laughed and then winced, a hand quick to his stomach. "No, no, nothing like that. I was just urging them to come to Sanctuary. I told them the First One hadn't forgotten them."

"That doesn't exactly sound offensive to me," Loch said.

"You're not from around here, are you?" Flynn asked.

"No, no I'm not," Loch said. "But still."

"Are you a believer?"

Loch looked at the ground. "Uh . . . you mean like in the First One?"

Flynn nodded.

"Well . . . I grew up in Anglinore," Loch said. "We uh, we attended Sanctuary every Halfinday. I mean . . . I . . . well, he is up there, the First One, I mean. Seems right and all."

"Listen," Flynn said. "I owe you more than talk. Why don't you come to Sanctuary tomorrow morning, Loch. Obert McAusland'll be there. He's very wise."

"You mean the Sanctuary down there?" Loch pointed. "I thought it was abandoned."

It was Flynn's turn to stare at the ground. "Not quite," he said. "Eight strokes. Come, won't you?"

"Uh . . . well, yes," Loch mumbled.

Flynn trotted off. "See you then, Loch."

Well, thought Loch. *I wanted to get to know my people. What's the worst that could happen?*

CHAPTER 28

SANCTUARY

"When Myriad is empty of faith and my Sanctuaries are left to rot, darkness will rush in to fill the void. Every foul thing, every reeking abomination will converge upon this land. There will be suffering unlike any that has come before. Men will beg one another to dash them with stones. They will cry out to Allhaven. And into this mire my Halfainin will come."

—From Canticles (XXIV.iv), Barde Salinder (r. 846 AO)

15 AVRILL 2238

By the seventh stroke of Silverglen's clock, Loch was barely out the door of the tavern. The breakfast had been too good to cut short. He was wiping powdered sugar from his beard as he stumbled across the weedy walkway and trudged up the stairs. On the stoop, he brushed out the wrinkles in his tunic and smoothed back his hair. In truth, it had been a long time since he'd attended Sanctuary. And given the primping nature of most of the Silverglen folk, Loch felt a little underdressed.

One of the twin arched doors was ajar. Loch eased it open only to hear its rankling squeak, something akin to cats being tortured. Loch squinted and slid into the building. He wanted to sneak in as he did some days in Anglinore, but the noise had ruined that. At least he could slip into one of the back pews and—he gazed around the room. There were no pews.

There was a motley collection of single chairs and sitting in most of them were an even more motley collection of parishioners. Men and women, some old, some young. Some wearing rags; others rich garments. Some of the men were bald. Some were sick, hacking away where they sat. Some bore the fitness and bearing of soldiers. Dark skin, light skin, even one blue-skinned Marinaen—as varied and peculiar as the Grand Council after the Ceremony of Crowns.

Flynn popped up from one chair and, with a grin that seemed to span the room, bounded up the aisle. He took Loch by the shoulder, led him into the center of the room, and gave Loch the chair he'd occupied just a moment before. Loch sat and watched Flynn disappear down a basement stair. There was a terrible racket of things being tossed around, and then Flynn reemerged carrying an old wooden chair.

He plopped it down next to Loch, sat without the slightest hint of self consciousness, and turned toward the platform which might once have been a beautiful altar. A man sat there in a peculiar-looking chair with wheels. He wore a plain leather jerkin, and his legs were completely covered by a thick woolen blanket. He held a sizable book thick with ragged pages in his lap and held up one hand as he spoke.

At first, Loch didn't pay much attention to the man's message. He found himself wondering about the man. He looked Vespal Wayfolk, certainly the ears. But his thinning hair was sandy brown, odd for one of the Wayfolk who tended to have solid hair colors: dark brown, black, golden, deep red, or bright blond. His skin too looked more weathered and stretched than the perpetually youthful-looking Wayfolk's complexion. *Weathered*, thought Loch. That was the perfect word for this man. He looked like he'd been through war and storm and the strain of life, almost like Mosteryn the Old. *And what happened to his legs?*

The man said something sudden and loud. Loch blinked and started listening.

"Of course, that's what most people will tell you," he was saying. "Oh, they'll say they are comfortable with what the First One says. But really, they are only comfortable with a vague recollection. A vague recollection of what some person said about the First One. Not what the First One said Himself. There's a grave difference, you know. The difference is often life or slavery, life or death. And I wonder how many of this generation know the difference at all? Or do we rejoice in our bondage, smiling hopefully even as our flesh begins to rot?"

There was a murmuring in the makeshift congregation, a few words: "Yes, yes" or "Ah huh" or even "Tell it, Obi!"

"So, this morning," he went on, "don't listen to me. Listen to the word of the First One quoted directly from Canticles." He opened up the thick book on his lap, and when he spoke again, there was a subtle change to his voice. The pitch was lower now, the pronunciation sharper than before, a bright zing of conviction in every word. "This is what First One declares: From deepest darkness, a light has come to Myriad. But Myriad has turned away from the light because it did not want its deeds exposed. 'Who will come to me?' asks the First One. 'Look to my light. Look to my Halfainin. Though every deed of yours be black as night and every word from your lips a curse, I stand ready to forgive.'"

"Not my words," said the man. "These are the immutable words of the First One."

With that, Flynn bounced up, took his chair, and went up to the platform. He took the book of Canticles and disappeared behind a curtain. He came back with a tall viol and gave it to the speaker. Before Loch could blink, Flynn had a tall harp. Three others had brought their seats to the front and produced instruments: a lute, a flute, and a kettle drum. In moments that old, dilapidated Sanctuary came alive with music.

Flynn's fingers flew over the harp. The speaker they called Obi bowed the bass line and sang. Each of the other instruments added something unique to the masterpiece. When it was all over, Loch couldn't remember the words to the song . . . only a subtle, sweet memory of the melody. And Loch found that he'd been crying.

Obert McAusland wheeled from the wood stove over to Loch and poured hot tea in his cup. "So, you're from Anglinore?"

"How did you know that?" Loch asked, a sliver of ice in his gut. *What else does he know?*

"Word gets around," he replied. "Amazing luthier from Anglinore playing at the Pipe and Tabor, that kind of thing."

Loch relaxed a little. "Oh," he said.

"You play, then?" Flynn asked, stirring his own cup and sniffing blissfully at the vapors.

"Since I was seven," Loch said. "It came naturally. But you guys . . . this morning, that was . . . that was stunning. I've never heard music so . . . so . . ."

"Blessed?" Obert suggested. "None of us alone are anything much, but together for the common purpose of giving the First One a smile, well . . . it all seems to come together."

"What did you think of the message?" Flynn asked, his blue eyes gleaming . . . and searching.

Loch instantly found his cup of tea infinitely compelling. Well, it was a delicious cup of tea. He hadn't really planned on anything past the morning service in the Sanctuary. Obert's invitation for tea was out of the blue, but somehow irresistible. It would have been rude to turn the man down. "The message," Loch repeated. "It was . . . well, it was interesting. I've been thinking about it."

"That's a good place to start," Obert said. "We're glad you decided to come."

"What happened in Silverglen?" Loch asked.

Obert cocked an eyebrow. "What do you mean?"

"The Sanctuary," Loch replied. "It's huge, bigger than several in Anglinore, and that's saying something. Why is yours in such a state of disrepair? Why were there only a handful of people— where are the blasted pews?"

"You sound indignant," Flynn said.

"In a way, I guess I am," Loch said. "Not sure why. It just seems wrong."

"It is wrong," Obert said, but his expression held no rancor. "Silverglen is a unique village, but unfortunately in this respect, not all that different from a lot of Myriad. I don't know how much you get abroad, Loch, but Sanctuaries are drying up. Many are left completely abandoned. Others turned into inns . . . or worse. It happened slowly here. Year after year as our affluence grew, our gratitude diminished. Now it's just a shell of what it once was, and only us outcasts worship there." He laughed sadly. "The pews were scavenged. Most of them are in the Pipe and Tabor now."

Loch remember the grand bench seats and felt somewhat guilty for admiring them there. "Oh." He went back to sipping his tea.

"Hey," Flynn said, "if you don't have to rush off, I'd like to show you something." He looked at Obert. "Do you mind?"

"Of course not," Obert said.

"Uh, yeah, okay," Loch said.

Flynn was up and led Loch out of the kitchen and threw a parlor full of all manner of decorations. It went by in a blur, and Flynn didn't stop for a moment, but they looked like trophies, medals, ribbons, scrolls, etc. Loch couldn't tell what the awards were for and to whom they'd been given. Flynn exited the cottage via a back door and descended a gentle hill into paradise.

Or so it seemed to Lochlan. The Gardens of Anglinore were legendary. The floral fields of Llanfair were a spectacle. But Loch found himself in speechless awe of the garden behind Obert McAusland's cottage. The ingredients were common: stately trees, patches of dark green ivy, all manner of flagstones, hillocks of tall grasses, white lattice work, a hundred varieties of flowers—Loch had seen it all. But the intimate arrangement of it all gave the garden an otherworldly atmosphere. Trees grew up from the ivy and cast perfect shadows over the gently waving grass. Small bridges spanned the narrow trickling brook that roamed playfully around the property. The flowers lovingly spilled color down one hillside but not another; climbed one trellis but left another bare; danced among the roots of one tree but left others alone or to the ivy. And throughout it all, laid out in the most welcoming fashion, were the stepping stones. They dotted the entire landscape, inviting travelers to explore and relieve their weary hearts.

Loch found himself wandering the paths alone. For how long, he wasn't sure. When he returned to the hill behind the cottage, he found Flynn sound asleep on bench of stone. He blinked awake as Loch approached. "Beautiful, isn't it?"

"The word doesn't nearly do it justice," Loch replied.

"Obi did it all, you know," Flynn said. "Well, he and his wife Chyrin."

"Was she in the cottage?" Loch asked. "I didn't see anyone—oh, she's . . . she's not—"

"No, no," Flynn said. "Chyrin's quite well. Off to east side, I reckon. Lots of sick there, you can imagine."

Loch nodded. "How, uh . . . what happened to Obert's legs?"

"Ambush," Flynn said. "Obi fought for Chaparrel during the Gorrack War and got his legs pulverized in a surprise attack. The Shepherds might have saved his legs, but some oozing sickness set in. Obi cut them off himself."

"His . . . own . . . legs?" Loch swallowed back his lunch. "Stars!"

"Never met a man like him," Flynn said. "C'mon, then, let's go back inside."

On the way back in, Loch stopped Flynn in the parlor. "What's all this?" he asked, pointing to the awards.

"Obi's," Loch said. "He's a champion archer, you know. Not just war time."

"No, I didn't know."

"Ah, he's won every contest within a month's ride. Even now, he could shoot the whiskers off a raccoon from a hundred paces."

"Oh," Loch said. "He must be quite the celebrity around here."

"Celebrity?" Flynn laughed. "He'd get a kick out of that. No, not hardly. Most of the townies sneer at Obi. He's the king of us outcasts."

"That's the second time I've heard the word. What do you mean? Is it because of your . . . your faith?"

"Partially, but haven't you noticed? Everyone looks good in Silverglen? Rich fabrics, jewelry, all that? And the hair, ah, don't get me started on that. Any man without a full head of lush locks . . ." He ran a hand over his smooth pate. "Well, we're pretty much pariahs around here. And old Obi, well, since he can't walk, they treat him like trash."

Loch's knuckles whitened and cracked as he tightened his fists. "That's not right," he said, each word feeling hot in his mouth. "Someone should do something about that."

"We've tried," Flynn said. "But all we can do is love them and tell them the truth."

"What about your music?" Loch asked. "Seems like Silverglen thrives on that kind of artistry."

"Ah, no," Flynn said, shaking his head. "You don't know what it's like."

"Hmph, no," Loch said. "You're right. I don't. But I'm learning." Thoughts flooded into Loch faster than he could keep up with them. But in a few breathless moments, a plan emerged. "Let's go talk to Obi," he said. "I have an idea I'd like to run by you."

Loch sat on the edge of his bed back in his room at the Pipe and Tabor. His lute was perfectly tuned, but still he plucked the courses to make sure. The common room downstairs was absolutely jammed. After all, it was Halfainday, the night of the big contest. Loch was going to compete. He could care less about the gold. He was after a far greater prize.

Bartles had told him to come down toward the midnight, near the end of the show. Loch had spent the time in his room at times listening to the competition, at times running through miscellaneous scales and melody lines. But when he heard the clock tower chime half past eleven, he figured he'd waited long enough. A sister team was just finishing on the stage. One sang. One played a flute. They were beautiful, and their music matched their appearance. Still, there was something hollow about it, something superficial. Loch shrugged. Maybe his own music would sound that way to them.

The twins earned a healthy dose of cheers and applause. They bowed deeply, earning more applause especially from the men in the audience. *Well, that's not quite fair*, Loch thought. He looked up to Bartles and the tavern owner took center stage.

"A real treat for ye now," Bartles said.

More than you know, thought Loch.

"This lad's come all the way from Anglinore, he has," Bartles went on. "Lute's his game, plays it like he was born to it. By the way, he'll be in town fer just this week, playin' here at the Pipe and Tabor, afternoons. Uhm, case yer wonderin'." Bartles made a brief bow that earned a smattering of applause, far less than the twins had earned.

Loch made his way on stage. Before he took his seat, he glanced stage left at the back door. The audience gathered at the Pipe and Tabor seemed well pleased with the night's performances so far, but one could never be too careful. Loch sat down and studied the well groomed customers. *Prepare to be blown away*, he thought. And then, he began to play.

He began with one of Maiocco's most popular minuets. It was a whimsical piece, perfect for limbering his fingers, and featured a repetitive melodic phrasing that was ideal for dancing. Loch noted a few couples spinning each other in the corner near the kitchen. Loch smiled. He was winning them over. With no discernible break in the music, Loch melded the minuet into Maiocco's Dark

Sea Symphony, taking the audience on a voyage among tempests and rogue waves. Loch could almost feel the rocking of the ship as it rolled across the swells, and he knew the customers could too. And then, he came to the part of the song where the storm unleashed its fury. This required a frantic, deep bass line that was far below what Loch could reach on the lute.

But the bass line came exactly on cue. Loch didn't turn. He didn't want to draw attention. But he knew that Obert McAusland had just wheeled himself through the back door and begun to bow his viol. The song became furious and the tension in the room rose to a fever pitch. Loch hadn't played with accompaniment in years. Thrill surged through him and he played unconsciously, the notes resonant with passion. Up, up, up the tension went. The room held its collective breath.

Then, the clouds cleared out and the sun shone down on the ship that had miraculously survived the stormy night. Allhaven had shown mercy to the vessel, and Loch needed more than his lightest touch on the lute. He needed a harp. And he got it. Flynn entered by the same back door and was playing before he sat on the edge of the stage. The three instruments voiced the melody such that notes fell on the crowd like drops of sunshine. Loch forgot he was playing an instrument, feeling instead that he must be dancing in Obi's garden.

The symphony finished with the viol stair-stepping down the scale while the lute and harp climbed up, the final notes sounding a perfect harmonic chord.

The gathering room of the Pipe and Tabor fell utterly silent. Loch hadn't been sure what to expect. He'd welcomed two of Silverglen's outcasts right on to their center stage. He thought maybe they'd throw food. Or maybe they'd toss them all out on the street. The silence was harder still because of the uncertainty. What did it mean?

But somewhere beneath the pipe smoke, in the shadowy back of the chamber, someone started to clap. Others in the same are joined in. Soon, applause rippled through the room, and like its own symphony rose to a fever pitch. People cheered and hurrahed and stood and whistled. A gold coin sailed out from the direction of the kitchen and clattered at Loch's feet. He snatched it up and strode over to stand behind his new friends.

Slowly, the applause died down. Loch took a deep breath. "People of Silverglen," Loch began. "We are honored for your appreciation. Did you enjoy our music?"

Loud cheers and calls. More applause.

Loch went on. "In a village where music is a way of life, that is the highest praise any minstrel might hear. This music that has blessed your ears tonight. Do you not know that you could have this music whenever you desire? Or do you not see who it was who played for you this way?" Loch gestured to Obi and Flynn, and muttering began at several tables in the audience.

"These men are among the most gifted among you," Loch pressed on, "and yet, you spurn them, call them outcasts, and revile them! How could you? Aren't we all brethren?"

There was no applause this time. No cheers. Much more murmuring. Angry faces dotted the audience now.

"Open your hearts to each other," Loch cried out to them. "Give them the right hand of friendship that they deserve."

"We'll give them what they deserve!" came a bitter low voice.

A very ripe tomato splattered on the wall behind the stage. Loch opened his mouth to speak again and suddenly found a bit of a carrot stick on his tongue. Before he could blink, hearty boo's and hisses spewed from the crowd. And every imaginable bit of food matter burst toward the stage.

"Time to leave!" Obi called, rolling quickly toward the back door.

"Come on, Loch!" Flynn called.

A radish bounced off Loch's forehead. He spat the carrot out and raised a fist just in time to catch a gravy soaked mound of mashed potatoes. Crusts of bread, bulbous elgar sprouts, bits of beef, tomatoes, potatoes, and even a few pastries spattered, splattered, or bounced around them.

Loch had a mind to reveal his identity right there and order them all into stocks. Of course, they might not believe him. And short of drawing blood, there didn't seem to be much he could do. So, in order to avoid being pasted by all manner of fruit and food matter, the High King Overlord of Myriad fled the stage.

"Things were going so well," Loch said. "Until I opened my mouth, that is."

Obi laughed and wiped a bit of tomato from his brow. "There's a good lesson to be learned there," he said.

31 AVRILL 2238

"They pelted you with vegetables?!" Maren exclaimed.

"If they only knew," Sebastian said.

Loch laughed. The memories were almost a blur. The days had streamed by so fast. "I almost told them."

"The rules, Loch," Sebastian reminded.

"I know, I know. I didn't say a word. No one knew me."

"So is that it then?" Maren asked. "Have you had your fill of your people?"

"Not at all," Loch said. "Have to take the bad with the good, right? And truly I met some remarkable people in Silverglen. Flynn is a good soul, and Obi is ... well ... never met anyone like him. I shall be thinking of his words for a very long time."

"He sounds very wise," Maren said.

"What about Cardiff?" Loch asked suddenly. "Has he caused any trouble?"

"Nay," Sebastian replied. "No sign of him in Anglinore for quite some time. Perhaps, we misjudged him."

"I wonder," Loch replied.

"So where will you go next time?" Maren asked.

Loch strode over to the map on Sebastian's chamber wall. "Ellador, I think."

"Nowhere near Lyrimore, I hope," Sebastian said. "Queen Briawynn would know you in an instant, and she's rather famous for visiting the surrounding villages, especially near the lakes."

"Well, of course, not Lyrimore," Loch said. "Hmm, maybe some small village in the west. I don't know. I'll need to think it over."

"Do not take too long to plan," Sebastian said. "There is an opening for your next venture in a few weeks, but not for quite some time after that."

"Really?" Loch nodded, still looking intently at the map. "Several possibilities," he said and turned to leave.

"Where are you going?" Maren asked. "To bed?"

"No," he said. "Not yet. I'm going to spend a little time in Clarissant Hall."

"I think I know how he's managing it, Mother," Baron Cardiff Strengle said as he traced a finger across a wide sheet of parchment.

A blank-faced elderly woman with long curling locks of silver hair leaned forward from the throne a few yards behind the baron. The seat was burnished gold, accented with cyrium and jewels. "Did you feed my fish?" she asked.

"Wh-what?" Cardiff asked. Then he sighed mightily. "Yes, I always feed your fish."

"I like to look at them . . . betimes," she said. Drool bubbled out of the corner of her mouth and fell to the waist of her gown. "Cardiff?"

"Yes, Mother?"

"I'm cold."

"I'll fetch you a blanket in a moment," Cardiff replied, exasperation tightening his words. "Didn't you hear me, woman? I said I think I know how Lochlan is doing it."

"Betimes . . ."

Cardiff ignored her. "He's got his Shepherd manipulating his schedule, blocking out times for him. No wonder the High King never misses a council or a trade meeting. No wonder he's there for every visiting dignitary . . . except for me, of course." He ran a finger slowly down his sideburns and then clapped his hands together. "Now . . . now, I know. I'll simply pay Lochlan a visit when he has nothing planned on his royal schedule. Then, I'll make waves greater than the Dark Sea can churn up. How does that sound to you, old woman?"

The baroness blinked awake. "Cardiff," she said, "did you feed my fish?"

CHAPTER 29

THE FALL OF REL-VIGIL

*And so Quevara, Queen of Cragheath Tor and ruler of the Eight
Hinterland Provinces, decreed that no citizen of her great city should
ever go hungry. She invited all the less fortunate to a great banquet
in a new, specially constructed hall high on Saurius Tor. Thousands
came. The queen spared no expense, feeding her people the finest
meats and slaking their thirst with strong wine. When the meal had
concluded, she inquired of these as to which of them would like never
to feel the pain of hunger or thirst again. Upon their universal expression of this wish, Quevara complied. She had her army of Slayers
board up the banquet hall and set fire to it.*

—From the Annals of Cragheath Tor,
compiled by Cleric Zajak Picard

8 SOLMONATH, 2238

The military outpost of Rel-Vigil was a vast stone and iron network of towers, keeps, manor houses, and turrets, surrounded
by fortified walls and bastions. All of that had taken Stonehand,
Spriggan, and Human stonewrights just one hundred twenty
years to build. The platform upon which Rel-Vigil sat in the

middle of the northwestern quarter of Lake Ioma, by contrast, required almost four-hundred years.

The fortress had been designed and built as a last refuge. When all other safe places failed, the surrounding villages could flee across the Viaduct, the great bridge from the mainland, or via boats and find shelter. And so, with rumor of the Red Queen's return, battalions of Cragfel soldiers shepherded civilians to Rel-Vigil. And now everyone, from Knight-Commander Brell down to the lowliest child, kept watch.

"The water is quiet this evening," Brell said, looking out from the parapet balcony of the southernmost tower.

"Clearly, even the water is in awe of this sunset," Kallor said, putting his arm around her shoulder. They gazed out over the gently undulating waters of Lake Ioma. The quiet water reflected back the bright orange on the horizon, the darkling blue gray of the cloud banks directly above, and the brilliant fingers of golden sunlight that burst through the clouds in places. Commander Kallor drew Knight-Commander Brell close and kissed her. When their lips parted, he said, "It's not often that a Commander gets a kiss from his superior officer while on duty."

"Given its rarity," Brell said, "I suppose we should savor this next kiss for a while longer." She leaned up to kiss him, gasped, and jolted backward. "The sky!" she exclaimed. "The sky is red and burning!" She pointed over Kallor's shoulder to the northeast.

He turned and gaped. "What is that?" he said. "Look!"

Out of the burning red sky above the mountains, a scarlet streak flared, getting larger by the moment. "It's coming this way," Brell said.

"I'll alert the guard," Kallor said, leaping the rail to the stairway leading below.

"Archer Core first!" Brell commanded. "This threat is coming from the sky."

Rel-Vigil bristled with arrow and spear, catapult and ballista. Five thousand fighting men and women, Stonehand beside Spriggan, Spriggan beside Human—they lined the walls and bastions and watched the approaching bloody scar grow and take shape. Broad membranous wings, muscular, almost human torso, snaking neck and tail—and then, as it glided near they saw more detail: a raptorish head with curling horns and black eyes, each stabbed through with a fang of yellow, crimson mane streaming out behind, long limbs full of coiling muscle and tipped with ebony talons—and every inch of flesh covered in hard-scale.

Townfolk still streaming across the Viaduct and into stone refuges shrieked at the sight. Some of the elders called out, "Raudrim is come! Raudrim is come again!" Thousands of resident birds, sparrows, gulls, jay, and woodthrush took wing and surged in massive wheeling flocks out over the water.

Knight-Commander Brell wasn't about to let this beast get any closer. "Now!" she cried. "For Queen and freedom, for our people and for peace! Now!"

Raurdrim-Quevara swooped low over the Viaduct and raked her claws over the fleeing townsfolk. She glided just above the bridge's entire length. Those who could in time, dove off into the water. But many unfortunate hundreds were shredded and thrown into the lake. A ghastly pool of red spread wide on either side of the bridge.

The dragon rose right into the teeth of Rel-Vigil's first volley. "Aim for the wings!" screamed one Forward Commander.

"For the eyes!" came another.

"The belly of a wyrm is soft!" cried one more.

The profusion of projectiles that swarmed into the air did all of that and more. Arrow and bolt found the dragon's eyes, surged into her gut, stabbed her limbs, and pelted her vast wings. The dragon seemed devastated by the initial onslaught and hovered directly in their line of fire. It seemed almost suspended there, unable to flee.

"YES! YESSS!" Knight-Commander Brell cried, her fist high in the air. Her celebration was marred by the loss of so many mainlanders, but to fell the creature outside of the city? That was more than she could have dared to hope.

It was also more than the stark reality would allow.

The great beast rose high above the battlements and, for a breathless moment, no one fired. Not even a single arrow streaked toward the dragon. All stood in shocked silence, realizing as quickly as their minds would allow that the monster was completely unharmed. The lake beneath Raudrim-Quevara was full of the flotsam of broken bolts and shattered arrows, but nothing had penetrated her armor.

"CANNONS!" Knight-Commander Brell screamed, but the tears on her cheeks belied her fear that it was already too late.

A stark roar rang out, and the creature crashed onto the parapets. Sword, spear, pike, and hammer fell upon her but she batted her attackers away like insects. The red dragon swept up a handful of warriors in one massive claw and slammed them into the side of a battlement. She crushed others beneath her feet and slashed dozens more with her talons. The forward guard was in disarray. To attack the creature was like tossing themselves from a cliff to be dashed upon rocks below. The cannon teams were afraid to fire for fear of striking down their own.

But from a lower tower, a catapult team launched the best shot of their lives. The arm whipped forward and flung a jagged hunk of stone in a perfect shallow arc toward the dragon. It struck the creature such a blow upon its jaw that the stone shattered, and the dragon's head was knocked backward and hung loose for a moment. A tremor passed through the creature, and its head swung back around. It's black eyes flashed with gold, and its brow lowered. Then the winged beast leaped to the air and careened toward the offending catapult tower. It fell upon the war engine, snapping timber and twisting iron. Then, with violent precision, she seized the catapulteers and tore them to pieces with her teeth.

Knight-Commander Brell had seen enough. She leaped the rail and sprinted down the stairs. She nearly crashed into Commander

Kallor coming the other way. "Cannons!" she yelled. "It's our last shot."

"The dragon's staying low," he countered. "Among the towers, keeping soldiers near. We can't fire."

"YES, we can. We just can't miss." She lunged away, leaving her husband gawking behind her.

The cobbled stone streets and alleys were cluttered with shrieking townsfolk seeking shelter. Many ran this way and that, unsure of where to go. "Get to the keeps!" Brell commanded. "At the base of every tower!" No, she thought. Not all the towers. "Stay to the southern towers! Everything dockside!" People began to form coherent groups and streamed toward the south. Brell hoped it wouldn't come to that . . . abandoning the city, but far better to get the people in position.

"You almost lost me!" Kallor said as he skidded to a stop beside her. "Where are you going?"

"To the cannons."

"What? You've got to stay in command position."

"Husband," she said. "I know my responsibilities, but there is no one in this city who can fire a cannon with precision like I can."

"Brell," he said. "That may be, but . . . ." He found no more words with which to argue. "Go," he said. "I'll watch your back."

"I love you," she said, and with a flickering sad smile, raced off. She drove herself forward, her heart pounding as if it might burst from her armor. She knew her city well and ducked between buildings, rounding turrets, and streaking up alleys. The cannon ranks were mounted on the north, east, and west bastions, generally aiming out to where anything might approach from land. Brell made for the western cannons, but as she ran, she heard the creature's roar ring out from the center of the city. She cornered a manor home and, though her view was limited to the span between two tall towers, she saw the dragon. Brell came to a sudden stop, and Kallor thudded into her. They stared.

The red dragon hovered slowly and began vomiting streams of blood red flame at those fleeing—townsfolk and soldiers alike. It was like watching a slow-moving storm over a field. The dragon's head swayed, and the ruinous fire came. Whole crowds that had been in motion—were gone—consumed in writhing red flames.

Brell heard a broken scream of despair and was shocked to realize that it was her own voice.

"Don't look!" Kallor yelled. "Get to the cannons and kill this thing!"

He took the lead for a moment, but his wife was faster. She raced by him and ignored the pleas of the soldiers at the base of the west-most tower. She raced up the spiraling stairs and burst out onto the turret. "MOVE!" she yelled, leaping to one of the cannons, and cranking the aiming wheels this way and that.

"What are you doing?" cried one of the cannoneers. "You can't fire over the city! You'll kill hundreds."

He started to move, but Kallor restrained him. "Leave her be!"

"But the people!"

"Will all die if we don't hit this thing with something harder!" Kallor gave the man a forceful shove. "Take a cannon or get out of the way!"

Brell looked up from the wheels and watched the dragon as it drifted slowly south. She spun the wheel on the right, but didn't like the elevation. She wound it back a few turns. Then she leaned back, grabbed a torch, put it to the fuse, and darted out of the way.

The cannon rocked backward in its wheel ruts and slammed into the restraining stocks. The thirteen pound ball crossed the city in an instant . . . and the dragon drifted right into its path.

"Impossible shot," muttered the cannoneer.

The shot hit the dragon in the back exactly between its massive shoulders. With a roar and a jet of red flame, the creature disappeared from view. Cheers rose up from the city, but they were short lived.

Claws appeared on a distant turret and that tower, wrought of stone and toughened over hundreds of years, was torn asunder. Brell, Kallor, and the cannoneers watched as the creature rose up again, leaping from the tower's rubble into the air and thrusting towards them.

Brell leaped to another cannon. "We've got to get—"

"The people out by the cutters," Kallor said, finishing her words. "But I'm not leaving you."

"We'll go," the cannoneer said, gesturing towards his men. "One cannot do it in time. We'll get the word to them . . . or die in the attempt."

"You have my thanks," Knight-Commander Brell said.

The cannoneers turned to leave, but their commander said, "All the cannons are loaded. Blast that thing out of the air!"

"If it can be done," Brell said.

"Six cannons left," Kallor called out with a grin. "I'm not in your league, but I'm feeling pretty good today."

"What . . . what are you talking about?" she glance up at the approaching dragon. It was closing.

"I'll take three, you take three," he said. "The most hits wins."

"Wins what?"

"The usual stakes," he said, spinning the aiming wheels. "Full back rub. You in?"

With a flood of sadness, she realized what he was doing. They were both going to die, but he would not let them die hopeless and afraid. They would die together, challenging and enjoying each other just as they did the day they met. She had a flash of that day, the challenge on the archery range. "You're on!" she said, wiping the tears away.

Kallor fired first. His shot was low, but took the creature in the knee, sending it into a dive toward the clock tower. Debris exploded at the collision, and the tower collapsed upon itself. The dragon rose up just in time to catch Brell's next shot full in the chest. The dragon fell backward, spewing red fire high into the air.

"That looked like it hurt!" Kallor said as he raced to the next cannon.

"We're even!" she called back. "Don't give the beast time to breathe!"

Kallor didn't. As soon as it reared its hideous maw, he fired. The cannonball struck the keep wall broadside just above the creature's shoulder, creating a landslide of rubble. Chunks of stone rained down on the dragon. "That counts!" Kallor yelled.

"Of course!" Brell called. "You should get a bonus point for the trick shot!" She fired her cannon on instinct, hoping the dragon would leap into the air again. It did, and the cannon shot struck its wing. But it didn't tear through the membrane as it should have. Instead, the dragon tilted its wing at such an angle that the cannonball slid beneath the wing and fell into the city behind the creature.

Brell closed her eyes and lowered her head. But Kallor was there and lifted her chin. "one more shot each," he said. "Wait till it gets close."

She nodded and went to her last cannon. Kallor was by her side at his final cannon. They could hear the dragon's wings and smell the smoke on the wind. It was just a hundred paces away and drifting closer.

"Steady!" Brell called. It wasn't so much about aiming any longer. No, wait! She had a sudden burst of hope. "Aim for its chest, fire at the same time. We may not pierce its foul hide, but maybe we can stop its blasted heart."

Kallor made a few minor adjustments to his aim. "Ready."

The dragon closed. So near now, its massive size became utterly clear. They saw its black eyes and those terrible yellow-fang pupils.

"FIRE!" Brell screamed.

Husband and wife lit their fuses and dove into each other's arms. The cannons fired. Both shots hit the beast center chest, one cannonball right after the other. The beast's roar choked in its throat, and it plummeted. The city fell utterly silent. Kallor rose first. He helped his wife to her feet, and they moved tentatively to the wall. "Please," Brell whispered. They looked over the edge . . .

. . . into a scalding wave or red flame.

The dragon poured its fire onto the tower until even the stone seemed to burn. Then it leaped into the air and flew to the highest tower in Rel-Vigil. There she perched . . . and melted. The Red Queen stood now on the tower, and when she spoke, her voice was so low and so loud that anyone near could feel it in the stone. "Bow down to me!" she commanded. "Queen Righel, the usurper, is dead! I am Raudrim-Quevara, Queen of the Hinterlands. No one will defy my rule. NO ONE!! Bow down, prostrate yourselves! It is due homage, for I hold your lives in my fist!"

Of those left alive on the streets below, many fell to their faces immediately. Still others bowed down slowly. A very few ran away as fast as they could.

Raudrim-Quevara smiled and her form became that of a dragon once more. She leaped from the tower and glided down over the bowing masses. And then, she unleashed her fire once more. Soon the streets were littered with the burning corpses of thousands.

The dragon began careening from turret to turret, slamming into each with her bulk or ramming them with her stolid horns until they collapsed. She barreled into the outer walls, cracking them a little at a time until they crumbled. Then she dropped into the middle of the city and began clawing at the cobbled stone, ripping up house-sized chunks and tossing them aside. Soon she had burrowed deep enough for her talons to strike the under-foundation, the bulwark of mighty darkseed iron. There her claws could do nothing. But Raudrim-Quevara had an answer to defiant metal. She reared back and unleashed a torrent of bright red flame, flash-boiling the cold water into steam and eating away at the iron. The cloud of steam hid her from view and did not relent.

The dragon Raudrim-Quevara burst up from the cold waters of Lake Ioma just sixty yards from Rel-Vigil. She surged away over the surface, chasing the long line of townsfolk trying to escape in longboat cutters.

What was left of the city shuddered and began to founder. Ever-widening crevices spidered out from the breach in the center of the city. Huge plates of stone upended and cracked open. Towers fell, walls collapsed, and water surged in. Rel-Vigil, the monument of Hinterlands craft and industry that had taken half an age to build, sank into the lake in a matter of minutes.

Raudrim-Quevara flew southwest. She had decided to visit each of the other seven provinces, to tell the tale of Drinaris and to quell even the slightest hints of rebellion. An ounce of prevention . . . she thought whimsically.

She banked hard to the right, toward the mountains. She saw a strange rock formation. Irregular slabs of stone stabbed upward and slanted so that it almost looked like an immense rose, except for the tall, spike in the center. Sharp, deadly sharp, like a stone lance.

Her thoughts became suddenly marbled and confused. If I climb high enough and dive fast enough, she thought, I might succeed. I might be free of this—

NO! She dropped her left wing and soared away from the stone rose and its single deadly thorn.

Angry and somewhat startled, Raudrim-Quevara hastened south. It will be time soon, she thought, time to venture beyond these borders that have penned me in for so long. Time to see what manner of blood flows on the other side. But for now, I will be content with the blood of my homeland.

CHAPTER 30

CROSSING PATHS

A note found on the The Board at the Venture Inn, Ellador, 2164
AS: "Wanted: Warrior(s) to deal with surly, tentacled haggath in my
chimney. Good pay. Room and Board. Must be willing to lose a fin-
ger or two."

4 CELESANDUR 2238

"Three seconds!" Meli clapped. "A new record!"

Tango took a bow. "Thank you, thank you." He gave a careful look around the Venture Inn. Except for a young Elladorian couple in the corner by the fireplace, the tables were empty. In the months they'd worked there, Tango had never seen the place so deserted.

"Don'na ya worry, Tango."

"Matron Tess would box me ears if she caught me fooling around."

"Well, you're not fooling around, really." Meli winked. "Ya just set a record for washing and drying a tankard."

"I suppose that's right," he said. "Just increasing efficiency. Never mind the two broken tankards."

"She won't mind them, Tango. She'll just take them out of your pay."

"Just take what out of your pay?" Matron Tess asked, entering the great room. "You didn't break more mugs, did you, dear?"

"Can'na slip one by you," Tango said.

Matron Tess patted her ample belly and looked around her establishment. "You've done nice work here," she said. "As clean as I've seen it."

"That's because hardly anyone's been in this afternoon," Tango admitted.

"Slow day," she said. "That'll change tonight, and don't I know it." There were footsteps in the hall. Clarisse Graymane and Grindle Freeman came in. Matron Tess nodded to them and said, "Take a break, Tango, Meli. Let's sit and talk a spell."

The Spriggans hopped away from the mug stands and water barrels and joined Matron Tess and the others at one of the big oblong tables near the bar. "Tango and Meli, I can't tell you how grateful I am to have had your help here at the Venture Inn." Matron Tess patted Meli's hand. "You're two of my hardest workers, and no argument there. But I'm afraid that I'm going to have to let you go."

"Let us go?" Meli echoed.

"What do you mean?" Tango asked. "Like out of a job? Like out on the street? But I thought—"

"No, not like that," Matron Tess said. "Sorry, dears. I am not firing you. Not hardly. I'd keep you if I had the heart to." She saw their blank looks. "Now, don't ya just stare at me like that. How many times have you told me of your troubles? And Clarisse . . . and Grindle . . . and anyone else who would listen? And, Tango dear, you only post your need once on the Venture Board."

"Oh," Tango said. "Sorry."

"That's okay, my lad. I think I've finally got them all." She laughed.

"I don't understand," Meli said. "Why can'na we stay?"

"I think Clarisse would be best to explain."

Clarisse leaned forward and her raven black hair fell over one eye. "Grindle and I have left the Venture Inn with new quests for nigh on fifteen years now, and mostly just to fill our pockets."

"More of a satchel thing for me," Grindle said. "My kind, well . . . we don't do pockets much."

Clarisse winked.

Tango felt his stomach flutter.

She went on. "In any case, we've earned plenty of wealth in that time and not without a lot of risk. But after hearing your tale: a tale of Spriggans and betrayals and some monstrous dragon thing, well, we got to thinking that maybe we ought to go take a look for ourselves."

"And if there is some meddling wyrm," Grindle said, "we aim to kill it and free your land."

"You're going to go to the Hinterlands?" Meli asked. "Did'ja hear that, Tango?"

"I heard it," he said. "And I'm glad. But, pardon my saying so bluntly, but no matter how good your two are with a blade, I don't think you'll have a chance against this thing."

Grindle roared with laughter. Clarisse did too but was a little more discreet.

"What?" Tango looked around the table.

"Granted," Clarisse said, "I've not faced too many wyrms, but I daresay I'd know not to take one on alone. Not even with brawny Grindle here."

"That," Grindle said, "is why we've invited a few friends. C'mon in lads!"

The heavy thumps in the hall told the tale. Bulwar Zanderose was coming. He ducked his head under a chandelier and entered the great room. Behind him came a dozen other warriors, and behind them a dozen more. More and more besides. Male and female, human, Stonehand, Wayfolk, Elladorian, and even a few Marinaens, a small army entered the Venture Inn. Some Tango and Meli had seen before. Some were regular customers. But many more were completely unknown to them. Beyond their smiles, they were a dangerous looking crowd.

Maybe, thought Tango, *just maybe they could take on that ole dragon.*

"Of course," Bulwar thundered, "we'll all need to be fed before we leave." The room erupted in cheers.

Matron Tess stood up and tightened her apron. She called back to the kitchen, "Stoke up the fires, lads! Break open the larders! We're going to need a right merry feast!"

"YOU GOT IT!" the kitchen lads answered.

Tango was still grinning and looking around when Clarisse took his hand. He turned and found her face very close to his. His heart leaped into his throat and did a little dance.

"I don't think it was by accident that you and your sister climbed into *my* wagon," she said. Her dark blue eyes, filling with tears, deepened still. "I'm so sorry for all that you've lost. I know something of what that feels like. And I want you to know I'm going to do everything within my power to put things to right in your homeland."

19 CELESANDUR 2238
(MUCH LATER THAT SAME NIGHT)

"Looks like I missed the party," Loch said.

Matron Tess stopped sweeping and blew some unruly hair out of her eyes. "Matter of fact, ye did. What can I get ye, dear?"

"Uhm . . . a job?"

Matron Tess beamed. "Well if you didn't just happen to be in the right place at the right time. Grab a broom. You're hired."

Matron Tess fell into a booth seat. "Whew!" she said. "You've been at it non stop. Why don't you take a rest, Loch?"

"The job's not finished," he said, grabbing up five mugs in one hand. Seven in the other. He dunked them all into the barrel of sudsy water by the bar. Then, he pulled out and dried three at a time and hung them on the high racks in a blink. "I don't mind cleaning, really."

"That makes you a rarity, then," Tess said with a dry chuckle. "I don't suppose you can keep the bar? I had a good one, but he's just run off on an errand. Don't know when he'll be back."

Loch stopped washing. "What's involved?"

Tess walked behind the bar and smacked a barrel with her palm. "Take orders from the maids, from me, and from customers at the bar. Fill up the right tankards from the right barrels. When it's slow, talk to folk. Let 'em know their welcome here. Be friendly."

"And when it's busy?"

"Same thing . . . only faster."

Lochlan laughed. "I think I'd like that. Get to meet some interesting people that way."

"Very interesting," she said. "But not often all that friendly, and well, some don't know their own limit. It can get ugly."

"The last guy didn't get killed, did he?"

"Bulwar? Stars, no." She laughed. "No one messed with Bulwar. But they might give you a try."

"I'd be alright with that," Loch said. "I've handled trouble before."

Matron Tess looked him up and down and lingered on his eyes. "I imagine you have," she said.

"But, you don't . . . uh, you don't sell Witchdrale, do you?"

Matron Tess looked like she almost bit her tongue in half. "Anyone brings that death in here . . . I'll strangle him myself."

"Not if I get to him first," Loch said.

"Good enough," she said. "You up for trying tonight?"

Loch shrugged. "Sooner the better. But you should know, I'm only in town for a week or so."

"That's fair," she said. "If you handle it well, it'll give me some time to find a more permanent replacement. Welcome to the Venture Inn." She held out a hand.

They shook. "Thank you," he said.

"Meantime," she said. "Fetch me a sack of barley, would you?"

"Where are they?"

"In the deep cellar." Matron Tess smiled winningly.

9 CELESANDUR 2238

"Three fairywaters, love!" Ella called. Loch spun left.

"Six kingsmeade!" ordered Sabine from the other side of the bar. Loch spun right.

"Can I get me a Fordham Brown?" a customer behind Loch asked.

Brown, right, Loch remembered. The man behind him had only one eyebrow. *One Brown for the one brow.*

Loch filled three mugs in his left from one barrel, six mugs from another a barrel and passed those off. The Brown was kept cold in a cask beneath Loch's feet. He dropped to his knees, whipped open the trapdoor, and filled a tall tankard. He was up in a flash, spun around, and knocked the bottom of the tankard against a barrel rim. He juggled it for a moment before emptying its contents all over the man with one eyebrow.

A bell rang somewhere in the tavern. Everyone cheered. Except the man with one eyebrow. He glared at Loch for the longest three seconds he'd ever experienced. "Might I have another?" the man asked quietly.

Loch went to work with his towel, wiping furiously. "Of course, Sir. I'm very sorry. Very sorry." He looked up at the man and considered wiping him as well. But then, he thought better of it and went down to pour another tankard.

He came up much more carefully this time and placed the tankard, in the most precise fashion, directly in front of the customer. "Again, sir, very sorry," Loch said. "This one's on me."

The man picked up the tankard and poured it over Loch's head. "It is now," he said.

Matron Tess whooshed by. "I'll need three Browns," she said. "That is, if you haven't wasted it all."

Loch shivered as the cold liquid ran down his back. *And so begins my stay in Ellador.*

After closing, Loch stared up at the scraps of parchment tacked to the wall. "So, these are all real adventures . . . real needs?" he asked.

"Aye, lad," Tess replied, whisking across the floor with a damp mop. "Far as we know." She smiled as if considering a fond memory. "Oh, we've had a few practical jokes. There was the time an old friend, a Windborne by the name of Grindle Freeman, posted about a giant string bean that ate his horse. And there's a running joke started by one of the kitchen lads, something about a cheese monster. Never fails to get laughs. But everyone knows it's meant to be serious business. That's just what the Venture Inn's been about for over two hundred years."

"Hmph," Loch said, studying the posts. "Monster spiders in Woodshire?" Loch shivered. "No thank you. Wyverns threatening the Kelly's farm in Dancaster. What in the Stars is a wyvern?"

"Oh, they're nasty things, they are. Like flyin' wolves. Just one could do a number on a herd of goats. More than one—why that'd be a terror. I sure hope High King Lochlan does something about it." She leaned on the mop. "Funny now, isn't it? You've got the same name as the Overlord. Think your folks named you after 'im?"

Loch nodded without turning. "Pretty safe bet, that." He was anxious to change the subject. "Maybe I'll try one of these adventures."

"Don't take it unless you're serious, lad. There are people out there desperate for help."

"Good to keep in mind," he said. "But I won't take it if I think it's over my head."

"That's a good man."

"This one looks . . . well, it looks like a littlin' wrote it." He leaned closer to read the post. "'Big, nasty dragon thing. Only way to kill it is to stab it into its ear. Please save . . . my Hinterlands'? Is this for real?"

"Ah," Matron Tess said. "Must have missed that one. It's real, but it's also been taken."

"Stab it into its ear," Loch whispered humorously. He looked through a few other posts. "Hmmm, this one I think I could handle. Seems a serpent has been frightening away all the perch in the Wetlands village."

"I dunno, lad, serpents can be a handful."

"So what do I do, just take it off here?" He pulled out the pin and took the parchment scrap.

"Don't forget to ring the bell."

Loch picked up the tiny hammer and struck the bell. It filled the room with its clear resonance.

"Not quite a cheer," Tess said, "but, YAY, Loch!"

10 CELESANDUR 2238

The man had sat at the bar staring at Loch for quite some time. He'd said his name was Oliver, that he was a local tradesman looking for a hand with some odd jobs.

"I don't understand why you think I can help you," Loch said, filling up the bench seat with his long legs. "I'm just a tavern keeper."

Oliver smiled. Quick as a striking snake, he grabbed one of Loch's hands. "The calluses on your palm, here and here, speak to me something different, my friend. The toughened skin on your knuckles, the bones beneath—broken and healed many times, I think—these speak to me of fighting."

Loch ripped his hands free and sat up. "Look, Oliver, I don't know what you're driving at," he said, his voice measure, quiet but tense, "but I've worked very hard to earn my position here. I don't need anyone casting suspicions on me. Understand?"

"Do not worry, my friend. Your secret is safe with me. In fact, I have a secret of my own that I wish to keep totally between the two of us. Should I put your reputation here in jeopardy, you could destroy mine."

"I'm listening."

Oliver glanced toward the busy common room, then leaned forward and began to whisper. "I have an embarrassing problem, you see. And I find myself in need of a fighting man, but someone noble, someone who will not be judgmental."

"You mean someone you can manipulate."

"Not at all," Oliver said, his face melting into distaste. "But perhaps, I was wrong, and you already judge me." Oliver stood up and turned to leave.

Loch grabbed his hand. "No, wait. I'm sorry. But I'm vulnerable here, and I don't like that. Not at all."

"Nor do I, my friend," Oliver said, returning to his seat. "Nor do I. Will you hear my proposition?"

"I will."

Oliver nodded. "Good. As I say, I have a situation that requires a fighting man. I live on the southern edge of Ravensgate."

"Down the slope?"

"Yes, precisely. And after the rains flooded out the Tangles—that is what we call the thick briar forest just south of us—well, after the flood, my wine cellar has been overrun . . ." He lowered his voice even more. "Overrun with scalix."

"Scalix?"

"Shhh, yes." Oliver held up his hand. "Do not speak it aloud."

"What in the Stars are they?"

"I do not have the words," Oliver said. "And I do not have the skill to be rid of them. I managed to kill one of them. I can show you. Will you come?"

"I'm intrigued," Loch said. "It's rather slow today. Let me check with Tess."

Minutes later, Oliver spurred his horse leading Loch on a meandering path across Ravensgate. They passed Oliver's shop and a dozen others like it. They passed the old Sanctuary and the stockade next door. Soon, the road plunged down into a more crowded village setting. Oliver brought his steed to a trot, hopped off, and led him by hand the rest of the way into a narrow stable. Loch followed and did the same.

Loch emerged from the stable and whistled. "You've a nice place, Oliver."

"Oh, thank you, my friend. It is home."

Some home, thought Loch. It was a mansion, a royal manor in appearance. Three turrets, sections of sloping roof at four different elevations, and a trellised garden in back—it was really a beautiful place to live. Oliver directed Loch to follow him to the side of the manor where a narrow alley cut a notch between Oliver's home and the estate next door. There, the base of the southernmost turret bumped out and created a cleft of darkness.

Immediately, Loch caught the smell.

"Right here," Oliver said, pointing to a tarp. "It is rotting, but whole enough to give you the idea." Oliver closed his eyes and his lips moved as if he was praying. Then, he removed the tarp.

Loch backed up a step. "That . . . that is horrid!" He was repulsed but he could not take his eyes off the scalix. Long as a Dark Sea thresher shark with similar smooth gray skin on top of its serpentine form, the creature had hundreds of pairs of tube-like appendages along its body. On one end, presumably its abdomen, it bore a pair of long pincers. On the other end, there was a segmented thorax and a large, egg-shaped head. It had two empty, bulbous eyes and a huge slimy maw full of long, interlocking membranous teeth. "Stars bless you," Loch said. "You have these things in your cellar?"

"Dozens of them," Oliver said. With a sneer, he threw the tarp back over the dead creature. "Nasty creatures, tails full of venom. Deadly if they get you on the ground."

"How did you kill this one?"

"Crushed its head in the door. Blasted thing tried to chase me up the stairs."

"I guess I still don't understand, Oliver. You're living in the greatest city for intrepid adventurers, why don't you put a note up on the Venture Board. Someone would have your cellar cleaned out in no time. Why, Bulwar Zanderose could finish them off in a half hour . . . he'd probably eat them."

"No, my friend, do you not yet see my predicament?" Oliver shook his head. "I have lived in this town of champions for a long, long time. For the warriors who come through here every day, scalix would be nothing. Can you then imagine what would be said of me if Oliver, the most successful weapons merchant in Ravensgate, could not manage to rid his own cellar of scalix? I'd be a laughing stock. My sales would be cut in half. That conniving Slakin Frostbourne would run me out of town on reputation alone."

"I see your difficulty," Loch said. "But with all your weaponry, surely—"

Oliver held up a hand. "This is the worst thing, you see, I cannot wield a sword. What would become of a weapon merchant who cannot use a sword?"

"Hmmm . . . that would not be good for sales."

"So, will you help me? I promise to make it worth your time."

Lochlan smiled. This was just the sort of thing for which he'd left the throne. How many times did I tell Sebastian I wanted to be among the people of Myriad, working side-by-side and getting my hands dirty with them? From the look of that scalix, Loch felt pretty confident he was about to get his hands dirty. "Alright, Oliver, I'll see what I can do," Loch said. "And don't worry. Your secret is safe with me."

"Ah, Lochlan, you are a prince among men."

You're close, thought Loch.

The lavish nature of Oliver's abode became more apparent once inside. Gilded mirrors hung on the walls along with tapestries so intricate they must have taken thirty years to make. The furniture was all dark woods: maple, cherry, hickory, and oak. Expensive, Loch knew. After all, he'd designed and crafted many such furniture pieces for Anglinore Castle. The chandelier over the long dining table appeared to be made of Amaran crystal. If sold, it would be enough to feed a family for several years.

"You've done . . . uh, quite well for yourself, Oliver," Loch said as they passed through a parlor.

"I travel far and wide to acquire the weapons and armor I sell," he replied, just a hint of indignation in his tone. "And though I live in modest opulence, my profits do not only benefit me."

"I meant no disrespect," Loch said.

"Nor did I, my friend. We each have our stories, do we not?"

Loch wasn't sure if Oliver expected an answer, so he kept it to himself. Oliver strode past a double-wide stair that led to a landing where it divided and climbed to heights unseen. On the side of the stairs there was a recessed door. Oliver slid three bolt-locks back and opened the door.

"Down these stairs," he said, "you will find another door with several locks of this variety. The wine cellar and the slithery interlopers are within. "Kill as many as you can quickly. They move slowly at first, but once they are roused, they are quite swift. Beware their venom and their teeth. Do not let them surround you. And, whatever you do, kill them all."

"How will I know?" Loch asked. "How will I know when I've killed them all?"

"Ah, now that, my friend, is simple enough. When the rest are all dead, the queen will attack."

Loch swallowed. "You never said anything about a queen."

"Did I not?" Oliver shrugged and grinned. "Perhaps I neglected to mention it because I have never seen her myself. She will let her drones fight for her, but if they are all dead, she will come forth. Still, with your fighting skills, it should be nothing to you."

Loch laughed with little conviction. Likely to get my hand bloody as well as dirty, he thought as he descended the stairs.

Unlike everything else in the house, the door to the wine cellar was not in good shape. It was cracked and boarded with some kind of metal caging at the foot of it. Loch found two bolt locks at the top of the door and three on the side. He slid each back, took the torch from its base, and then, he opened the door.

When Oliver said the creatures were in his wine cellar, Loch had imagined a cozy chamber with a trellised rack of dusty bottles on one wall. What he found was a vast catacomb three times the floorspace of the mansion above with gleaming racks of bottles as far as the eye could see. *I shouldn't be surprised*, Loch thought. *Oliver doesn't do small.*

Loch shut the door behind him and looked about for the beasts. Seeing no immediate threat, he put his torch to the nearest brazier. It flared to life as did the next two Loch found as he crept into the deep cellar. The room was dank and smelled faintly of mildew and something else Loch couldn't quite place. And unlike most underground places in Ravensgate, there were no rats . . . at all. He'd traveled some forty feet into the shadowy basement and had seen nothing of the creatures. *Odd*, he thought. *Perhaps now that the flood waters have dried up, they've gone away.*

Loch rounded a pillar and ducked an arch. A wide span of darkness yawned open in front of him. He halted suddenly. There was an odd clicking sound. It undulated with its own peculiar cadence, filling Loch's thoughts with all sorts of images. *Nothing worse than the terror you don't see*, Loch told himself. He tossed his torch into the center of the chamber.

It came to rest among glittering forms and cast its flickering light over slithering, writhing shapes—segmented bodies, clicking pincers, macabre toothy grins.

The scalix—hundreds of them.

CHAPTER 31

A KINGLY GIFT

Of all the races dwelling in the Hinterlands, Spriggan-kind are the most resilient and longest lived. Rumored to have sprouted up from deep within the world, Spriggans are a little people, standing three and a half feet to four at their tallest. They are generally considered close cousins to the Stonehands, but are less stocky and broad. Prone to extremes of emotion, Spriggans are never a 'little' anything. Hopping mad, bouncing happy, chittering nervous, or drunk with peacefulness, most Sprigs like to work hard and play hard. They take special pride in the building and crafting of their delshroom homes. Oh, and they like cheese.

—From Bergle Finche's Catalogica Culturim

10 CELESANDUR 2238

"Oh, crud."

Kill them quickly . . . Loch heard Oliver's words in his mind . . . before they become aroused. "Good thought, that," Loch muttered. He strode into their midst and unleashed his blade, creating a blur of carnage. He hacked into the center of the largest creature, splattering himself with foul-smelling paste. He stabbed another through its thorax. There was a popping sound and the thing cracked open. Then he spun and clove another beast's bulbous head. The clicking increased its rhythm and its volume. The scalix began to raise up around him. Loch's blade swept through each one, sending bits of shell, limb, and gore in all directions. He kept his strokes short, imparting just enough force to penetrate their husks. With so many of them in such close quarters, he couldn't afford to waste motion or overextend.

In just moments, he'd cut down more than a dozen creatures. But now, the clicking became loud and uneven and was joined by an otherworldly hissing. A beast rose up in front of Loch, its stubby limbs, like short tentacles, rippled from back to front. Its pale, empty eyes smoldered and its jaws opened wide, revealing slime-covered, interlocking finger-length teeth. It lunged. Loch dropped to a crouch, and the thing sailed just above his head. But its pincers flicked down and sliced a gash into Loch's upper back. Even as the pain began its burn, Loch arched his back and lashed out. The offending creature fell to the ground in two pieces.

The others came on at once, a rapidly tightening noose of teeth. These things weren't polite duelists either. They did not wait their turn, they did not hesitate, they did not announce their attacks. Loch came to his feet and spun, his blade turning round the room like a scythe through chaff. He danced left, lunged forward, and leaped backward. He couldn't stay in one place long. There were simply too many. The clicking sounded now like an avalanche and the hissing was a slithering roar.

Loch hacked his way to the perimeter of the creatures' den and did his best to wipe his hands and the hilt clean of the membranous goo. "Stars, but these things bleed!" Loch muttered. He turned to face another rush of the beasts, but as he plunged the blade into the gaping mouth of one creature, he felt an unnerving tingle on the back of his right shoulder. It was like the strength was draining from the muscles in that area of his upper back. The venom!

Loch switched the sword to his left hand and swept through another creature. He stabbed through one and then slammed a leaping beast to the ceiling. It rained gore from that one, and Loch found himself skidding into a spin. He smacked one with the flat of his blade before regaining his footing and coordination. He backed toward a pillar, hacked into the throat of a creature and then bludgeoned another with the sword's heavy pommel. Just then, a hissing came from the side. Loch felt pain lance up his leg as a scalix's jaws closed on his shin like a bear trap. Out of pure reflex, Loch brought his sword crashing down, severing the creature at its midsection. But still its jaws clung to Loch's leg.

Loch's eyes flickered down to the pain still burning his leg and found his breeches dark and glistening. It diverted his attention for only a moment, but it was enough. He heard the sound, but turned too late. A scalix larger than any he had yet seen curled out from the pillar and struck. Loch yanked his sword up, but the lunging creature hit his fist. The gore-slicked weapon came loose and cartwheeled away. Racing after his weapon, Loch skidded in the blood. As he fell, the scalix barreled into his side. They rolled together toward one of the wine racks. Loch hit the ground hard enough to steal his breath, and the creature fell on top of him.

Loch used both hands to keep the creature from getting at his throat, but he couldn't see the beast's pincers. A new spike of white-hot pain pierced the flesh on his leg, and Loch screamed out. With no other alternative, he slammed his knees and ankles together, holding the creature's stinging pincers in a vice grip. Its jaws snapped free of Loch's grip and drove toward his neck. Loch wriggled, and the thing bit into his shoulder. Loch cried out again, more in anger than in pain. The thing reared back again to strike. Loch had no blade, no weapon. The gaping jaws opened and the beast shot forward.

In the same moment, Loch did the only thing he could do: he grabbed a huge bottle of wine out of the rack and shoved it into the creature's mouth. The neck of the bottle went deep into the creatures throat, and initially its jaws couldn't close. Loch used the diversion and heaved the thing off of him. Then, his left leg numb, his right bleeding, he hobbled to his sword. He grabbed the blade left-handed and turned. The hissing and clicking became a symphony of malice as the creatures closed in on Loch. He had backed into a corner. There was nowhere else to go.

There came a crack and a shriek. Loch watched as the scalix crunched the wine bottle in its teeth, splashing the deep red wine all over itself and onto the floor. The creatures creeping closer to Loch rose up high on their flanks, turned, and dove at their wine-soaked comrade. Pincers flashed, jaws crushed and slashed.

It didn't take Loch long to understand what had happened. He snatched out another bottle of wine and lobbed it onto the naked stone close to the writhing mass of creatures. It shattered on impact, and the monsters reacted, immediately slithering into the spilt wine. Loch launched another eight bottles, giving the creatures plenty of things to play with. Then, one deft slash at a time, Loch killed the scalix. Soon, the cellar floor was awash in blood and wine.

Loch exhaled and fell against the pillar. He closed his eyes and sighed. Everything that wasn't burning or stinging was numbed by the venom. Loch felt sick to his stomach and dizzy. "I can't believe this," he muttered. "Those stupid, nuisance beasts nearly killed me!"

The sound Loch heard next chilled his blood. A muffled shrieking hiss rose up from somewhere below. The Queen.

Loch strode out into the center of the floor, crunching on scalix carcasses and broken glass. Suddenly, not four feet from Loch, the flagstones of the floor popped free of their mortar borders. A massive head rose up, bulbous like the others but armored with sections of shell like a helm. And the teeth, each one was as long as Loch's forearm. "Forget this!" Loch yelled. He wasn't about to wait for the creature to fully emerge. He charged it and, with both hands, he chopped down with all his might. The blade crashed into the shell-helm, cracked it, and sundered the head. But in the process, Loch's sword blade snapped in half.

A roar from behind made Loch jump ten inches off the ground. He spun in time to see a second head, exactly like the first. His racing thoughts converged on the reality that the queen had two heads, one on either end of its long, segmented body. Loch lifted what was left of his sword just as the perilous creature swung forward on top of him.

Oliver had listened for long enough. He'd heard the creatures hissing and clicking. He'd heard Loch grunt and the wet impact of his sword. From there it had all turned to chaos. Shrieks, screeches, crashing, splatters . . . and then complete and utter silence. "Loch!" Oliver called through the crack in the door. "Loch, are you . . . can you hear me?"

No answer. No sounds at all.

"Stars forgive me," he said. "What have I done?" He drew his daggers and barged through the door. He found the initial portions of the cellar relatively clear compared to the last time he'd ventured within. He strode into the various corners and alcoves of the vast basement area, finding nothing at first. But then, in the deepest recesses, he began to find the ruined carcasses of scalix.

Oliver approached them slowly, lest some not be truly dead. The things had a nasty, deceiving tendency to look dead while only dormant. As he came closer, however, Oliver was relatively certain that they were all dead. "Great Stars of Allhaven!" he exhaled, looking at the carnage. Gooey chunks of the creatures were scattered all about: a head here, pincers there. A few whole corpses remained, but these had skulls cloven in two or smashed-in in the most brutal fashion.

Had he done it? Oliver wondered. Had Loch killed them all? "Loch?" Oliver called out again. "Loch, are you there?"

Oliver came round a pillar and gasped. A massive creature's torso lay among a cataclysmic mess of dead scalix. A relentless chill crept over him. The last time he'd ventured into the cellar there had been fifteen creatures, maybe twenty. But they had multiplied many times over. No one man, no matter how skilled, had a chance against so many.

And yet, Loch had slain them all, for this behemoth corpse could only belong to the Queen. Its body had several segments, each a barrel's thickness, and it seemed to have writhed out of the very ground. It lay very still and—

"Loch!" Oliver cried out. "Loch, my friend!" He saw the human hand just visible between the creature's many appendages. Oliver dropped to his knees and heaved against the creature's torso. The thing weighed more than Oliver thought possible. Still, with renewed effort, he managed to shove the thing off. It hit the floor with a wet thud and rolled over, revealing a sword, driven to the hilt, in the creature's chest.

But then, Oliver's hands lingered in the air uselessly over Loch's stricken form. The warrior's clothing glistened in the torchlight. There were angry wounds on his legs, his shoulder and neck. He was deathly pale. "Curse my foolishness!" Oliver cried out. "I should never have gotten him involved. I . . . I should have doused the whole cellar with oil and let it burn!"

"Would be a shame, that," came a weak voice. "Waste a lot of good wine."

"Loch, my friend, you live!" Oliver took Loch's hand. "Ha, ha! Stars be praised! You live!"

"Barely," Loch said, coughing weakly. ". . . could barely breathe with that thing on top of me." Loch's eyes opened and blinked clear. "Can't feel my leg . . . or my shoulder."

"The venom," Oliver said. "I have something for it, my friend. Come, let me help you upstairs."

"No good," Loch said. "I can't get up."

"Ah, but you must, my friend. We must make you well. I will pour you a bath . . . a warm bath."

Loch sat up immediately. "Ah, that does sound nice. Let . . . let me try."

Oliver helped Loch to his feet and supported the wounded man's weight. They traversed the cellar slowly, and as they passed through the door to the stairs, Loch said, "That was ridiculous, Oliver. Much harder than you let on. I might have died."

"Alas, you are correct, my friend. I am an idiot! But I did not know they had increased in number like that." Oliver shook his head. "I rue the moment I got you into this, Loch. But may it be some small condolence that I will reward you for your efforts."

"Ah, Oliver," Loch said, not thinking of his words. "I have no need of gold."

Oliver paused a moment and raised an eyebrow curiously. "No need of gold," he echoed. "It is a rare man who says such things. Fortunately, the reward I have in mind has nothing to do with gold."

Oliver was better than his word. He prepared a luxurious bath of soothing hot water in a porcelain tub Loch could have swam in. While Loch cleaned himself off and relaxed, Oliver went to work in the kitchen. He prepared a sumptuous feast for Loch, including a glorious brazed hunk of beef and seared potatoes with garlic and onion. Along with the filling meal, Oliver also whipped up a half dozen medicinal elixirs. Loch drank them all and found himself regaining his strength and feeling quite alert. In fact, he felt like everything was right with the world. He wanted to laugh and smile and grin. He pushed his chair back from the table and did just that. He bellowed out such an infection guffaw that Oliver joined him.

"I don't feel the pain as much," Loch said. "I feel pretty good."

"You find the effects of the jasmine elixir exhilarating, do you not, my friend?"

"Oh," Loch said. "Is that what it is? Ha, ha! Should have known. Sebastian makes the same stuff. Hoo, boy. Did I mention I feel pretty good right now?"

"Yes, I believe you did." Oliver wiped his mouth with a linen handkerchief and stood apart from the table. "Shall we see to your reward?"

"That sounds remarkably good," Loch said, following his host back down the stairs to the place that had nearly claimed his life.

Oliver handed Loch a torch and kindled one for himself. They passed through the cellar door with much less trepidation than before. Oliver placed his torch in a holder by the far wall and went to the vast wine rack there. He seemed to be counting the bottles from left to right and top to bottom. Then he grasped a dusty black bottle and began to slide it free.

"You're going to give me a bottle of wine?" Loch asked, his tone somewhat deflated.

"Ha," Oliver laughed in reply. "Not hardly." Holding the bottle in his left hand, Oliver leaned into the rack, his right arm disappearing up to the shoulder. "Though my collection is quite unsurpassed, my real treasures lay hidden." He grunted.

Loch heard a heavy metallic thud. Then, the narrow seam between two racks widened a bit. Oliver replaced the wine bottle and then pushed on the rack to his right. To Loch's surprise, the entire right half of the wine rack swung inward revealing a curving corridor beyond cobbled out of blue stone. Oliver took his torch out of the holder and ducked under the newly revealed arch. "This way," he said.

Loch followed Oliver and found the air in the corridor quite cold. The path ended with another door. Oliver turned his back to Loch there. His elbows moved up and down rapidly, there was a click, a whirl, and another click, and the door opened. "Prepare to be amazed, my friend," Oliver said, swinging wide the door.

Loch came forward and gasped. The torchlight played of the glittery contents of a narrow but very deep chamber. Within stood coats of armor, some hundred or more. There were racks of weapons mounted on every wall: swords, axes, bludgeons, spears, sycthes, flails, glaives, and halberds. Huge, precise piles of lumber rested in the back corner along with cast iron fixtures. Loch wasn't certain, but they looked like the pieces to several catapults. Joining the other occupants in the room were more than a dozen closed chests. Loch could only guess what might be in those.

"Uh, Oliver," he said, "are you planning to raise an army?"

"Ha, ha! No, my friend," he replied. "But when you are the leading supplier of arms and weaponry in the most adventurous city in Myriad, it pays to be prepared. It pays very well."

He placed the torch in a holder on the right hand wall and strode to a long, burnished cedar chest that looked like it was made for treasure. With his back again to Loch, he clicked several latches, but rather than the arched roof of the chest swinging open like a traditional chest, several wide drawers slid open from the base.

"You know, it is amusing how things work out," Oliver said as he worked with something inside the drawer. "The whole time you were gone, I was thinking of what to give you. No, it must not be something ordinary. For you have rescued me from a horrible dilemma. But just what it would be, I could not decide. It would seem the First One has decided for you. In destroying that bestial queen, your own sword was broken. It might be reforged, I suppose. But the very notion that it broke at all is troubling to me. So therefore, I give you this: a blade that is as far superior to your former weapon as the sun is to a simple torch."

Oliver turned and handed Loch a long sword whose blade was covered by a black velvet sheath. The grip and crossguard looked ordinary enough: the tang was wound tight with a beaded black material while the guard was some kind of brushed silver metal, thick at first but tapering to a dulled point four inches on either side. The pommel was unique, however, and Loch found he could not take his eyes off of it. It seemed an impossible melding of metal and gemstone. The jewel was not simply set firmly in clasps of metal but rather it was as if a sparkling blue sapphire had bloomed within a bud of steel. Strands of each entwined the other. It was mesmerizing and beautiful.

"Will you not see the blade?" Oliver asked.

Loch blinked. "I . . . uh, of course." He took hold of the hilt and pulled the velvet covering off of the blade. Unlike the pommel, the blade did not have any sort of hypnotic effect, but it was peculiar. It had a teardrop shaped rain guard from which a three inch wide blade emerged, curving outward to a little more than four inches and then tapering gradually to its razor point three feet of metal later. The shape and design were not completely unique, but the metal itself . . . Loch had never seen such an alloy.

He held it very close to his eyes and began to study. Its fuller, the narrow, beveled channel that ran up two thirds of the blade, was a rich dark green. And all along the groove, barely visible were tiny, pale green veins. "I have seen a lot of sword blades," Loch said, "but I don't think I've ever seen this kind of metal. What is it?"

"It is bywydirium ore," Oliver replied. "The 'singing metal,' or so it is called where it is mined and smelted."

"And where would that—ow!" Loch plunged his thumb into his mouth and mumbled, "Mmph, sharp." He stared down at the blade where a perfectly rounded drop of his blood glittered like a ruby. Suddenly, it rolled into the fuller and disappeared. Loch squinted and ran his finger into the groove but felt no wetness.

"You were saying?" Oliver prompted.

"This metal, I've never heard of it," Loch said, still eying the blade. "Where did you get it?"

"I am sorry, my friend," Oliver said. "But I cannot reveal this source, not even to my most trusted customers. I have sworn to keep it a secret. But I will tell you this, you will never wield a finer blade. It is, as you have seen, razor sharp and it will never lose its edge. And while supple and agile, the bywydirium blade will not break. Not ever."

Loch laughed.

"I am quite serious," Oliver said. "Not if it were lain up against a castle wall and a rock giant were to pounce upon the blade would it break."

"A weighty claim," Loch muttered. "Even so, I wish I had had this weapon today . . . for the scalix."

"Alas that you did not have it then, Loch, but forever more, it will be at your side."

There was something odd about the way Oliver had emphasized the word forever. Loch shrugged and slid the blade into his own sheath. "Ha, it fits," he said.

"Even so," Oliver said quietly. "Even so."

Lochlan awoke from a strange dream. He blinked and gazed around his moonlit loft. He'd thought for a moment he'd heard someone talking. It was an odd voice, inflected in awkward places and not very precise.

Things were still lively in the common room two levels beneath him. Maybe that was it. He glanced at his work table and his new sword that lay upon it. The moonlight glimmered on the facets of the pommel and on the inch of blade that had slid out from the sheath.

Laughter erupted from downstairs. A deep voice rang out, chuckling between each word.

Loch turned over and closed his eyes. No wonder I'm having strange dreams, he thought. Listening to this kind of bantering nonsense half the night. Even as sleep began to reclaim him, Loch wondered. The voice had sounded so close, certainly loud enough to be in the room. He could almost remember what that odd voice had said.

"I never heard you before this today, but now I have heard."

Loch shook his head, closed his eyes, and melted into his pillow.

CHAPTER 32

GRAVE TIDINGS

And there will be those whose great learning in my Lore will inflate their pride 'til it be, for them, a stumbling stone and a hindrance. For they will use my Lore which is meant to lift burdens, to give life, and grant freedom—to shackle those less learned. Bereft of love, such as these will speak guilt, scorn, and blame. They will claim my door is shut tight against the very poor, imperfect ones I have invited to my table. They will speak with stolen authority as if they know my mind! But I say to you, it would be better for these to tie a castle turret around their necks and sink into the sea . . . rather than face my wrath.

—From Canticles (XXVIII.ii), Barde Talaursis (r. 919 AO)

42 DRINNAS 2238

On the curling trade road hidden beneath the deep green canopy on the eastern face of Vulmarrow Keep, a strange caravan made ready for departure. A team of heavily armed Stonehand warriors toiled around three covered wagons like hornets around a disturbed hive.

"You understand your orders, Borix?" Cythraul asked.

The Stonehand leader leaped down from the wagon and adjusted the backhanger straps that secured twin axes to his back. Borix snorted. "I would'na last long in this business, if'na didn't."

"Spare me the professional pride," Cythraul quipped. "This isn't about satisfied customers. This is about survival." A crow screeched somewhere in the trees above. Cythraul didn't smile, but he showed his teeth. "Your survival."

Borix swallowed. "Right, then. I understand, lord."

"Repeat them to me."

Borix rocked uneasily on his heels. "Uh, right, well . . . first, we need t'deliver the cargo safely to our moines in the Verdant Mount'ins."

A Stonehand with a tuft of wild red hair dropped to the ground beside Borix. "We guard it day'n night," he said. "No one gets within a 'undred paces of it. No one sees it."

Borix nodded. "Right ye are, Dreft," he confirmed. "No one even speaks of it. The cargo waits in the deep moine until the appointed delivery date. Then, we set our fer Anglinore City."

"Take it right to the guards, then," Dreft continued. "Leave it with them and disappear."

"What will you tell the guards?" Cythraul asked. "They will demand to know how it came into your possession."

"We unearthed it in a mine, we say," Borix explained. "And, well, once we realized what it was—what it was made of— we made straight for Anglinore. Simple mining clans like us, would'na know what t'do with such a perilous thing."

"You know it by word at least," Cythraul said. He gestured to the first wagon. "Galnan, come here at once."

A bristle-bearded Stonehand with upper arms thicker than young tree trunks came bounding between two wagons and bowed low. "My lord?"

"Each of you drives one of the wagons," Cythraul explained. "Two troop carriers and the cargo between them. You suffer no interference as you travel. One odd look . . . one lingering glance from anyone, and you end them. I advise you to avoid populated areas unless you wish to swim in their blood. Do you understand?"

Borix, Dreft, Galnan nodded and bowed.

"I hope that you do," Cythraul said. "I've paid you each enough kingsgold to retire in luxury. But payment is not your motivation. Should you err in any facet of these instructions or arrive one day late to Anglinore, I will know. I will find you, and I will bring you down to my Bone Chapel. I will string your entrails from one altar to the next and keep you alive while my pets consume you."

The three Stonehands shifted nervously and cast furtive glances at each other.

"Stick to the eastern roads or perhaps venture further south," Cythraul commanded. "Stay clear of the north road . . . trouble is coming by one of those ways. Now, get you gone."

Borix, Dreft, and Galnan scrambled each to his own driver's seat and took his reigns.

"Be aware, my friends," Cythraul called as he mounted his black horse. "One of you three is my personal spy. You won't know which one. He will not reveal it. And there are others . . . among your soldiers. I will be watching through them."

"We would'na cross you!" Borix yelled.

"One more thing," Cythraul said. "Before you depart for good, I want you to ride circles around all of Vulmarrow Keep. Dozens of times. Spoil any trail."

"Expecting more company?"

"Perhaps." Cythraul showed his teeth once more and then yelled, "Come Sköll!"

The enormous blackwolf leaped out of the nearby foliage and, with a mournful howl, raced after his master.

33 FEFTIN 2238

Alastair and Telwyn were glad to come upon Vulmarrow during the light of day. Even so, the skeletal ruins and the yawning main gate were enough to give even the sturdiest man pause.

"You used to work here?" Telwyn asked.

Alastair laughed grimly. "Asking in that way, you almost cast my service under Morlan in normalcy, like I was a clerk or . . . or a baker. Believe me, Tel, dwelling in this place was a nightmare from which there was no awakening."

"I believe you." Telwyn trotted his mare toward the main rampart. "Do you really think he is here?"

"After the war, Anglinore sent soldiers to scour this place," Alastair said, absently rubbing the crisscrossed scar on his cheek. "No sign of Cythraul was found. Of course, since I killed him, no one expected to find him here."

"No remains?"

"Ah, lad, you heard the blackwolves. Any meat left to rot would soon be scavenged by those . . . or worse things."

Telwyn swallowed. "That is an image I didn't need."

"You asked," Alastair said. "So, by one means or another, Cythraul's body was never discovered. But I wonder if the Anglish Guard spent much time searching the Vulmarrow's catacombs. I doubt that any were anxious to explore the Bone Chapel. So many years have passed now. Vulmarrow's legend grows. It is haunted, some say. Others claim it will drive a man mad. Still others will tell, when gathered around campfires, that a monster dwells in its depths. Maybe all three are true. We will find out. Come."

With the jagged turret watching from high above, Alastair and Telwyn traversed the rampart and unknowingly followed King Ealden's path almost precisely. The horses could not fit through the wrecked portcullis. They had become so skittish anyway, it was impossible to know if they would have entered the keep even had the gate been open and a hundred paces wide. Tel tied off the horses loosely. If wolves or any such things came upon their mounts, they could free themselves and run.

Alastair kindled a torch and tossed one to Tel, and they entered Vulmarrow Keep. Wreckage lay strewn across their path, and they picked their way into the vast hall where chains hung from the vaulted ceiling. They walked hundreds of yards in silence when Telwyn pointed, "Stars! What is that?"

"The better question," Alastair said, as he looked to the chamber floor, "is what was that?" He held up his torch and cast light on bones jutting this way and that in a mangled mess of gore. Some kind of black pelt had been shredded and cleaned of meat, and dark blue blood stained the floor ten feet in every direction. "I do not know what sort of creature this was," Alastair said at last. "Blue blood . . . some kind of reptile, perhaps."

"I am not afraid of it," Telwyn said. "But whatever did this to it . . . that is what I fear."

"Oh, no," Alastair muttered.

"What is it?"

"Dead men," Alastair replied. "What's left of them. Wayfolk, it looks like."

Telwyn drew close. "This looks recent."

"I thought so as well," Alastair said. "But I wonder what they were doing here. In any case, Tel, stay alert."

They moved on from the gory sight, picking their way and each thanking the First One for the blessing of daylight. They came to the stair chamber, and Alastair and found more carnage . . . bones and old blood stains. Alastair took the center stair that he knew led to the throne room. Halfway up the stair, Telwyn called out. "Look there, MiDa. Do you see it? A glimmer?"

Alastair turned and waved torch back and forth. "I see it," he said, "But—" It was too late. Telwyn scampered down the stair and vaulted the railing at the bottom. "Tel!"

Alastair bounded down after him. "Tel, don't touch anything!" He found him kneeling over gleaming metal.

"It's a glaive, MiDa," Telwyn said.

Alastair sucked in a sharp breath. "It is not just any glaive," he whispered. "It belongs to the lord of the Prydian Wayfolk."

"King Ealden?" Tel gasped. "He is here then?"

Alastair nodded. "Or was . . . at least. I cannot fathom what could possibly disarm Ealden, lest it be Cythraul himself." He fought internally. Ealden could lay wounded and dying nearby. But to call for him could alert anything to their position. "Let's search the area," he said at last.

But after an hour or more scouring the broken stone and every crevice or alcove, they came away with nothing. "Bring the glaive," Alastair said. "Let us hope to return it to its owner."

Telwyn, picked up the dual-bladed weapon and turned it absently. "MiDa, look." He held up the glaive. "It gives off light."

"Emberstones," Alastair muttered. "Come."

They took the stairs once more, and upon arriving at their eventual destination, found the archives completely wrecked. Once orderly bookshelves and scrolls were cast down and torn asunder. What black deeds had been recorded on all these ancient pages? Alastair could guess. More than a few with his name upon them. He shuddered. The atmosphere of the room weighed heavily upon him. He led Telwyn as quickly as he could to the rear passage, the one that led to the throne room.

Their torches flickered and a sour breeze wafted through the corridor. "Odd," Alastair said. "There's no opening to the outside by this way."

They emerged at last in the throne room, and felt the chill of dusk settling over the chamber. It was immediately clear where the chill breeze had originated. Wreckage of the vaulted ceiling lay strewn about the chamber, a large section of stone had crushed Morlan's old throne to shards. It looked as if some mountainous creature had risen from the chamber, bursting through the ceiling to make its escape. Where there had once been a vaulted ceiling with a cunning mechanism built to open and close at Morlan's command, there was now just sky . . . sky and the waving high boughs of black trees. Alastair and Telwyn were thankful for the natural twilight, but it revealed no sign of Cythraul, or anyone else, in the throne room.

Alastair found himself bewitched by the flight of stairs leading up to what was left of the throne. How many times did I bend my knee at this abominable seat? How many baleful orders did I assent to here? How many times did I storm out of this chamber with bloodlust burning within me?

"MiDa?" Telwyn said, putting his hand on Alastair's shoulder. He waited to gain eye contact and said, "The old has gone, MiDa. You are no longer what you once were."

Alastair blinked back tears and said, "Was it that clear on my face? I . . . I'm sorry. I know what Canticles says, but the past doesn't die easily."

"It is dead," Telwyn said. "Leave it buried."

"You are right, of course. How did you get so wise?" Telwyn didn't answer, and Alastair was reminded full force of old suspicions . . . older hopes. He looked at Telwyn and shook his head. "Let us leave this place." Alastair led Telwyn up the stairs, beyond the remains of the throne, and into the back right corner of the room. A rectangular opening yawned open from the floor before them. Stairs descended beneath the surface and curled out of sight.

They took the stairs and traveled in pregnant silence. Alastair felt a heavy presence, like watchful eyes upon him, but no matter where he angled his torch, he saw nothing but the glistening walls of the stairwell. The steps wound downward and spiraled sharply before emerging in a breathtaking open chamber.

Telwyn gazed up at the vast ceiling some hundreds of feet above. Then, he saw the Bone Chapel. He held King Ealden's glaive in one hand and drew his own sword in the other. "This place," he said gazing at the macabre structure before him, "this place is an atrocity."

"It's worse than that," Alastair said. "But this is our destination. If Cythraul is here, I will add his bones to the structure. This way."

Alastair circled the Bone Chapel until he found what he was looking for: a pair of black iron doors and a strange orb of polished stone. He removed his gauntlet and put his bare hand on the stone. It warmed to the touch, and there came a grating slide of metal from somewhere beneath their feet. He kicked open the outer doors and ventured into the building. The smell hit them both like a wall: sickly sweet, sharp and burning, old and decaying all at the same time. Alastair unsheathed the Star Sword and held his torch aloft.

They came into the main sanctuary, and Alastair marched over to the candles. "They have been lit," he whispered, "within the week at least . . . if not more recently." The time for secrecy had ended. "Cythraul!" Alastair yelled. "Cythraul come out and face my sword once more!"

His voice echoed but nothing else answered him. "Cythraul Scarhaven!" he yelled with such force that his voice cracked. "Answer me, unless you be afraid!"

They both heard the groan from somewhere near the center of the chamber. Telwyn started forward, but Alastair held him back. "Advance slowly. I'll go first." They came to the experimentation table and found a headless body torn and partially devoured.

That sound certainly wasn't from this poor soul, Alastair thought, stepping forward. He nearly slipped, his foot sliding in something wet. He moved his torch and saw a slick of dark blood. It trailed away from them. Alastair followed it past the table. A few paces later, he found a most curious site. There were two dead blackwolves. At first, Alastair thought they were sleeping, for there was no overt wound. But as he came closer, Alastair saw that each of the creatures had had their eyes driven deep into their sockets.

"Ealden had been unarmed," he muttered. "Ealden! Ealden, call to us!"

A weak groan answered them from just ahead. Alastair and Tel rushed forward, but they pulled up short. King Ealden lay sprawled upon his back. His chest rose and fell slowly, and the one eye that wasn't caked shut with blood, stared out somehow aware. How Ealden lived, Alastair could not tell. His blood stained everything nearby, and his abdomen had been torn open.

"King Ealden," Alastair whispered. "Lord of the Prydian folk, what . . . what befell you here?"

Ealden's arm flopped out to his side, and his hand curled once at the wrist. Alastair and Telwyn came to his side.

"No . . . no time," he whispered. His eye rolled loosely. "Cythraul . . . Cythraul lives."

"Where is he?" Alastair asked.

Ealden jaws worked, but at first no sound came. "Gone . . . a day . . . or more . . . I, I don't remember. Wolves came. I killed them, but went to sleep."

"Do you know where? Where did Cythraul go?" Alastair asked urgently.

"Nay, Alastair . . ." Ealden said. "Gone."

"Here, lord," Telwyn said. He placed the glaive upon Ealden's breast and helped the stricken man put his hand upon its central grip.

Ealden's lips curled into a peculiar smile. His head turned back and forth, and he took his own hand free of the weapon and nudged Telwyn's hand to grasp it. "No longer mine," he whispered. His eye seemed to lose focus and he said, "With . . . his twin-blade he will darken the eye . . . of the deceiver."

Alastair blinked. "What?"

"T-take it, Telwyn Hal—" He coughed suddenly and wrenched his head toward Alastair. "Listen to me, Coldhollow . . ." He screamed in agony. "Cythraul . . . he is Pureline . . . he cannot . . . die." Again, Ealden screamed out, but the sound died away. "Ah . . . burning . . . burning . . ." The breath hissed out. He lay still now, his eye staring . . . fixed. King Ealden, Lord of the Prydian Wayfolk was dead.

Telwyn clutched the glaive and stared up at Alastair. "What did he mean?"

Alastair blinked away tears. "I . . . I do not know."

"What will we do now, MiDa?"

Alastair stood. "We won't leave him here for scavengers to take," he said. "We will bear King Ealden's body to the nearest town, Denham, perhaps, and hire a team to bring him back to his people."

"And then? He said Cythraul cannot die."

"And then we continue the hunt."

"But—"

"This changes nothing, Tel!" Alastair shouted, louder than he meant to. "If it is true . . . what Ealden says, I will cut Cythraul into a thousand tiny pieces, seal each one into a small iron box, and drop them all over the Dark Sea. Then . . . I will be content."

CHAPTER 33

VOICES

The sharpest quill of grief is in the terror that one unique individual,
vital and beloved, peculiar to that soul alone, is irretrievably lost.

—A Myridian Proverb

14 CELESANDUR 2238

Memories of his stay in Ravensgate swam in Loch's mind as he sat down to breakfast at the Troll's Bottle, a little hole-in-the-wall inn half way between Ellador and Anglinore. He wouldn't have stopped but somewhere on the hard ride, his pack full of smoked meats and cheeses had fallen from Chalaren's saddle. And Loch felt half-starved.

A swarthy man sorely in need of a shave brought Loch a heaping plate of food. He'd not expected much, so when he looked down at the mounds of steaming hash browns, the generous rashers of bacon, the fluffy dollops of eggs, and the husk of bread with butter seeping in, he gasped. "Thank—you—sir!" Loch exclaimed.

The man burped and walked away.

Loch dug in. "Unbelievable," he mumbled, crunching on a third slice of bacon. "Inns like this are all over—just takes a little exploring."

Unbelievable.

Loch sat up straight. He looked at the two old gaffers sitting at the table adjacent to his. "Did one of you say something?" he asked them.

"Eh?" said one.

"Whassat?" said the other.

Loch repeated, "Did one of you just say something?"

"I said 'Eh'."

"And I said 'Whassat'."

Loch turned back to his food. "Well, that was pointless." He slathered some of the eggs onto his bread and took a colossal bite. He closed his eyes and savored the experience of pure bliss.

Pointless.

Loch's eyes snapped open. His head swiveled. "Who said that?" No one answered. Loch looked up to the man behind the counter, the one who'd delivered his breakfast. He burped again but didn't look up. *I need to get more sleep,* Loch thought as he took a bite of hash browns. *Hearing things.*

The potatoes took his mind off it. They were fried golden brown on the outside and yet still full and flaky on the inside. Loch counted garlic, onion, bell pepper, basil, rosemary, and parsley among the delicious flavors mingling in that bite. "Allhavenly hash browns," Loch muttered. "I may have to have hire the cook away from here."

Hash browns.

Loch pushed away from the table and stood so suddenly he knocked his water over.

The unshaven fellow behind the counter looked up. "Whad'ya see, a rat?"

"Well, no," Loch said. "But . . ."

"But what?" He snorted. "There a hair in yer eggs?"

"Ew, no," Loch said.

"What? Would'na been the first time."

Loch felt his stomach wrenching. "No, no, nothing like that . . . at all." He reached into his coin pouch and left a kingsgold coin. "I need to step outside a moment. Leave my food. I'll be back."

Loch strode out of the inn, hopped down off the landing, and raced around the backside of the building. This last time, he'd heard the voice plainly. It had an odd metallic ring to it and was quite a bit higher than Loch's own voice. *I must be losing my mind,* he thought anxiously. *But why? With these trips among my people, I'm as relaxed as I've been in years. And if I'm going insane, why is my inner voice repeating what I've already said?*

Loch paced one end of the building to the other. Maybe if I hear it again. "Speak, confound you!"

What should I say?

Loch jumped, slamming his back up against the inn. He looked left and right, up . . . and then down. Down at his side. The sword Oliver had given him for getting rid of the scalix.

"My queen!" Paige Martin called, banging his way into Clarissant Hall. He didn't see her at first. "My queen, where are you?"

"Here," Maren said, standing slowly. "I fell asleep while praying."

"Come quickly! It is urgent!"

Queen Maren blood ran cold. "Is it Loch? Is he hurt? Is he—"

"No, no, my queen. I have not seen King Lochlan all day." Paige Martin scratched his short, curly hair. "Come to think of it, I don't think I've seen King Lochlan in over a week."

"Never mind that," the queen said, rushing to meet him. "Tell me what's happening?"

"We've had a delivery," he said. "Looks like a piece of furniture to me, but some of the Anglish Guard were all bent out of shape about it. They sent for Sebastian and sent me to fetch you. Best you see for yourself."

Paige Martin led the queen to Anglinore's central armory. She nodded to the first guard, setting off a chain reaction of bows through the hundred or so soldiers gathered outside the armory and in. She found Anglinore's High Shepherd within.

"Sebastian, what's going on?" she asked.

"Something of a miracle," he replied, lifting his gnarled staff to scratch the side of his head. "I really cannot believe it."

"A Shepherd doubting a miracle?" Queen Maren laughed. "But, if a miracle, why all the guards?"

"Come and see," he said.

The soldiers parted for them, and they passed deep into the armory to a vault where Anglinore's treasures were kept. Anglish guards stood on either side of a pair of iron doors that were sealed closed by wickedly interlocking mechanisms. The soldiers glanced warily at each other and then back at their esteemed visitors. Then they turned and began to labor over a number of levers and wheels. To Maren, it seemed they worked in a kind of precise synchronized tandem, something they must have practiced hundreds of times. One guard turned a wheel and, immediately upon stopping, the second guard pulled a lever down two slots to the left and one to the right. Just before that movement was complete, the first guard pressed in a fist-sized panel at his chest height and another closer to his waist. It was a coordinated movement of more than a dozen separate actions. The guards stepped away, and the vault doors swing inward.

Light shone down upon the contents of the vault, and Queen Maren gasped. "Is this . . . after all the years . . ."

"The Eye of the North," Sebastian confirmed.

Queen Maren's eyes bulged, and her hand flew to her lips. "How . . . how comes it here?"

"Stonehand traders," said the Shepherd. "They discovered it in an abandoned mine in Ellador, covered in years of dust and grime. Once they cleaned it off, they realized it was vaskerstone and brought it here."

"And you believe them?" she asked.

Sebastian nodded. "Guardcaptain Broadward questioned them thoroughly," he said. "Besides, these Stonehands are far to young to be the original thieves."

"Thief, you mean. The Wayfolk convicted an apprentice . . . Xanalos, Ealden's apprentice. But they never recovered the table. Have you sent word?"

"Of course," the Shepherd replied. "By Windborne courier— directly to Ealden—he should be the first, after all he's been through."

Queen Maren nodded. "That was wise. We don't want a misunderstanding between our peoples. Wars have been started for less."

"Much less, unfortunately."

The queen stepped up to the table and gazed at her own reflection in the polished black surface. She ran her hand along one corner. "Have you . . . have you tried to . . ."

"No," he replied curtly. "I will leave that to the Wayfolk. Vaskerstone is a remarkable substance, but even after so many ages, we do not fully understand its properties. And this . . . The Eye . . . is the only one of its kind. By all accounts it contains perilous power. If I might advise you, I should not make use of it at all until Ealden comes."

Maren pulled her hand away. "As you wish, Sebastian."

15 Celesandur 2238

Loch found Sebastian deep in thought in his tower chamber. He eased the door shut behind him and bolted it. The Shepherd didn't move. He seemed sculpted of marble.

"Sebastian?"

The Shepherd blinked. "Loch . . . you've returned."

"Yes, I've returned. Else I wouldn't be standing here." He laughed.

"Right . . . my apologies. It's been a very, complicated day." Sebastian took a deep breath and exhaled slowly. "So, tell me, how was Ellador? Ravensgate, was it?"

Loch grinned. "It was splendid. I became a tavern keeper, a place called the Venture Inn. Have you heard of it?"

"By reputation," he said. "Stars, I think I know where this is going."

"I guarantee, good Shepherd, that you do not." Loch glanced back at the door.

Sebastian followed his gaze. "Did you . . . did you bolt my door?"

Loch nodded.

"Why would you lock the door?" the Shepherd asked. "Cardiff hasn't been here for some time now."

"I've brought back something from Ellador, something unique." Loch placed the sword upon the Shepherd's desk.

Sebastian raised an eyebrow. "A sword?"

"Not just any sword," Loch said. "Unsheathe it. But careful. It's very sharp."

Sebastian looked curiously at the pommel a moment. "Unusual," he murmured. He took hold of the black ribbed grip and slid the blade from the sheath. He noted the teardrop shaped rain guard and the dark green fuller running up the blade, the strange veins of pale green . . . "Is this a Master Blade?" he asked. "Like General Coldhollow's Star Sword?"

Loch shrugged. "I wish I knew. Oliver, ah the merchant who gave this to me, said it was one of a kind."

"The metal . . . is strange to me."

"Bywydirium ore," Loch said. "The singing metal."

"I've never heard of such a thing," he said. He started to hand the blade back. "Well, it certainly is a magnificent gift. But, if you'll excuse me, Loch, I have a few pressing matters—"

"Wait," Loch urged. "Wait. I want to show you what it can do." He waited for Sebastian to put the sword back on the desk and then he said, "Go on, then."

Sebastian misunderstood. "What? I put it down. Was I not supposed to?"

"No, no, not you." Loch stared at the blade. "Go on, say something." Sebastian's eyes became small. He glanced from the blade to Loch and back.

Loch frowned. "Speak confound you!"

Sebastian laughed. "My lord, if you please . . . I really do not have time for jesting—"

"It's not a joke, Sebastian." Loch picked up the sword. "You hardly shut up the whole trip back—and NOW you won't say a word? Go on, will you?" Silence rang loud in the round chamber. Loch felt hot blood rushing into his cheeks. "Sebastian, I know how this must look, but I'm telling you, this blade is alive! It speaks!"

Sebastian spat out a hard laugh and guffawed for several moments before wiping his eyes on his robe sleeve. "Ah, ah, thank you, my king. I have been in need of such levity. Too serious of late. This . . . this was most amusing."

Loch sheathed the sword with a growl. "Shepherd," he hissed. "I am not joking!" Without another word, Loch threw back the bolt, wrenched open the door, and stormed out of the chamber.

Sebastian leaned back in his chair and blinked in astonishment. "What in all the Stars is that all about?" he asked his empty room. *Either the lad is pulling off an ingenious prank or he has gone stark, raving mad.* The Shepherd wondered about the tavern. Perhaps Loch had sampled a little too much of the Venture Inn's products. Sebastian would speak to Maren about it later. But for now, there were more insistent things on his mind.

He stared beyond the trellises and the dark red flowers blooming there, out through the window into the night.

The voices on the wind.

Since just before the Ceremony of Crowns, Sebastian had heard nothing of substance. A recent correspondence from Shepherd's Hollow reported much the same. But now, Sebastian heard them distinctly; there were frightful whispers . . . two separate voices. One seemed to be coming from the far west. The other—and this made no sense whatsoever to Sebastian—came from the north. But there was nothing there . . . just the endless black water of the Dark Sea.

"Well thank you for making me look like a lunatic!" Loch growled. He sat on the edge of his bed in his own chamber. He'd triple locked his door. The sword was in his lap. "Why didn't you speak?"

"I'm shy."

"Oh, that's just . . . wonderful!" Loch huffed. "Look, sword, you have to understand something. In this realm, I am the High King. You must do what I say."

"I want to be king."

Loch threw his head back and barked out a huge laugh. "You are a piece of metal. People hit you with hammers and throw you into the fire!"

"Tell me about it. You have no idea."

Loch thought about that for a moment. "Did . . . did you feel it?"

"Did you feel it when you cut your finger on me?"

"Of course," Loch said.

"It was the same with me, only much more pain."

"How can that be? I mean, you speak, you think, you feel? How . . . how can metal . . ."

"I am a living being. How I am what I am, I do not know. Metal, hmph!"

"Well, I'm sorry," Loch said. "But you cannot be king. I already am."

"Can I be the king's sword, then?"

"I suppose," Loch said. "I already had a blade, but I think you're better."

"Of course, I am better. I stay sharp. I will not tarnish or mar. Best of all, I never break."

"So you say," Loch quipped.

"You will see."

"But this talk-don't-talk nonsense has to stop," Loch said. "Sebastian must think I've gone loopy."

"I am sorry. But, I probably should not speak in front of just anyone."

"Why?"

"Beings like you tend to steal rare things. I changed hands many times before Oliver took me in and put me in that vault."

"Did you speak for them . . . the others?" Loch asked.

"No. I could not."

"Why?"

"Blood. I sampled them all, but there was no match until you. Then, I listened to your words, learned them."

Loch sat up straight. He remembered the bead of blood vanishing. "Blood, is . . . is that how you feed?"

"No, that's how I mate."

Loch stood up, aghast. He held the blade at arm's length. "You what?"

"I am . . . how do you say it? I am meant for someone. Is mate not the right word?"

"NO!" Loch said. "No, sword, it is not."

"I do not wish to be called 'sword.' Will you give me a name?"

Loch placed the sword on his bed and paced. "What sort of name, I wonder? The Master Blades are all named. Star Sword, Sun Sword, etc. What would you be? How about Singing Sword?"

"No. Not a name like that."

"What kind then?"

"Something like your name. Lochlan or Oliver or Tess or Sebastian."

"Oh, a person name. Hmm." Loch thought of people he knew. "Ealden, Drüst, Flynn, Obert, Telwyn . . . any of those?"

"I do not think so. None of those strike me . . . as me."

"Alastair, uhm, Galeal, Chesterton, Martin . . . Itzjaak, Jornth, Roth, Alfred, Gander—"

"Fred!"

"I didn't say Fred," Loch replied. "Alfred. It's from my sword trainer, Alfred Adelbard. That would make sense, you being a sword."

"No, not Alfred. Alfred is your sword trainer. Fred. Fred is me."

"How odd."

"Yes," Fred replied. "But I like it."

"Alright, Fred, from here on out, speak when I tell you to, but not before."

"I can do that."

The hour was late, but Maren was certain the armory would still be well-attended by guards. Even the adjoining hallways were watched by treble its usual complement. Each soldier of Anglinore bowed or nodded as their queen passed. She came to the vault. The two guards there looked up, startled.

"Your majesty?" one said.

"I wish to see the table," she said.

The guards eyed her strangely but bowed and went to work on the doors. Once opened, Maren stepped inside. She turned back to the guards. "I presume the doors open from the inside without all the machinations?"

"From the inside . . . uh, well, yes." The guard stepped forward and pointed to a curving bar that ran along the backside of the door. "Push this forward," he said. "And then pull. The doors will open. But—"

"That will be all for now, thank you," the queen said. "Now please close the doors."

Trading questions in their eyes, the two guards leaned in and closed the vault.

Maren went straight to the table. She understood little of its use but knew that vaskerstone was activated by touch. She placed her hands on either side of the black stone surface and waited. Nothing happened at first. She let her mind wander. The Eye of the North, missing over a hundred years, returned at last. *A gift from the First One,* she thought. *But to what end? What do we need to see now?* Queen Maren had no idea, but above all those other mysteries, pulsed one question that had gnawed at her mind for over twenty years: *why?*

Her hands began to tingle. She felt suddenly very tired. Green light began to whirl within the table. It was as if she were looking through a dark window into a deep chamber. The green light was like a writhing mist within, and there was suddenly a figure there, walking. He drew nearer, and Maren caught her breath. "Aravel!" she gasped.

And he was there, just on the other side of that thin window. He looked older, a little more gaunt, hair shot through with more gray than she remembered. But he smiled and looked up at her knowingly. "Ah, Maren," he said. "You have come to me at last."

"How can this be?" she asked, tears rolling down. "You . . . left this world. You died."

"My love," he said, "would I ever depart to such a place where you could not follow?"

"What are you saying?"

"Why have you waited?" the ghostly Aravel asked. "What has stayed your hand? I long for you to join me."

She caressed the table. "Oh, oh Aravel, I linger only for Lochlan but I must stay for him. Our son needs me."

"Does he?" Aravel asked. "Does he need you more than I need you?"

"You cannot force me to choose between a husband and a son. That's not fair."

His eyes flashed with white-hot anger. "Death is not fair," he said, his features softening. "Come to me, Maren. There are so many things I long to show you. Come and be with me . . . forever."

Maren let go of the table, fell backward, and gasped as if surfacing from deep water. She got to her feet and backed towards the vault doors. She threw them open and raced out of the armory without a word to anyone.

"Did you see the queen?" one of the vault guards asked the other.

He nodded. "Stricken, I thought. And ghostly pale."

16 CELESANDUR 2238

Loch spent the better part of the next afternoon staring sullenly at the calendar. *Sebastian had said it would be some time until my next venture, but this?* Drinnas and most of Octale too—all completely consumed with kingly duties. "My luck the serpent creature will be slain before I set foot on Wetlands soil."

"Serpent?" Fred echoed. "Wetlands? Are we going to a place where there is much water?"

"Eventually," Loch groused.

"I do not much like much water," Fred explained. "If I fall into it, I sink."

"I will be careful with you, Fred. No one likes to sink."

CHAPTER 34

The Wetlands

How do we know when we have truly loved another? It is when we realize that others can give only their own kind of love—not our kind—and we accept that.

—An Elladorian Proverb

6 Octale 2238

"What's going on with my mother?" Loch asked himself. He leaned over the port rail, stared down at the waves, and shook his head. "Did you meet any nice ladies yet, Loch? Are you sure there isn't a special someone? How could you go to Ellador and not find some exotic beauty?" He laughed, more out of exasperation than in humor. "The very LAST thing I need right now is a woman to complicate things."

"Are you sure?" asked Elsa Taerinin, the captain standing behind him. "I don't mean to pry, but you say you don't want a woman in your life . . . and yet you chartered a ship named The Relentless Wench?"

"More than a little irony, I suppose," Loch said. "Didn't really pay attention to the name. Just looking for a ride to Chapparel."

"So what's in Chapparel for you?" asked the captain. "If not a woman?"

"A serpent," Loch replied.

Captain Taerinin walked away without another word.

"That sounded creepy," Fred whispered.

"Fred?"

"Yes?"

"Please shut up."

"I'm sorry, sir," Skappy said, yawning. "But who did you say you are?"

"I am Baron Cardiff Strengle of Avon, and I do not appreciate being held up like some peasant begging bread at the gate! I wish to see my cousin, High King Lochlan on a matter of utmost importance."

"Ohhh, right . . . right," Skappy replied, adjusting his stance so that he was no longer leaning against the gatehouse wall. "It's the Baron, Fez. Why didn't you remind me?"

Fez scratched behind his ear. "I dunno, Skap," he said, squinting at Cardiff. "We get lots of folk round 'ere askin' to see the High King. But yeah, come to mention it, I fink I've seen you before."

"Several times in the past year," Cardiff muttered. "Now, if you'll excuse me, I aim to see King Lochlan. Please send word for us to meet in Clarissant Hall."

"I'm right sorry, Baron," Skap said, consulting a logbook. "But, eh, King Lochlan has a rather lengthy council with Shepherd Sebastian Sternbough. He'll be tied up for the foreseeable future."

Baron Cardiff kneaded the bridge of his nose with his fingers. "That will not be acceptable," he said. "Send word immediately that I will meet with High King Lochlan or else I can meet with the senior Guardcaptain."

"As I said, King Lochlan is well and truly occupied," Skappy explained. "Grimgall is the senior Guardcaptain on duty, but if it's as serious as you make out, then ole Grimgall won't do you no

good. He can't make high and mighty decisions like King Lochlan. Heh, heh."

"Yeah, don't he wish!" Fez laughed so hard he wheezed.
"He'd probly rename this Grimgall City, he would!"

Baron Cardiff waited until both guards calmed down. "I
believe the Guardcaptain is precisely who I need," he said. "You
see, I wish to bring charges of treason."

"Charges?" echoed Skap. "Gainst who?"

Cardiff folded his arms. "Against Lochlan Stormgarden."

"I seek an Elder . . . uh," Loch said, looking quickly to the
parchment scrap in his palm. "Elder Justinian, I think is the
name."

The woman put down a huge basket of jumbled clothing, licked her palm, and brushed the hair out of her eyes. She
smoothed the waist of her dress, smiled, and said, "You aren't
from around 'ere, are you now?"

"No, I am not," Loch replied. He waited. She waited. I feel
like I'm on display, he thought. "My travels brought me to the
Venture Inn in Ravensgate." She shrugged. "In Ellador."

"Oh, Ellador, now that I heard of," she said. "What brings
you to the Wetlands?"

"Elder Justinian does," he said. "Does he still live here?"

"Well, where else would he be?" she asked, squinting as if the
numbers she'd been adding didn't sum correctly.

"I don't really—look, Miss, is he here . . . in this village . . .
right now?"

"Yes."

"Could you please point me in his direction?"

"Oh, well certainly," she said. "Why didn't you say so, handsome?" She winked and strode off.

Reluctantly, Loch followed.

She strode across the village, picking her way across a carpet
of pine bark—some pieces as big as a man's palm—and between
cottages and shops, bringing him at last to a woodland fortress

nestled among tall pines at the top of a wide hill. Loch craned his neck to take in the facade. He'd never seen a building of this construction before. It was seemingly built from alternating layers of timber—whole trunks—slate gray stone, and a peculiar white mortar that glistened as if still wet. Magnificent mansion, Loch thought. And that's what it was . . . a gigantic, ostentatious house framed by a few turrets and defendable parapets. He stared up at the wagon-wheel sized chandelier that hung above the front stairs.

"This way," the woman said, curling her fingers in a way that might have been cute if Loch hadn't felt so awkward around her. Nonetheless, he followed her inside. They passed through a corridor over-decorated with paintings, etchings, engravings, and plaques. Mostly portraits. The occupants of the Elders' mansion seemed to be pretty fond of their own faces. Loch rolled his eyes. If I ever see another painting of me, I'll vomit.

The woman went to a rich mahogany desk at the end of the hall, picked up a small silver bell, and gave it a brief shake. "I must return to my duties," she said. Loch didn't turn around as she left.

He was still looking at the decor when another woman entered the corridor. Loch tripped over his own feet but caught himself before he went down. Blush burned up his cheeks, but Loch still couldn't keep from staring. The woman standing there was a vision of raven-haired allure. Tall, svelte, and shapely, she wore a steel-blue gown that hung within an inch of the floor. Her hair was pulled back, bound twice by silver wraps, and fell like black silk down her neck. It framed her ivory skin perfectly and fed her dark eyes with symbiotic power. Her lips were deep red, almost plum. And they were moving.

Loch suddenly realized she had been speaking. "I am so sorry," he said, delivering an odd bow. "What were you saying?"

She returned the bow with a slight tilt of the head. "No, my lord," she said. "Do not apologize to me. It is my pleasing service to repeat my words . . . as many times as you wish. I was simply asking about your business with Elder Justinian. He is rather busy this afternoon."

"I've come to inquire about the serpent," he said. "Is it still a nuisance?"

"More than a nuisance," she said. She offered her arm: a slender, delicate thing of beauty, Loch thought, and he took it. "I am Mistress Eveara, the Elder's handmaiden. I will see you to him."

Handmaiden? Loch thought. And she seems proud of it. Dare calling a woman in Anglinore such a thing, I'd get smacked silly . . . if I wasn't king, that is.

Mistress Eveara escorted Loch into a large parlor full of dark furniture and one robed man. His back was turned and he seemed intent on a volume from one of the bookshelves. His hair was once blond but had gone mostly gray. He wore it short and it bristled in places. He closed the book and turned. He blinked at Loch, glanced to Mistress Eveara and back.

"Do I know you?" Elder Justinian asked.

A chill like frozen lace settled on the back of Loch's neck. No, he thought. I've never seen this man before. Still, he may have come to court in Anglinore. Loch lifted up the scrap of parchment he'd taken from the Venture Inn. "Did you leave this offer?" he asked. "I was at the Venture Inn, and I'd like to answer it, if I may."

Elder Justinian left the book spinning on a nearby desk and took Loch's hands in his own. "My good, good man," he said. "First One bless you for coming. We've done everything we can, short of poisoning the lagoon, but that would defeat the purpose, you see."

"Actually, I don't see," Loch said. "All I know is you have a serpent interfering with your fishing."

"Ah," the Elder said. "It's more than that. Eveara, fetch us tea and cakes. Come, sir . . . your name?"

"Loch."

"Yes, yes, a good, sturdy name. Come, Loch, come and sit. I will explain." He led Loch to a pair of chairs with a small, gnarled table resting between them.

Mistress Eveara returned that moment, placing a tray generously laden with small cakes: frosted, unfrosted, crumb-topped, fruit-topped, and more. Two steaming cups of tea waited as well.

She turned to leave. The Elder hadn't even said so much as a thank you, so Loch did. "Thank you for serving us, m'lady," he said, earning a curious glance from the Elder, as well as, a heart-melting smile from Mistress Eveara.

Loch watched her leave and then turned back to the Elder expectantly. But Elder Justinian seemed content to stare, quietly sip tea and munch cakes. Loch waited . . . and waited. Finally, as the Elder started on his third cake, Loch said, "Elder? About the serpent?"

"I beg your pardon," he said. "Lost in thought, you know. Now, the serpent. Foul thing. We don't know where it came from, but it arrived last Solmonath after a terrible storm. Huge thing. Massive thing. Much like a fennigator but a better swimmer . . . and much bigger. It's eaten the perch population down to almost nothing and driven the rest out to the deep shoals where we cannot get to them."

"Forgive me, Elder," Loch said, "but I know something of this region. Your hunters' reputation has spread far and wide. How is it that . . . what I mean to say is, well, why haven't you killed it yet?"

Elder Justinian put his tea cup down, a slight tremble in his hand. "It's armored, and it's elusive. We've spent thousands of shafts trying to skewer that thing. We've tried netting it, spearing it. We've even tried to explode it. The closest anyone got was Millard Key. Crazy lad, bless him. Felt guilty for some problematic business he was involved in this past spring, I suppose. He actually dove into the lagoon and wrestled the thing. He gashed its forelimb, but it took his arm."

Loch found the lagoon with little trouble. As instructed, he took the forest paths until they opened up onto the sand. Then, he followed the shoreline until he came to black, water-pocked stone formations, clambered over them, ducked under the strange, lilting pines and dropped to the ground.

Loch's feet sank several inches, and he looked down. It wasn't sand, really but rather a thick, pure white clay. Loch knelt and touched it with his fingertips. It was positively smooth and, with some effort, quite malleable. He packed a ball of it into his palm and then hurled it at a tree trunk. It gave a satisfying smack and stuck fast to the tree. Loch shrugged and padded on, following the water's edge. Fist-size, golden crabs skittered out of his path as he came.

Then Loch stopped. "Oh . . . now that is something," he muttered. He'd envisioned the lagoon as a small inlet pool, forty or fifty yards across. What he found was more like a small bay, five hundred yards across if it was an inch.

"That is much water," Fred said. "You promised to be careful."

"I will, I will. And, for me at least, the water isn't the problem. It's what's in the water."

The blazing midday sun brightened the half of the lagoon that wasn't under canopy cover. And there, just at the border where the shadows began, something created its very own wake.

A very large wake.

Loch sprinted across the packed white clay to point on the waterline nearest to the disturbance. He dropped his bag, leaned against his bow to string it, and nocked an arrow. *I don't know what the Wetlanders use for arrowheads,* he thought, *but I can't imagine a hide that would stop a cyrium tipped head.*

Loch took aim, watching the troughs and eddies in the water. Whatever was under there, moved a lot of water as it circled. White spray erupted, and a dark shape blasted up from the water. It looked like a narrow whale but was longer and had large spade-shaped fins and a massive triangular head that reminded Loch of a venomous snake. Loch heard a distant cracking sound as the creature's jaws opened. It snatched a gull right out of the air and then fell back to the water with a thunderous splash. Loch let the arrow go far too late. It sailed in a high arc and fell harmlessly into the sea.

"Stars," Loch exhaled. "That thing's big." He looked at his bow, shook his head, and cast it up on shore.

He went back to his pack and rooted around. "Let me take him!" Fred demanded. "No serpent will deny my edge!"

Loch laughed. "I am sure you're right, if only we could persuade it to come upon shore. Remember? The danger of sinking? What if I lost you? Then where would I be?"

"Lose me?" Loch thought sure he heard Fred actually gulp. "Lose me in the sea. No, that would not be good at all."

"No chance of that," Loch said. "For I am leaving you with my pack." Loch loosened his belt and lay Fred in the pack.

"I would try," Fred said, "if you asked it of me."

"I know you would," Loch replied. "But today, it's spear work."

He took out five foot-long lengths of wood and began assembling his spear. It was fitted with threaded iron couplings and screwed together quickly. He hefted the weapon, and it felt good in its hands. Its cyrium-tipped spearhead looked vicious, gleaming in the sun's light. He took a tight coil of treated rope from his pack and knotted one end to the eyelet on the back of the spear.

No way to avoid getting wet on this, Loch thought. Just hope it's with water and not blood. He plopped down onto the white clay shore and pulled off his boots. He took off his tunic next and kept going until all he had on were his breaches—and those he rolled up to his knees. Rope in one hand, spear in the other, Loch jogged down the curving beach. He watched the creature's wake and tried to figure out where it might come closest to shore.

After some indecision, Loch chose a hillock of beach grass, clay, and more of those twisted pines. It over hung the water dangerously, but Loch needed to get close. And he needed the trees. He took the other end of the rope and secured it to the gnarled trunks. Then, he waited.

The serpent seemed to be following a spiraling circular pattern. It slithered through the waves near the surface, but would dive occasionally. Loch watched curiously on one such dive. The serpent had been deep for just a moment when a ten-foot spread of bubbles shimmered to the surface. The sea birds dove down a few yards closer to the water. Then, WHOOSH. The serpent leaped up from the surf and got himself a little more lunch.

Smart serpent, Loch thought, mentally noting that he'd better not underestimate this thing.

Farther and farther out it came, tracing concentric circles until it was almost in range. Loch hefted the spear, letting it bounce in his palm. Then it was close enough. The shot was there. Loch backed up a step, lunged forward, planted his left foot, and heaved the spear. Loch's momentum nearly carried him off the hillock, so he didn't see the spear hit home.

But he heard it.

Combining the roar of a stoked kiln and a the grinding of a dull blade against a spinning whetstone—it was a terrible, shivering sound. Just as Loch clambered to his feet, the rope went taut and the entire hillock shuddered and dropped a few inches. Loch sunk his fingers like claws into the white clay and turned his head back to the water. The spear had been well-thrown. He'd pierced the creature's tough hide just below what would've been the left shoulder blade of a human. But he'd missed the creature's heart—*wherever that might be on such a thing,* Loch thought—for the beast showed no signs of fading. Instead, the serpent thrashed its long, membranous tail, kicking up fountains from the sea. The hill shuddered again, and Loch couldn't get to his feet.

The rope was Angle-braided by Syngal Grommet, the Anglish Guard's own supplier. It wasn't going to unravel or snap. And the old gnarled pines looked like they had a death grip on the clay. No chance of those snapping. The only thing with any give was the soil itself. And pretty soon, the entire hillock broke free of its foundation and began to slide.

"Forget this!" Loch yelled. He released his grip, jerk-twisted his body round, and pushed off the foundering hill with his legs. In midair, Loch unsheathed his serrated dagger. He fell like a stone on the serpent's back, the weight of his fall driving the dagger seven inches into flesh. Dark blue blood bubbled up. The serpent thrashed, bouncing Loch hard. He hit his head on the pommel of his dagger. His thoughts swam a moment, but he held on to the knobby ridges of the thing's back. That's when the serpent started to spin.

Unable to break free of the thorns that impaled it and anchored by a huge hunk of root and clay, the creature slashed its tail and alternated thrusts of its fins. Loch straddled the serpent, went under, came up, went under again—faster and faster. "Bad idea!" Loch yelled, spewing out gulps of seawater.

The creature roared and flailed, its tail bludgeoning the water. Loch's hands, arms, shoulders, thighs—the burning strain would turn to muscle failure soon. He went under. When he came up, he yanked out the dagger and slammed it home in another spot. Clutching the beast with strength born of desperation, he went under again. Every time Loch came up, he plunged the dagger in. Every time he went under, he held on for dear life. Slowly, he inched his way through the fresh-flowing bluish gore toward the beast's head.

No way I can take much . . . more . . . of . . . this, he thought, going under again. When Loch came back up, he lunged and drove the dagger into the base of the creature's skull. Only the blade didn't penetrate. It slid off to the side and carved a hunk of flesh off the bone.

"Ohhhh, no!" Holding on with just his legs, Loch went under again. He came up sputtering and spluttering, knew he didn't have much choice. His chin pressed into the beast's brow, Loch practically hugged the creature's head. He sawed the dagger across the thing's throat. It barely cut in half an inch. Loch strained, arching his back, trying to press the blade into the beast's neck with both hands. It was no good. He couldn't force it in, couldn't find any lethal spot to hit. Under. Loch hadn't timed his breath. He sucked in a quart of water and nearly fell away.

When the serpent came topside once more, it flung back its head. Desperate to hold on, Loch fumbled with the dagger. It slid from his hand. He snatched at it, almost got it back. But his hand, slick with gore and sea water, had no traction, and . . . he just lost it. The blade fell into the water. Over now, Loch thought. Once the serpent put him in the water, Loch knew what would happen.

Out of options, he did the only thing he could think of. He wrapped his arms around the creature's neck and tried to strangle it. Loch had trained in grappling, and he'd broken a mans ribs once with a bear hold like this. But even so, Loch had to laugh at himself. There was no way he could—

He heard a crack. The serpent went still so suddenly that Loch almost slid into the water. Loch couldn't believe it. He'd killed it. Not by suffocation, not hardly long enough for that. I must have broken its neck, he thought, feeling relieved and more than a little impressed with his own strength.

Then, he saw the arrow.

Buried to within an inch of its fletchings, a thumb-thick shaft protruded from the serpent's eye socket.

"I . . . CAN'T . . . BE . . . LIEVE . . . IT!!" someone shrieked, anger burning in the tone.

Loch spun and fell off the creature. When he surfaced and wiped the water from his eyes, he spotted a young woman more than fifty yards away on shore. She had her fists dug into her hips. She also had a bow.

"I take it I have you to thank," Loch called to her, "for saving—"

"I leave for an hour," she growled. "ONE HOUR, just to get a few more coneys for bait, and I come back—and someone's beaten me to it!" She lifted her face to the sky. "Do you just HATE me?" Then, she looked back at Loch. "What were you even doing here anyway? You aren't from the Wetlands or from Chapparel."

"I answered a summons," Loch replied. "Elder Justinian gave me the job."

"Of course he did," she replied. "That's just perfect."

While she muttered, Loch swam to the shallows. "But m'lady," he said, emerging from the water. "You saved my life."

"Did I?" she asked.

"Undoubtedly."

"What a pity," she said. "You ruined mine."

"Pardon?" he said. "But I don't even know you."

"Noooo." She buried her face in one hand. "No, that wasn't fair. My life is already ruined. You simply ruined the possibility of life getting any better for me, that's all." She growled and then kicked a dead rabbit fifteen feet out into the water. She made some small whimpering noises. "Don't look at me!" She peeked through her fingers to make sure.

Loch turned away, feeling foolish and somewhat reluctant. In fact, he couldn't help looking. Whoever she was, she was not glamorous. Nothing at all like Elder Justinian's handmaiden. But there was, in her collection of features, something very interesting. Her eyes, half hidden now, glimmered cornflower blue with hints of storm gray. Her eyebrows canted toward the bridge of her nose and were oddly darker than her golden tresses. She had tiny red rose lips and an unbearably cute tiny cleft in her chin.

Loch banished those thoughts as best he could and said, "Please, may I know your name . . . and how I've wronged you?"

She wiped her brow left and right and stared hard at Loch. "Ariana," she said. "And I was trying to kill the serpent that's been plaguing my village. If . . . if I had, well, I thought that I might gain a measure of respect."

"But you did kill the serpent."

"I finished him," she said, in almost a hiss. "I saw what you did. Anchoring him with the spear? That was good thinking. I never could get it to stay on the surface long enough to get a good shot. And the way you dove onto the creature and stabbed it with that dagger, well . . . that was brave. Foolish, but brave."

She picked up the rest of the dead rabbits, spun on the clay, and started to march away. "This was my last chance."

"Look, my la—Ariana—I know what you think you saw, but I'm trying to tell you that you killed this beast."

"Don't patronize me."

"Patronize you?" Now Loch was growing angry. "I'll march to the Elders right now and tell them it was you who slew the serpent."

"No," she said. "I've been down that road before. It was your kill." She picked up her pace and disappeared into the wood.

"We'll just see about that," Loch muttered. Then he yelled out, "And my name is LOCH by the way!"

He kicked the sand. Why am I so angry? he wondered. It might have been because the stubborn girl refused to listen. Or it might have been because she never asked for my name. Loch refused to admit to himself which one. He turned and jogged around the waterline to fetch his sword.

CHAPTER 35

MOONLIGHT AND STEEL

Very little of the original document survived. Burned a' purpose, to be certain. The Shepherds labored long over bits and pieces, words and phrases, and charred blanks. It was enough. The traitors of our order, the so called Dark Shepherds had taken everything from the Wayfolk of Grayvalon. Their dreams, their futures, even their bodies. It was a pact made in the Pits. The only question left is: why?

—From Shepherd Druval Celigion,
on *The Fall of Grayvalon*

6 OCTALE 2238

Cythraul found the crevasse that Morlan had entered twenty years earlier. A black gash gaped open at the peak of a stony tor, the highest of many haphazard collisions of rock in Cragland Hills. Cythraul breathed out a sigh of pure awe. "There is nothing left," he whispered. "No sign at all." The destructive force was beyond imagining. More than two ages ago, in the span of just a few days, shifting stone and quaking earth had reduced the magnificent Wayfolk city of Grayvalon to ruins and then swallowed it whole. That there was still any coherent way to descend into the crushed ruins—that was something of miracle. *Cythraul laughed at the thought. Sabryne rarely gets his due credit for miracles.*

Cythraul tied off his horse at the last living tree in the area and then scaled the rocks to the yawning gap. Without hesitation, Cythraul dropped down into the murk. The sun was almost directly overhead, so that provided some light for the initial descent. That would change soon enough. Levels of sharp, jutting stone, blocky clefts, and sandy ridges appeared and fell away as Cythraul descended. Soon, the snaking hole fell into darkness, and Cythraul kindled a handful of emberstones. He affixed one on specially made clasps for each wrist and another on his belt. The dizzying rocky depths flickered into view, and Cythraul wasted no time clambering down. Time passed without reference. Stony chill settled over him, and the air itself seemed somehow alien: thin and vaporous, barely life-sustaining.

The whispers.

Ah, he thought. *I wondered when I would hear them. How peculiar.* It reminded him of . . . the dying gasps of the subjects he experimented on in the Bone Chapel. Be they Stonehand, Windborne, Human, or Gorrack, bodies tended to release what little breath remained through saliva that pooled in the back of the throat. The sound was beyond unnerving to most men, and it was unmistakable: the death rattle.

Cythraul stopped on a cleft of stone and cast about, looking for the crack. He scraped at the layers of dust with his boot until, at last, he found a root of darkness where the stone had split. He followed the hairline fissure to nest of sharp, protruding blades of stone. He reached within it, cuffing his knuckles more than once. Finally, he found the box and extracted it. Made of some dark metal Cythraul did not recognize, the box had a simple hinge for the lid. When Cythraul opened it, an image flashed into his mind: hooded figures bearing torches stood around a strange design graven into a stone floor. They raised their fists, and Cythraul thought they might have been chanting. Fire rose up from the ground, and the vision was gone.

"Odd," Cythraul whispered, committing the images to memory. He wanted to know more about them and thought he might know who to ask.

He removed a single candle and put the metal box back in its resting place. He gave the wick a quick twist, watched it spark and sizzle. Like luminous blood, a tiny dribble of red rolled down the wick and vanished into the shaft of the candle. The entire candle began to glow, faintly at first, but then it kindled to a glowing flare. And then, it seemed to go out. But Cythraul knew better.

One by one, he unfastened his emberstones and dropped them into a pouch on his belt. The darkness reclaimed his vision for a moment, but then, even though the candle did not seem to emanate light of its own, a profound scene materialized before him, illuminated with spectral light. There stood an arched gate of stone. Runes of Sunderell ran up one side, across the arch, and down the other. Cythraul recognized it as a trapping rite. Then, he saw the pale figures milling about on the other side. Male and female, military and civilian, more than a dozen ghostly forms waited. Their mouths were moving, gaping open in wordless moans. An endless death rattle.

They held out their hands as Cythraul moved through them, but he paid them no heed. The candle held high, Cythraul found himself in the midst of the fallen city of Grayvalon. There were buildings, but they were all somewhat irregular: walls at odd angles, roofs shifted or tilted, doors and windows in strange places. It was altogether wrong, and the beings all around Cythraul seemed well aware of its broken nature, for they were part of it. Cythraul pressed on.

But soon, the ghostly figures began to thicken in number. They crowded in on Cythraul as if they might bar his way. But he paid them no heed. He burst through them, feeling the touch of cold liquid on his exposed arms. The death rattles increased their volume and, somehow, their intensity, but Cythraul charged ahead. He looked to the ground and found the heavy lengths of chains that led away from each of the ghostly beings. The chains were the trail to follow.

Cythraul quickened his pace. He was not frightened, but rather thrilled. He was getting close. Around a gradual curve, he went, the Wights moving aside whenever they crossed his path. At last, he found where the luminous chains led. A massive chamber gaped open, and the chains disappeared into a sheer wall of stone. Many Wights were gathered there, pulling at their chains and writhing in quiet agony. Some clawed at the stone, others at the shackles on their ankles. But none of them found relief.

Cythraul stood among them and looked up at the long passages of Sunderell. Long ago, Morlan had described this very scene, and Cythraul stood there for many long moments. *It is all true*, he thought. Not that he doubted the word of Sabryne. But he'd often wondered if perhaps Morlan had embellished the tale. He had not. It was all there, written in stone. The Dark Shepherds had caused it all, and in so doing, they had cursed themselves to wait beneath the surface, to wait in exile until the ending of time.

With this precious new knowledge, Morlan had turned back. It had been a different errand. Cythraul needed to go on. And so, he stepped forward and passed directly through the wall. No Wights existed on the other side, and the cavernous chamber choked down to a single corridor. The chains continued, however, and Cythraul followed them through the passage. At last, he emerged in a larger chamber that was unlike the rest in that it seemed to be more or less intact. Huge pillars of stone rose on either side of the wide room. There was a short stair ahead, leading to a throne. It was empty, but as Cythraul stared, a shrill scream rang out. This was not the rustling, deathly whisper of the Wights. This was an explosion of sound, an agonized wail fraught with sharp notes and tainted with weeping.

8 SOLMONATH 2238

King Ealden's battered body had been delivered to a merchant family Alastair knew in the town of Denham seven leagues north of Vulmarrow. That diversion had cost Alastair and Telwyn much precious time. But it couldn't be helped. Ealden deserved to be returned safely to his people. The merchants would transport Ealden by boat as far north as the Fordan River would take them; then the long journey through Tryllium, across the Nightwash into Amara and, at last, home to Llanfair.

Alastair and Tel had returned to the jumbled mess of tracks encircling Vulmarrow Keep. Parsing that had proved impossible, so instead they'd scoured the outskirts of the trampled concentric circles . . . and found the trail they'd been looking for: one man and one monstrous wolf. Cythraul and Sköll's trail was quite cold. But it was there.

"If we keep going northwest," Telwyn grumbled, "we'll be almost back to Denham again."

"Not quite," Alastair replied, slowing his steed. "But not far off either. If only we'd had some inkling . . . we might have saved ourselves precious time."

"Where then is Cythraul headed?"

"Bell Farthing perhaps, maybe Cragland Hills, though there's nothing there." Alastair shrugged. "Impossible to say."

Alastair sighed. "Yes, probably. But it would help if we had even the vaguest notion of whatever errand Cythraul might be on."

They rode in silence for many minutes until Telwyn asked, "Do you think MiMa is safe?"

"I pray, Telwyn. I pray." Images of his beloved Abbagael faded in and out of his mind's eye. And something akin to volcanic fury began to bubble deep within the cauldron of his soul. That a sick villain such as Cythraul should haunt Abbagael's dreams . . . her thoughts—that was the blackest of tragedies. Alastair felt himself trembling with rage.

"Is something wrong, MiDa?"

"We must find him," Alastair said, his quiet voice taut like a bowstring. "We must find him and end him."

6 SOLMONATH 2238

The scream bled away, but its echoes had been enough for Cythraul to follow. In the forward left corner of the chamber, crushed and almost completely buried by a ruined pillar, was a woman. Only her head, a shoulder, and one arm were exposed. Cythraul could barely believe what he was seeing. For the woman blinked, and her arm flailed about, gesturing for him to approach. He held the candle behind him a moment and realized with certainty that she was not a Wight. The candle seemed to have no affect on her at all. Cythraul fumbled for a moment in his pouch, pulled out an emberstone, and shook it up. With the actual light, he drew near and saw that this woman was beautiful, but in an artistic sense . . . like a statue. In fact, she seemed to be hewn from some kind of smooth gray stone. Everything but her eyes. Her eyes were large and dark and altogether real. She blinked again, and thin tears made dark trails on her cheeks.

Her mouth dropped open. "Water," she said, her voice pitiful and thin. She reached up to Cythraul.

He affixed the emberstone in the clasp on his belt and then drew a water skin from around his neck. "Drink, Queen Aelyrion," he said.

She eyed him suspiciously but took the water and gulped it greedily. Trickles ran from the corners of her mouth, and Cythraul realized why she looked sculpted from stone: she was covered in dust. Many layers of dust . . . many years worth of accumulation. She stopped drinking a moment and poured some water in a slow circle on her face. She wiped a kind of gray mud from her face until pale flesh came through at last. "You know my name," she said. "But we have never met."

"You are the last Queen of Grayvalon," he said. "It wasn't hard to guess."

"Who are you?"

"I am Cythraul Scarhaven of Vulmarrow. I have undertaken a long and arduous errand and am now just nearing its halfway point."

"And yet, you seemed surprised to find me here . . . alive."

"I've read the histories," Cythraul said. "I've heard the legends. But none of them suggested you are Pureline. I see it in your eyes, and yet, it is strange to me."

"Is it so odd to meet one of your own kind?" she asked.

"Rare . . . and unlooked for here." He shook his head slowly. "How . . . how did you become . . . trapped like this?"

She winced, and closed her eyes. "The whole world shook . . . my city . . . it collapsed around me."

There weren't many things that could send a chill through Cythraul Scarhaven. But this revelation did just that. "You mean, you've been pinned beneath this rubble . . . since the fall of Grayvalon? But that would mean . . ."

"That I have been here alone for a very long time." She opened her eyes, and fresh tears rolled out. "The Wights dwell beyond the curtain, but they cannot pass." She lifted her hand and pointed weakly.

Cythraul held up the ghost candle and observed innumerable chains pouring through the the wall. They stretched across the chamber floor and converged at the throne. Cythraul looked back to the queen and began to guess why the chains were tied to her seat. *All this time*, he thought, *and she has lain here alone with her guilt but for the Wight's chilling moans. No food, no water, no solace . . . and yet, unable to die.* Cythraul was beyond pity, but even so, he shuddered.

"I owe you a great debt, knight," she said. "Had I a kingdom still, it would be yours for just a drop of this water. But, I am afraid my debt is greater still, and I have nothing to offer in return."

"What of the Moonblade?" Cythraul asked. "I was told I could find it here."

Her eyes flickered toward the edge of the fallen stone monolith that pinned her. "Who told you that?"

"A friend," he replied. "A very old friend."

"Did your 'old friend' tell you about the Moonblade . . . what it is . . . what it can do?"

Cythraul knelt. "It was a master sword, forged by a Stonehand Shepherd many long ages ago of a craft surpassing even that of Synic Keenblade. It was given thee as a token of fellowship between Grayvalon and Umbar the old capital city of Tryllium."

"It is more than a master sword, Knight Scarhaven," she said. "Use it at night and, with it, you could cut stone. Use it during a full moon, and you will be nigh unbeatable."

"During the day?"

She laughed quietly. "If the sun has risen, the blade is just another old sword."

"I want it."

"And you may have it," she said. "But . . . you must release me from this everlasting tomb."

Cythraul appraised the massive pillar that lay upon the queen. "You said the Moonblade could cut stone, but this . . . this granite column . . . it must be mightier than a castle bulwark."

"Nay, I am beyond that sort of freedom. You also are one of the Pureline. You know what must be done."

"How?"

"Go to my throne," she said. "Search behind it. There is a hidden compartment built into the base. There I kept . . . certain important things."

Cythraul left her and went to the throne. He banged on its base with his fist, and dust rained down. He found the hollow sound he had been seeking and used the blade of his dagger to pry open the compartment. Dead spiders greeted him, white and curled up in rigor. But two other objects shared that space: a folded leather pouch and an oblong wooden box.

"Take the wooden box," she called to him, her voice strained.

"I have it," he said, taking out the box. He removed the leather pouch as well and slid it into the waistline of his breeches. His tunic covered it completely. He strode over to her and opened the box. Within, he found a gleaming metallic instrument. There was a silver ball, about the size of a small apple. A long, narrow spike protruded from it, stretching the length of the box. A stubby lever extended from the side of the ball, and, as Cythrual carefully removed the device, he noted a matching lever on the opposite side.

Queen Aelyrion sighed, and it turned into a quiet sobbing. "It is intact," she cried. "I was afraid. But wait, how full . . . how heavy is it?"

"What do you mean?"

"Jostle it," she said. "But do not depress either of the levers. There should be fuel . . . fuel enough for . . ."

Cythraul gave it a gentle shake. "I feel the liquid within," he said. "I suspect it is at least half full."

She sighed once more. "It is enough," she said, and Cythraul thought she looked at him strangely.

"Do I understand these mechanisms correctly?" he asked. "I plunge the spike into your heart, depress one lever for the spark, the other for the fuel . . . and it is sufficient to burn out your heart?"

"You have experience with such devices." It was not a question. "Will . . . will you do it? You, of all beings in this broken world, must understand. Your footsteps echo forever among those who come . . . and go . . . while you remain. Even if you are not trapped like I am, you are still trapped." Her words cracked. "I . . . I can bear it no longer."

Cythraul grew weary of her voice, the sound somehow grating and raw. Every word she spoke felt like the tearing of a scab from a wound. "I want the Moonblade," he said.

"It is yours to take," she said. "But it is here at my side . . . beneath the stone. But . . ." She craned her neck and seemed to struggle with her free arm now out of sight. "It is wrenched within . . . I cannot free it. With your strength, your leverage, I am certain you could."

Cythraul placed the ghost candle and the wooden box on the floor, but he kept the burning device in his right hand. He slid close to her and started to reach beneath the cleft of broken stone.

"Wait," she said. "Promise me . . . I want your word that you will use the fire . . . burn my heart and release me."

"You have my word," Cythraul said.

She smiled, a sad little smile born of relief and something else Cythraul couldn't quite understand. "The Moonblade waits. Reach here," she said.

Cythraul dropped down to both knees and lowered his body to almost prone. He held the burning device back in his right hand and turned his shoulders so that he could plunge his left arm deep beneath the stone. He felt the cold of her flesh, the softness of her neck on his bare arm.

"You are . . . almost there," she said. "A little farther down."

Cythraul wrenched himself awkwardly, searching for the hilt. He thought maybe it was there, but—

A sudden pressure on the side of his chest. A sharp and stinging pinch. The blade drove easily through his tunic and the flesh of his chest. It plunged between his ribs and pierced his heart. Cythraul grunted and yelled, trying to back himself off the blade. But something held him. It was Queen Aelyrion. She had his belt in a vice grip and pulled him forward. The blade sank deeper and widened the wound. Blood gushed from the opening, and pain threatened to knock him unconscious.

"What are you . . . doing?" he screamed.

"Easy now," she said, her voice firm but strangely soft. "Just lay back and accept it."

"You're mad! Unggh. That blade is . . . in . . . my . . . heart."

"Do you not see?" she said, twisting the sword's blade. "I am doing you the favor you've made possible for me. We are the misbegotten of this world, abominations! We cannot go on forever! Do not struggle, Knight Cythraul. There is enough fuel in my device for us both."

Cythraul's world threatened to gray out. He reacted in a cloven heart's beat. He dropped the device to the floor. He knew she would reach for it. The moment it clattered on the stone, she did.

Cythraul moved swiftly. He thrust himself farther onto the sword's blade and backhanded the queen on the corner of her jaw. It was a crushing blow. She moaned and her grip on the sword loosened. In that moment, Cythraul grabbed the sword by its inverted hilt. He yanked it and the queen's device from her hands and skidded backward on his side . . . out of her reach.

"No!" she shrieked, and her hand found his boot and latched on like a claw. "No! You don't understand. We were never meant to be. We must die!"

Cythraul didn't have the energy to resist her. He could barely stay conscious. Ever so slowly, he eased the Moonblade out of his heart and out of his chest. Blood spouted up like a fountain, and he coughed out several red-misted breaths. But the flow stopped seconds later, and Cythraul found himself breathing more deeply. He tried to kick her hand away. When that failed, he curled up at the waist and let the sword fall upon her wrist. To his shock, the Moonblade cut cleanly through the bone of her arm and sliced several inches into the stone floor.

Queen Aelyrion screamed. Her blood spattered and mingled with Cythraul's. Her severed hand flopped about like a disoriented insect until, at last, it fell close enough to her wrist. Fleshly tendrils soaked in blood stretched from stump and hand, and soon, the hand was reattached. "No, no, no . . ." the queen sobbed. "You don't understand . . . you don't understand . . ."

Cythraul finally gained enough strength back to stand. Trembling with sheer rage, he thought about what he might do to her with the Moonblade. But then, he had a better idea. He took his old sword from its sheath and tossed it at the throne. It carved a chunk from one of the armrests and then clattered onto the stairs. The Moonblade fit his sheath perfectly. *Almost as if I was meant to wear it,* he thought. He put the queen's device into a satchel he had slung over his back. He looked about on the floor and grabbed up the ghost candle. Then, he turned to leave.

"Wait!" she yelled. "Where are you going?"

He ignored her.

"No, please! Please! I'm sorry," she cried. "I shouldn't have done that without your leave. I'm so sorry, but believe me, I was thinking of you. No one should have to endure such a long time. But maybe, you need to make that choice! Please, just kill me! I won't try anything more. Please!"

Cythraul stopped and half-turned. "I have no plans to die," he hissed. "Not now. Not ever! And . . . neither will you."

"Noooo!" she cried. "You can't leave me like this! You don't know what it's like!" Her voice became thick and desperate, shrill and half-choked. "Nooo! NOOO!!"

Cythraul turned and walked away. When he at last emerged from the crevasse on the tor's peak and saw the stars overhead, Cythraul began to gather massive fallen stones, dead branches, and soil. When he was finished, no one would ever guess there was an opening there. He mounted his horse, and as he rode away, he thought he could hear the faint echo of a haunting scream.

CHAPTER 36

THE GROVE OF GOLDEN LIGHT

Dara strolled past the man three times and wondered if it would be in poor taste to ask him such a question. But being only nine, she gave in and inquired, "Sir, why do you stand there holding a string that goes up into the clouds?"

"I am fishing," he replied.

Dara's eyebrows leaped. "Fishing?" she asked. "For what?"

The man didn't answer, but his arms jerked, and he pulled the string sharply back. There came a strange warbling trumpet sound from above, and something dragged the man across the field.

—From Greenshire Tales, Hans Fablemeister

6 OCTALE 2238

I sat in my favorite spot and leaned against my favorite tree, but the Grove of Golden Light wasn't so golden at the moment. It was near Gray Hour and that, in and of itself, brought me nothing but pain. And given the events of the afternoon, it seemed that pain was pretty much my way of life. I thought I'd planned it all out perfectly. No one had been able to kill the serpent or drive it away. And anyone who ended up in the water with it, got hurt. I winced, thinking of Mill and his poor arm.

Getting the thing to stay on the surface was the trick. The coneys were working too. And then HE shows up. I slammed my palm against the moss. "Ah, if only—I'd—killed it." I'd have used my father's axe, cut its head off, and dragged it triumphantly into the center of the village. I closed my eyes and growled. It would have been so sweet to have old Plebian Scandeer have to swallow his venom and hand me the Scarlet Bow.

I thought about that bow. I'd held it once. It was short for a recurve, but had more tension than any bow I'd ever pulled. Carefully worked rosewood was unmatched for bow crafting, but it was incredibly hard to carve without cracking an internal grain. Do it right, and you've got yourself the only bow you'll ever need for your entire life. Do it wrong, and you've got one expensive mess of broken wood. What I could do . . . with that bow.

I sighed. It wasn't about the bow, not really. It wasn't even about putting Scandeer in his place. After the Huntmeet fiasco, the failed Archer's Guild . . . and poor Starke, I just wanted to do something to help my village. And I wanted to be able to walk through my village again and not have everyone treat me like I'm diseased. It was bad enough before, when all I was was the little girl whose parents got taken. It was bad enough when I was the teenager who wanted so badly to be a hunter, but couldn't. But after all that I'd done and everything that had happened, every single day was filled with dirty looks and comments under the breath. If only . . .

I rested my head against the tree.

"Ariana!" someone yelled. "Ariana, are you up here?"

It was Mill. I was sure of it. I heard heavy footfalls in the grass on the hill behind me. Mill came lumbering up over the edge, tripped, and sprawled right beside me. I think I bounced when he hit the ground.

"Oh, Ariana, here you are."

I ruffled his shaggy hair. "What are you doing here?"

"Lookin' for you, of course." He made a face and pinched at the little patch of whiskers below his bottom lip. "I didn't think you came up her 'ceptin' for the sunrise."

"Mill!"

"Kay, kay, I've come lookin' for ya to thank ya and cheer for ya and get ya back to the village!"

I stood groggily. "Wha—?"

"You did it, Ari," he said, rolling back to his feet. "You really did it! Ah, I'd hug ya if I had both my arms. Forget it, I'll hug ya anyways." He grabbed me round the waist and swung me around like a toy.

"Mill, put me down. What are you talking about?"

He plopped me to my feet and stared at strangely. "The serpent, ya dunce! Honestly, I don't get you sometimes. The whole village is waitin for ya. Come on!"

He grabbed my hand, and before I knew it, we were half-rolling, half-bouncing down the hill.

When Mill dragged me into the village, all the shops' lanterns were still lit, which was odd since it was well past Gray Hour. Minstrels played merry music up on the auction stage—and that was odder still because it was Celester, and the minstrels only hit the stage on Sennet and Soliday nights. But most odd of all: the people of my village were happy to see me.

They cheered when I entered the courtyard, and I got separated from Mill. Taken from him actually and escorted through the jumble of smiling faces, pats on the back, and clapping . . . all the way up to the stage. Suddenly, the Elders were there, and the music stopped. I thought I smelled something odd, but I couldn't think much about it. More and more cheers came, but Elder Justinian came forward and lifted his arms to shush them. The crowd obeyed for the most part.

Elder Justinian asked, "Where have you been all day, Ariana Kurtz?"

"Uh . . . I was—"

"Are you so humble that you would miss your own celebration?"

Someone from the crowd yelled, "We love you, Ariana!" *Okay, that was weird.*

"Yes, yes, we do," Elder Justinian said. "For you have rid our village of its bane." He stepped to the side. Several burly men carried something up to the stage, something covered in a gray tarp. "At last! The serpent is dead!" Elder Justinian whisked the tarp away. And there was the massive, ugly triangular head of that creature, my arrow still protruding from its eye socket.

The cheers were so loud and so powerful that I thought I'd be blown off the stage. I held on and scanned the expressions on the Elders' faces. Except for Scandeer, they were all smiling and nodding. I knew it was fake, but I didn't care. I looked out into the crowd, all the people I'd grown up with, and somehow it was as if the Huntmeet, the Archer's Guild had all been forgiven. I saw that horrid Choiros Greenshambles. He was slinking away from the village square. One day, he'd pay for the senseless killing he'd committed. But for now, this celebration would be a down payment. Then, I saw Mill. He was hopping like his feet were on fire. He waved. I rippled my fingers back.

Then, I saw him. A green tunic covered the muscle in his chest and shoulders now, but I recognized him instantly. That rogue who took the serpent kill away from me . . . somehow, he had found a way to give it back. He mouthed something I didn't catch at first. He repeated it. *I told you so.*

"And now," Elder Justinian said, "and now for your prize! High Elder Scandeer, please bring forth the Scarlet Bow!"

Looking like he'd just sucked a lemon, the High Elder who'd called me a disgrace and a wench, among other things, brought me that gorgeous rosewood bow. He placed it in my shaking hands and said, "For your bravery, sacrifice, and heroism, I thank you. And I hereby grant you this, the symbol of Wetlands craft. May you . . ." He cleared his throat. "May you . . . hunt well."

The crowd erupted. My heart swelled. And the dance began.

Mill asked for my first dance, of course. I nearly had to beat him off with a club, but I needed to see Elder Justinian first.

"My lord!" I called to him before he vanished behind the stage.

He reappeared and looked curiously at me. "Did you call to me?"

"Yes. Could I have a moment of your time?"

"Of course, of course, for our village hero." He motioned for me to join him, so I walked around to the backside of the stage. It wasn't nearly as loud there.

"How did you know?" I asked.

"I don't follow."

"About the serpent? How did you know I'd killed the serpent?"

"Oh!" He laughed. "The man you saved, Loch is his name, I think, he told me. He cut off the beasts head and brought it back as proof."

Whatever it was that came over me at that moment, I am not sure, but I hope it doesn't become a habit. "Elder Justinian," I said, hesitant but determined. "I don't know how to tell you this, but . . . I didn't kill the serpent. That man, that Loch did."

I don't think any of the Elders have put a hand on my shoulder since the night my parents were taken. But Elder Justinian did now. He leaned very close to me and said, "Loch told me you would say that, Ariana Kurtz. But he explained the whole situation to me. He told me how he speared the thing and how he dove onto the serpent's back. He tried desperately to kill the creature, but could not. It never occurred to him to stab it in the eye, and, in any case, he dropped his dagger in the lagoon. That creature had dunked Loch under the water a dozen times. If you hadn't come along and made that one-in-a-million-shot, the serpent would likely have killed Loch. He owes you his life, and we owe you much of our livelihood."

I felt dizzy. I thought I'd been hit in the head, but I was still standing there. Still breathing. "But . . . but, I thought the creature was already dying . . . I thought—"

"Young woman, did it ever occur to you that you may have misjudged?" Elder Justinian patted my shoulder and said, "We all owe you an apology, Ariana, especially Scandeer. To think we have so discouraged you from being a hunter, and yet, if it weren't for your obvious gifts, half our village's food supply would remain compromised."

"Have the perch returned?"

"Yes, yes," he said. "They returned within hours of the creature's death. I think those fish are brighter than we give them credit for, though not bright enough to avoid landing on my dinner plate. Which, if you'll excuse me, I'm late for that dinner."

In a daze, a deliriously happy daze, I walked back around to the front of the stage. I did it. I actually killed the serpent. I only wished my parents could have seen me. Maybe they had. Maybe they had guided my arrow into the creature's eye. *No, no,* I told myself. *They're still alive . . . out there . . . somewhere.*

Loch was waiting at the corner of the stage. He looked very handsome and very proud of himself.

"May I have this dance?" he asked, holding out his hand.

I almost said yes, but out of the corner of my eye, I saw Mill. He was standing stock-still some six feet from the stage with all those other merry villagers dancing around him. "I am in your debt," I told Loch. I thought quickly and had an idea. "But, I have a debt to an old friend to repay first."

I left Loch with his hand still held out. I danced half the night with Mill. And we talked while we danced. We talked a lot. I just hope he understood.

7 OCTALE 2238

"Wake up!" Fred barked at the cocooned lump on the bed.

"It's still dark outside, Fred," Loch growled back. "Now leave me be or we're going to the blacksmith."

"That is not amusing," he said, his tone wounded. "Now, get up, will you? There's a girl at the window."

Loch bounced up, was too tangled in the blankets to stand properly, and fell hard to the floor. "Oofmph!" He broke free from his wrappings and knelt on the bed by the window. Ariana stood just outside, looking smug in the starlight.

Loch pulled up the latch and pushed the window open. "What are you doing . . . here . . . this late?"

"It's not late," she said. "It's early. Get dressed and come out here. I want to show you something."

Chaotic thoughts ricocheting around his skull, Loch closed the window, hopped to the floor, and go the rest of his clothes back on.

"Ooh, going out with a girl," Fred chirped. "Can I come?"

"No, you can't come." Loch rolled his eyes and quietly left the inn.

"C'mon," Ariana said, bounding up the hill. "I thought with all those muscles you'd be a little faster."

Loch puffed and lunged his way, but remained several paces behind. "It must be all the sleep that I didn't have!" Her giggles rained down on him in response. *Where is she taking me?* he wondered.

Finally, he crested the lip of a partially wooded flat land. He looked back over his shoulder at the Wetlands village. A few cottages were lit now. Shops getting ready for the day.

"You made it," Ariana said.

"It was no trouble, really," Loch said. "What, with all my muscle, that is."

They shared a laugh, and Ariana said, "You can see a lot of stars from here."

Loch looked up. The black velvet of night held innumerable diamonds and sapphires. "Is that what you brought me to see?"

"Not exactly," she said. "We'll have to wait for it."

"For what?"

"You'll see." She pointed to the blue-gray shadows of the pines and maples whispering on the east side of the plateau. "That's where you're going to want to be looking. Shouldn't be too long. We can sit here. The moss is soft."

She eased down to the moss, and Loch noticed for the first time what she was wearing. It was a gossamer white tunic that fit her well enough to emphasize her femininity without being revealing. There must have been tiny jewels or colored glass at the collar because she sparkled when she turned at certain angles. She had dark breeches, blue or green. Probably green, Loch thought. He thought her eyes captured something from the early morning twilight, and then he realized she was looking at him. He turned quickly to look at the trees.

"My father used to bring me here," Ariana said.

"Oh? Was he at the celebration? I don't think I met him."

She bowed her head. "No . . . I wish he could have been. He . . . he and my mother were taken in the raids. Do you know of them?"

We just spoke of them at the Council of Crowns, he thought. "Yes," he said. "I've heard stories."

"It'll be thirteen years ago this summer," Ariana said. "I miss them still . . . it's like a hollow deep within. I thought it would go away, but it hasn't."

Loch rubbed the chill from his arms. "I think I understand that hollow place," he said. "My father died when I was very young. I never knew him."

"I'm sorry."

"Time continues to pass," he said, finding a sprig of grass to wind around a finger.

It grew quiet until, Ariana said, "Look, the sky is getting lighter."

And it was. The darkling plum sky had ripened somewhat. Fewer stars. A definite glow somewhere behind the trees. "Is that the sea down there?" Loch asked.

She nodded.

"Ah, I see," Loch said. "You want to show me the sun rising over the sea." He felt bad. How could he tell her that he'd seen the sun rise over the sea for just about every day of his life? *My expression will give it away.*

"Not exactly," she said. "Sunrises over the sea are pretty. This is better."

"Oh," Loch replied.

Her hand found his, and Loch felt as if a bolt of lightning was crackling up his arm. "You don't understand what you did for me today," she said.

"I told the truth," Loch somehow found the words to say.

"You did. Many men wouldn't have, especially not here. I don't know what it's like where you come from, but here women don't get to do much."

"What do you mean?"

"We're kind of afterthoughts. Look pretty, mind the laundry, cook, have children, and mostly keep quiet. We can't vote in the council. We certainly can't become Elders. And, among other things, we cannot hunt. What you did by convincing the Elders that I killed the serpent . . . well, it may change things. Elder Scandeer still looked at me like something to scrape off of his shoe. But Elder Justinian, well . . . he looked at me differently. He saw me, I think." She turned and started to say something else, but caught her breath. And Loch saw the glow on her face.

He turned. The sun had risen above the horizon and just high enough above the eastern rim of the plateau to spill blazing golden light through the trees. It kindled the maples and pines, silhouetting them in morning sunshine. And it set a brilliant fire spreading between all of the varied tree trunks, creating a surreal entanglement of light and shadow.

Loch swallowed and couldn't pull his eyes away.

"Welcome to the Grove of Golden Light," Ariana said.

Loch said nothing and kept staring until the sun had risen high enough to be almost entirely caught by the trees. At last, he found words. "This seems a very special place, and very private. Why did you bring me here?"

"To say thank you."

Loch smiled. He suddenly realized her hand was still on his own. "I feel I am in your debt," he said. "I just wish I had more time."

Ariana took her hand back. "What do you mean?"

"Well, I came here to answer the summons. I have to return home."

"Where's home?" she asked.

Loch hesitated. *Tell her. Tell her,* his inner self urged. But he remembered Sebastian's code. "I live in Anglinore, and I must return to work."

"Oh," she said, her face expressionless. "I . . . I thought, well . . . no matter." She stood. "We ought to be getting back then. The day beckons."

"I think you mistake me," Loch said. "I want to come back."

"Why?" she asked bluntly. "Why do you want to come back?"

"Well, for one thing, the wildlife is certainly exciting." She laughed, so he did too. Then, he took both her hands in his. "But if I must speak plainly, I want to come back and see you. We've only just met, but . . . uh, well . . ." Loch ran out of words. Then, he bowed and kissed her hand. "I will come back."

8 OCTALE 2238

"How was your stay in the Wetlands?" asked Captain Elsa Taerinin, stepping lightly down from the forecastle of the Relentless Witch.

Loch stared west over the rail. "It was interesting."

"Did you find the serpent you were looking for?" she asked.

Loch smiled. "Why yes, I did. And more besides."

9 OCTALE 2238

Loch had just returned to the castle of Anglinore. He'd come on the dockside and meandered his way back to the main hall. He hurried to Clarrisant Hall, hoping to find his mother at prayer. She wasn't there. She wasn't in the gardens either. But as Loch moved through the central hallway of the castle, he saw his mother coming the other way.

He held out his arms as she approached and embraced her. She felt strange. Stiff and somewhat cold. They separated. "I am back from the Wetlands," he whispered conspiratorially.

She looked up at him, her eyes on him but somehow still unfocused. "I am . . . glad," she replied.

"I have a bit of a surprise," Loch said. "I met a young woman there. Someone I am quite fond of."

"That's nice, my son," she said. "But if you'll please excuse me."

Stunned, Loch watched her go. He wandered the halls of Anglinore aimlessly but noted that there were fewer guards on duty than usual. He decided to check the nearest barracks, but found it empty. *Something is very wrong*, Loch thought. *I need Sebastian.*

On his way to the High Shepherd's tower, he met a squad of knights marching double time. They nearly plowed into him.

"It's him," one of the knights said.

"Finally," the Guardcaptain said, his voice like the release of pent up steam. "I'm sorry to 'ave to do this, sir. I really do like you, but I've got orders to follow."

"What are you talking about, Guardcaptain?" Loch asked, his blood chilling in his veins.

"High King Lochlan, by virtue of the ancient codes, we must escort you to Carellian Hall."

"Carellian Hall?" Loch blurted out. "But that's the magistrates domain, well . . . that and the stockades."

"Again, sir, I'm sore apologetic here," the Guardcaptain said, "fer what I 'ave to do. Please come with us."

"It doesn't feel like I have much of a choice," Loch muttered. He found himself wandering in a haze of bewilderment. The passages and chambers went by in a mute blur until two massive wooden doors opened before him. Cavernous Carellian Hall was filled to bursting with soldiers. The vast chamber was strange with sudden silence as if Loch's entrance had interrupted a hundred heated discussions.

"This way, sir," the Guardcaptain said. The sea of knights parted for Loch as he was led forward.

The High Bench rose up before him. Loch thought absently, "I never knew how tall this was." Indeed the High Bench towered over him as if it might slam down upon him.

Sebastian came abruptly to his side. "Loch, we'll figure this out," he said. "It won't stand. I won't allow it."

Loch blinked. "What won't stand? I don't—"

"Lochlan Stormgarden!" a voice rang out. And there, standing next to the gray-headed First Magistrate, was Baron Cardiff Strengle. "You are accused of abandoning your throne in violation of the ancient statues, a clear act of treason. How do you plead?"

CHAPTER 37

MANY TRIALS

"Each and every decision you make places another league before your feet."

—A Myridian Proverb

9 OCTALE 2238

"How do I plead?" Loch spluttered. "Cardiff, you lecherous, backstabbing—"

"Your majesty," the First Magistrate interrupted. "Please . . . you must confess or deny."

"Treason?" Loch thundered. "I deny it!"

A loud murmur traveled through the crowd of soldiers and magistrates gathered there. The First Magistrate leaned to his right and spoke to someone Loch could not see. "Let the chronicle read that High King Lochlan Stormgarden denies treason in any and all forms."

"Do you deny then," Baron Cardiff said, "that you did knowingly defy the statute by leaving the throne of all Myriad without consent of the High Council?"

"He had my consent!" Sebastian exclaimed. "And that of his mother, the Queen. Lochlan did not shirk any pressing kingly duties. He didn't leave Anglinore unruled. He did not take 30,000 of our troops away and leave us open to invasion or some such. He left Anglinore to meet his people. There is no treason in that."

"Except that he broke the law," Cardiff muttered smugly. "Or is the king above the law?"

The crowd rumbled. Loch started to speak, but Sebastian touched his arm. "Above an archaic law, yes!" Sebastian yelled, but he quickly mastered his emotion. "He is the High King of Myriad. If he wants to go and visit his people, he does not need to drag all of the other rulers across the world just to give him permission."

"The law says he does," Cardiff said.

"Enough!" the First Magistrate commanded. He turned to Cardiff, "Are you certain you wish to proceed with this?" he asked. "It is, after all, a very old law. Only the long-lived Shepherds—well, and you—seem to recognize it. In all my studies and training, I don't recall ever coming across it."

Cardiff turned his head slightly left and then right, seemingly swallowing back bile. He said, "With all due respect, First Magistrate, we must proceed. The law is the law."

"Don't you understand?" Sebastian asked. "I am surprised, Cardiff. I mean, it is very clear—to me at least—that you've searched the statutes long and hard and yet, you did not discover the context of the law. You see, Anglinore City was in its infancy, infinitely more vulnerable than the teeming military realm that it is now. Elorvorn made a terrible mistake, and he went against the advice of his aging parents and his Shepherds. It might have been tragic. The law was simply a knee-jerk reaction. Did you know?"

Cardiff mumbled something, but no one could decipher it.

"No," Shepherd Sebastian said, "I thought as much. You see, First Magistrate, I believe this is treason, but not Lochlan's. Nay, it is Baron Cardiff, the ever ambitious, attempting to subvert Loch's rule and eventually . . . supplant him?"

The crowd erupted. Some soldiers hurled angry words and curses at Cardiff.

"Order, order!' the First Magistrate called. "There will be order in this hall!"

"Me?" Cardiff exploded. "I've done no such thing. I've simply come to call on Lochlan and found him often unavailable, by that I mean, illegally absent from the city. And no one seemed to know. That is irresponsible and dangerous, and as we all know, Lochlan is very young and inexperienced. I do not wish to see him off the throne. I simply believe he needs someone older and wiser to rule with him. If that be me, so be it."

"So be it," Lochlan mimicked snidely. "So you'd reluctantly accept worldly power . . . if you must. Your plan is laid bare, Cardiff. What do you have to say for yourself?"

"I am not the one on trial," Cardiff replied.

"Excuse me, Baron," the First Magistrate said, "but neither is King Lochlan. This is a formal inquiry, not a full Council. There will be no ruling until the High Council can be summoned."

"You mean to go through with this, then?" Sebastian said. "We're really going to pull all the other rulers away from their duties to their realms for this . . . for this mockery?"

"I am with you in sentiment," the First Magistrate said, "and it is my hope that the High Council will do their duty and strike this ancient law from the scrolls. But until such time, we must attend to the laws as they are written." He leaned once more to his right. "Enter into the chronicle that the High Council will be summoned and convene here for trial in one month's time."

"One month?" Sebastian mumbled a bit and his eyes darted back and forth in thought. "Wait, that's not going to work. The Shepherd's Council takes place in Shepherd's Hollow one month from today. We celebrate the Cyrium Anniversary of the founding of Shepherd's Hollow. I cannot be in two places at once."

"I'm sorry, High Shepherd," he said. "I suppose you'll have to choose." The First Magistrate stood and, with a whirl of his dark blue gown, was gone.

15 OCTALE 2238

"Have you lost your mind?" Sebastian bellowed. He shut his chamber door and glared at Lochlan. "You're going on trial in a few weeks for treason, and you want to leave Anglinore once again?"

"Cardiff is ridiculous," Lochlan replied. "You said yourself that this law is archaic and no longer necessary. The High Council will undoubtedly overturn the old law and cast out the charges, won't they?"

Sebastian's eyes bulged. He took a deep breath and seemed to calm. "This is where youth and maturity so often collide," he said. "Lochlan, you are wise for your age, and you see so much of the picture, but your view is skewed by your passions. You do not see all of it. If you go errant once more, it will seem to some that you are thumbing your nose at the High Council and abusing your powers. You're assuming a favorable outcome to the trial may actually force a not-so-favorable outcome. Do you see?"

"I see," Lochlan said, "I see my wise advisor, the High Shepherd of all Myriad, turning his back on his own wisdom to keep his own robes out of the fire."

"Lochlan Stormgarden," the Shepherd said sternly, "I will forgive you that slip in courtesy. I care not for my own consequences. I fear for you, your throne, and all of Myriad."

"But you agreed, Sebastian," Lochlan argued. "You were behind this. You handed me an hourglass and warned me not to live a life I'd look back wondering what might have been."

"I know that's what I said," Sebastian replied. "And it was true, but—"

"Sebastian, I've met someone . . . in the Wetlands village," Lochlan said. "Ariana is her name. Smart, spirited, beautiful—I think she might, well, she might be important. If I don't go back, I may never know just how important. There's something about her."

Sebastian spun in the middle of his chamber and stared out through his window. "Aravel was similarly smitten with Maren," he said. "I do not blame you, for indeed Maren and I hoped that, on your journeys, you might find a bride. And yet, Lochlan, now is a wickedly inopportune time. You are not some squire in training for the Anglish Guard. You are the High King of the known world."

Lochlan was silent for some time. "What . . . what if I just went for a few days, a week including travel. I could bring Ariana back to Anglinore, you and mother could meet her. And then, once the High Council puts down Cardiff's halfwitted charges and that ancient statute, I can be more free. Surely you can keep order here for just a week's time. My mother would help."

Sebastian did not turn around. "My . . . lord . . . will you open your eyes? Have you not seen your Maren recently?"

Loch frowned, his stomach knotting. "I've seen her. She's distracted is all . . . by the charges against me, I suspect."

"Maren wasn't even present at Carellian Hall," Sebastian said. "Your mother is very ill. Once more, she is withering in grief. And now also, there is some inner struggle that eats away at her like a phantom blight, affecting her emotions, her judgment. She is not fit to rule!"

"What was that?"

Sebastian and Loch spun. Queen Maren stood in the now open doorway, her expression blank, but green eyes blazing. "Who is not fit to rule?" she asked, her voice thin but pointed.

"Forgive me, your grace," Sebastian said. "But while that comment was meant to be private, I meant it nonetheless."

"How dare you," she hissed. "Think you that I have lost my mind? My reason?"

"I think no such thing," he replied. "But I can see with my own eyes that you are depleted. Once more, you aren't eating enough. You aren't resting enough either. I have come to check on you, betimes late at night, only to find your chamber empty. Tell me, Maren, where have you been going in the quiet hours of the watch?"

"That," she said, "is none of your concern. I am High Queen of Myriad. I need not answer to you, Shepherd."

"No," he replied. "You need not heed my concern or listen to my wisdom. But you used to . . . willingly."

"Mind your place, Shepherd!"

"Mother!" Loch exclaimed. He watched her waver. Then she started to go down. He swooped in and caught her. "Mother, what's wrong?"

"Tired," she whispered. "Just tired." She righted herself and moved away from Loch. "Listen to me, son. I heard your plans. You go. Go and meet this young woman—."

"Ariana."

"Yes, meet Ariana." She cast a withering glare at Sebastian. "I will be fine in your absence. We will hold off Baron Cardiff, if necessary." She sighed and her eyelids fluttered. "Now, if you will both excuse me. I will retire to my chamber."

Loch watched her move slowly down the torchlit hall. He turned back to Sebastian. "I see it now. She is like a shadow of herself. What's wrong with her?"

"There again is grief," he replied. "Once more, she pines away for Aravel, gone these many years. They were so close, Loch. I wish you might have seen how they loved one another, how they carried one another along through life. But there is something else, something new."

"What?"

"I have spoken to the guards in the armory. They tell me that your mother has been going to the vault late at night."

"The vault?" Loch eyebrows shot up. "Whatever for?"

"The Eye of the North," Sebastian replied.

"What?" Lochlan exclaimed. "The great table? It's been found?"

Sebastian nodded. "While you were away, Stonehands mining in the Verdant Mountains brought it here."

Loch blinked. "The Eye of the North . . . it, well it seemed like an old legend to me. I've only read of it." Loch sighed. "Amazing."

"I believe Maren has been using the table," Sebastian said, striding to his his desk.

"But is that so bad? It's vaskerstone, right? We have vaskerstone all over the castle. What of it?"

"That, Loch is the pivotal question." The Shepherd went to his windowsill and caressed a few of the new blooms. "The Eye was a boon to the Wayfolk and helped us shepherd Myriad from all manner of threat. It has been used before and for long durations, and yet I have no record of it ever affecting anyone like this. Perhaps it somehow amplifies the user's emotions? Ah, I do not know. And no word from King Ealden. I am certain he could answer many of my questions concerning the table. The Windborne couriers report that Ealden rode off on a very private mission. He had not returned as of the most recent correspondence from Llanfair. I am tempted to just deliver the table to the Wayfolk. Let it rest in Llanfair and trouble them. Perhaps that would help Maren."

"Perhaps the vault should be off limits," Loch said.

"Off limits to the High Queen?" Sebastian asked.

"Right." Loch stared at the floor. After some thought, he looked up and said, "I am worried for my mother. But, you know, meeting Ariana might cheer her some."

"I imagine it would," the Shepherd replied. "You are going then?"

"I will not ask your blessing," Loch said, "but yes, I am going."

"You need not ask my blessing," Sebastian said. He drummed his fingers on his desk. "But I will ask the First One's blessing on us all. I feel uneasy about all of this. There is an unwholesome feel to the way circumstances seem are coming together. So you go, Lochlan, discover more about this Ariana and, if she is what you suspect, bring her back to Anglinore. But if you would heed any of my words, I implore you to stick to these two conditions: You've seen a broad swatch of Myriad, and I know you've grown from it. But you must settle down to kingship now. Let this journey to the Wetlands be your last venture—ever, unless the law is abolished. Agreed?"

Loch nodded. "Agreed, and the other?"

"Your second condition is that you should return by Octale the 33rd."

"The 33rd?" Loch exclaimed. "But that is less than a week. If I leave tomorrow, that will give me just five days. Three days really, when you consider the ship rides both ways. Why so short?"

The Shepherd sighed. "The High Council has been summoned already. I suspect some of the kings and queens will begin arriving within the week, and I am certain that they will want to speak to you before the trial."

"I see your point," Loch said. "Very well. I agree."

"Good, Loch!" Sebastian clapped him on the shoulder. "Good, lad. Now get going. Go see your Ariana. If she is the one you love, bring her back to Anglinore. She should know what she might be getting into."

Loch frowned.

Sebastian's eyes widened. "You . . . you haven't told her?"

"You TOLD ME NOT TO!" Loch's eyes bulged.

"I did no such thing."

"It was there in writing . . . rule number seven, I think. You said not to reveal my identity for the honor of my station might be at stake."

Sebastian rolled his eyes. "That was so that you don't drink too much at some tavern and disgrace the throne! Of course, if you find someone you might marry . . . you tell her! You can't hide something like that and hope to have a relationship."

"Now you tell me!" Loch exhaled a breath hot with exasperation. He turned to leave. "This is going to be a fun trip."

27 OCTALE 2238

"I told you I would come back," Loch said, grinning mischievously.

Ariana gaped. "I wasn't sure you would come," she said, "and certainly not so soon."

Loch smiled, waiting. "Oh, oh," she said. "Would you like to come in?"

Loch bowed and came inside Ariana's cottage.

"I was just making tea," she said. "I'll get you some."

"Thank you." Loch sat down at the small table and found a leather bound journal. "What's this?" he asked.

Ariana put down the kettle and strode quickly to the table. "It's one of my journals," she said, gently removing it from Loch's hands. She walked crisply to the fireplace. When she returned, the journal was gone.

"Do you write often?" Loch asked.

"Almost every day," she said. "I began when I was very young, after my parents were taken. It hit me, then. I didn't want to forget them. So I wrote down every memory I ever had of them. Now, I guess it just stuck so I keep writing."

"Amazing," he said. "How many journals do you have?"

"Dozens . . . I've lost track of how many. But they are precious to me."

She brought their tea and joined Loch at the table. He sipped his tea. "Delicious," he said. "Would you like to go on a trip?"

Ariana slurped her tea and coughed. "Wh-what?"

"On a trip . . . with me? There's a place in Amara, western Llanfair actually, that I've always wanted to visit."

"What's there?" she asked.

"Only the famed fields of flowers," Loch replied. "Though, this late in the year, it's likely that only the snowbuds and blue arnets are in bloom."

"Flowers?" She squinted at him. "You're taking me to see flowers?"

"Well, that's part of it," Loch said. "Can you spare the time away from your duties?"

"For flowers?"

"Well, and for me," Loch said, feigning insult. "I thought we might get to know each other a little better, if we went somewhere."

Ariana smiled. "I like you, Loch. But, I don't know . . . I haven't left the Wetlands . . . uhm, ever."

Loch thought for a moment. "Well, what if I told you that, if you come with me to Llanfair, you'll be able to meet the High King of Myriad? Would that get you away from here for a few days?"

"The High King?" she exclaimed. "Do you know him?"

"Oh, yes," Loch replied. "We grew up together. I'd go so far as to say I know him as well as anyone."

"Really." She whistled. Then she laughed. "You both have the same first name."

"Yeah," Loch said. "I get that a lot. So will you come or not?"

"Let me talk to the Elders," she said. "When did you want to leave?"

"Oh, in about an hour," Loch replied. "I have a ship waiting."

"You put me on a ship called the Relentless Wench!" Ariana crossed her arms and glared. "Is that some kind of hint or something?"

Loch held up his hands. "No, no, nothing like that. But I trust the captain. She sails with a steady hand."

"She?" Ariana looked up to the forecastle. "There's a woman captain?"

Loch nodded. "Uh, yes. She's quite capable."

"We don't have very many tall ships in the Wetlands," Ariana said. "But the ones we have, well . . . just men in charge. Like everything else in the Wetlands."

"Perhaps," Loch said. "Perhaps we can talk to the High King about that. You deserve better."

She blinked and rose colored her cheeks. "Thank you," she said.

Deck hands took the ship's gangplank in. Dockworkers threw up the ropes. Soon the Wench took a bite of open sea and surged away from the Wetlands. It was a short jaunt to the Horn of Ipswich, but Loch had payed extra to get Captain Taerinin to skip Ipswich port and even Brightcastle. They'd sail directly for the port of Llanfair.

Loch and Ariana leaned over the rail and looked out to sea. Amazing, Loch thought. He glanced sideways at Ariana. Almost as soon as we pull away from land, it feels like we've left the world and all its troubles behind.

30 OCTALE 2238

Ariana looked up at the city of Llanfair and gasped. "I've never seen anything so huge, besides mountains, that is." The city began not far from the water's edge and climbed, vast-sculpted-terrace by vast-sculpted-terrace, up a foothill. Low walls on each terrace defended clusters of cottages, manors, and keeps at each level. There were trees and gardens everywhere, though, as Loch suspected, only a few flowers bloomed. Still, there were shimmering patches of white and blue. And the tall trees had not lost their leaves.

Loch and Ariana left the ship and ventured into the port. Not far from the docks, Loch found a few merchants and hired out a pair of horses. "You ride, don't you?"

Ariana frowned. "Of course." She leaped up on the blotchy gray mare. "But, why rent the horses? We're right here in the city. I wouldn't mind a walk."

"This isn't our final destination," Loch said. "And time is not exactly plentiful."

"What do you mean?"

"You'll find out soon," he said, tightening the saddle straps.

CHAPTER 38

THE IMPERIAL INN

Bogle, the maneater made of festering
earth. Firbolg, the fire daemon that comes
when hatred calls. Nixy, mischievous sprite,
in the deep wood plays. Lich, the creeping dead
thing, lingers for lost souls. Shade, bonefinger
wrapped in shrouds and fear.
Ghuls, dread-bird, roosts in eyries high
bane of mountain's pass.
Banshee, hag warrior, with a perilous
wail and eyes aflame.

—From Catalogue of Beasts (16:9)
Drake One-Eye (b.524)

31 OCTALE 2238

"A friend told me of an inn not far from here with a perfect view of the fields," Loch said. He didn't want anyone to reveal his secret to Ariana before he could, so he guided her away from the main roads and hamlets. "It's called the Imperial, and if my understanding of the map is correct, it should be just over this hill."

"Care to race?" Ariana asked. Loch was about answer when, she cried out, "Hya!"

She was gone in a flash, racing up through the browning fields as if she were the wind itself. Loch gave his steed a little kick and took off after her. It was a lost cause. Ariana crested the hill first with ten seconds to spare.

"Where did you learn to ride like that?" Loch asked.

Ariana didn't answer.

"Ariana?" Loch turned and found himself speechless as well. The hill's long ridge flowed down into a vast undulating valley. Though winter was coming on and snow might come in the near future, the snowbuds and blue arnets were still very much in bloom. The entire landscape was awash with pristine white and rich dark blue. And it was all in motion, swaying gently as if giant invisible hands were sweeping through the fields. Here and there a few evergreen trees poked up, and in a thatch of those, with its chimney puffing out white smoke, was the Imperial.

"I . . . love . . . it," Ariana said. "The color is so rich . . . it's like feeding without eating anything."

Loch smiled. "That is just the right way to say it. Maybe you can write about it."

"I brought a journal with me." She reached around and patted one of the packs strapped to the back of the saddle.

Maybe there will be a lot to write about, Loch thought. Immersed in a sea of blooms, they rode down the hill to the Imperial Inn.

After they'd tied up the horses near a watering trough, Loch led Ariana around the front of the inn and pushed open the door. There was a tall counter up front with a jacket thrown over the side. To the left, they found a cozy dining area, just a few tables built into little dark wood stalls. A merry fire crackled away in the far corner. A few paintings lined the walls: most of hills rolling with flowers. A couple of the paintings were of a single flower, a deep red bloom that peeled open like a lily. Near its center deep, royal purple spread out, and tiny golden-yellow clusters of pollen jutted up.

The section to the right was a museum of sorts. A museum of farm equipment, lovingly preserved: plowshares, harnesses, planters boxes, and tools of all kinds. There were dozens of square bins filled to near overflowing with flower bulbs. The room had a pleasant earthy smell.

A snort and a cough made Loch and Ariana jump. What they had taken for a coat on the front counter was actually a living person. He rose up on his thin elbows, threw back his hood, and said, "What? Oh, oh, well, hullo dere." He quickly straightened himself and brushed off his coat. Then, he ambled around the counter and shook hands with Loch and with Ariana.

"Welcome to the Imperial Inn," he said. "Named after the beautiful Imperial Lily first farmed here in 2939 AO! So sorry not to give you's a proper greeting. Sound asleep, I was, and no mistake. But business is slow this time a' year. Again, welcome! New marrieds, eh? Well, have I got a room for—"

Loch cleared his throat. "Uhm, sir, we're not married."

"Sir? What's this 'sir' stuff? M'name's Peebles. If you need anything, you's just shout, 'Oh, Peebles!' and I'll be out lickety-split."

"Do you have a pair of rooms?" Loch asked. "Close each other?"

"Oh," he said. "I get ye. Sure we do. Up the stairs, take a left. End of the hall there are two rooms. They both look out over the fields if ye have a mind."

"That'll be spectacular," Loch said.

"Uh, how many nights?" Peebles looked up expectantly.

"Three," Loch replied.

Ariana looked up sharply. "Just three?"

"Uh, maybe more," Loch said.

"Shouldn't be a problem, not a problem at all," Peebles said. "Payment's in advance. And can I get you something to eat?"

Loch paid the man, and they placed orders for food. After unpacking Loch and Ariana emerged from their rooms and met in the hallway, nearly running into each other.

"Oh," she said.

"Hi," Loch said.

They bounded down the stairs, went to the hall, and took a table. Peebles was out in a flash with a platter of bread, cheeses, and some very salty olives. Half way through the meal, Ariana put her hand on Loch's and said, "Thank you for bringing me here."

Her smile was so absolutely adorable that Loch couldn't think straight.

"So . . . when do I get to meet the High King?" Ariana asked. "I thought maybe he was in Llanfair City."

Loch blinked. Not yet, he thought. "He'll be along soon, I think."

Ariana looked at him skeptically. "The High King of All Myriad is really coming way out here, the Imperial Inn?"

"I believe so," Loch said, trying his hardest not to laugh.

They ate and talked the rest of the afternoon into evening. Late at night. Ariana gave Loch a kiss on the cheek.

Back in his room, Loch fell back on his bed and touched the wall. She was there, he knew, on just the other side. Six inches away at most. He sighed.

"She kisses you and you go to pieces," Fred said.

"How did you know that she kissed me?"

"I have told you before. I am aware of things. I am aware that she kissed you."

Loch smiled. "Yes, she kissed me." He put his hand back to the wall and thought he was going to enjoy the next couple of days. The kiss had been just what he needed to bury the fear tumbling around in his gut: fears that Ariana might not take the news of his real identity very well, fears that it could drive her away.

32 Octale 2238

Another day had gone by in a flash. Loch and Ariana had spent the time horseback riding, exploring the Llanfair countryside, and of course relaxing at the inn. Here and there, Ariana spent time writing in her journal. She never said what she was writing. Loch hoped some of it, at least, was about him.

But on that last eve, Loch found himself in turmoil. He sat alone in the dining area of the inn while Ariana rested. He wanted to kick himself for not telling Ariana the truth about himself. At first he'd thought it would be easy, but the deeper his feelings grew for her, the harder it became. He put it off and put it off some more. And now, their time was almost up.

What if she's angry that I kept it from her? What if she never trusts me again? There was more to it than that, of course. *All she's ever known is the little Wetlands village. And suddenly the king of the whole world wants to whisk her away to the biggest city in the realm? It might overwhelm her. What if it frightens her away?*

Not enough time, not enough time! He put his head in his hands.

Peebles cleared his throat and sat down. "What's wrong, son? You and the little lady seem to be gettin' along just fine."

"Ah, no," Loch said, grateful to have someone to talk to. "It's not that."

"What then?"

"I have something very important to tell her," Loch said. "But I don't know how . . . when . . . or where?"

"Ohhhh," Peebles said with a wink. "I get ye, now. Well, then, I think I just may be able to help." The innkeeper leaned forward and whispered conspiratorially, "There's a stream, in the pine wood barely a league from here. Finest little babblin' brook ye ever did see. Anyhow, there's a beautiful old stone bridge built over it. Been there forever, made by some folk long forgotten, I'll wager. Take her there! Now, I'll grant ye, it's not as green and full a' flowers like it would be in spring. But stand on the middle of that bridge and stare out. It's like lookin' down a tunnel through time. Then . . . then ye' ask her the question."

"You are a genius, Peebles, thank you," Loch said. "I'll do just that."

"This doesn't make any sense, Loch!" Ariana's voice warbled as she bounced on the mare.

"What doesn't?" Loch's stallion was doing a better job keeping up on this morning's ride.

"The High King of Myriad . . . is somewhere out here, out in the deep woods?"

Loch laughed. "I know it seems odd, but let's just say, he is very motivated to be out here."

"If you say so," she replied. "But seriously, Loch, it's okay if he's not really coming. I'd be mad, but I'd get over it."

"He'll be here," Loch said. "I promise."

They rode on in companionable silence until they reached a hill sloping down into a fairly dense pine forest. Loch rode along the trees and spotted the trail in short order. "This way!"

He slowed his horse to a walk until he saw the stone bridge up ahead. He dropped from his saddle and tied off his horse where it could graze on ferns. Ariana did likewise and followed Loch up the path.

She took his hand from behind and walked by his side. He led her to the foot of the bridge and said, "Would you look at this!"

"It must be ages old," she replied.

Loch ran his hand along the stone rail. "It's still smooth." He bent at the waist to see the details of the stonework, etchings in every panel, mostly trees and mountains. "Marvelous."

Ariana let go of his hand and walked to the middle of the bridge. She gasped. "Stars, Loch, come look!"

Loch joined her at the top of the arch, and they gazed over the stream. As far as the eye could see, it seemed that great round flagstones had been laid the length of the stream. The chilled fresh water cascaded musically from one level to the next . . . on and on. It was hypnotic, and the trees magnified the effect. A hundred varieties lined the banks of the stream with trunks of black, brown, gray, white, green, blue and most any mixture or pattern one could imagine. And they all leaned in, forming a natural arch over the stream. A perfect natural arch. The symmetry was as undeniable as it was stunning.

The effect did not wear thin, but Loch's mind buzzed with all he had come there to say. He reached out for Ariana's hands, received them, and then said, "Ariana, I wanted to bring you here to this place because, well . . . since I met you, I've been stricken, and—"

"You mean when I yelled at you about the serpent?"

Loch laughed. "Funny, but you know something? That is part of it, part of your spirit. Please don't misunderstand me. I am drawn to your beauty—Stars know, I am drawn to your beauty. But you are so much more than that. You have a fierce spirit for living. You have overcome so much and dare to grapple against the day with such grace as I have scarcely ever seen."

Ariana stared up at him, her blue eyes glimmering. Loch had to catch his breath. "You know when I went back to my home that first time. I thought about how you didn't dance with me at the celebration."

"I'm sorry," Ariana said. "I never meant to—"

"Never apologize for being noble," Loch said. "How long have you known Mill?"

"All my life," she said.

"And he is a true friend, isn't he?"

"The First One broke the mold after making Millard Key. He is going to make some young woman a splendid husband one day."

"But not you."

"But . . . not me."

"Then I read it correctly," Loch said. "You might have accepted my offer to dance, but it would have crushed your friend. So you proved your loyalty to him, even if it meant offending a promising, rather handsome stranger."

She smiled and brushed the hair from her eyes. "Mill knows," she said. "We talked about things while we danced. Funny thing is that we had a fantastic night dancing . . . as friends."

"That is a marvelous part of your character, Ariana. And . . . I'm afraid I'm falling in love with you. How can I not? You are smart and talented and hardworking and—"

She kissed him, hard, on the lips. When they finally parted, she said, "You talk too much."

He blinked for a few seconds. "I . . . uh, I . . . uh seem to be at a loss for words at the moment."

They both laughed. The sounds of the brook took over for a moment, but then Lochlan said, "I am afraid I need to annoy you with my speech a little more. For I have more than one confession to make."

"I know," she said. "The High King isn't really going to be here. You're just going to offer to take me to Anglinore to meet him."

Loch shook his head. "No, I'm afraid that's not it. You are going to meet High King Lochlan Stormgarden today." He took a deep breath. "I am him."

Ariana dropped his embrace. Her blue eyes worked restlessly and her brow knotted up. Then, she smiled. "You almost had me for a minute there. Loch I—"

"Ariana, it's true. I am the High King of Myriad." He reached into the pouch at his side and took out a ring. His signet ring. He showed it to Ariana and then placed it on his finger. "Do you see? That is the Stormgarden family crest. This was the ring worn by my father Aravel until three years ago when my mother, Queen Maren gave it to me."

Ariana tilted her head. "The crown."

"What?"

"If you're really High King. I want to see the crown. It's made of pure cyrium with a black methecet—"

Loch opened the large pouch on his hip and removed his crown. "Inlaid with black methecet and blue sapphires, actually. This is the crown of the High King. It is my crown." Loch couldn't read her expression, and without thinking, he said, "Oh, and I have a talking sword."

"Hello!" said Fred.

Ariana jumped backward. "Who said that?"

"I did."

Loch unsheathed his blade. "I am Fred," it said.

Ariana reached out a tentative hand and touched the blade but jerked it back when it said, "Careful, I am sharp."

"The blade is alive?" She laughed. "Is there any more wonder in this world?"

"You . . . you aren't mad at me?" Loch asked. "About not telling you?"

Ariana laughed. "Are you kidding? Loch, I am grateful you didn't tell me. If you had, I would have fled before I came to know you. But now . . ."

"Now?"

"Now, I'm terrified. I'm in love with the king of the entire world."

"Am I so frightening?"

"Not personally, but there's so much about your kingly life I know nothing about."

"I was hoping you would come with me to Anglinore. You could learn for yourself about these things."

"Loch, I . . . I—"

"Please, my lady. I am due back in Anglinore. I must leave no later than this evening, and I would not be parted with you so soon."

"I want to come . . . to please you," she said. "But my life is in the Wetlands . . . I need to think about it."

"Ariana, I'm sorry for placing such a burden upon you."

"Burden?" She laughed. "You idiot, this is a wonderful blessing . . . the most amazing thing to ever happen to me." She cocked an eyebrow. "Wait, I just called the High King of Myriad an idiot. You could probably have me executed for that."

"No," he replied. "You are far too beautiful to execute."

Hand in hand, they walked back to the horses. And as they rode back to the Imperial Inn, Loch's mind was awash with possibilities, but chief among them was a question: Have I found my queen?

CHAPTER 39

FIRE IN THE SKY

The beat of our wings is swift and it sings
Of a life lived only in part.
For our days race away like a wish gone astray,
A sign of our swift-beating hearts.
Windborne taste of the sky for just a blink of the eye
While the grounded endure on and on.
When the sun sets today, we dream and we pray
That the morrow will not find us gone.

—From the Ballad of the Windborne, but Skymaiden Elis

31 OCTALE 2238

The Hinterlands had been cowed in a matter of months. And now, Raudrim-Quevara had a debt to repay. How long would she have remained dormant if Cythraul hadn't summoned her? She shuddered to think. He had rescued her, given her another chance to rule. And for that, she would go to the ends of the world . . . and beyond. And so, with Cragheath Tor in Vilnus' capable hands, the Red Queen had taken flight and flown to the end of the only world she had ever known. She descended to the foot of the Impasse Mountains, where Cythraul claimed there was a way through, a passage to beyond.

It took some searching, but the Stonehands gave it away. Apparently they had been duped into thinking my treasure vaults were theirs for the taking, thought the Red Queen. She found a regular train of them, their carts loaded with her treasure. She devoured the Stonehands whole, leaving carts and wheel barrows full of riches sitting out in the open daylight. Then, Raudrim-Quevara passed into the shadows within the mountain.

Much to do, the Red Queen thought as she crawled slowly through the darkness. And it all begins with a part of the realm called the Windbyrne Eyries.

There were places beneath the mountain where she could not easily fit through, so she assumed human form and walked. But when she at last spied daylight and saw the foreign land for the first time, she spread her vast wings and took to the skies. Once airborne, she found the terrain just as Cythraul said it would be. It was nearly a straight line north, soaring along the border of the mountains.

Hours later, she found the wide river Cythraul had called Nightwash. There would be a vast forest, and beyond that the tall knives of stone would stab up into the sky. Knives . . . an interesting image, she thought. Knives and new streams of blood.

32 OCTALE 2238

Aerial combat. Raudrim-Quevara relished the thought as she glided high above the Myridian realm known as Tryllium. Ages ago, before all the ancient wyrms fell dormant, there were such battles. She remembered, or at least part of her did.

As terrible as her strength was upon the land, as fierce as her talons could be, as vanquishing as her fire could be . . . she was far more dangerous in the air. She had owned the skies. And that was long ago, before her strengths had been fortified in the Compromise.

Of course, Cythraul had warned her not to underestimate this foe. The Windborne, he had called them. Deft flyers, clever and well organized, and equipped with an array of unique weaponry— no, she would be wary of them. Fighting an enemy commensurate with her own size was one thing, but battling dozens—even hundreds—of smaller foes presented its own challenges. Raudrim-Quevara remembered scrapes with wyverns and drakes that had not gone so well.

A shrill siren from the distance, scattered her thoughts. Ah, they are aware of me. Good, let it begin.

Drüst closed his eyes.

Jornth looked up suddenly. "What is it, Uncle?"

Drüst did not answer. He'd heard the safety latches removed far above Galumet Chamber. He knew there was no drill scheduled for today. He knew what was coming.

The siren rang out with deafening clarity, not echoing within the cavernous space, but filling it with such resonance that the air seemed thick with it.

"A threat by air?" Jornth exclaimed. "An attack? Who?"

"We will know when the Skyflights return," he replied, flexing his iron gray wings. "Command the Sky Captains. Time is the critical element."

Jornth leaped into the air and began shouting commands. Galumet Chamber became like to a hive of hornets disturbed by a stone. Windborne surged to and fro, disappearing through narrow openings in the conical stone, while others appeared and sped to interior supply depots.

Drüst found himself smiling at the blade-sharp symmetry. They had drilled for literal ages to hone such precision. And though, to the untrained eye, the movements of so many Windborne may have appeared a tempest of chaos, Drüst knew better.

He knew that weapons were being armed, stormshields were being dropped into place, sorties were being formed, and most importantly the skymaidens and fledglings were being prepared for evacuation. It was all happening in a matter of minutes. But how precious were those minutes. As ever it has been, Drüst thought. He took to the air and raced to his command position at Galumet Peak.

As ever it has been.

Raudrim-Quevara's keen eyes spotted them miles out: sorties of small creatures, closing fast. Fourteen in each line, stacked vertically and spreading as they approached. She flexed her neck and shoulder muscle, forced drag into her wings, and swiftly increased her altitude. Then she saw the other threat. High in the clouds, just the vaguest of unnatural shadows.

Clever indeed, she thought. She pinned her ears back to the side of her head, drew in her wings, and dove. Exulting with sheer velocity, she smashed into the first line of the Windborne, knocking several warriors spinning away into the sky. Spears and other projectiles pelted her from all sides. The hidden flyers had dropped out of the clouds behind her and now sought to attack from their perceived advantage. She laughed to herself, feeling their useless weapons bouncing from her armor like so many twigs. But she had to admire her adversaries' velocity. Impressive speed, Raudrim-Quevara thought. Very impressive for small-wings.

She continued to accelerate, leading them, knowing they would follow. Discipline and organization were of inestimable value in combat, but there was a downside. It could be predictable.

Suddenly, she changed the angle of her broad wings, slewed to a hover, and rose on a draft. The Windborne, far more numerous than the dragon had first thought, raced by, themselves slowing with realization. But it was too late. Raudrim-Quevara drew in both wings and dove toward the cluster of turning Windborne.

As she plummeted, she unfolded in one of her wings and began to spiral. And then, she unleashed her flames.

Blazing crimson streams poured from her maw, bent with the wind, and curled around her. She cork-screwed through the Windborne, her fire bleeding out into them, blinding all and igniting the wings of many. They burned like kindling and fell from the sky in smoking trails. But Raudrim-Quevara was far from finished. She pulled out of the spiraling dive, banked hard to the left, and turned on her remaining opponents. Her talons took some. Her jaws took more. The bony ridges of her vast wings took the rest. She roared at the empty skies.

Then, she pulled at the air and raced toward the distant peaks.

"The Skyflights have not returned!" Jornth growled, leaping from one ledge to another. His black wings spread and collapsed as he moved. "Why have they not returned?"

"Because they are dead." Drüst spoke these words in a low, flat tone.

"An entire Skyflight?" Jornth asked. "Just like that?"

Drüst nodded. "Send the reserves."

"How many?"

"All of them."

Jornth gave the command. Windborne Sky Captains leaped from their perches and fled to the other peaks. Sirens broke out all around. In moments, clouds of Windborne fliers raced away to meet the inbound threat.

I exceeded their expectations, Raudrim-Quevara thought as she spotted the massive storm of enemies careening towards her. Now, let's see if they change their tactics. She climbed once more and dove, but not in a straight line. This time, she came at them on a gentle curve—though, it was not so gentle on the Windborne.

The dragon's arc took her surging across the face of their oncoming lines. She flew with her arms pinned to her chest, but gnarled hands turned palms out so she could rake them all with her talons. At that speed, and with the force of the Windborne's approach, her talons sliced deeply. Few in that front line survived, flailing for lost limbs or helplessly attempting to close wounds far too wide and deep.

The Windborne cloud wheeled and dissipated, coordinated arms of combatants surging in seven directions at once. They rose and arced in precision, picking up speed, generating closure, and aiming to shoot her from behind. Several of the enemy even had the temerity to land on her body, slamming down their pikes and axes futilely.

Raudrim-Quevara lowered her head, arched her neck, and the opened her jaws. She fired a stream of red flame into the air just above her head. It washed back over her, erasing the Windborne from her scales and singing all those who trailed her.

The peaks were just ahead, but the mass of flying soldier were curling to the east. Drawing me away from their home, she thought. Just as Cythraul said they would. Fine. I'll play.

She careened after them and was ready when they turned. She swung her head among them like a flail weapon, bludgeoning several with her horns, and then opening up with more fire. Their weapons continued to bounce off of her armor like hail. Then, they did change their tactics.

Raudrim-Quevara felt something wrap around her right leg near the ankle. She jerked at it but felt cords wrapping around her other limbs as well. They sought to immobilize her, force her from the sky. But even with ten Windborne to a strand, they could not match her strength. And, they had failed to restrain her wings. The dragon dove straight down, rolled, and then she yanked all of her limbs inward toward her body. The combination of her irresistible strength and the sudden wind sheer collapsed the Windborne in upon themselves. They shattered upon each other and fell away.

The dragon turned her fires upon them even as they fell. Then, she banked back toward the peaks and gather all the speed she could muster for a deep dive.

"A dragon . . ." Jornth exhaled, staring east at the massive silhouette growing ever larger. "Our ancient bane. All my reading, all the history—it never prepared me for this sight."

"Nor I," Drüst said. "Get the word out: forget the bolts and spears. Go immediately to the chain nets."

Jornth gave the commands and began to hoist his battle rig over his shoulders.

"What are you doing?" Drüst demanded.

"Preparing to fight, Uncle."

Drüst flew to Jornth and grabbed him by the shoulders. "Fool!" he yelled. "You are to be Windlord. Your job is to preserve your people. Get off this peak and see to the evacuation."

"But, Uncle . . . sire of old, I am torn! Our people fight and die out there. I should be with them."

"Why?" Drüst asked. "To die and leave them leaderless?"

"But they have you!" Jornth returned.

"My years are upon me, Nephew," he said. "I have no time to apprentice another fledgling. You are the Windlord of this generation. No, you will not fight this day. I will fly against the dragon in your place. See to the evacuation. Get our people to our Homeland of old. Go, now!"

"Is that an order?"

"It is," Drüst said. "My last."

But before he took to the sky, Drüst put one hand on Jornth's forehead. "Jornth, I confer to you the station of Windlord, unquestioned leader of all the Windborne. And whatsoever blessing I have to offer, it is yours. May your skies find peace in your day." After saying this, he took his lordship ring from his finger and placed it on Jornth's finger.

Jornth looked up with tears in his eyes. "Like a father you were to me."

"And you, a son, to me." Drüst drew his war axe, flexed his wings, and took to the air.

Drüst had one goal in mind: get the dragon within range of the nets. And, at the rate the creature was closing on the peaks, that didn't seem like it was going to be much of a problem. Amazing, he thought. The beast is swarmed with our Skyflights, but still moves unhindered.

Drüst flexed his wings as he had not for many years and drove himself to killing speed. He dodged under a burst of fire, curled under a talon swipe, and sailed up into the creature's face. He gave his axe a mighty swing into the dragon's black eye. The blade bounced, and the vibration burned Drüst's hand.

Even its eyes are protected? Drüst felt the bottom drop out of his stomach. What manner of wyrm was this? Still, whatever days he had left to live, he planned to spend them all in this one attack. He would smite this creature no matter the cost.

Though his stroke to the dragon's eye had not harmed the beast, it had distracted it. Drüst fled toward the peaks, and the red dragon followed. His movements were insane by Windborne standards. He dove, banked, climbed, swerved at angles he knew would exhaust him sooner rather than later. But he had to move that way, for the creature's flames reached out from behind. Drüst whipped around the southern face of Galumet Peak and screamed in defiance.

The flames suddenly stopped. Drüst pulled up and turned to see a third clump of chain netting launch at the dragon. It spread wide and fell upon the creatures right wing. Drüst knew the chains were heavy and intermittently linked with clasps that would enclose upon any other strand of chain they touched. The dragon roared and then plummeted from the sky.

Jornth felt the tremor in the stone beneath his feet. He looked away from the continuous line of departing sky-vaults, the carriages used to ferry fledglings who could not yet fly, and turned to see if one of the other peaks had somehow collapsed.

But to his surprise and great joy, the peak still stood, and the dragon was no where to be seen.

Raudrim-Quevara blinked open her eyes. She hadn't felt such pain for a thousand years. She lay crumpled on the ground at the base of one of the mountain peaks. Windborne had descended upon her like locusts. They smashed away at her chest, stomach, legs—every limb. When, she sensed movement around her head, she reared up suddenly and belched out a weaker jet of fire. It was still effective enough, incinerating a few Windborne on her chest.

She rolled over, crushing foes beneath her girth. Then she rose up on her netted limbs and withdrew a hurricane's breath. She sent forth a wave of reddish-white fire upon the chains that held her. And they flash melted to nothing. She roared once more and catapulted herself into the air.

This time, she rose up the shaft of the peak and poured her fire out at the very first sign of movement. The peak wreathed in flame, she wheeled about and surged toward the next high finger of stone. And there was that gray-winged gnat again. It bounced its tiny blade off her eye shield once more. And then, with vexing precision, it disappeared from her view.

Drüst careened away from the dragon's eye. His broad axe still hadn't put a scratch on the creature, but it seemed to annoy her. And that was something. He looked over his shoulder and saw the dragon's neck crane back, saw its jaws open wide, and heard the furious roar. But he'd also seen something else: soft flesh.

Never guessed I would go out like this. But somehow the thought of it made him laugh. Cackling like a lunatic and muscles pulsing, Drüst went into a shallow dive and drove down beneath the creature. His timing had to be perfect, but with his burst of speed, he knew it would be. He pulled up suddenly, just as the dragon yanked its head around and struck like a cobra.

Drüst didn't try to evade. The beast's great maw opened wide before him, and Drüst propelled himself inside. For once, time seemed to slow down for Drüst. He stood in the furrow between the dragon's jawbone and its tongue. And there, he summoned all the strength of his people: for Jornth, for the fledglings and Skymaidens, and for his own blasted self. And he buried the axe in the roof of the dragon's mouth. Black blood rained down on him. Drüst yanked the axe free and hacked into the tongue. Drüst roared in defiance and readied a third stroke.

TWICE the insect had bitten her. Raudrim-Quevara had never had such an insult. She had never had an enemy in her mouth.

The pain was excruciating, and she wasn't sure what manner of weapon had cut into her mouth. She didn't know if slamming her jaws shut would push a blade deeper into her flesh, but there was no time to think. She simply reacted. She bit down as hard as she could, feeling the satisfying crunch within her jaws. Then, she opened wide and let loose her fire.

This foe had wounded her, but now he was naught but ashes. Raudim-Quevara turned and continued her onslaught, visiting fire, tooth, and talon upon the foundering enemy. And then she saw what she had been looking for: the Windborne were fleeing. She could see their evacuation trains streaming to the west. Cythraul had been right all along. The Windborne would fight viciously, but only for a time. If enough losses could be inflicted, they would run. And that's what Cythraul wanted. Eliminate the threat from the air, he had said. It will cut their lines of communication. Then seek out their ground forces.

Raudrim-Quevara circled the peaks, spraying them with fire until all of the Windbyrne Eyries smoldered. Then, she turned to the northeast and raced away with all speed. If Cythraul had spoken truly, there were tens of thousands of soldiers to bleed.

CHAPTER 40

Stars and Moon

*While hunting delk in the high grasses upon the Naïthe, I had
sighted one, a full muscular buck, grazing in the hollow between two
hills, when all of a sudden, I scented something odd and unnerving.
There was something large and dead nearby. Keeping the delk in
sight, I followed the smell. And, in a bit of a ditch where no grass
grew, I found a delk larger than the one I'd been tracking. But it had
been so mauled that it was scarcely recognizable. And its killer, a
voraelion near twice its size, was still there. Fortunately for me, the
big cat already had a meal. I will be more careful on the Naïthe from
now on. I had no idea that voraelions had migrated so far east.*

—From the journal of famed hunter
Ham Nessingway, 15 Solmas 2237 AS

18 Octale 2238

Alastair and Telwyn had tracked Cythraul and his blasted wolf
as far west as they could go, to the outskirts of the known world.
With the unscalable Impasse Mountains of the Hinterlands looming ahead, they'd discovered a profound mystery. Cythraul had
entered the desolate land called Cragland Hills, and in those

windswept broken fields, his trail disappeared into a massive cairn of rock and soil that looked like it'd been there for ages.

It was too much to accept that perhaps Cythraul had been killed and buried there. Perhaps he was slain, Alastair had thought as he examined the setting. But if Ealden had been right, Cythraul would have just slithered out of his grave and gone about his business.

It had been Telwyn who found his exit trail. And so had begun an exhausting trek across northern Fen into the mountains and forests of Tryllium. Leagues passed by the dozens and more besides. They took only short breaks to rest the horses or search for the trail. Alastair wondered what had driven Cythraul to such careless speed. His trail couldn't have been more obvious. His need for haste must have been great. The alternative was too troubling to consider: Perhaps, Cythraul wanted to be followed.

When Alastair and Telwyn skirted Thel Mizaret and continued north toward the Nightwash river, Alastair began to fear that the alternative had become almost assured. For, if the trail continued on its present course, it would lead Alastair and Tel into the Felhaunt.

21 OCTALE 2238

Alastair knelt and stared at the foliage . . . at the soft ground. "He's near, Tel," he said. "These are maybe an hour old, not more."

Telwyn examined the wide paw print in the soil and nodded.

"You remember the plan, you've seen it through in your mind?" Alastair asked.

"A hundred times," Tel replied. "I take out the blackwolf, leave Cythraul to you."

"Don't underestimate Sköll," Alastair warned. "I've seen what that creature can do. Swift, agile, and in the shadows, he'll double back on you before you blink. No matter what shot he gives you, even an open kill shot, don't leave your neck unguarded. And watch your hamstrings too. If he can wound you, impair your movements—"

"I know," Tel said. He didn't show anger. "Remember, I'm fairly competent with beasts."

"I suppose if you can handle a snow drake . . ." Alastair didn't finish the sentence.

Alastair crept onward, Tel diagonal behind him. They followed a very clear trail through the depths of the Felhaunt for what felt like hours until Alastair held up his hand. "Do . . . do you smell that?" he whispered.

"Smells like garlic." Telwyn felt around through the low ferny foliage. "There may be some growing here. I can't tell. Too dark."

Alastair squinted into the gloom beneath the trees. "I've smelled a lot of things in the Felhaunt, but never garlic."

"What now?" Telwyn asked.

"We move," Alastair said, and they crawled onward. Alastair found himself thinking of Abbagael. He longed to be with her again . . . to work on their home together . . . to see her smile untainted by fear. Alastair blinked back his focus. That, of course, was what all this was about: putting an end to fear. Cythraul was fear incarnate, and Alastair planned to put an end to him by whatever means necessary. But how? he wondered. Cythraul survived a hundred foot fall. He survived being run through to the heart. What would kill him? Ealden might have known something, but if he had, his knowledge had died on his last breath.

A flickering light appeared between the black boughs far ahead. Alastair turned but didn't say a word. Telwyn had seen it too. A fire. They spread apart as they grew closer to the blaze. Sköll, that blasted blackwolf, certainly would have already picked up their scent by now. The only question was, what sort of trap had Cythraul set for them?

The fire was much smaller than it had first appeared. It was little more than a campfire. Alastair drew his Star Sword. He glanced to the side and saw the gleam of Telwyn's glaive. A few more steps, and Alastair was right at the edge of a small pocket-clearing.

"Come forward, Coldhollow," came Cythraul's impossibly low voice. "Telwyn also, I expect."

Alastair froze in midstep. He could see his enemy now in the clearing. Cythraul reclined by his small fire. Steam rose from a round black pot that hung over the flames. Sköll rested under Cythraul's left hand.

Alastair stepped into the clearing. "Decided to surrender?" he asked.

Cythraul laughed. "What good would it do? You wouldn't let me."

"You're right."

"Would you like some stew?" Cythraul asked. "I'd hate for you to fight in a depleted state. It's quite savory, though you probably shouldn't like to know what sort of meat is in it."

"I'll pass," Alastair said.

"Pity," Cythraul muttered, rising lightly to his feet. Sköll stood, stretched, and yawned. "And what of you, Telwyn Coldhollow? Or . . . do you fancy yourself Telwyn Halfainin, the coming one?"

Telwyn stepped out of the treeline. "Only a fool speaks glibly about things he does not understand."

"Well," Cythraul said. "That settles things." He shook his head. "To think Morlan, in all his wisdom, thought you might be the foretold Pathwalker, the mighty hero of antiquity. Not much to look at, are you? And worse still, bearing a dead man's blade. And you, Coldhollow, you sold your soul long ago. What in the name of your so called First One made you think that you could ever—EVER—be the Caller?" He sneered. "Pathetic."

A triangle of burning gazes formed. The only sounds came from the crackling fire and the bubbling cauldron.

"Sköll!" Cythraul shouted. He darted to his right even as the blackwolf lunged for Telwyn.

Alastair lowered his blade and took a step forward, but something snared his boot. He found himself on his back, sliding, then curled up and saw a chain wrapped around his ankle, a curved blade at the end digging into his boot. He wrestled for a split second with the buckles on his boot. But by some preternatural swordsman's sense he glanced up, saw the movement, and then threw his upper body backward, slipping under Cythraul's violent slash which would have swept his head from his shoulders. Cythraul hissed and kept pulling on the chain that he'd slung around a thick tree, using the trunk as a pulley. Alastair couldn't get to his feet. Somewhere in the trees, the blackwolf snarled. Telwyn yelled.

"Keep my boot!" Alastair yelled. He flicked two buckles, pointed his toes, and let the boot fly off. He rolled to his side and then slammed his blade backhanded to the turf where he'd just lain. Cythraul had been charging for him. When the boot came off and there was no resistance, Cythraul fell forward. And Alastair's cold Star Sword came crashing down.

Only to be met by Cythraul's Moonblade. White and pale yellow sparks rained out from the collision. Alastair kept the pressure on the blade as well as he could as he clambered to a knee and then to his feet. Cythraul propelled his sword upward with a great thrust and rolled out from under Alastair's push back. Then, they faced each other, blade tips just inches apart.

"Do you know what this is?" Cythraul asked, brandishing his weapon.

"I'm not very good with riddles," Alastair replied dryly. "But I'm going to say . . . it's the feeble hunk of metal I'm going to shatter before I kill you."

"Droll but ignorant." Cythraul lunged. The Moonblade flashed high and fell like an ax. Alastair blocked steadily but felt the blow up into his shoulders.

"You see? This is a master sword to more than match your own." Cythraul laughed. "I see recognition in your eyes. It is false. Synic Keenblade did not make this weapon. He had not the skill. This blade was forged by those from whom Synic learned his trade."

"A special blade," Alastair said, circling to Cythraul left. "All that means is it will not break in half when I strike it. You forget

I know you, Cythraul. You're no swordsman. Your expertise is with sickening little toys. Leave the bladework to your betters."

"Ahharrrhhg!" Cythraul's furious attack was much more complex this time. He crashed high, spun back to slash at Alastair's feet, pulled back and then stabbed for the chest.

Alastair blocked the high blow, leaped over the slash, but barely deflected the stab. Cythraul's blade slid by Alastair's midsection, grinding sparks off of Alastair's sword. Cythraul curled and threw a left handed punch into Alastair's jaw. The Iceman staggered backward and shook his head.

"I've learned a few things," Cythraul hissed.

"It won't matter," Alastair said. "I am going to kill you."

"Like you did in Vulmarrow twenty years ago?" Cythraul pounded the armor over his heart. "You know where that blade thrust went, don't you? Straight through my heart. I should have bled out . . . should have died. And yet, I live. What does that do to your thinking? Why do you even fight me when you have no chance of killing me?"

On the last syllable, Alastair came in so strong and so fast that Cythraul stumbled. Alastair pressed in, always toward's Cythraul's left hand, and unleashed a flurry: low to Cythraul's left knee, up beneath the left shoulder, a spin to his right side—Cythraul blocked them all. But that was what Alastair wanted. He charged through the final block and, from behind, delivered a thunderous backhanded stroke into Cythraul's unprotected left shoulder. Blood sprayed from beneath the sundered armor, and Cythraul curled the wounded arm to his chest.

"So maybe you won't die," Alastair said, wiping the bloody sword on his pants leg. "I've spent a great deal of time thinking of alternatives to death, but at last, I believe I've stumbled upon the right choice. I'm going drop you like last time by puncturing your heart. Then, I'm going to spend the rest of the day, hacking your body into pieces so small they could never do any harm. But just to be sure, I'm going to feed your flesh to ten thousand different carnivores all over Myriad and mortar your bones into every castle wall in the known world. If you can climb out of ten thousand piles of excrement, gather up your bones, and come get me . . . well, more power to you. But, I'm betting you can't."

A lone blackwolf was not nearly the threat of a pack of black-wolves, but Sköll was an unusual exception. Trained from a pup to be in Morlan's employ, his company and then, after the exile, to follow in Cythraul's sick footsteps—Telwyn knew there was likely no other beast so vicious in all the wilds of Myriad. Sköll had all the blackwolf instincts: the sharp eyesight, speed, and agility and twice the size and strength.

Telwyn sidestepped the beast's initial lunge and whirled the glaive at Sköll's shadow as it passed into the treeline. The blade caught fur but did not bite, did not draw blood. The creature rounded on him and charged again. Tel drove himself forward and leaped. The beast passed directly beneath him. Too close for the glaive, but Tel drew his dagger left handed and dragged it along the creatures spine.

Sköll snarled and yelped. Dark blood matted its fur. Telwyn landed, rolled, and came to his feet. He felt a curious sting and looked at his left arm. A puckering, ten-inch slash bled freely from his wrist to his elbow. Teeth or claws, Tel didn't know, but the blackwolf was faster and more cunning than Tel expected. He took a step backward. Sköll leaped, but he didn't land on Telwyn. He landed in the crook of a tree and bounded from there, crashing into Tel's side. He felt like he'd been hit by a castle turret. He flew backward, breaking branches and ripping through thorny bram-bles. He slammed into the ground with the beast on top of him.

Blood and saliva oozed from Sköll's jaws, and his teeth snapped dangerously close to Telwyn's throat.

C ythraul smiled, but he wasted no more words.
The Moonblade came swiftly at Alastair's right side, but he saw the chain drop down from Cythraul's left sleeve. Another one of his toys, Alastair knew. He saw how it would play out, saw

the moves required to escape, and then the acrobatic move that would give him an open shot at Cythraul's neck.

Alastair dropped the Star Sword into a underhanded knife grip and took Cythraul's full blow. If not for the strength of the Star Sword, Alastair knew the stroke would have cut him in half. Sparks exploded outward, but the blade held.

Alastair planted the Star Sword in the turf like a spike and used it to vault upward. Instead of snaring Alastair's legs, Cythraul's chain weapon wrapped itself around the sword blade. Alastair used the sword as a pivot point and drove his one booted foot into Cythraul's chest.

Cythraul careened backward, the chain jerked taught, and Alastair let it pull the Star Sword up from the turf and toward his prone enemy. Alastair took his blade in two hands and cast himself toward Cythraul. If I'm going to cut him to pieces, he thought, might as well start by removing his head.

Sköll's jaw's shut fast. Telwyn twisted the handle of the dagger and pressed it harder into the blackwolf's chest. The beast leaped off Telwyn's weapon, its hind paw pushing off of Telwyn's face and opening a gash on his cheek. Telwyn yelled, partly from pain but mostly in anger. He'd somehow allowed this creature to cut him twice. No more.

Telwyn rolled away, grabbed a tree, and yanked himself to his feet. The beast paced ten feet away. It pawed at its chest a moment, releasing a ululant cry. Telwyn knew he'd hurt it. Sköll shook its massive head and turned its open maw toward Telwyn.

Suddenly, Tel was back in the courtyard at the Castle of Anglinore, and the young snow drake stood before him. Tel had felt a compulsion to hold out his hand to the beast, to touch its snout. The creature responded and was instantly tame. Telwyn blinked. Sköll lowered its head and pawed forward. It came within three feet, and Telwyn held out his hand. It ducked its head several times but kept watching Tel. There was something in its eyes, the gold all but consumed by the growing black pupils. The eyes weren't softening. They were still the eyes of a predator. The muscle in the creatures shoulders grew taught.

Tel drew back his hand, whirled the glaive, and, even as Sköll lunged, drove the blade up through the bottom of the wolf's jaw straight through to the center of its skull.

"I already have a pet." Telwyn said. He yanked the glaive free and watched the blackwolf tumble away. Then, Tel raced out of the trees to find Alastair.

Cythraul severed his own chain weapon, sheering through it with the Moonblade to avoid Alastair's comeback stroke. It worked, and Cythraul slid beneath the Star Sword.

Alastair dove over his foe and rolled to a crouch behind a massive skagmaple. Something spattered across his cheek, and he found the Moonblade embedded in the tree's flesh, just inches from his face.

Cythraul hissed and yanked the blade free. "What an oddity you are," Cythraul hissed. "Charmed and yet cursed at the same time." He poured on the attack, driving Alastair back toward the campfire. Their swords were a blur in the flickering light, colliding in dozens of short, measured blows.

Alastair was careful not to be lulled by the combat rhythm, but still, he had to think moves ahead. He'd never expected Cythraul to have acquired so much skill with a long sword. And yet, it was not so much skill. I should have finished him by now, he thought. And it was true. Cythraul had improved, but he was still short of mastery. It's those cursed surprises. Hidden weapons and tricks.

Alastair saw progressions he might use—but shied away because those complex moves left himself open to Cythraul's hidden treacheries.

"I am here, now!" Telwyn yelled. "Sköll is finished."

"Hcythhhh!" Cythraul glanced to the side. "You lie!"

"Shall I fetch his head?" Telwyn asked.

When Cythraul's eyes came back to Alastair, he saw the stroke coming. He lifted the Moonblade to block, but fell for the feint.

Alastair dropped low and drove the Star Sword through the top of Cythraul's thigh. Then, Alastair ripped it up through the muscle. Cythraul's leg buckled, but Alastair wasn't finished. Continuing the upward thrust, he slammed the Star Sword's pommel beneath Cythraul's chin. He fell backward into the campfire, sending the cookpot rolling across the turf and orange sparks scattering. The fire was full of white-hot embers, and Cythraul's tunic and hair ignited.

Alastair moved in, but Cythraul flailed about in the fire, jerking himself out onto the turf and rolling. He tore off his tunic, his leather armor, and stood. His head, half burned bald, still smoldered. He flexed his wounded leg, shrugged his smoking head to his shoulder until his neck cracked, and then glared at Alastair. "Bludgeon me, stab me, cut me, burn me—it makes no difference. You cannot win."

Alastair glanced at the fire and wondered. Then, he saw Telwyn take a tentative step into the clearing.

"Let's put him down together," Tel said.

"No!" Alastair held up an urgent hand. "Remember what I said. Just watch him!" Alastair could see the indecision on Tel's face. The lad didn't understand. "Just watch!"

Now bare chested, Cythraul charged, and their blades met again. The battle ranged all over the clearing, in and among the trees as well. Telwyn kept clear of the blows and watched Cythraul's every move. He made no sign to pull forth a hidden weapon. Perhaps, with his tunic and armor gone, there were no more surprises.

Alastair labored on, controlling the tempo of the duel, but never getting the opening he was looking for. Cythraul's taunts didn't bother him so much, but the truth behind them did. He'd managed to wound Cythraul: a slash across his ribs, the shoulder cut, the massive leg wound—none of it seemed to weaken Cythraul for long. And as the battle wore on, Alastair felt himself begin to grow weary. He glanced at the sky and noted the moon was long gone. Through the eastern treetops, there was even a slight pinkish tone. That's when it occurred to Alastair. With startling clarity, he knew what Cythraul was doing.

"You will not wear me down!" Alastair yelled, releasing a flurry of jabs and slashes.

Cythraul countered them all and backpedaled. He too glanced at the lightening sky. "Finish me then!" he yelled.

To do so, Alastair knew he would have to take some chances. Cythraul seemed to have run out of chain weapons and wore nothing now but breeches and boots. Alastair scrutinized the way Cythraul was moving, the angle of his Moonblade, the length of his strokes, and the distance he traveled when he lunged. Then . . . he had it: the winning approach. It was there, but it was as athletic a series as Alastair had ever attempted. The battle had gone long, and Alastair felt somewhat depleted. But *I've got to try.* He glanced to Telwyn.

"MiDa!"

"Goodbye, Cythraul," Alastair whispered. He stabbed forward, angling the blade for Cythraul's thigh once more, bounced off the block, spun, and hammered a two-handed stroke at his opposite shoulder. The Moonblade parried without an inch to spare. Alastair slid off and chopped the Star Sword down at Cythraul's knee. As Alastair predicted, his enemy sidestepped and prepared his own backhanded attack.

This is it! Alastair's mind barely registered the thought. He had to be liquid, lightning fast, and precise to an eyelash width. Cythraul's weak backhanded stroke arrived. Alastair grunted, sucked in his wind, and arched his body into a C shape. The Moonblade's tip cut a shallow line across his tunic and stomach. Alastair winced, wrenched his body to throw his Star Sword, a powerful stroke, into the Moonblade as it passed. This tripled his enemy's momentum, throwing the Moonblade far to Cythraul's right, and opened Cythraul's torso. Alastair whipped his blade back and sawed across Cythraul's chest. The deep gash wept blood immediately.

Cythraul's instinct would be to cover the wound, to defend. Alastair knew it. Cythraul jerked his right arm, wrenching the

Moonblade back toward his torso. Alastair summoned all his might, shifted his hips, and rotated into the open-stanced stroke his Wolfguard associates had once called the "widowmaker." The blade carved across Cythraul's chest, right-to-left, making a bloody "X" of his wounds. That had been easy, but Alastair knew what he had to do. His eyes narrowed. Every muscle, tendon, and sinew in Alastair's arm followed his unconscious demands. He tilted his wrist and carried the stroke to meet Cythraul's. Alastair knew the follow through would decide life or death . . . for them both.

Telwyn had never seen Alastair's hands move so fast. The Star Sword flashed high and low, whipped left and right. And suddenly, blood was pouring from Cythraul's chest. But on his follow through, Alastair did something Tel didn't think possible. He slammed the pommel of the Star Sword into the cutting edge of the Moon Blade. The pommel shattered as if it had been made of ceramics not iron, but the blow completely stunned Cythaul's stroke. That gave Alastair the second he needed to draw his elbow back to his side and gather his strength . . .

. . . to drive the Star Sword into Cythraul's chest.

The blade plunged six inches from the hilt and the tip burst through Cythraul's back. Cythraul's head lolled and he arched his back. His arms fell out to his sides, and the Moonblade seemed to dangle.

"YESSSS!" Telwyn exulted.

Alastair plunged the blade into Cythraul and watched his enemy's head fall backward. Watched the blood gurgle and spray from the wound. Watched the villain's arms fall out to his sides. But when he went to twist the blade, something was wrong. It wouldn't move. Must be caught in the ribs, he thought. But he tried to twist it the opposite direction. No movement . . . at all. Then, he tried to pull the sword out. It stayed fast.

It was as if his sword were encased in stone.

Alastair gazed at the bloody chest of his enemy. The pale flesh had coalesced into something akin to scales. No, more like ridges on a block of granite.

Cythraul's head rose. That mottled, half-burned, skullish countenance lifted until his bone-gray eyes locked with Alastair's own. His thin lips curled into a wretched sneer, and he said, "Goodbye, Coldhollow."

Alastair's felt his breath seep away from inside. Fire erupted on his chest and seared through his body. He stared down at the Moonblade that Cythraul had driven into his body. His hammering heart became erratic. His mouth dropped open and he mouthed, "How?"

"I have many secrets," Cythraul whispered. But the word was scarcely out of his mouth when Telwyn appeared and placed his palms on Cythraul's chest. "It is too late!" Cythraul hissed. "He is slain . . . while you watched and did nothing. He is slain! And you can do . . . NOTHING to move me!"

Cythraul's expression changed as if he'd been struck by lightning. Dumbfounded, he stared down at Telwyn's hands. Those hands seemed to blur as in the superheated vapors that rise off a castle wall in the heat of high summer. Fingers, knuckles, and palm, they began to smolder. Licks of flame appeared outlining Telwyn's hands in crimson.

"Nooo!" Cythraul cried. "Impossible!" He wrenched and squirmed, trying to free himself, but he was held fast by both swords. His stoneskin seemed to melt. The blades slid out. Alastair fell away. And Cythraul fled into the forest.

Telwyn dropped to the ground at Alastair's side. He looked at the seeping wound. "Alastair," he said, tears cresting his eyelids and streaking. "Alastair, why didn't you let me help?"

"Fire from stone . . . you, you're him," Alastair whispered. He blinked back tears of his own. "After it all . . . you're him. But why, Telwyn? Why didn't you reveal?"

Telwyn took Alastair's hand into his own and wept out the words, "It was not yet my time."

"Still . . . I am glad," Alastair said. But his eyes opened wide. "Cythraul's getting away. I promised Abbagel. I promised . . ."

"Call me."

"What?"

"Call me forth, Man of Ice."

Then, Alastair smiled. He clutched Telwyn's hand. "Telwyn Halfainin!" he cried, his voice raspy and wet but still strong with conviction. "Foretold Pathwalker . . . come forth and fulfill your eternal oaths."

Sunlight spilled through the thickest trunks and boughs, bathing Telwyn in the golden light of the morning sun. Alastair heard a voice, but Tel's lips weren't moving. *This is my beloved Halfainin. Let his journey begin.*

Telwyn opened his eyes. "Thank you, Alastair," he said. "Allay your fears. I promise that Cythraul will never harm Abbagael. I know his secret." He started to stand, but Alastair grabbed at his arm.

"Telwyn Halfainin," he cried. ". . . I am dying . . . and all I've done . . . still haunts me . . . so many transgressions—"

"That have all been forgiven, long before this moment." Telwyn eyes glimmered and he said, "When the time comes, Allhaven will welcome you."

"Th-thank you!" Alastair choked on the words, and started to close his eyes. They snapped open with horror. "Tel—"

Cythraul slammed a heavy, backfist into Telwyn's temple, and he crashed over his own knees and rolled onto his side not far from Alastair. Cythraul stood over Telwyn, gripped the Moonblade in both hands, and raised it high for a killing stroke. Telwyn blinked to clear his vision. He struggled to reach for his own sword, but found a stone instead. He lifted his hand, and a sunbright inferno kindled in his fingers. Liquid fire streamed forth from the stone and engulfed Cythraul. He shrieked, slammed sideways into a serpentwood trunk, and careened away.

Telwyn tried to sit up, but his mind swam. Night filled his vision, and he fell still.

22 OCTALE 2238

The sun had risen to mid morning when the gray rider came. His tall gray steed barely made a sound as it picked its way among the trees' roots and fallen boughs. He stopped not far from two fallen warriors and slid out of the saddle to the ground. There he stood for many silent moments, his hooded cloak hiding his face. Then, he reached past the hilt of a sword at his side and removed a pouch from his belt. He untied the pouch and shook a few ounces of powder into the palm of his gloved hand. Then, he stood over Telwyn and tilted his hand. The powder spilled over and seemed to vanish in the air over the prone warrior.

The gray rider put away the pouch and went to kneel by Alastair's side. Without any noticeable strain, he lifted Alastair's body from the ground and gently laid him across the back of his horse. Then, the gray rider mounted up and rode away.

Telwyn awoke and found sunlight shining directly overhead. He practically leaped to his feet and scanned the area. Cythraul was gone. Alastair was gone. He checked the ground for sign. It was a confusing jumble of prints and marks and blood, from the duel of course. Cythraul's prints seemed to race away to the south. But there was no other sign of anyone leaving that place.

Telwyn bowed his head. *Did Cythraul take his body?* he wondered despondently. *No!* His next thought was *Abbagael.*

CHAPTER 41

PARADISE LOST

27 OCTALE 2238

Telwyn rode to the feet of the Windbyne Eyrie peaks and found utter carnage. A battle had raged there some time ago, that much was clear. A day . . . two? He wasn't sure. Windborne corpses lay all around, many burned to black husks. The smell was almost too much to bear.

As he moved slowly among them, several mysteries suggested themselves. Where are the enemy's dead? He wondered. And why aren't any of these pierced with arrows? Where are the survivors? He looked up to the still smoking peaks and wished he could fly. There might be answers up above, but Telwyn would not have access to them.

He knew the Windborne were not warriors by choice, but they served many critical roles in the kingdom: transportation and reconnaissance being chief among them. Losing them would be a crippling blow to Myriad's security. Cythraul. Somehow, Cythraul was behind all this.

Telwyn winced, the image of Alastair impaled by Cythraul's blade flashed into mind. And yet, no body to bury. That gnawed at Telwyn like an unseen rodent. He'd wanted so badly to go back to the Bone Chapel, to search it . . . to make sure. But he couldn't risk leaving Abbagael alone.

Telwyn spurred his horse. The road was long, and lingering among the dead was doing nothing for his hopes.

33 OCTALE 2238

Wayfolk scouts surrounded Telwyn with spears and glaives just half a league from his home. "Let me pass," Telwyn demanded. "I have urgent news."

One of the scouts stepped forward. "I am Fendror of the Prydian scouting caste. Declare your business within."

"My business is with my mother, Abbagael Coldhollow, and Uncle Jak," Tel replied. "Are they safe?"

Fendror bowed low. "Forgive us our vigilance, master Telwyn," he said. "I did not realize it was you. Yes, yes, your mother and uncle are quite safe. We saw them riding just this morning."

Telwyn sighed, and if felt as if ten anvils had slid off his shoulders. He dropped lightly to the ground next to the Prydian. "I am afraid I bear evil tidings to all who might listen," Telwyn said. "I have come leagues beyond number with tragedy weighing on my mind. Not a fortnight ago, King Ealden Everbrand, your lord was murdered by the assassin Cythraul."

"Murdered!" Fendror's face went ashen. Scouts seen and unseen cried out in dismay.

Telwyn held out Ealden's glaive. "I would give this to you as a token of your king, but with his dying breaths he gave it to me."

Fendror's eyes were riveted to the glaive. "Ealden . . . slain," he whispered. "Why did he go on this journey with so few?"

"I cannot answer for him, but Fendror, I need you to be perfectly lucid. King Ealden's passing, grave though it may be, pales to the other news I bear. The Windborne have been utterly defeated. The Windbyrne Eyries are burned out, and there was no sign of the living."

"How can this be?" Fendror asked, his voice pinched and high. "Those peaks are unscalable!"

"This we must discover. Now listen, Fendror, I know you have been tasked with watching our property, but I beg at least a few of you to return to Llanfair bearing this news. It may be that Ealden's body has already arrived. Alastair and I tasked a merchant family from Denham to bring the king home."

"But Telwyn, you've spoken of the Windborne and of Lord Ealden, but what of Alastair?"

Telwyn lowered his head.

"We all will grieve this day," Fendror said.

"But we must act," Telwyn said. "Act now, or I fear more will grieve. Whatever annihilated the Windborne could lay low Llanfair City, Anglinore too perhaps. Couriers must be dispatched to Anglinore at once. Windborne couriers if any yet remain in Llanfair. If not, by ship."

"It will be done as you say," Fendror said.

Tel leaped up into the saddle. "Prydian friends," he said. "I am sorry to bear you such grievous news. First One sustain us all, for I go now to Abbagael. This will be hard. Go now. I will come when I can."

Fendror eyed the second horse, the horse with no rider. He nodded. "Farewell."

Telwyn moved very slowly, tying up the horses. He trudged up to the cottage's front door. It took him more than thirty seconds to turn the door's knob. When he pushed open the door, he found Abbagael and Jak laughing over pastries and cups of tea. Tel didn't say a word. Their eyes met, and Abbagael's face went sheet white. Her cup shattered on the ground. Her mouth opened and her chin trembled. Her hands, bent like claws, flew to her the sides of her head. A low ululating moan rose up from her throat.

She would have fallen to the floor, but Jak and Telwyn were there to catch her.

As they eased her to lay on the couch, Telwyn saw a swelling in Abbagael's usually trim waist. Stunned, he looked up at Jak, who nodded back. "Found out just after he left," Jak said.

Uncle Jak became a hurricane of efficiency, packing up all the essentials: tools, nonperishable food, warm clothes, Books of Lore, and, of course, weapons. Telwyn waited by Abbagael's side. When she revived, she shook her head at Tel. "No, no, no," she wept. "He cannot be gone . . . he cannot. He is my husband. He promised never to leave me." She buried her head in Telwyn's chest and wept bitterly. "How?" she whispered.

Choosing the gentlest words he could find, he told of the four month search for Cythraul, of Alastair's heroic deeds in the Felhaunt, of their grim discovery of Ealden, their arduous journey across Fen and back, of Alastair's fall, and of the terrible fate of the Windborne. But Telwyn said nothing of Alastair's missing body. There was no need to feed Abbagael's nightmares beyond what they already would be.

"The horses are packed," Jak said. "We should go."

"What?" Abbagael looked from her uncle to Tel and back. "Where . . . where are we going?"

"Llanfair City," Tel replied. "King Eal—the Prydians have a massive standing army and as strong fortifications as any outside of Anglinore. We need protection and we need news. What happened to the Windborne, troubles me greatly."

"And we won't be waitin' around here for Cythraul while all this is going on," Jak said. "Pity I couldn't pound him into mush when I had the chance."

Telwyn helped Abbagael to her feet. "Are you fit to ride?"

"For a few months more," she replied. She took Telwyn's hands. "I didn't know . . . until after you went away, Tel. Twenty years of trying . . . and failing . . . and finally, I can bear him a child . . . and, he's gone. Why?"

Telwyn led her from the room, down the steps, and to her horse. When she was safely in her saddle, he said, "There is no answer to 'why?' None that would pacify our hearts or persuade our minds. But I am convinced that the First One is good and wise and perfectly just. He will not let these events be wasted, and one day . . . one day, someone will answer for all the evil of our time."

Loch and Ariana saw the black smoke twisting into the eastern sky over Llanfair. A strange gray haze had fallen over the sun, and dark clouds roiled at the horizon. Loch rode up beside Ariana and said, "I don't know what we'll find ahead. Very likely there is danger, but I need to ride on."

"And I'm going with you," she replied. "I know that male code talk for leave the woman behind. You can forget it."

Loch reached for her hand, received it, and gave it reassuring squeeze. "Actually, I was hoping you would say that. Having you with me brings me comfort." He frowned at the scene ahead. "Still, there may be fighting ahead."

"And I'll have the Scarlet Bow nocked and ready." She kicked her horse to a full gallop. Loch caught her, and they rode on to Llanfair.

The red dragon swooped low over Llanfair City's towers. Red fire streamed down, igniting the trees outside Jurisduro Hall and sending trails of fire climbing as high as the vaunted dome. "First One, save us," Loch whispered, reigning in his horse. "Have the wyrms of old risen from their rest at last?"

"What do you mean?" Ariana asked.

"There are living dragons in the wild," Loch said, "but small, mostly drakes. This . . . this creature is like something of legend. Its wingspan is . . . is . . . vast."

"Will the Prydians defeat it?" she asked. "Loch?"

"We can only hope. Come on. Stay to the south. That ridge will guard our approach." They rode off swiftly, trying not to watch the destruction the creature wrought over the city, but they were unable to tear their eyes away. A smoking tower fell with a sound like thunder. Loch and Ariana were beginning to be able to hear the buzz of battle, shouts, weapons fired, crashing, breaking, burning, and shrieks of agony. Loch spurred his already exhausted steed and raced around the southern wall of the city. The dragon banked hard taking its wing directly over Loch and Ariana's heads. Their horses reared, and they had to fight to keep them from bolting.

"Down!" he yelled. "This is no good. To our feet!" They leaped down and sprinted toward the ruined gatehouse. Fires burned uncontrolled, and the heat was withering, as they picked their way into the city.

"Loch, get down!" Ariana shrieked. She dove for him and dragged him behind the wreckage of a wall. The ground shuddered beneath them as the dragon landed not fifty paces away. Nearby a manor home engulfed in fire collapsed, pieces of burning rafters blasting almost to their feet.

"Thank you," Loch whispered. He peered around the stone. "There are soldiers on the other side there, and armory, maybe? I couldn't see them until that building went down."

"Try to get to them?"

Loch nodded. "Wait until the creature turns or takes to the air."

The dragon spread its wings to their full reach, covering some two hundred paces of Llanfair's central thoroughfare. It roared and shook its head. Then, to Loch and Ariana's astonishment, the dragon spoke. "Burrrrnnnnnnnn!" it hissed, the sound less a voice and more like the grating of stone or cracking of a mountainside in an avalanche. Every syllable seemed to shake the world. "I am Raudrim-Quevara, archwyrm of my race," it said, "devourer of nations, and conqueror of the eight provinces of the Hinterlands!"

Hinterlands? Loch's mind seized onto the word and spun madly. But nothing concrete, just vague threads of something he felt he ought to be able to remember, but couldn't. He tried to pull one of the threads, but calamity in the road yanked his attention away. A phalanx of tri-wound ballistas launched a hail of post-sized bolts, heavy and razor-sharp straight at the beast. But the timber shattered on impact, their only effect to turn the creature to the north to unleash its deadly fire upon the offenders.

"The thin shelter of your world is pierced forever!" the dragon shrieked. "Burrrnnnnn!"

Cannon fire opened up, deafening and continuous, for almost a full minute. Loch shouted, "GO!" But Ariana heard only the thunder of the cannons. Loch grabbed her arm, and the two raced for the soldiers in the armory. They stumbled through the smoke and the wreckage, twice coming dangerously close to the flames. The cannon shots began to hit home, delivering a crushing report and explosions. Smoke engulfed the area and fine debris fell like ash from a volcano.

"Hail, Prydians!" Loch yelled as he and Ariana leaped over a low ridge of stone, and bolted into the armor.

Several warriors looked up, but no one answered. There was a tremendous explosion in the road. They all turned. Something in the impenetrable murk fell to the road. Something heavy. They all gaped at the road, waiting for what seemed an eternity. The smoke writhed and whirled . . . and began to fade.

A massive silhouette appeared, and the dragon's roar rang out. It leaped into the sky, turned east toward the outer bailey where hundreds of civilian cottages lay.

"High Scholar," one of the soldiers shouted, "what will we do? The dragon's heading toward Market Town, and our bows, cannons—nothing seems to harm it!"

"Nothing seems to harm it, Sedge!" answered a taller Prydian, wearing similar leather armor, but with white trim and a dark blue cloak. "But that does not mean that nothing can harm it." He stormed over to a huge diagram of the city that had been hastily strewn upon the far wall, traced his finger across an area near the top, and then, he began barking orders. "Scout Vestigen, mobilize the Brindale Heights cannon brigade. Make their load heavy, but no incendiary shot, understand? Tell them, intermittent fire. Move a block at a time, west to east. Mark me: west to east!"

One of the scouts near the door sprinted away. The High Scholar moved sideways across the diagram, lifted his hand high, and tapped his finger against the map. "Here! Scout Daigolos, see the powder reserves! Get the east-enders to empty their armory. Plug the barrels with short fuses. Let's blow this haughty beast into the water! That ought to quench its flames!"

Loch recognized the commander. Veior Moon-something-or-other, King Ealden's second in command. But Loch said nothing. He stared at the diagram of the city . . . the tacked up symbols denoting troop concentration, cannon brigades, weapons caches, and the like. It reminded him of the Venture Inn. Loch stared . . .

"First One, save me!" someone shouted. "High King Lochlan, what in the Stars are you doing here?"

Loch didn't answer. Even when someone grabbed his hand and shook it, he didn't answer. Ariana was suddenly at his side. "Loch, Loch what's wrong?"

Lochlan blinked. "I don't believe it," he said. "It's real."

"My lord?" Veior asked. "Are you well?"

Ariana bobbed her head near the High King as if she might be able to see into his eyes and figure out what was wrong with him. "Loch?"

Loch gripped the Prydian's hand. "I am sorry, Veior. Yes, yes, I am quite well considering the circumstances. But I think . . . by supreme Providence, I know how we can kill this thing."

"We are trying to drive it down the cliffside," Veior said. "Into the water."

"Good, good," Loch said. "But that won't be enough. I learned something of this beast while traveling in Ellador. Listen, on the docks, the ships carrying cargo, do they have any massive nets?"

"I should think so," he said. "But nothing that could hold that beast." Light flashed from the windows. Thunder boomed and rumbled.

"We don't need to hold it for long," Loch said. "I know its weakness."

CHAPTER 42

A Weapon of Three Strands

Since the split in 2116, the Vespal Wayfolk lived only on the out-skirts of Llanfair City. They generally had their own neighborhoods, their own shops, their own entertainments, and certainly their own Sanctuaries.

—Histories, compiled by Gilthanor Wren

33 Octale 2238

Under a blackening sky, Raudrim-Quevara landed in the center of Market Town, crushing a bakery and a smithy. She sprayed the fleeing Prydians with crimson fire and laughed as they fell. Lightning flickered overhead, and thunder blasts rumbled. But only part of that sound had come from the storm. The Brindale Heights cannon brigade opened up, and the first seven shots struck the dragon in nearly the same spot in the small of her back. Roaring in pain, she crashed forward and crushed a three story inn. Her reckless momentum nearly took her over the edge of the eastern wall, a fall of over a hundred feet to the Waterfront region. She flung out her talons, grasped at wreckage, flexed her wings and rose back up. She smashed a cottage with each fist and roared at the cannons. Then she leaped into the sky.

Still, the cannons continued to fire, tracking the beast as it hovered over the market. The marksmen were gifted, hitting more often than missing. And with each strike, the dragon jerked backward.

"They're punching her pretty hard," Loch said from the second story balcony of the keep east of Jurisduro Hall.

"Our cannon brigades are brutally accurate," Veior said. "Still, I don't think we've broken through the thing's armor yet."

"Nor will we," Loch said. "But we need to drive her to the waterfront."

"How long will it take your men to prepare dockside?" Ariana asked. "Will they do it in time?"

"We Prydian folk can work very swiftly when motivated," Veior said. "And I cannot contemplate more motivation than this."

As they watched, the cannon brigade advanced. One line fired, stopped to reload, and a second line rolled forward and fired. They repeated the procedure, pummeling the dragon with heavy iron. That's when everything went wrong.

Raudrim-Quevara fell upon the cannon brigade like a hawk on a hare. Her claws flashed. Prydian soldiers, torn and broken, flew into the air. Red fire engulfed much of the city block. She crushed cannons under her heavy fists, and devoured those who tried to fire them.

The dark clouds roiled above, and the rain came. It poured in sheets, and the wind howled. Raudrim-Quevara looked up suddenly, turned, and flew over the east wall. She dropped from site somewhere dockside.

"She's there!" Loch yelled. "We need to go now!"

High Scholar Veior, Loch, Ariana, and a dozen scouts fled the building in haste and leaped upon the scormounts tethered there. Loch heard the dragon's roar as he drove his mount hard, following Veior through the unknown streets and byways. Down the rampart, they flew, unable to see below due to the high bulkheads on the east side. Loch's heart pounded. His mind spun. So many variables. So many details had to fall exactly into place for Ariana to get a clean shot. It began with getting all ballistas lined up. Then, the netting had to be piled up so that it wouldn't catch or tangle. The Prydians would see to that, Loch thought. But everything depended on getting the dragon to the right spot on the quay. Loch wiped rain from his eyes and spurred his horse. He thought he saw light ahead, the opening to the quay. High Scholar Veior turned the final corner first, the others just behind. Fierce lightning flashed. Thunder crashed. And they came face to face with Raudrim-Quevara.

Something struck Lochlan hard. He flew from his saddle and crashed onto the rampart.

Ariana screamed.

The dragon roared.

Loch shook the cobwebs from his mind and rose to his elbows. When he looked up through the rain, he saw a very tall, pallid man standing just a dozen paces ahead. He was bald, but for patches of half-burned gray hair, and his pale gray eyes seemed almost to glow in the stormy twilight. He wore all black, and a chain with a curved blade at the end dangled down from one sleeve.

"Your majesty," said the man, his voice registering as low as the thunder. A smile formed at the edge of his thin lips. "What a fortuitous surprise."

"First One in Allhaven!" Uncle Jak exclaimed. "Llanfair's in flames!"

Telwyn said nothing, but shut his eyes tightly. *Just like the Windbyrne Eyries. I am too late.*

"What's happened here?" Abbagael asked, her voice shrill. ". . . to this beautiful city?" No one answered. "Tel?"

"Something terrible has come to Myriad," Telwyn said. "It is unlike anything I've ever seen."

"Are we just goin' t'sit here?" Uncle Jak asked. "Or are we goin' t'see if anyone needs help?"

"You are a good man, Jak," Telwyn said. "Be wary, and look out for Abba—"

"I can take care of myself," she said, her voice quiet but not to be disputed. A low roll of thunder rumbled in the distance.

Telwyn spurred his horse, and they rode swiftly to the ruined gate of Llanfair City. Within, they found many fires still burning, in spite of the heavy rain. But to their surprise and joy, they also found survivors. Prydian scouts, foot-soldiers, and citizens moved to and fro among the wreckage.

"Prydian Wayfolk!" Telwyn called. "What happened here?"

A scout looked up. "Go back!" he cried. "Go back the way you've come. The dragon . . . it's still here!"

"Dragon!" Uncle Jak exclaimed. "Not some little drake like Icy. Look at this city."

Telwyn said, "Where? Where is this creature?"

Several of the Wayfolk pointed to the east. The one who'd spoken before said, "It has gone beyond the eastern wall, to dockside. We've heard its roar still. You should ride away as fast as you—what are you doing? Sir, do not go that way!"

Telwyn thanked the man but rode forward anyway. They traveled through Llanfair and found that some parts of the city remained largely intact and undamaged. The rain had quenched some of the smaller fires, and Wayfolk labored hard to put out the others. But the fallen towers, shattered turrets, and crushed cottages showed the power behind the attack for what it was: devastating.

Night had fallen behind the boiling clouds, but not even the darkening, stormy sky could hide uncounted scenes of misery from Telwyn's eyes. Bodies lay tangled in rubble, often surrounded by grieving families. Wayfolk, bleeding and battered, limped from place to place . . . sometimes aimlessly. Telwyn found himself riding faster and faster through the city. He longed to help all of these people, but he had to see the beast . . . to see if he might find some way to stop it from hurting anyone else . . . to end it.

Tel drove his horse forward through a debris-strewn alley and right to an edge from which there would be no return. The parapet had been broken in places such that nothing lay between Tel and a stomach-wrenching drop. Abbagael and Jak rode up on Telwyn's left, but he held up a hand to halt them. Lightning split the sky. Thunder exploded a split second later, a sudden stunning blast that rolled until it blended with another sound: a haunting roar.

Jak unslung his hammer and pointed. "Great Stars in Allhaven!"

"It . . . it is the size of a castle keep," Abbagael whispered. "Telwyn . . . Son, we can't go down there. We can't."

"Precious lady," Tel said. "You do not understand. I am needed there. I have to assail this beast." Telwyn turned his horse and drew the glaive King Ealden had given him with his dying breath. He began to whirl it about, and the emberstones kindled, forming a luminous golden spiral.

Abbagael held out her hand. "Tel?"

He did not answer, but rode off to find a rampart leading down.

"Don't!" Uncle Jak yelled. But Abbagael paid him no mind and followed after her son.

"Who are you?" Lochlan demanded.

The man tilted his head so that one of those ragged tufts of gray hung out to the side. "You do not know me by sight, do you?" he said. "No, of course not. Does the name Cythraul mean anything to you?"

Cythraul. A hundred stories flashed through Loch's mind, each one more horrifying than the last. Loch swallowed. His hand drifted to his side.

"That's better," Cythraul said. "You do know me." He began to swing his chain weapon in a slow circle. "If you wish to keep that arm, I'd advise you not to touch your sword."

"He can touch me whenever he wishes," Fred said, and then he yelled, "KILL THE FREAK!"

Cythraul hesitated, puzzled by the voice. An arrow with blue fletchings slammed into his chest, and he staggered, staring up at the golden-haired maiden who was nocking a second shaft.

Loch didn't hesitate. In that moment, he loosed Fred, rolled, and slashed Cythraul's chain. It split instantly. Loch jumped to his feet and leveled the blade at Cythraul's throat. "You were saying?"

Cythraul's dagger swept up, knocking Loch's sword far enough away to allow him time to loose the Moonblade. Their swords met in a spray of glittering sparks.

"That hurt."

"Fred, shut up now!" Loch cried, spinning under Cythraul's high swipe. Loch jabbed for Cythraul's gut, but he deflected it and leaped backward.

"Your majesty," Cythraul said, tearing the arrow from his chest, producing a gout of blood. "You do not seem to understand, I would very much like to have you alive and in one piece."

"You won't have him at all," came a voice from behind Cythraul. A glaive blade suddenly lay against his throat.

But when Cythraul willed his skin to meld into stone, he screamed in dire agony. "You!" Cythraul turned and saw Telwyn . . . and flames. "No! You cannot . . ." He didn't finish the words. He threw the back of his rock-hard fist into Telwyn's jaw and sprinted away down the rampart.

"Don't let him escape!" Telwyn yelled. But it was too late. All became chaos.

Raudrim-Quevara had not been idle, but somehow Veior had gotten by her. His horse had been slaughtered, but Vei was as fleet of foot as any Wayfolk scout. He flew up the quay, yelling "Steady! Steadeeee!"

But the dragon grew weary of the chase and unleashed a rope of red fire.

"NO!" Loch yelled.

Raudrim-Quevara's wings flexed, and she wheeled about so fast that no one else could escape the rampart. She lifted her arm as if to strike the Prydian soldiers standing there. But Telwyn stepped in front of them and held up his hand.

"Telwyn!" Abbagael screamed. "Run!"

"What are you doing, Tel?" Loch yelled.

"Stand down, beast!" Telwyn commanded. His eyes bored into Raudrim-Quevara's reptillian orbs. "You will fight no more this day."

The dragon's head seemed to fall toward the ground, but she caught herself and resisted. Her massive body shook. "Who are you to speak with authority to me?" One of her wings folded and fell. The other wavered. "Who are you?"

"I am Telwyn Halfainin, wyrm," Tel said, his voice resonant. "And it is given to me to tame all beasts such as thee."

Abbagael gasped. "Alastair was right," she whispered. "All along, he was right. He called you . . . didn't he, Tel, before he died?"

"The Man of Ice fulfilled his promise," Telwyn said. "I will fulfill mine."

"Only if that be the promise to die!" Raudrim-Quevara rasped. "Think you that I am only dragon-kin? Nay, insect. I am more." She strained as if an unseen hand held her down, but suddenly, she changed. Her vast wings, long neck, and massive torso began to bubble like melting wax. Before their eyes, the dragon was gone and, in its place, a tall woman stood. She was shapely and beautiful. Her long red hair rippled in the storm-driven winds. She held up an accusing finger and said, "Much more."

"Ariana!" Loch yelled. "An arrow, now!"

The Red Queen turned. Her hand seemed to boil. A pure white talon lanced toward Ariana. Lochlan had already been running. He dove, pushed, Ariana from harm's way, and took the talon-point in the shoulder.

"Dare do harm to the High King!" yelled Uncle Jak, sweeping his war hammer into the Red Queen. He caught her in mid-transition. Her body flew into the air, shimmered, and transformed into the immense dragon. She pulled hard at the air with her outstretched wings and gained some altitude, but one of her arms hung limp.

"I don't understand," Telwyn said. "Woman? Dragon? Which is she?"

"Both," Abbagael said. "Somehow, Tel. That's why she broke free of your control."

"To the quay!" Loch yelled. Rainwater rinsed bright red blood down his wounded shoulder. He clutched his arm into his side and sprinted down the end of the rampart. The others followed. A wicked bolt of lightning struck the mast of a Prydian ship moored a hundred paces from where they now ran. The mast cracked and fell, burning a few moments before the sheets of rain put it out.

Raudrim-Quevara circled above them, and then plummeted to crush them beneath her. Veior, Loch, and Ariana escaped on one side, Telwyn, Jak, and Abbagael on the other. But a pair of Prydian scouts weren't so fortunate. They lay crumbled and still beneath the beast.

"We'll never get a better shot!" Loch yelled. "Veior! Now!"

The High Scholar lifted his glaive and tossed it high in the air. A nearby cannon fired, but that was only a signal. Between the stacks of crates and barrels, more than forty ballistas looses their darts. They sailed in a high arc, each one with a trailing rope line leading back to one seam in the massive cargo net. The lines went taut, and the net flew skyward over the dragon. The ballista darts fell harmlessly to the other side, clattering on the bulkhead at the water's edge. Teams of Prydian scouts hoisted up the projectiles, pulled until the ropes were tight, and wound them around the bulkhead pilings.

Raudrim-Quevara was snared beneath the cargo net. She tried to rise on all fours, but with so many individual lines adding threads of strength to the net, she could not rise up.

At Ariana's side, Loch said, "Just like the serpent . . . make this shot count." As she drew back the fletching to her ear and aimed,

Loch thought back to that day at the Venture Inn. A small scrap of parchment tacked to the wall. A message written in a child's script: 'Big, nasty dragon thing. Only way to kill it is to stab it into its ear. Please save . . . my Hinterlands.' "Go ahead, Ariana, put this shaft into its wretched ear!"

Ariana released the arrow. It flew straight and true right at the sleeved pocket of Raudrim-Quevara's left ear. A fraction of a heartbeat before the arrow struck, the dragon flattened the ear to the side of its head. The arrow struck the outer sleeve and bounced away.

"No!" Loch yelled and then winced. His shoulder burned, his right arm felt weak.

And the dragon began to claw at the netting. Her talon cut through one strand and sawed at another. "Again, shoot again!" Loch cried.

But Ariana made no move to draw a new arrow from her quiver. She stared out to the Dark Sea and stood still as a grave. "No," she whispered. "It, it cannot be . . ."

"What, what is it?" Loch asked her. "You've got to shoot now! You've—" Then, lightning flickered, and he saw . . . past the waves that crashed against the bulkhead, ships . . . dark ships, a fleet. Too many to count. Who? Loch's mind reeled. Then, he knew. The Council debate. The Wetlands. Ariana's parents . . .

The Gray Hour Raids.

Ariana began to shake violently.

"Veior!" Loch yelled. "Look to the seas! Invaders coming! Get whatever defenders you have left!"

The tall Prydian's eyes went white. He raced away toward the northern rampart.

The dragon roared. There was a sound like a whip cracking. Loch spun, saw that the dragon had cut through three more net threads. An arrow sailed right over Loch's head. Another clattered a few yards to his right.

"For the ear!" Loch cried. "Aim for its ear!" Loch knew only the most precise sharpshooter would have even a ghost of a chance.

"Ariana," he said, taking her by the shoulders. "Ariana, don't look at the sea. Look at me! You have to shoot again."

"They're coming for me . . ." Her eyes fluttered strangely. Tears mingled with rain.

"Please, Ariana, the dragon will break free," he pleaded. "We need your aim. We need the shot!"

"I . . . I'll try." She nocked an arrow, took aim.

Loch turned to watch, but the dragon wasn't holding still for this shot. With the broken strands, the creature could move her head somewhat. Ariana let the arrow go . . .

It sailed six feet in front of the dragon. Loch looked out to sea. The dark ships were close. Some close enough to moor. "Again!" he yelled.

Ariana glanced at the ships. "NO!' she screamed, and the way her voice rose in pitch, Loch was afraid.

"Again, Ariana!"

"Loch!" she screamed. "Take me from this place!"

"One more shot!"

She made a small whimpering sound. Her eyes were huge and haunted. But still, she lifted an arrow, put it to the string, and let fly. The arrow raced through the rain. Loch almost leaped for joy as it struck home.

But it hadn't. A twist of the beast's head saved it. The arrow clattered off its neck armor. "This is no good," Loch said. "The dragon's not still enough. Only one other way." Loch drew his sword, winced again, hefted the blade.

"What are we doing?" Fred asked.

"Loch, what are you doing?" Ariana demanded, grabbing at his arm.

He looked up, saw dark figures moving down a gangplank from one of the ships. His blood ran cold. The dragon roared. A crimson flash lit the quay. The dragon had burned out a patch of the net. "No other choice!" Loch said, and he started to run. "Get to the Prydians! They'll get you to safety!"

"Loch!" she shrieked. "No, no, no! Don't leave me alone! Not all . . . alone . . . ple . . . he . . . hease!"

As he ran, Loch felt as if part of his heart was being torn away. He glanced back to Ariana once and saw only a little blond haired girl, her hair matted with rain, face streaked with tears. And behind her the dark ships and a surging wave of shadows invading.

But still Loch ran toward the dragon. He clambered up the netting, dodging holes, and dove for the dragon's neck. If it hadn't been for the creature's thick red mane, Loch would have slid off immediately. But like a spider, Loch clambered up the creature's hair, closing in on its ear. Raudrim-Quevara roared, loosed a burst of flame, and then, its neck and head were free of the netting. It flung back its head, hoping to toss Loch. He swung out from her neck but held on to the hair. He slammed back into her and took the sword in his left hand. He tried to angle it into the scaly sheath of its ear, but the beast wouldn't hold still. It flung Loch back and forth. He swung out and crashed back in . . . again and again. His ears rang, he couldn't see much, and his grip was slipping. He almost dropped the sword, but got a finger hooked over the crossguard. He swung out on the hair, and tried desperately to drive the sword into the ear canal. But he missed.

The dragon unleashed another gout of flame and flung its head hard and high. Loch clutched the sword and the creature's hair, knowing that the violent downswing of the dragon's neck would likely throw him.

"Be STILL, beast!" a commanding voice called.

The dragon's head slowed, and it emitted a half-strangled growl. Loch glanced right and saw Telwyn with both hands outstretched toward the dragon. How's he . . .

Loch never finished the thought. He clambered up closer to the dragon's ear and straddled the creature's neck. He took the hard ear sheath in his right hand and drove his sword into the canal. This will finish it! he thought.

The blade slid in ten inches but stopped. Loch pushed with all his might, but it was stuck. "Fred, do something! You've got to go deeper, pierce its foul brain!"

"It's too narrow, too hard," Fred called back. "Drive me with greater force!"

"Do it!" Telwyn yelled. "She's breaking my hold!"

Loch felt the dragon stirring, its head rising. He tried again, slamming the sword with both hands into the ear sheath. He might as well have been trying to drive the blade into concrete.

"I cannot fit!" Fred said. "Try the dagger!"

The dragon roared. Loch fumbled with his sword, had to pin it under his arm to reach around for the dagger. The smaller blade caught on his belt. The creature was breaking free of Tel's hold. It arched it's neck—and suddenly, the dragon's head dropped to the ground like a stone.

The force of the impact flung Loch off. He hit hard, knocking the wind from his lungs, and Fred clattered to the ground beside him. Loch blinked open his eyes, expecting to see the beast's taloned claw come crashing down. But the dragon had gone still . . . and silent. Dead.

What? How? Loch stared. Then, he realized. She did it. Ariana did—he rolled, grabbed up Fred, and started running.

He saw her standing there, the Scarlet Bow still in her outstretched hand. Her eyes seemed so small and far away. Shadows were moving all around her. Loch yelled as some massive dark thing seized Ariana and took her away.

CHAPTER 43

THE COUNCIL OF SHEPHERDS

*The steep rocky coast of Anglinore is often called the "Storm Coast,"
for its sheer walls and even the city itself must often bear the brunt of
the storms that howl in from the Dark Sea.*

—Thurber's Alamanac, Spring 2116

32 OCTALE 2238

"Confound it, Lochlan Stormgarden!" Sebastian growled to his
empty chamber. The sun had set on the sixth day. Now, unless
a pair of Windborne could be found, there was no chance to get
to Shepherd's Hollow for the Council on time. "I should have
known better! Love messes everything up!"

He grabbed his staff and hastened from the room. Down the
spiral stairs, he flew, and raced to Queen Maren's chamber. He
knocked softly. No answer. He rapped a little louder. Still nothing. He pounded so loud that the guards down the hall turned
to look. But Queen Maren did not come to the door. "Of course
you're not in your chamber."

He visited his fury on the guards. "Prove to me your vigilance," he demanded. "Where has the queen gone?"

"I don't rightly know," the younger guard replied, sweat already dribbling down the bridge of his nose. "You, Skap?"

The older guard said, "Fez and I 'ave been 'ere all day, Master Shepherd. All we know fer certain is that she left 'er room 'round noon, she did. Rather late for 'er, I thought. Wasn't two months back, she'd a' been up at dawn to prayer. Maybe, check Clarissant Hall?"

Sebastian eyed them both a silent moment, not in reproof, but in careful thought. It seems everyone has noticed a change in the queen . . . except the queen herself. "Thank you," Sebastian said, whooshing away so fast the nearby torches fluttered.

Sebastian stormed up to the tall double doors outside Clarissant Hall and said simply to the guards, "Is she?"

They nodded.

The Shepherd took a deep breath and went inside. He found the queen, but she was not kneeling in prayer. She sat alone on the first pew right at the center aisle. Sebastian brushed by her and took a seat to her right. She turned slowly, and Sebastian winced. Her face was pallid, shriveled to the point of being skeletal. Her eyes had once glistened like polished emeralds, but now they seemed dull, almost murky.

"Ah, Shepherd," she said, her voice surprisingly crisp. "Good of you to join me. I've been here . . . some time. Come to think . . . think of many things."

"Think?" he asked. "Not to pray?"

She gave a weak smile. "Have I not worn my knees to calluses enough for your satisfaction? You know the words of Canticles. 'For everything, there is a time.' A time for peace. A time for war. A time to pray. And, a time to think."

Sebastian nodded. "All too true," he said. "Indeed, seeing you now, makes me thoughtful. How . . . how are you, Maren?"

Queen Maren laughed, a tired, brittle sound. "Well met, Sebastian," she said. "I should know better than to spar words with a Shepherd." She put her hand on Sebastian's. "I know I look a fright. I'm afraid I've spent too much time indoors of late. But . . . I feel well enough. My mind seems so much more clear this past week. Do you ask in general? Or is there a particular reason?"

"Both," he said. "Loch has not returned from the Wetlands. He has broken our agreement."

She sighed, but smiled. "And you expected less? The boy is in love." She paused a moment. "And you know, he is king of Myriad. He honors your agreement out of devotion to you, not to legal necessity."

"That may be true," Sebastian replied. "But integrity requires that one adhere to one's word. And if Cardiff gets a sniff of this, it will all be up."

"Aptly spoken," Maren said. "But had my Aravel ignored his heart for the sake of such as Baron Cardiff, we might never have wed. You remember, don't you?"

Sebastian shook his head. "Yes. I will never forget." The conversation drifted like a low fog into his thoughts:

"Have you seen her?" Morlan asked. "From Tryllium, I think . . . not royalty, but a queen nonetheless. She is beautiful."

"I don't know brother," Aravel replied. "I may have seen her. But I've been rather busy with my studies of late. As you probably ought to have been as well." He laughed. "What does she look like? What is her name?"

"Maren. Pale, but like to porcelain, bright green eyes, dark hair. Ah, I am done for."

"So it sounds. Careful, brother. Giving your heart away is a dangerous thing."

"Promise me," Morlan said suddenly. "Promise me you will leave Maren alone."

"What? I don't even know her. Besides, I'm not concerned with women these days. That can wait."

"Promise me, Aravel."

"I don't know why you need such assurance. I prefer blonds anyway." He laughed.

"I am serious. I want your word," Morlan said. "Because if she meets us both, she might be swayed by the crown. They always are. Promise me . . . I implore you."

"Fine, if it will make you shut up about it, I promise."

Sebastian remembered it well. It was one of many bitter thorns that consumed Morlan in the end. "Still, in Aravel's defense, it was you who decided between them. Aravel would have walked away if you had chosen otherwise."

"Well do I know this," she said, her voice faltering somewhat. "I never really loved Morlan. He was . . . interesting. But something within him always warned me off. And, of course, there were things he did—and said—that I could not forgive. I chose rightly."

"You did," Sebastian agreed. "So help me choose rightly in this. The Shepherd's Council will be underway in a day's time, the Cyrium Anniversary. Every known Shepherd in the realm will be in attendance. Mosteryn the Old sent a courier just this past week to make sure I would be there . . . and on time. And yet, Loch has not returned, and his trial is forthcoming. Ealden and Drüst have not arrived, but others have."

"So go, Shepherd," she said easily. "I can deal with the dignitaries and the trial. Loch will return soon. Perhaps he'll bring a new bride home with him."

"That would please you, wouldn't it?"

"Infinitely so," Maren replied. "He is a young man of many passions . . . like his father."

"But if I leave . . ." he said.

"Sebastian, go. Go to your celebration." She gave his hand a gentle squeeze. "I may not be tan and robust, but I can rule a few days without your assistance. Besides, I have every Anglish Guard, a formidable army, at my beck-and-call."

Sebastian stared at her in silence. She certainly sounded clear of mind. More lucid than in many weeks. *Perhaps . . . perhaps it will work out. I will alert the guards to watch for her, and Daribel, I will command her most oppressive pressures for the queen to eat as she should.* "Very well then, Maren," he said. "I will depart at once."

"Good, good," she said. "Fear not for queen or country. We will be fine."

Sebastian stood and bid her farewell. As he left Clarissant Hall, one thing troubled him still: her hands. Her hands had been so cold.

33 OCTALE 2238

"I don't suppose either of you think our relief will actually come on time?" Shepherd Velebrimbir asked, leaning against the rail overlooking the treeline on Shepherd Hollow's northern flank.

Shepherd Galea laughed, the sound rich and musical. "Oh, they'll probably come on time," she said. "We Shepherds are nothing if not punctual. I suspect they'll show up in such a state that, in good conscience, we cannot let them take sentry!"

"Sampling too much of Mosteryn's strawberry vintage, like as not," Shepherd Surrand agreed. "Ah, hearing the music and not being able to go and enjoy it seems such a crime."

The woods were dark and quiet, and the three Shepherds listened to the exquisite faint notes of the symphony drifting out from the great stained glass windows of Guardian Hall.

"Well," Shepherd Surrand said. "At least we have each other for company."

"Good for your two," Velebrimbir groused. "My date is inside, dancing with who-knows-whom."

Surrand laughed and took Galea into his arms. "So sorry, old friend," he said. "It must be somewhat maddening."

"Somewhat . . ." he replied flatly.

"My dear," Surrand said. "What do you suppose would happen if we wed? Given our gifts, I mean. My molten rock . . . and your water working?"

She nestled into his chest. "No doubt it would be steamy," she said.

"What was that?" Velebrimbir asked. "I saw something, there by the stream. Something leaped over it. I'm certain."

Surrand and Galea separated. They gazed into the trees. Surrand looked to the west. "There's danger afoot," he whispered urgently. "Uri and Ronin are not at their posts."

Velebrimbir motioned, and the three Shepherds descended one of the spiral stairs. Keeping ten paces apart, they moved stealthily closer to the edge of a snaking stream that surrounded Shepherd's Hollow like a moat. They found an undersized figure in a dark, hooded robe. He stood erect, but with his head bowed and his arms crossed and hidden within enormously wide sleeves.

"Who are you, and what business have you in Shepherd's Hollow?" Velebrimbir demanded.

Without looking up, the small figure uncrossed his arms, and from his left fist dangled a small black lantern. There was no oil supply or candle evident, for this lantern held something vastly different from fire. Shimmering waves of black and purple twilight spiraled out of its pulsing center, casting the Shepherds in ethereal violet hues.

"I warn you!" Surrand yelled. "You are in great peril!"

"Surrand!" Galea called. She stared up into the trees on the other side of the stream. Dozens of dark shapes bounded down the leaf-strewn hill. No, not dozens. Hundreds. And as they leveled out, they too revealed glowing twilight lanterns.

Velebrimbir pulled a fist-sized stone from the pocket of his robe, tossed it into the air, and exerted his full will. The stone fell to the ground. He stared and tried again. *You are mine to command!* he declared in his thought. He could see the fabric of the stone, saw every junction, every breaking point. It should have shattered into a thousand pieces—a thousand weapons—to propel at the intruders. But again, nothing happened.

Surrand held his hands out to his sides, palm down and called to the flows of molten rock deep beneath the surface. He could feel the pulsing veins of liquid stone surging. It would take a matter of a few seconds to incinerate the intruders . . . but nothing came. Nothing moved at his word. "My gift!" he yelled. "Nothing's happening."

Galea shook her head in frustration. The stream was ten paces away. It should have leaped into the air to bend and surge by her will. But it continued to flow along its course undisturbed. Almost as one, the three Shepherds abandoned their gifts and drew swords . . .

Only to find a dozen blades and more troubling weapons leveled at their own chests. The Shepherds had no chance, but they did not lower their blades.

The Shepherds could not see the faces of even a single foe. "Who are you?" Galea demanded.

"Drones . . ." a raspy voice whispered.

The crowd of enemies parted in three places. Three much taller, cloaked figures advanced through those narrow breaches. They advanced to within striking distance of the Shepherds and lowered their hoods.

Velebrimbir gasped, gazing at the being before him. Its face was eel-like, pale, and stretched . . . the countenance of a drowning victim. Its hairless head was misshapen, and its mouth was crudely sewn shut with strips of flesh. It's nose was a mere skullish cavity. And where two eyes should have been, there was a horrifying sideways crescent. It might have been a single eye, but it had no pupil or iris . . . only a pale yellow light whenever the flesh parted.

Aside from a variety of scars, pocks, and folds of loose skin, the three taller beings were of like kind. They stood motionless before the Shepherds as if daring them to strike. Then, all at once, the air about them began to stir. Tendrils of leaves took flight and spiraled around them. Suddenly they had weapons in their gnarled fists, narrow scepters, hollow at the ends with crowns of sharp edges.

The Shepherds unleashed their weapons, but it was too late by far. The eel-like beings took awful blows: a slash to the neck, a thrust to the chest or gut. But these impacts had no visible effects. With almost casual ease, the three menacing figures drove their strange weapons at the Shepherds.

The army of cloaked figures stepped over the bodies and advanced on Shepherd's Hollow.

"Where in the Stars is Sternbough?" Mosteryn the old asked his goblet. It was one of his own making, beautiful, intricate lightning glass. He whirled the plum colored liquid inside and harrumphed. "He'll be late to his own party."

Mosteryn looked out over his people assembled in Guardian Hall, his flock. He was the senior Shepherd, the highest ranking member and leader of the Shepherd Order. The Shepherd of Shepherds.

It gave him great pleasure to watch them all. Some dancing, some singing, some had joined the orchestra and played. Others mingled or sat at long tables overloaded with every delicacy the realm of Myriad had to offer. The vast granger-wood chandeliers—each with a thousand candles—hung high above their heads, casting warm light upon them. Festive light that flickered happily on the stained glass and reminded Mosteryn pleasantly of the month of Advent.

It was an unprecedented celebration. The first time since the founding of the Order that every known Shepherd in Myriad had left their charges and gathered in one place. It had been a monumental task to pull together, even just to arrange the courier system that could safely notify so many over such a large geographical spread. The invitations had gone out just a week ahead of time, giving the exact date of the three day celebration. And everyone had come.

Except Sternbough.

Mosteryn drained his glass. *Perhaps, I should rethink nominating Sebastian as Leader of the Order.* He thought ironically, that punctuality had been one of Sebastian's most persuasive traits. A stray thought came on like an icy fingernail pressed into the soft flesh of the back. *There could be trouble in Anglinore.*

No, no, not likely, he thought. *Stop it, old man. You're doing your level best to taint this celebration.* Mosteryn signaled for an attendant to refill his goblet. His glass heavy once more, Mosteryn sat back in his high chair to watch his people celebrate.

But as he recognized the closing notes of the minuet, he remembered somewhat sullenly that he was to give his welcome speech at this end of this piece. He put down his goblet, stood and wiped the crumbs from his robe, and waited. An attendant tried to hand the old Shepherd his staff, but Mosteryn waved it away. The music ended, and so did the dancing. Quiet conversation lingered until polite awareness made its way around the hall.

Mosteryn raised his hands and motioned for everyone to be seated. He waited. One thing I hate more than speaking to large crowds, he thought, is having to wait for large crowds to quiet down so I can speak. But on the very first word he spoke—nay, the first syllable—all fourteen panels of stained glass in the chamber imploded with a deafening shriek.

Shards of every color sprayed inward and fell upon the screaming Shepherds. And all at once, all ten thousand candles blew out. The last thing Mosteryn the Old saw before the loss of light were dozens of hooded figures streaming in from every door. Now, in the terror-filled darkness, hundreds of strange purplish lanterns kindled to life. Screams of agony rang out.

Mosteryn called out for lightning. But there was no answer.

The King's Courtyard on the far eastern side of Anglinore Castle had been all but abandoned for twenty years. Ever since the skeletal remains of High King Brysroth had been discovered in the well there, most of the Anglish royalty and citizenry had stayed away from the once beautiful site. There were rumors that the courtyard was haunted. And at times, Anglish children on a dare, would come to the gated arch and look in. But they would rarely step foot past its gate. It was weed-strewn and unkempt, full of cracked flagstone walks, and overgrown benches of white marble. And, of course, the well.

Cobbled of dark stones and marbled together with ages of mortar, the well stood four feet from the flat ground and had an arched wooden roof overhead, supported by thick columns of dark wood. The rope and bucket for drawing out water were long gone. No one would dare use that foul water anyway.

But, as the Gray Hour waned and night came on, the foul dark water in the bottom half of the well slowly drained away.

Had any children been there at that time, staring wide-eyed through the gate, all their haunted suspicions would have been confirmed. For from the well, there came a grating sound. And then, from within the well's depths where the should have been only darkness, a pale light shone.

CHAPTER 44

FEAR

Grayvalon was once the Wayfolk capital city, and during the Age of Origin, it served as the capital city of all Myriad. It was an architectural phenomenon, and from many leagues around, people would come to see its famed tiered courtyards or marvel at its pillared fortresses. There had never been such a city, and those who visited left with just that impression. But those who lingered, or even remained to call Grayvalon their home, soon came to realize that the city was like a whitewashed tomb.

—From Myridian Antiquities
Sage Josephal (w. 2119, D)

33 OCTALE 2238

Loch caught up to Ariana's captor and hammered his back with Fred's pommel. It lurched forward and turned, and Loch finally saw what it was. A manlike thing with no armor, but its flesh looked like sun-baked clay, bulging and cracking. It was seven feet tall and full of lumbering muscle. Its canted eyes glowed with pale light, and its mouth looked more like an open wound. It let out a gurgling roar that was abruptly cut short, for Ariana had plunged her dagger into the thing's eye.

The creature dropped her. Loch lifted Fred and leveled a powerful two-fisted stroke that swept through the creature's giant hand and lopped off its head. The massive creature fell backward and shattered into ten thousand fragments.

There came a shriek from behind. When Loch turned, he saw the form of a woman with fire for eyes. She seemed to float. When she reached out her arms, showing her long, sharp fingers, Ariana yelled, "RUN!"

Loch blinked awake, took her hand, and they sprinted for the center rampart. Horrors from every nightmare surged behind them. They heard men and women screaming. And worse, they heard howls, and moans, and trilling wails—the cries of things Lochlan had never heard in his life.

Something brushed Loch's elbow and his flesh went icy cold. He turned and saw what looked like the skeletal upper torso of a large man. Bluish flesh and tatters of black fabric hung off the bones, and it reached for Loch. The High King of Anglinore wanted no part of this thing's plan. A slash of his blade took off one of the creature's arms at the elbow. Then with a powerful high to low strike, he clove the thing in two.

"LOCH!" Ariana screamed.

Loch ducked and a fist the size of an anvil swiped over his head. He rolled, turned, and saw another one of those mountainous clay creatures. It arched its back, leaned forward, and roared. Three more just like it strode up from behind.

"Come on, Loch!"

The young king stumbled but regained his balance and began to churn his legs as hard as he could. He met Ariana at the bottom of the rampart and they pounded up the slick slope. Loch heard the wet slaps and thuds of many footfalls behind him, but he did not turn. It wasn't until they reached the top of the high eastern wall, that Loch looked back. And now, as he stared out over the parapet, he saw how many ships had moored. He saw the black tide of invaders spilling across the entire quay. "Telwyn," Loch said. "Abbagael, Jak . . . I hope you got out . . . somehow." But as he scanned Dockside, the only thing he could make out were small pockets of combat. And of course, the carcass of the great red dragon. Creatures streamed over it like ants.

"They're coming!" Ariana exclaimed.

Loch heard them. They picked their way through the wreckage of Llanfair City, warning any Wayfolk they saw to flee the coming invasion. As they ran, the sound of the clamoring dark horde was always behind them. Closer to the gatehouse, Loch spotted a stable and they made for it. In spite of the pouring rain, harsh red fires still burned. The scormounts inside were have mad with terror.

Loch with his sword, Ariana with her dagger, they cut the scormounts free. Loch went to hand her the reigns of a scormount, but she shook her head. "No," she said. "I'm riding with you!"

Loch nodded. He leaped up into the saddle and helped her up behind him.

"Where . . . where do we go?" Ariana asked.

"Port of Brightcastle," he said, clicking his heels on the scormount's flanks. The beast responded with a quick trot. "From there a ship to Anglinore. We'll be safe there."

Her fingers tightened on his shoulders. "Anglinore?" Her voice was shrill and strained. "Loch, what about the Wetlands? They need to be warned, the Gray Hour is happening all over again!"

"Ah, blast this evil day!" Loch yelled. "Ariana, we don't know for sure what's happening . . . and where. I've got to get back to the throne and mobilize my armies."

She swallowed hard. Tears rolled down her cheeks. At last, Ariana said, "I . . . of course, you're right . . . Anglinore is the only hope against such a dark tide as this. We need to go to Anglinore."

Loch drove his scormount to a full gallop. Outside of the city gates, he turned south. They needed a ship to Anglinore. But Loch wondered about Brightcastle. It was one of the coastal cities attacked those many years ago.

Long before they entered the borders of Brightcastle, Loch and Ariana ran into the villagers of Brightcastle. On horseback and scormount and even on foot, they fled by the thousands. When Loch and Ariana finally got someone to stop for them, the news was not good.

"The city is burning!" a man said. He held a baby daughter to his chest. His wife next to him had a wounded arm. "Things came ashore! Like twelve years back, it is, but in far greater numbers!"

"What about the Horn?" Loch asked. "Is the Horn of Ipswich taken as well?"

"I don't know," he said. "We've had no word from the south."

"We're making for Llanfair," said his wife. "King Ealden will know what to do."

Loch cringed inwardly. "Is that where most of you are headed?"

They both nodded.

"Sir, listen to me," Loch said. "Llanfair city has fallen."

"No!" the woman cried. "The city?"

"Where can we go, then?" he asked.

Loch swallowed. "I do not know what way is safe, now. If you do continue north, I advise you to hug the western coast, steering clear of the major trade routes from Llanfair City. Then, head inland, deep into Amara. Maybe Thistle or Graymere."

"But where are you going, Sir?" the wife asked.

"We are going to attempt to sail from the Horn to the port of Anglinore," he said.

"Anglinore!" she exclaimed. "Well, you tell King Lochlan to put the Guard on these monsters!"

"That I most definitely will," Loch replied. Ariana gave his shoulder a squeeze.

"Thank you, sir! Thank you for the warning about Llanfair. May the First One guard you."

"And also you!" Loch yelled after them. "Spread the word to the others from Brightcastle!"

Loch and Ariana turned south once more, praying that the Horn of Ipswich was yet a free port.

Soldiers—some in dark armor, others shrouded in strange, spectral wrappings—rose up out of the well in the courtyard of Anglinore Castle. One after another, a seemingly endless train, they emerged. The darkest shadow among them, their commander, rushed to the east parapet, held something aloft that flashed like lightning reflected in a mirror. Far below, on the shore, small flashes rippled up the coastline.

The ships had all arrived. Forces were in position and ready. The commander cast something over the wall, something that this time burned red. It flared brightly as it fell beyond the cliffs. He raced back to the horde still gathering in the courtyard and gave the order. And even as one black mass fled into the castle, another of equal size had already begun filling the courtyard from the well.

"Where are all the ships?" Loch demanded of the woman hastily closing up her shop on the Horn's eastern shore. "We have dire need for passage to Anglinore!"

"Sorry, lad, but they've sailed," she said.

"All of them?" Loch asked, crestfallen.

"Any as are seaworthy," she replied. "But I can't say if Anglinore is where ye should be a'headin. Bad goings on there, by all accounts." She threw down a heavy piece of timber as a bolt lock and then hurried to another room. Loch followed.

"What kind of bad goings on?"

"Horrible, if old Dagspaddle's t'be believed," she said, fighting the wind to keep the shutters closed so she could latch them. "Fleet a'dark ships as far as the eye can see under this sky . . . bound for Anglinore."

"Anglinore? Who would dare attack m—our capital city?"

"Dagspaddle's weren't the only one sayin' it," she said. "Now, move on. I've got t'lock up and lock out, as they say."

Loch followed her onto the shop's front porch. "Surely there must be one ship left in Ipswich?"

"Ships, no," she said. "I've got a little sloop round back. If the wind hasn't blown it away, it's all yours."

"Thank you," Loch said. "You've no idea how important this is."

She stopped at that, seemed indecisive for a moment, and then said, "Uh, listen. Ye seem like a nice lad. Pretty little lady there too. And whatever's ye got goins on, sounds real important. But I wouldn't try goin' to Anglinore, I was you."

"Thank you, but I'll take my chances with the rumor of dark fleets," Loch said.

"That's not what I mean, lad," she said. "I'm talkin' about takin' a sloop out into the high Dark Sea. Rough out there. Dagspaddle said it almost turned the Mynx. You wouldn't get past the shoals in my little sloop."

Loch looked out at the rough waters. "Where's the sloop?"

"Suit yerself," she said, taking small steps away. "Back a' the shop, there's an old shed. In there. Sorry it's all I can do fer ya. I've got a fleet mount all packed around front. Stars guide you." And she was gone.

Loch met Ariana out by the road. "There are no ships," he said.

"I feared it so," she said. "This is a port town, and not even a single mast rises from the docks. What do we do?"

"Change in plan," Loch said. "Follow me."

They found the sloop in the old woman's shed just as she'd described it. It was a twelve-footer and in decent shape. The headsail was new, but the main sail was torn and would be virtually useless in the wind.

"We're going to sail this to Anglinore?" Ariana asked.

"I did say a change in plans," he replied, tossing a couple of long oars into the boat. "It would be suicide to take this out into the heart of the Dark Sea. We're going to sail to the Wetlands. If it weren't for the storm, we might be able to see your home from here."

Ariana practically tackled Loch into the boat. She held him for several long breaths. And then, she released him and said, "Thank you, Loch . . . thank you."

"There may yet be seaworthy vessels moored on your side of the bay," he said. "If so, we'll warn your people, take as many as you can, and sail to Anglinore. But . . ."

"But what?"

Loch shook his head. "That woman, she said that Anglinore might be under attack as well. A fleet of dark ships."

"No, Loch," she said. "Is there any place safe?"

"I can't think of any place more fortified against invasion and attack . . . than Anglinore," he said. "We will find our way there . . . and see."

"But what if there are no ships in the Wetlands?"

"Then, we'll try Chapparel," he said. "And if not there, we'll head straight south, then east through Woodshire. It's a day and a half, maybe two from the Chapparel to Woodshire. Another four days to Anglinore. That's almost a week." Loch sighed.

Ariana whispered, "So much can happen in a week."

Skappy and Fez were off duty, sopping hard rolls in their stew at a local pub when they heard the tower bells ringing madly over Anglinore City.

"That can't be right," Fez said, wiping gravy from his mustache. "They're ringin' for All Guard."

"Right or not," Skap replied with a snort, "we got t'report. C'mon, lad, up we go!"

They left a coin spinning on the table and raced out of the pub. They found the city in an uproar, folk running about in every direction almost as fast as the rumors. Gorrack invasion some said. Pirates, said others. The night watch had seen dark ships, a fleet approaching the coast—that much had been agreed upon. Skappy and Fez gave up on trying to calm folks down. There was no use. Fear swept over the city like a tidal wave.

They had to fight through a massive outpouring of Anglish Guard from the main gatehouse. This was the reserve rolling out to fortify the city barracks and walls. But Skap and Fez were castle guard, so they struggled on.

"This is ridiculous!" Skappy yelled. "We're getting nowhere fast. Come with me."

Fez followed and Skap ducked into an old stable just off the main thoroughfare.

"Brilliant!" Fez exulted, seeing the horses.

Skappy mounted up on a brown mare. "Now, we'll get somewhere."

The horses had indeed made travel through the seven gates much faster. Soldiers and townfolk who wouldn't step aside for pedestrians, leaped out of the way of the tall steeds thundering their way. Once they reached the castle, Skap and Fez tied off their borrowed mounts and raced inside the main gate.

"I don't like this at all," Skap said. "There's no one here."

"We need to find a Guardcaptain," Fez said, "find out who's supposed to be on duty."

"Right," Skap said. "This way. We'll go thru barrack's way. Faster."

The two long-time Anglish guards raced through the halls, down a long stair, and around a sloping ramp to the main barracks section of the castle. The first two barracks, they found empty, which was no surprise as these were the dock guard. If enemies did come by sea, they'd be the first legions deployed.

Skap and Fez were puffing by the time they climbed the stairs to the next flight of barracks. "Old Grimgall's here," Skap said. "He's been through it all. He'll know what's what."

Ducking torches and trying not to trip over each other, they careened up the hall, turned the corner into the first infantry barracks . . . and froze. The hundred-yard hall was full of soldiers . . . but nothing moved. Near a thousand knights, there were, but not even a breath of sound. Skap moved forward as if walking was brand new to him. Fez followed slowly. Anglish soldiers were everywhere, but sprawled in all manner of unnatural poses: draped over chairs, fallen forward at tables, hanging half-tangled from bunks.

"What in the First One's name . . ." Skap whispered.

"They're all . . . all dead," Fez muttered. "How? I don't see any blood . . . no wounds . . . nothing. How can they all—" Fez retched and doubled over, spilling his stomach's contents on the cobbled stone.

Skappy walked into a group of soldiers splayed out in a semi-circle. *They all died with their eyes open,* he thought. He'd never seen anything like it in all his life, not even in war. The men, the looks on their faces: eyes bulging, jaws locked open, muscles taut, hands and fingers bent into claws—abject terror. "It's as if they all died a'fright," he whispered.

A crash from the far side of the barracks made Skap and Fez jump. "C'mon, lad," Skap said, drawing his sword. "Sounds like the fight's ahead of us."

"But, Skap, who could . . . how could this happen?"

"Draw yer blade, man!" Skappy commanded. "There's nothing for it. We'll do our part." Skap ran to the door on the other side. Fez followed, half limping and stumbling.

They left the barrack by that far door, turned into the corridor just in time to see—something—pass by the flickering torches at the far end of the hall. Whatever it was turned the corner, a glistening mist trailing behind it.

"What the—"

"I don't know, Fez." But Skap led his friend on. They moved as silently as two terrified soldiers could move and tried not to look at the dead knights who lined the hall like broken dolls.

But Fez couldn't help but look down at one man. He lay on his back, half-draped with his own green and black cloak. His wrists were crossed at his throat and his fingers had pressed so hard into his neck that blood trickled from several wounds. He looked as if he'd been choking. Then Fez saw much more than he could handle. Like so many of the others, the dead man's mouth was wide open. But with this man, his mouth was filled with a pool of vomit. And as Fez watched, it bubbled twice.

Fez looked away and retched, but he had nothing left. Fez hadn't liked Baron Cardiff Strengle very much, but he wouldn't wish this end on anyone.

From around the corner, came another crash and a blood-curdling shriek. With Fez a few footsteps behind, Skap turned the corner. He stopped immediately. His sword clattered to the floor.

"Skap!" Fez yelled.

But his friend would not turn. Fez couldn't see around the corner, couldn't see what Skap saw. But Skap's mouth hung open, his tongue lolled out, his eyes blinked in rapid fire spurts, and his arms shook at his sides. Some kind of vast sucking sound escaped Skap's throat, and for just a split second, his eyes darted toward Fez. In that singular moment, when their eyes met, Skap's right hand jerked, a sudden flicking motion. With a labored breath unlike any Fez had ever heard before, Skap whispered, "Go!"

Then, Skap collapsed in a heap. Fez took a step toward him. But he heard movement. Something in the other hall, coming closer. "I'm sorry, Skap," Fez cried. "So sorry." Then, Fez ran for his life.

Queen Maren had stood in the very same spot in Clarissant Hall for more than three hours . . . debating. Something was very wrong in Anglinore, this she knew. She'd heard the heavy marching of the Guard. She'd heard shouts. She'd heard rumbles and knew they were separate from the storm's angry report.

But her debate was about something different entirely.

Why have I come here? she wondered. *Is it merely habit . . . that so often, in times past, I have come to offer prayers to the First One? Should I pray now? Should I try . . . again?* She stared at the place on the wall where the original altar had once stood. Had Aravel made a mistake taking down, having the new altars commissioned? Or, as the Eye of the North had suggested, had Aravel done only what was needed?

And what of the Eye? Could the things she had seen in the table be trusted? *Was the voice really . . . really him?* It was maddening. *Madness,* she thought, *is likely where all this will lead.*

Then, in a rare moment between the ending of one thought and before the beginning of the next, Queen Maren knelt on the stairs and called out to the First One.

She heard the doors open behind her. She heard footsteps on the stone. Long, confident strides. They stopped. Someone stood behind her, maybe at the side of the first pew. Maybe closer.

"Hello, Maren," a familiar voice said. "I have missed you."

Ariana climbed out of the boat and stepped to the shore. Loch leaped behind her. There was a tremendous kerr-rack! And the boat began to sink.

"That was as close as possible," Loch said.

"If we had tried to sail it to Anglinore . . ." Ariana didn't need to finish the thought.

"Here is where I am out of my element," Loch said. "You lead the way."

With the morning sun maybe two hours off, Ariana led Loch on a chase upon soft, sandy white soil and through incredibly dense reeds and sea grass. They passed into a forest of those gnarled pines, and Loch thought he recognized the path to the lagoon where he'd battled the serpent. Several wooded twists and turns later, Ariana stopped suddenly.

Loch tripped on a root and planted his face into a patch of ferns. He sat up and was about to speak when he saw Ariana's expression.

"Oh . . . oh, no," she said. "They're already here." She crouched very low and pointed through the trees.

Loch saw now, in the eerie predawn twilight, tall ships—two, three, even four masts—all crafted of dark wood, were moored just off the coast. Smaller, fifteen foot cutters, scores of them, were slicing swiftly through the waves in the shallow waters toward shore.

"No," Loch said. "I . . . I don't think they've been here long. I think they are just arriving, but there will be no escape, at least not by ship."

Ariana was up and running. "We've got to warn them!" her voice fell back over her shoulder.

"Ariana, wait!" he called, racing after her. She was right. They needed to warn the village, but not by running heedlessly into danger. He caught her at the edge of the village, just behind the Elders' mansion. He pulled her down and said, "We look first."

From that vantage, far up the hill, they could see shadowy movement just behind the far side of the village. "There's no way we'll get to those cottages in time," Loch said.

"The bell!" Ariana broke his grip and tore off around the building. Loch ran after and found her inside the mansion shouting.

"Elders! Get up! We're under attack! Gray Hour is upon us again!" Then she grabbed a desk and, with strength that surprised Lochlan, she overturned the heavy piece of furniture, making a horrendous racket. Then, she left Loch standing in the hall and raced up spiral stairs that were hidden away in corner doorway.

Elder Justinian was the first out, hastily wrapping a robe around himself. "What's—"

The bell rang out, deafening and near. And it continued ringing, probably, Loch thought, much harder and much louder than it had ever been rung before.

High Elder Scandeer and several of the others, wives, attendants too—spilled into the hall. Loch didn't give them time for questions. "Every one of you, arm yourself as best you can. Get out into your village, and get everyone out! An enemy beyond your reckoning is on your doorstep!"

"We will not let them do this to us again!" Scandeer said, clenching his fist high. "We'll fight them!"

"And you will die!" Loch shot back. "These are terrors of legend, the same and worse than before! You may have to fight as you flee, but if you try to make a stand, they will wipe you out!"

"Where?" Justinian asked. "Where do we go?"

"Stay away from the coasts! I doubt Chapparel Village is safe. Go far south and inland. Make for Tryllium, perhaps Shepherd's Hollow. Yes, the Shepherds! Go there."

"What about Anglinore?" asked Mistress Eveara over Justinian's shoulder.

Loch shook his head. "I don't know. I hate to say it, but even Anglinore may not be safe."

Ariana joined Loch, and together, they emptied the hall. Then, they sprinted down hill, making for the cottages and shops on the far northeastern side of the village. Howls and moaning cries issued from the woods.

They had but moments. Loch had just ushered a family with six small children out of a cottage when one of the massive clay beasts caved in the roof. Loch raced down the alley, hopping wreckage, and then slammed Fred into the creature's lower leg. It took two swipes, but Loch managed to cut through. The beast fell backward with one of Ariana's arrows protruding from its eye.

The village became a hurricane of horrors. Loch and Ariana did what they could to usher people to safety, but in moments, there was no safety to be had.

A massive, hunch-backed creature with arms so long its fingers dragged the ground came shambling around the corner. One of the villagers came too close. He was snatched up, and the creature opened its lopsided, skullish jaws and bit into the helpless man. Loch turned away and found himself face-to-face with eyes of fire.

The banshee let out a low ululating wail that rose in volume and pitch all at once to a shrill blasting scream. Loch suddenly felt nothing. Numb. Paralyzed. The Banshee's black lips curled into a hungry smile, and she drifted closer, reaching out a curling gray hand.

"Do something, Loch!" Fred yelled. "Cut her head off!"

As if splashed with cold water, Loch blinked. With her sharp nails just inches from his face, he leaped back, drew his sword and swept it through the center of the creature. There was no shriek. No death cry. Only two wet thuds.

"Thank you, Fred!" Loch turned to run, saw Ariana to the south. She's heading for her cottage, he thought, and sped across the courtyard. He dodged claws and blades alike as he ran, stopping only once to hamstring a tall, cloaked figure. He went down, and Loch kept on running.

He came around the opposite side of a shop and found Ariana kneeling outside of her own cottage. "Mill's gone," she whispered.

"No, Ariana, I'm sorry."

"No, I mean, I didn't find him. I think he got out."

Loch sighed. "Good, good," he said. "What are we dealing with here?"

"I'm not sure. The door was is broken open, but I don't know what did it or if it's still inside."

"Let's find out," Loch said. Sword drawn, he crept up the stairs to the porch. Ariana came behind, silent as a whisper.

Loch made himself thin to slip through the door. No sense risking a creak or groan from the ruined wood and hinges. Once inside, they found an absolutely gigantic figure standing in front of the dormant fireplace. He wore a dark cloak and a sword was at his side. There was something odd about this being's profile, but Loch couldn't figure it. He motioned to Ariana and mouthed, "Arrow."

She mouthed back, "I'm out."

It'll be the sword then, Loch thought. He crept behind the figure and made ready to swing when the brute turned on his heel and swung a ham-hock sized fist at Loch's head. Loch ducked, heard the impact of the fist on the wall and wrenched his blade up at the only angle he had. It should have lopped off the intruder's left arm . . . only there wasn't one there.

"Mill!" Ariana yelled. "Loch, stop! It's Mill!" She ran to the figure and hugged him. "Mill, what are you doing here? Why aren't you already out of the village?"

He glanced back at the open hollow in the stone behind the fireplace. "I was gettin' yer journals," he said, pointing to a huge leather satchel at his feet. "You warn't here, and I know how much they mean t'ya. Oh, and I got yer father's axe too." He patted the broad-bladed weapon at his side.

"Mill, you are a miracle," Ariana said. "Thank you, more than I can repay."

"I think I got 'em all," he said.

Ariana fished around in the hollow. "Oh, one more. She removed a thin leather journal and placed it carefully in the satchel.

"I've got horses," Mill said. "Stashed 'em just outside." He looked at Loch. "Oh, just two of 'em. I gave the rest to families as needed 'em. You two will have to ride together."

"Millard Key," Loch said. "Remind me to make you a knight."

Mill scratched his shaggy hair. "Huh?"

Ariana spoke up, "Mill, this is Lochlan Stormgarden. He's not just some wandering swordsman. He's king of Myriad."

Understanding took several moments to appear on Mill's face. His mouth dropped open. "All this time? You mean . . . I mean . . . really?"

Loch nodded.

Mill's hand shot out. "Your majesty!" he said. "I've always wanted to meet you! But, uh, we might want t'get moving. Those things out there . . . I can hear 'em comin'."

Loch led the way with his sword. Ariana followed, and big Mill with the axe came after. They fought their way through the village and disappeared into the forest. The horses, two stout draught horses, were right where Mill had left them. Once they'd saddled up, they sped off south, deep into the wood.

"No good!" Lochlan shouted to the ragtag train of survivors from the Wetlands. He pointed through the trees. Chapparel was already burning.

"We've no choice then," Arian said, hovering over his shoulder.

Loch touched her forehead with his own. "No . . . we don't."

Mill rode up. "What now?" he asked.

"We ride east to Woodshire," Loch replied. "And then . . . we'll see."

Queen Maren rose from her knees, spun around, and gasped. "I . . . I heard your voice, from the table," she said. Then she ran to him and threw her arms around his neck. "Oh, my sweet Aravel . . . you've returned to me."

She felt his breath hot on her neck. "No," he whispered. "I am afraid not."

CHAPTER 45

UNHALLOWED GROUND

Gorracks don't fear much, and that's a fact. But my cousin Deedrick and I found one near scared to death. The brute beached up on the far western end of the Nightwash River. Seemed dead, but he was a biggun, all rippling with muscle, so we prodded him with a long branch. Tell you, he snapped awake and kicked up a cartload of gravel and sand backin' away from us. His slanted eyes were a'bulgin' and he held up his hands like t'keep us away. I couldn't figure it. I was staring at the bulky muscle on his arms and chest. If that Gorrack had had a mind, he could'a torn us limb from limb. But he didn't. Just sat there shaking. I actually felt sorry for 'im. Deedrick too, and he never went in for that war stuff. He reckoned he could get along with just about anyone, man or beast. So Deedrick, he eases on up to the Gorrack, talking all soft like ye might to a child. That's when the blasted Gorrack started talkin' back.

It was garbled, loud, and as hoarse as you please, but he was speakin' Anglish. Kept saying things over and over again. First we thought he was talking about some Gorrack version of Allhaven, but it didn't make sense 'cause he was so scared outta his head. Best we could figure, the Gorrack thought he might still be on some kind of a forgotten continent; a hidden refuge kept by something he called Shadelth. He said the Shadelth took him and kept him there, said they took things as wasn't theirs.

Maybe it was the not knowin' exactly what he meant. Maybe it was just seein' a Gorrack like him all a'tremble, but it got to me and Deedrick. Then the most peculiar thing I've ever seen happened. That Gorrack started bleedin'. Blood bubbled out of a jagged wound in his neck and a nasty deep cut in his gut. Then he died. Just like that. Swear we didn't see no wounds a'first. None at all. Later on, we got to someone in our village who knew a bit about the Gorrack language. He told us that the closest word to Shadelth in Anglish is 'witches.'

—From Deedrick and Val Allen Kensey,
A journal found in the ruins of Stonecrest (w. 2221, AS)

40 OCTALE 2238

"NO!" Loch yelled and slammed his fist to the table. A goblet crashed to the floor. The clamor inside the small Woodshire tavern vanished and all turned. "Sixty thousand fighting men in Anglinore City, and yet the capital of realm was overrun in a single night?"

The man sitting across the table scratched his beard and drained his tankard, his second since Loch had sat down. "Beggin' yer pardon, sir," he said, watching intently as the barmaid refill his mug. "But it's forty thousand we had . . . s-s-since the king's last decree. The invaders had twice our numbers. And, some'ow, they came at us from inside the castle. The poured over the walls in great masses, came up from the docks, and spread like brushfires. They had Shepherd gifts too. Fire an' blood an' green light—wicked things. Never seen anything like it."

"But the Anglish Guard," Loch argued, "they are elite, the best warriors of all Myriad. We should—"

"You weren't there, sir!" the man grunted. "Ye shut yer mouth if ye weren't there. Yeah, we're well-trained, but these weren't stinkin' Gorracks. They had numbers, they had the element of surprise, they had Shepherd gifts, and they had something else. I didn't see it. I don't know what it was or how it could do what it did. But I found scores of men dead of nothing but pure fright. I'm talking hundreds of men, thousands all told, barely raised a weapon and was dropped right where they stood."

"We've got to go back," Loch said. "We must liberate Anglinore."

The man laughed pathetically. "There is no going back," he mumbled. "The city is taken. Even had we ten times what we've got here, we wouldn't pass the first gatehouse."

"What he says is true," a man said, drifting toward the table. "I saw a whole barrack of our own, laid low like wheat. And . . . I lost me best friend." He raised his mug. "To old Skap!" He downed a deep swallow. There were more than a dozen Anglish Guard soldiers in the room. Each raised his own tankard and then drank quietly.

"Fez," Loch said. "Fezzel Crom, don't you recognize me?"

The guard blinked his reddened eyes. His mouth dropped open, and a little ale dribbled onto his beard. "Stars and thunder!" he cried. "King Lochlan, yer, yer alive!"

Loch began to smile, but saw a Fez's expression darken. He felt men moving up close behind him. "Pardon, my sayin's so," Fez muttered. "But where were you?"

Loch felt as if someone had swung a tree trunk into his gut. "What? I . . . I was, well, I was in Llanfair."

"What were you doin' in Llanfair, sir?" one of the guards asked from behind.

"Yeah," said another. "We needed you in the castle! We could'a used your command."

"I'll tell you what he was doing!" Ariana hissed, knocking a soldier out of a chair and taking his seat at the table. "He was killing an elder dragon with his bare hands—the same beast that laid waste to the Windbyrne Eyries and the city of Llanfair and would have brought its crimson fire to Anglinore, like as not."

Murmurs sifted around the room. "Believe me, Fez, believe me, all of you," Loch said. "I wish I had been there, if for no other reason than to stand by your side. But, had it been so, I fear my commands would have done little. I have seen some of what we're up against. In Llanfair, Brightcastle, the Wetlands, Chapparel—so many black ships, so many soldiers, dark things . . . nightmares. But this thing in Anglinore, this thing that bursts hearts with fear . . . I . . . I do not know." Loch put his head in his hands. When he spoke next, his voice was a frightened whisper. "Fez, what . . . what about my mother? Did she make it out?"

He looked up. Fez took a quick drink, wiped his lips and chin with his arm, and gave a subtle shake of the head.

Loch suddenly stood. He made no effort to wipe the tears streaming down his face. "Those of you with the Anglish Guard," he said, his voice booming. "Secure the people of Woodshire. It will not be safe here for long. We are too close to the coast. Get every horse, scormount, and pack mule; every wagon, every cart, every satchel. Get all the weapons, all the food and supplies we can carry. We leave in one hour!"

"But, King Lochlan," Fez said, "Where can we go?"

"We'll make for Shepherd's Hollow," he said. "They're our last hope."

Uncle Jak rode with Abbagael. Tel rode beside them, and Veior Moonglaive, his head and chest heavily bandaged, rode to his right. Hundreds more Wayfolk, Prydian and Vespal, followed in ragged lines trailing half a league behind them.

They'd been riding north for hours when Veior broke the silence. "My men, some of them say the enemy possessed gifts, like the Shepherds. One could hurl fire. Another breathed out poison. And those creatures! I saw things out of legend—how can this be?"

"I think that's plain enough," Jak said. "Those beasties came sailing across the Dark Sea, they did."

"But from where?" Veior asked.

"You are High Scholar of the Prydian Wayfolk?" Tel said. "And yet, you do not understand these things?"

Veior glowered and wiped a trickle of blood from his eye. "You do not mean to suggest . . ."

"The Convergence," Telwyn said. "The time is coming."

Veior had already been pale, but at this, his face went sheet white.

"The Convergence?" asked Jak. He frowned and smacked his lips as if he'd eaten something foul. "What's that?"

Abbagael surprised Tel by answering, "Canticles tells of a time when Myriad has denied the First One, a time when all dark and evil things will converge on one location."

"Was that it, then?" Jak asked. "All that back in the city?"

"Certainly not Llanfair," Veior said. "Canticles calls the location, the empty nation. That cannot be Llanfair . . . can it?"

Abbagael shook her head. "I wouldn't think so." Then she whispered. "I think the Convergence is supposed to be much worse."

Veior stopped asking questions. And they rode in gloomy silence for some time. But then Abbagael asked, "What do you think we'll find, Tel . . . up north?"

Telwyn replied, "A beginning."

The sun had risen, but the gray sky still had a wintery look to it. Not the glad fluffy winters of Advent season, but rather the dreary, barren months of Alpheus and Wenvier. The journey had taken Loch, Ariana, Mill, and all those from Woodshire two days without pause. But at last, the geography changed, and the steady decline into Shepherd's Hollow began.

Loch saw the thin tendrils of white smoke rising as they entered the tree path. And as they spiraled down into the wooded hollow, Loch smelled something foul that he could not identify. But when no Shepherd challenged their approach, Loch's stomach tightened and would not let go.

The smell became more pungent and pervasive as they descended. Ariana said, "I . . . I think I know what that is." But Loch urged her to say nothing. As they exited the trees and came to flat ground in the bottom of the valley, they found a vaporous white fog. It filled the dell like a ghostly lake and seemed to be swirling on the southern side of the Shepherds' fortress.

There a great burned mound still smoldered. Recognition of the charred bodies in the pile went from person to person like an icy thread. Quiet weeping spread behind Loch and several cried out in anguish. It was then that Loch noticed a frail-looking figure in a dark blue cloak hunched in the whirling mist a few paces from the mound. The man looked up, his dark eyes flashing.

"Sebastian!" Loch called. He leaped down from his horse, ran to the Shepherd, and helped him to his feet.

"They're all dead, Loch," he said, his voice brittle. "All of them."

Ariana and Mill eased up behind Loch. The travelers from Woodshire began to fill in behind them, but on the far side of the smoking mound.

"I'm sorry, Sebastian," Loch said, "I didn't get back to Anglinore . . . in time."

Sebastian shook his head. "I would be in that cursed pile," he said, "if it had not been for your delay." The Shepherd blinked and stared at the people behind Loch. "Anglinore?" he asked.

Loch shook his head. "Is fallen. The Windbyrne Eyries, Llanfair, and several villages too. Sebastian, who did all this?"

"Traitors," he replied. "We may never know how many or who they all are. But the slaughter here in Shepherds Hollow can mean only one thing: Morlan Stormgarden has returned."

Dozens of history lessons, as well as, the family legacy swirled in his mind. "That's impossible," Loch said weakly. "He was banished, sent—"

"Across the Dark Sea, yes, he was." Sebastian seemed to waver unsteadily. "And no one returns from that hapless voyage. And yet, I believe Morlan did." He looked grimly at the mound of the fallen. "I've had much time to think while I . . . labored . . . here. With each body I carried or carted off, I thought of this mystery. Who could stand against the full might of Shepherd kind? How could anything wipe them all out and leave no casualties of their own behind? And then, I came to the body of Shepherd Xangion. She was one of my favorites, you know." He stopped and seemed lost in thought.

"Shepherd Xangion?" Loch said. "I didn't know her."

"Shepherd of the winds," Sebastian said. "The First One raised her up to take Shepherd Draevan's place in Bell Farthing. Draevan went missing, you know . . . just before the war with the Gorracks . . . and Morlan's forces. Bell Farthing Manor was deserted. No body was ever found. It was as if Shepherd Draevan had vanished from this world. She was a wind Shepherd too. Very powerful. Much more so than Xangion."

"I'm not following you," Loch said. "How could . . . I don't see—"

"Morlan killed Shepherd Draevan," Sebastian said. "He discovered a secret known only to Shepherd kind, and he murdered Draevan and stole her wind gift. He needed dominion over the winds to get back."

Loch squinted. "Stole her gift?" he muttered. "How could he . . . such a gift cannot simply be taken. Can it?"

Sebastian looked away.

Loch shook his head back and forth, battling with denial. "But . . . if he could return . . . why did he wait so long? He could have used the wind power to sail back the very day of his exile."

Sebastian closed his eyes and leaned even more heavily on his staff. "I wouldn't have understood if not for the nature of the devastation here. I always wondered why Morlan was not more distraught at his sentencing. He was defiant, even as his ship carried him away. Now, I know: Morlan wanted to be exiled."

"Wanted to be . . . that's madness."

"Yes," Sebastian replied. "Morlan was utterly mad, but more cunning than anyone would have ever guessed. You see,

Morlan was not the only one to be exiled across the Dark Sea. Ten thousand years of villainy, Loch, untold numbers of Myriads worst scoundrels, marauders, and murders—they've all gone across. And worse still, the Dark Shepherds were sent across as well."

"Dark Shepherds?" Loch exclaimed. "I didn't know . . ."

"We Shepherds are a secretive lot," he said. "Myriad's histories do not record everything. The Dark Shepherds were just as powerful as the rest of us. Morlan must have discovered this . . . somehow. It comes close to stopping the heart, to think of some black continent out there across the Dark Sea. A place where the worst evil in Myriad has lived and festered and multiplied for ages and ages."

Loch thought about the horrors he'd personally witnessed . . . and worse that he hadn't seen.

"And then," Sebastian continued, "Morlan arrives and offers them a way back. I imagine that twenty years is all the time it's taken to build a fleet of ships large enough to bring them all back."

"The Gray Hour Raids," Loch whispered, glancing at Ariana. "He was testing our responses, our defenses."

The Shepherd nodded. "You know," he said, "I can almost remember Morlan saying something like that once . . . at a council meeting—that you had to take measure of an enemy before invading. Miscreant. Now, he's done it."

Except for weeping and a muted crackling from the smoldering mound, Shepherd's Hollow was silent. Loch stared out on the tiny remnant of his people: grieving, fearful, bereft of hope. He felt those same emotions within himself.

One of the Woodshire folk rode up, a man with two little boys looking wide-eyed behind him. "My lord," he said, his eyes constantly darting to the ground. "My lord, what will we do now?"

"We run," whispered Ariana.

Shepherd Sebastian nodded. "I am afraid . . . we have no choice."

Loch knew his people. And they were more dear to him now than they ever had been before he went errant. He could not . . . would not let them down. "No!" he declared, loud enough that all could hear. "We will be cautious, but we will not run. We are going to Ravensgate in Ellador. I know someone there, someone with a hidden cache of weapons. He will help us."

"You mean Oliver!" Fred piped up. "Hooray!"

"Fred, shhh!" Ariana put her hand lightly on the hilt.

"King Lochlan," the Woodshire man said, "What if the enemy is there too?"

"I do not think so," Loch said. "Morlan's forces attacked all our major cities and the coastal villages. Ravensgate is neither."

The man nodded, his expression grim but not as fearful. "Forgive me, my king," he said, "but what good will weapons do when we are so few?"

"We are not the only ones to escape the attacks. This I know to be true. There are more on the way from Llanfair and Brightcastle and the Wetlands! My soul stirs to tell me that there are more just like us all over Myriad! We will need every one . . . every last one."

"Why sir?"

Loch smiled at the man and winked at his two sons. "Why?" he echoed. "Because we are going to build a new army."

ACKNOWLEDGMENTS

I t's just a little after 3:00 am, and I've just wrapped up the edits for *The Errant King*; you, my wife, are to my left, sleeping somewhat restlessly. No doubt it's because your subconscious recognizes that I'm still up and likely to be exhausted tomorrow. This is the last day of a 3-4 week block where you, Mary Lu have taken on way more than your share of responsibilities for our family. I know a simple thank you just doesn't cut it. I hope you'll take pleasure out of every signing I do, every pat on the back I get, every stitch of reader mail—and know that you are every bit as much a part of this as I am. You are sewing seeds through every book that I write. Our children have gotten to see through you just what it means to be selfless. I love you. 1C13

Kayla, Tommy, Bryce, and Rachel: thank you for understanding this mission. I know it stinks when you want to play tennis or watch a movie with Dad, and all you see is the back of my head as I sit at the computer. I love you very much. Thank you for all the trips down and back up the stairs to fetch me a cup of ice water, a soda, a piece of gum, a mint, or even ice cream while I wrote.

Mom and Dad: This Dark Sea series feels to me like a kind of culmination. God willing these 7 books won't be my last, but still there's something special going on. Thank you for your unwavering support, oh, and for buying me all those Star Wars figures and comic books to fuel my childhood imagination. I love you!

Leslie, Jeff, and Brian—we're all entering different stages of life now, but somehow, when we're together, we're all kids again. I'm grateful for all that you are.

To dear friends/family: Ed, Deanna, Diana, Andy, Lorraine, Olin, Jordan, Christian, Matthew, Tyler, Abigail, Deborah, Annalise, Daniel, Samuel, Nikki, Ashley, Dillon, Patti (Lil Tyler), Sadie, Lochlan, Kaitlin, Josh, Kaleb, Luke, and Lydia. Doug, Christine, Chris, Dawn, Mat, Serrina, Susan, Alaina, Chris, Leslie, Jeff, Eric, Alex, Noelle, Todd, Dan, Warren, and so many others who enrich this adventure.

To Bill Russell, thank you for pushing over the first domino for me.

To the faculty and staff, my friends at Folly Quarter Middle, thank you for being amazing. Iron really does sharpen iron.

To my students past and present: you do realize that each and every day, you inspire me to write good stories. Pip pip cheerio!

Jill Peck for the name "Scandeer."
Jeff Hanson, Squid.org, Sam Stoddard at Rinkworks, and The Donjon for making the coolest fantasy name generators on the planet!

Cindy Dillon for the name "Choiros."
Sophie Bull for the name "Scalix."
Laura Jenae VanderWoude for the name "Fred."

Special thanks to the fine establishments that have allowed me to darken their doorstep with my laptop and consume tables all day and all night: The Banshee and Backyard Ale House in Scranton, the Brickstore in Atlanta, the Blind Pig in Champaign,

O'Llordan's in Westminster, Martin's Grocery and Panera Bread here in Eldersburg, and probably a dozen other places.

Jake at ArcheryCountry.com for most excellent demonstration of form and release.

The Bands that have fueled my creativity:

Theocracy, Nightwish, Inner Quest, Senium, Scarlet Citidel, The Orphan Project, Symphony X, Dream Theater, Anthriel, Darkmoor, Darkwater, DGM, Echoes, Eyes of Eden, Majestic Vanguard, Seventh Wonder, Within Temptation, Xystus, etc.

Sir Christopher Hopper, my brutha from anutha mutha. It's just not right that you live so far away. Somehow, God put our friendship together, and even from day 1, I felt I'd known you for decades. Now, it's just like having a kindred spirit just an email away. Thanks for being real and for radiating love to a world in need.

Thanks to Bob Vogel for listening to all my new "doubt bombs." Your wisdom has given me peace and stability.

TO THE ELVES: Endurance and Victory!

EaglesWings, Millard, The Seventh Sleeper, Jake, TAK, SciFiAuthor, Chris, Vrenith, Hark, The Golux, Manny, Brianna, Anduril, Seth, Anna, SilverLake, Alastrina, Jared, Pingpong, ElvenPrincess, Squeaks, Seth E, and Olivia—as always, you rock! But are you ready to be Among the Stars?

Thank you to Rick, Dale, John, Trevor, and all at AMG. You make a publisher feel like a real home. For Daryle Beam and all the talented artists who made The Errant King cover breathtaking.

And last but not least, thank you my publicist, agent, and friend, Gregg Wooding—thank you for all the sacrifices you've made over the years, for handling all that yucky business stuff, and for being the voice of calm when I'm ready to go crazy.